ten-thousand pounds all
dozen more dotted aroun
more weapons and passp
tions, along with a seri
could contact each other using a tried and tested technique
of keeping an email in a draft folder and using it as a
message page if they needed to, saving the draft when they
had finished and remaining under the radar. The email
would never even enter the ether, where any number of
foreign intelligence agencies or terrorist organisations could
intercept their communication and do them harm.

Outside, King's car was fuelled, well-serviced and a
small leather travel bag was permanently stashed in the
boot. Under the spare wheel a compact M4 assault rifle had
been scissored open as if for cleaning which enabled the
weapon to fit snugly in place in the recess along with a
detachable scope and three magazines filled with
5.56x45mm Swedish match grade ammunition. King had
chosen the Audi RS4 for its powerful engine and four-
wheel-drive system but had removed the satnav and emergency response button so that it could not be hacked into by
hostile forces to discover either his current location, or
where he had been. Likewise, Caroline's Mini Cooper S
was both anonymous and swift, but just like King's vehicle
the satnav had been removed. The couple had both reverted
to a more analogue world in a bid to disappear. Only now,
they had been found.

King watched as the vehicle was joined by another. It
was dark, just after midnight. He could hear the engine
switch off through the open window. The driver's door
opened, but no interior light illuminated. There was the
faint, red glow of the door lights opening on the first car, but

again, no interior light. The car in question was a BMW 3 Series and King already knew where the red convenience lights were located and that he was dealing with a degree of professionalism. But he would have done it differently. He would have had the bulbs of these lights removed and not just switched off the interior lights, and he wouldn't have parked so close.

King made his way to the rear of the house. Behind the property were several fields running to the natural border of a river in the valley below. He already knew that it was high tide and that the tidal creek would be deep enough for a boat of considerable size to find passage through. From half tide RIBs and rowing boats could easily escape the mud, which was all there was for an hour or so either side of low tide. A muddy creek with a sliver of murky water from the stream which ran permanently. But at high tide, and an hour either side, a boat with a five-foot draught could easily anchor close to the shore. King picked up the binoculars and switched on the night mode. He couldn't quite see the edge of the creek, but he did see the five, armed figures making their way across the fields. His heart started to beat heavily, and his breathing became erratic. He put down the binoculars and took a deep breath. And then another. Just like his mentor had taught him all those years ago. By the time he exhaled a third time, he was ready for the fight.

King was already dressed in black jeans and wore a black M65 style military jacket over a dark navy sweater. He had used a camo-cream stick on his face and wore a black beanie hat. He raced downstairs and picked up the crossbow, slipping the pistol into his jacket pocket. He had been watching the vehicle for two hours in the darkness and his eyes were well-adjusted to the dark. He assumed the approaching men would have some sort of night vision

DEAD MAN WALKING

A P BATEMAN

Dead Man Walking
By
A P Bateman

Text © A P Bateman

This book is a work of fiction and any character resemblance to persons
living or dead is purely coincidental. Some locations may have been
changed; others are fictitious.

Facebook: @authorapbateman

www.apbateman.com

Rockhopper Publishing

THE ALEX KING SERIES

The Contract Man
Lies and Retribution
Shadows of Good Friday
The Five
Reaper
Stormbound
Breakout
From the Shadows
Rogue
The Asset
Last Man Standing
Hunter Killer
The Congo Contract
Dead Man Walking

THE ROB STONE SERIES

The Ares Virus
The Town
The Island
Stone Cold

Standalone Novels
Hell's Mouth
Unforgotten

Novellas
The Perfect Murder?
Atonement
(an Alex King short story)

Further details of these titles can be found at
www.apbateman.com

For Dad.
I'll miss you every day...

ONE

He had first noticed the car four days ago. On the second day he had approached the driver in a casual manner before the vehicle had driven off. Not erratically, but certainly because of him making a beeline towards it. On the third day he had packed Caroline off to an aunt in the lake District, where she had cancelled her *Airbnb* bookings for the late winter die-hard walkers and welcomed her niece with open arms. Caroline had left her mobile phone and bank cards behind and taken with her the ten-thousand pounds that had been wrapped in a brown paper bag and hidden under a stair tread in their cottage, along with the basic burner phone and second passport under an assumed name. Hidden too had been the baby Glock and two magazines loaded with 9mm hollow points. One could never be too careful.

King peered through the edge of the curtain. The car was still there. The bulky and heavy Sig Sauer P226 9mm pistol felt comforting in his hand. The cash-filled envelope in his inside jacket pocket felt comforting, too. The same system, but as he cocked the 175lb pull crossbow and fitted the first bolt under the clip that would hold it in place next to the bowstring, he took some satisfaction in having a night vision sight fixed and painstakingly zeroed atop the crossbow.

Attacks should always use the terrain and darkness to good effect. Successful attacks incorporated both factors, and approach from multiple sides. But the most successful attacks always had the element of surprise. That element only lasts for a few seconds, but it can mean the difference between failure and success. King had both terrain and darkness. He couldn't cover multiple sides, but he had the element of surprise, and his attackers did not. They had played their hand and he had would call them on it. King knew that if he were to ambush a target at night, then he would do it somewhere between two and four AM. A person's sleep pattern had usually entered REM sleep at that time and waking suddenly would leave them groggy, their equilibrium still to catch up. He checked his vintage Rolex, the luminous dials faint and just visible in the darkness. It was not yet eight PM.

Outside, the air was fresh, and the night was still. Unusual for late winter in Cornwall. Last week had been eighty-mile-per-hour winds and driving rain. Next week would likely be the same. But the still air and clear skies could work for King just as well because King could be as silent as the grave and he would hear his enemies coming. He had been in this scenario many times, and he was still here.

King had landscaped the garden as best as his limited skills would allow, but he had excavated and laid paths of gravel through the rustic garden and apple orchard. He had used paving around the house, and he now crossed it silently, hearing the crunch upon gravel from one of his enemies as a boot crunched on the gravel chippings. King slipped silently into the shadows while the man crossed the gravel in three tentative strides. Behind him, King could hear another footstep in the still, night air.

They were surrounding the house. Closing in like a boa constrictor contracting its grip on its prey. King shouldered the crossbow and saw the man crouching beside an apple tree. Too small to afford him any cover. Strange that a man would think to conceal himself behind such a thing, but it told him another thing about his enemies. Anyone with military training would have been lying prone, following the tree's moon shadow. The man may have had darkness to his advantage, but he had forgotten all about silhouette. And the way he had chosen to cross the noisy gravel once he had trodden carelessly onto the path, so close to the house, told King that sound was another of the five S's he had chosen to ignore. He put himself inside the man's head. Most likely young and excited, scared even. Focusing on the weapon in his hands and getting the job done. Without ego, King thought that the men would have been thoroughly briefed on their intended target, and that briefing – should they have the intelligence to back up their actions – would have confirmed King as a highly trained and highly motivated individual with a track record of kills for his country in wars, foreign and domestic clandestine operations across every continent bar Antarctica. At a shade under six foot tall, around fourteen stone and well-muscled King had the build of a light heavy/cruiser weight boxer and had indeed fought in the ring when he was younger – although the only organisation to hold such information was MI6 and none of his former handlers or overwatch were still alive. King watched as another figure drew near and squatted down next to the first man. Both men now formed a sizeable dark mass in the garden he knew so well, and as the clouds parted and allowed a brief sliver of moonlight to project cleanly onto the ground, it was clear that his enemy were not equipped with comms and that they still needed to communicate verbally. King estimated the distance to be approximately seventy metres between them. He took careful aim and took advantage of the gift the two men had given him. The nearest man was training his weapon on the cottage. His right arm was bent with his elbow pointing downwards and his hand on the pistol-grip of the assault rifle. King breathed out steadily, held his breath while he adjusted his aim, then fired.

The crossbow made a dull and barely distinguishable thud as the bowstring sent the bolt out across the garden at eighty metres per second. Not even a second to reach the target, penetrate completely and go halfway through the second man. The first man stood up and started to run. He made it twenty-paces before his legs rapidly became more and more unsteady and he stumbled head forwards and lay still on the grass. The second man had slumped where he had been crouched, his rifle dropping into his lap. Neither man had made a noise, but their colleague had witnessed it and he opened fire on the cottage and within seconds had emptied thirty rounds of high velocity 5.56mm all over King's garden, and much of his house as well. King remained still as he watched the man dive flat onto his stomach and start to change magazines. King was sizing up his opponent and his magazine change was smooth, and the way he thumped his left palm onto the bolt-release button on the left-hand side of the weapon's frame told King the man was armed with an AR-15 variant rifle.

There were gunshots behind King now. Pistol rounds.

Short, sharp reports without the resonance of the assault rifle. Several rounds pinged close to King, and he lowered himself onto his stomach and worked the bowstring backwards. It was an awkward angle, and it took every ounce of strength that King had to cock the weapon without the foot stirrup attached to the fore-end of the weapon. King aimed at the third man, but he was already moving – running hard and fast across the open ground to a belt of evergreens. King quietly cursed. He had been meaning to take down the conifers and enlarge the orchard, but the thick, bushy trees hid the man once he stepped amongst them. Someone less experienced may have taken a hopeful shot into the foliage, but King knew the odds against that, and even a bolt fired from such a powerful crossbow could be deflected by the thinnest of branches. Besides, he only had four bolts remaining and was loath to waste one unless he had a clear shot. King turned and faced the oncoming threat, footsteps crunching on the gravel behind him. The man had focused on this too and came out shooting. Confused, King used the night sight to survey the ground behind him. Four men, but unlike the three who had entered from the direction of the creek these men were dressed in casual clothes, one of them even wearing a suit. King studied the weapons, fearing for a moment that the men could be police officers, but discounting that as soon as he identified one of the weapons as a Kalashnikov, given away by its long, curved magazine. He aimed at the furthest one and fired. The bolt reached the target within two seconds and the man doubled over and dropped to his knees. The men in front of him had no idea that they were a man down and King reloaded, taking a bolt from the quiver rack underneath the weapon and slipping the bolt between his teeth as he pulled back the bowstring, then slipped the bolt in place. His movements were methodical and fluid, but clearly not as stealthy as he would have hoped and bullets tracked across the grass in front of him, sending mud up into his face. King threw himself clear and pushed his way through the foliage and rolled to his right once he was clear. A volley of gunfire followed him through the bushes, but he was already clear as the gunman fired blindly, and his bullets headed for the creek beyond. King changed tack and backtracked around the cottage. He slung the crossbow over his shoulder on its sling and drew the Sig Sauer 9mm. He had only reached the gable end when a man running towards him stopped suddenly, his shoes skidding on the path. The man raised his weapon, but King dropped down and fired three shots from his hip. The man squirmed as the bullets struck him in the stomach and King straightened his arm, aiming true and shot him in the forehead. He changed over magazines despite still having eleven rounds remaining, but now with the last bullet chambered, he now had sixteen 9mm bullets at his disposal. King pressed on; his eyes well-adjusted to the gloom. He had timed blinking with each gunshot, the muzzle flash briefly lighting the rear of the house as if it were daylight and threatening to snatch his night vision from him. His ears were ringing, and despite having fired weapons thousands of times, there was nothing like the first salvo to assault your senses. King could see the next man firing across the rough grassy area at the front of the house, too unkempt to call it a lawn, but not a meadow by any means. King switched to the crossbow. No sense in giving away his position, and the night sight and shoulder stock of the crossbow made it a far more accurate prospect over the distance of sixty metres or so between King and the gunman. King aimed, but he did not tighten his finger on the trigger. What were the chances of a simultaneous attack by separate forces? But they were certainly opposing forces, as the battle on the front garden ahead of him was in full flow. King was about to fire, but the man moved forward. He soon found another target and took aim on a man wearing a leather bomber jacket and carrying a sawn-off shotgun. He fired and the bolt shot past the man's face and off into the night. The man turned and at the same time, he flicked on a head torch and King was blinded by a blue-white LED beam that cut through the night like something from a sci-fi movie. The man fired and King felt himself peppered with shot. King dropped the crossbow – far too slow to load now – and answered with the pistol. The man threw himself onto his stomach and fired again, but King was rolling across the grass and the wide spread of shot missed him and he heard the shot spraying the hedge behind him instead. King could feel the shot on him now, his clothing had taken the brunt of velocity out of the shot – and thankfully it was travelling at only four-hundred feet per second – but he knew that some of the shot had broken the skin as he could feel something warm and wet on his chest that he knew wasn't perspiration. King answered with three shots from the 9mm, and the bullets were travelling at almost four times the velocity as the shotgun pellets. The man went down and rested still, his headtorch beam shining a motionless searchlight in the sky.

King did not hear the helicopter approaching. The gunfire must have suppressed the sound, but he saw its belly in the beam from the man's headtorch, and when its searchlight illuminated the area in front of his home, the men firing at each other were caught in its beam and left looking panicked and unsure what they should do next. The helicopter banked and King saw the door slide open. A single figure leaned out with a rifle, and then the helicopter spun around, and the engine pitch and noise of the rotors changed, and King could clearly hear the report of the rifle above the din that a helicopter makes from such proximity. King watched and two men went down. Each man was from the other side, and almost at once the men scattered and set back out the way they had come. King watched as the helicopter carved out another turn and by the time it came back, there were no more gunmen to engage, and the aircraft lowered in a landing hover approach. Six feet from the ground and two figures leapt out. One figure was considerably larger than the other, and this beast of a man set out towards the road where the retreating gunmen were getting back into their vehicles. King heard several gunshots, but only for as long as the vehicles took to rev and wheelspin their way to escape. The smaller figure set out towards the creek, stopping and crouching to take three-round bursts at the retreating gunmen.

King remained in the shadows. The helicopter had landed on the unfenced paddock area beyond the garden. He watched as the two men regrouped and headed his way. Both men kept their weapons trained on the bodies on the grass until they had ascertained that they were no longer a threat. King watched as the two men peeled off their balaclavas and comms. The giant of a man was black. He was six-four and eighteen stone before breakfast. The other man was wiry and slim and Asian. Pakistani to be precise, although he had been born in Britain and had at one time been the youngest ethnic minority captain in the British army. Both men had served in the SAS, or 22 Special Air Service Regiment.

"I didn't think you would retire peacefully," said Rashid.

King stepped out from the shadows and onto the grass. "Where's the fun in that?"

The large black man, aptly nicknamed Big Dave beamed a set of brilliant white teeth against the darkness and said, "Get a brew on, mate. We've got a bit of news for you..."

TWO

King put the kettle on the stove. The stove was an oil-fired Aga and the kettle had been one of Caroline's whimsical purchases from an artisan kitchen shop. And from what King could ascertain, cost five times the price of a decent electrical kettle and took three times as long to reach the boil. But it had a whistle and King need never miss a cup of tea through distraction again. As he watched the steam start to waft from the spout, he realised just how much his life had changed since his childhood and those days of survival, dodging social service case officers and getting into trouble with the police, or worse.

"And you are confident that Caroline will be safe?"

King looked at Simon Mereweather, head of MI5. His short tenure at the Britain's counterintelligence and anti-terrorism service had borne huge success and wild failures, but the good had outweighed the bad, and working with King and undertaking a ruthless approach had shut down branches of the Russian mafia, rogue CIA operations on UK soil as well as Islamic extremism and interference from both wings of the Russian intelligence services. Despite the man's hardened stomach for the fight in keeping his country safe from hostile interference and attack, it was far from normal for Mereweather to arrive in such a manner and he had clearly taken a risk in being here. "I am," King replied.

"Where has she gone?" Mereweather asked.

King poured the hot water into the five cups and watched as the teabags puffed up and floated to the surface. "She's safe."

"I suspect you both thought that you were safe down here, too."

King didn't answer. He splashed some milk in then spooned in four sugars for Big Dave and one for himself. "I had it covered."

"I just need to know that Caroline is safe."

King fished out the teabags and tossed them into the sink. He stirred perfunctorily and handed the cups around. He took a packet of biscuits out of the cupboard, tossed them over to Big Dave and smiled as the man started to devour them by dunking them into his tea. The thump of the engine and rotors grew as the helicopter flew overhead, then its pitch altered as it started to descend. "Good timing," he said, then looked at Mereweather. "She's gone to her aunt's. Her family is estranged – some kind of falling out - and her aunt changed her name to escape an abusive relationship. Only Caroline is in touch with her now. Caroline has left her regular phone and cards, taken only cash and both of our cars have had the satnav removed."

"Yes, we know."

"You've been trying to find us?"

"Yeah, didn't know where to send a Christmas card to you both," Big Dave quipped.

Rashid laughed. "King's not exactly hot on goodbyes, either."

King shrugged. "But you're here now, so..."

"Yeah, but I don't think you'll be staying somehow," Big Dave said, then cursed as his biscuit fell apart on the third dunk and splashed into his tea. King tossed him the teaspoon and watched as the man set about salvaging the remains, but it was a lost cause. MIA. The big Fijian cut his losses and stirred the tea well, opting for a malty sludge instead. He was briefly distracted by a text which he looked at and sighed. He slipped the phone back into his pocket and tried the new tea recipe giving little away as to his thoughts.

"Another text?" Mereweather frowned. "That's about the fifth today. This is not the time for affairs of the heart. Your love life is of no concern to the service. Get your head in the game, Lomu."

Big Dave sipped another mouthful of tea, then said quietly, "We all have our problems, Mister Mereweather. Talk to me like that again and getting my foot out of your arse will be yours..."

There was an awkward silence, but eventually both King and Rashid laughed, and it went a little way to cutting the growing tension. Dave Lomu was a man mountain, and there was never any doubt that he would follow through on any threat he made. Mereweather seemed to realise this and shrugged, his lips just the right side of a smile. "Okay, point taken. But if you have a problem, you can share. Talk before it's too late."

"You sound like one of those mental health awareness adverts," Big Dave quipped. "I'm not sure sharing will find much caring in my case." He paused. "But duly noted..."

Mereweather shrugged and turned back to King. "Where is this aunt?" he persisted.

"Scotland," King lied.

Mereweather nodded, but he didn't seem convinced. He looked up as Leroy entered. He was a black man in his early thirties. Ex-army Air Corps and he went by the moniker Flymo named after the brand of lawnmowers that floated on a cushion of air, and because nothing or nobody could hover any lower.

"Hey, Flymo," King greeted him.

"Watcha. Bloody hell, it's carnage out there," he commented eyeing the cup of tea. "Is that mine?" he asked, not waiting for an answer as he helped himself. "They're long gone on the road, but I followed the boat, a mid-sized vessel. I think it's what they call a fast fisher. Twenty-five feet in length, cabin, berth, a working deck and a couple of large outboard motors." He paused, swigging down most of the tea which had cooled just enough to do so. "I coordinated with Falmouth coastguard and the maritime police, and they've intercepted the boat near the village of St. Mawes across the water on the Roseland Peninsular. No weapons found on board. The men say they were going night fishing."

"Dumped the weapons in the Carrick Roads," said King. The permanent body of water fed by three rivers and at least a dozen or so tidal creeks boasted one of the world's deepest natural harbours with a deep channel that went inland and was deep enough at all tides to moor seized transport vessels or ships waiting to be repaired in Falmouth Docks. Short of being scooped up by scallop dredgers, the weapons would be lost forever to the sandy and silty bottom. And considering that the only scallop dredgers allowed to operate on the water had to be wind-powered sailboats called *luggers*, he would have put money on the weapons being unrecoverable in the silt and mud.

"Get the police on the radio and give the order to

release them, but only after Sally-Anne and Ramsay are in position to follow. Let's see where these bastards go next…" Flymo nodded and left the kitchen taking his tea with him. Mereweather looked at King and said, "What was with the William Tell performance?"

"It got the job done," replied King.

"The paperwork is going to be interesting," Rashid smiled.

"Let Ramsay deal with it. I'll toss the crossbow in the river, and he can lay down the blame at both sides," King replied.

Mereweather nodded. "Ramsay will smooth it over. It's what he does so well."

King smiled. "That detective is still working with you, then?"

"Sally-Anne? Yes, and she's been invaluable of late," Mereweather replied. "The days are coming when we will be working more like police officers than surveillance specialists."

"I think we're way past that now. Until Charles Forrester brought me in, and we took the fight to the enemy head-on, the Security Service's remit was very clear."

"That's why we're not technically in it anymore…" Big Dave commented flatly. "A new department, a little less accountability."

King stared back at him. "What? Anyway, I thought you'd bailed and were lying low in Berlin…"

The big man shrugged. "I was. But when Ramsay came over and proposed another option to me, well, I guess I'd had enough of bockwurst and sexually uninhibited young women…" he grinned.

"His proposal must have been a good one," King ventured.

"It was," Rashid said quietly. "That's why I'm here, too."

King shrugged. "I guess I wasn't on the list..."

"You're on sabbatical. And after the last job, and what you said to me on the Embankment, I was giving you some time."

"So, what was the big proposal?"

"I'll let you know after we have addressed *this* issue. But in short, the Security Service returns to its remit and a small team with a short chain of command and little accountability keep the country safer than if we didn't exist."

King nodded. "Then with regards to Sally-Anne Thorpe, having a police officer's take on our work is a backward step." He knew he'd said enough. When all was said and done, Caroline had royally screwed the woman over and shown that the team had its specialities and was not only a vital resource, but a force to be reckoned with. King put his empty mug down. "Okay. It's time to level with me. What the fuck is going on?"

"You know something," said Mereweather.

"I know a lot of things." King paused. "Most of it pointless."

"But you know a hell of a lot of things that you shouldn't."

"We all do in this game," replied King.

Mereweather nodded. Like the rest of them, he had trouble sleeping sometimes. People like King, Big Dave and Rashid did the dirty work, but people like Simon Mereweather handed out the missions and with that came a different set of emotions and responsibilities. "You know a woman called Margaret Stewart, don't you?"

King cast his mind back, not familiar with the name at first, then feeling foolish that he had not associated her with his one-time mentor at MI6. Of course, he knew her. Stewart had often briefed King at his own home. Not everyone working for the SIS walked into the River House. King had only been there a handful of times in his dozen or so years with the 'firm'. Margaret had brought them tea and biscuits and sometimes King had stayed for dinner and one of Margaret's delicious homecooked meals. King had never really had a homecooked meal growing up and hadn't known the difference until much later in life. His mother had thrown frozen meals into the microwave or let him and his siblings use the account she ran at the all-night café. It was a dive used by market traders during the day and taxi drivers and prostitutes at night. Stewed tea, soggy chips and questionable meat content in the sausages, but a place with heat and light and a plate of food for a couple of pounds. She had an arrangement with the owner, and he cleared her account every Friday night. His mother had arrangements with other men, but not for such wholesome or admirable provisions as food and a place for her children to warm from their dank, freezing council flat with the mould on the walls and the persistent drip from the ceiling. His mother had been a junkie and her arrangements for a fix had led to her path to prostitution and eventually her own demise through drug addiction and recklessness. King and his siblings had entered the social care system, or at least King had until he was old enough and soon found himself in prison. His two youngest siblings had gone to a nice home, eventually adopted by their foster parents and his mixed-race brother had been found a place with an Afro-Caribbean couple who could address many of his needs. His sister Leanne had ended up on a slippery slope, destined to follow their mother's path, but King had intervened. He no longer had contact with any of his siblings, but that had been part of the deal and his new identity and work with MI6 had meant that King had left a shaky family life behind and been tossed into a world of isolation and secrets, with nobody to talk to and nobody who would ever truly understand. Outside of the service, he could not tell anyone about either his past or his employment. Margaret Stewart had seen this in him and when her husband had brought the young man into his home for their briefings between assignments, she had recognised a man who had needed a relaxed, warm environment, and had spoiled him with his favourite foods for dinner. King smiled at the thought. He had missed her over the years. King had parted from MI6 feeling betrayed by Stewart. The man had eventually made it up to King, and then some, when MI5 and MI6 crossed paths in an operation in the northern tripoint of Finland, Norway and Russia. King missed his mentor, but he missed the man's wife, too.

"I worked with her husband in the Secret Intelligence Service."

Mereweather nodded. "Yes, Rashid said this man Peter Stewart was at the ice hotel in Lapland." He paused, glancing at Rashid and back to King. "I gather the man paid his debt to you, in more ways than one. He was also instrumental in the operation's success..."

Success? King thought how it had eventually played out. How the asset was put on a submarine in a fjord and what had eventually transpired. Was there even a scintilla of success? King hadn't thought so, but they kept something out of Russia's hands, so that obviously marked a success in Mereweather's book. But it all came at a hefty price that had been paid in lives. "Stewart recruited me. He later betrayed me. The debt was settled," King replied tersely.

"Margaret Stewart was murdered," said Mereweather without a hint of emotion.

King looked at him. He had seen more than anybody's fair share of death, but the news that the woman had been killed, murdered in fact, shook him inside. He hid it, of course. That was what men like King did. His cold, grey-blue eyes didn't so much as flicker, but Caroline would have noticed the downward pull to his lips – the sign that he was upset – but it was already gone. He stared back at Mereweather and said, "Who the hell would murder such a lovely woman? She had nothing to do with the intelligence services."

"That's what we want to find out," Mereweather replied. "Because we think that they were after something of Stewart's, or something she knew merely by association."

"The man's dead!" King slammed a fist on the counter. Mereweather visibly flinched, but Rashid and Big Dave didn't even come close to spilling their tea. "What could he have there that would be of use to anyone?"

Mereweather sighed, "I said she was murdered, King. But I haven't yet told you how she died." He paused, watching the man's expression. There was more than a downward pull to his lips, and for the first time ever, he could see through the man's façade. The stare slipped. It was enough for a good poker player to bet their entire hand against him. "She was tortured, King. Over a long period and quite savagely. If she knew anything, had been trusted with knowledge that she shouldn't have, then they will know by now…"

THREE

The cars arrived and turned around in the driveway facing back out. Two Range Rover Vogues and a Land Rover Discovery. All liveried in black with tinted windows all round.

"Oh look, the drug dealers have arrived..." Big Dave chuckled.

"Subtle," King commented flatly. "I'll be in the Audi."

"They're from diplomatic protection," Rashid countered defensively. "The best I could do at such short notice."

"I don't get why we can't fly," Mereweather protested.

"You will fly. You can be safely above us at five-thousand feet, if you prefer," Rashid replied. "The vehicles are equipped with Kevlar sheets behind the panels and inside the doors, and ballistic resistant glass has replaced the standard windows and front and rear windscreens. I'll be taking up the rear in the Disco. Big Dave will be in the lead vehicle." He paused. "Most people wrongly assume that the VIP travels in the middle vehicle in a three-car cavalcade, but this isn't the case. The VIP travels in the lead car and if there is an ambush, the middle vehicle overtakes and blocks the front while the middle and rear vehicle J turn it out of there. We're going with the hope that they will assume King is in the middle vehicle. This is why the only person in there is a driver named John from the carpool. He knows the risks and he's onboard."

"Armed?" Mereweather asked, although it went way beyond any MI5 remit except for when operating abroad, and only for self-defence. As MI5 started to do more work in Iraq after the fall of Saddam's regime, the need to expand upon the weapon handling course that was once just used for officers working in Northern Ireland, was soon realised, but not before it had cost lives.

"A handgun. Self-defence only, or if he fears threat to life."

Mereweather nodded. "Okay. I can deny you lot, but when the carpool boys get involved, we need things to be done by the book."

"I don't think we've ever done anything by the book," Big Dave commented glibly. "Anyway, it's a plan. If we stick King on the chopper then he'll be safe, but we need the enemy, whoever they are, to make a move. We can't fight who we can't see and right now, we're blind. If we can get to them, then we can find out who they are, or who they're working for."

"Nice," said King. "So, I'm a stalking horse?"

"More like live bait, I guess," Big Dave replied.

"We believe that they think you know what Stewart knew and what he may have told his wife..." Mereweather explained.

"Margaret," King reminded him.

"Sorry, yes. What Margaret Stewart may have known."

King looked at him expectantly and said, "And this is all you've got?"

"It was short notice, man," Big Dave drawled. "An Armalite at both ends and a shit-scared driver in the middle, with a stuffed suit watching it all safely from the sky above..."

King shrugged. "Alright, just checking..." To be fair, King knew that he'd had less well-conceived plans spanning most of his career, and he trusted the men in front of him with his life. Which was exactly what he was about to do. Except for the fact that he would be following from a distance in his own car with a rifle of his own. The plan was workable, but he had speed and anonymity in his own vehicle, and he had left it parked inside his garage, so it was unlikely that the team of people watching him had any idea of its existence. Caroline had left in her own vehicle but had agreed to stop and switch to the set of numberplates that King had stolen from an identically coloured Mini Cooper S parked outside a local dealership.

"Any thoughts on what this could be about?" Rashid asked him as Mereweather walked towards the helicopter.

King shrugged. "It could be literally anything..."

"And what about Caroline? Are you sure she's safe?" He held up his hands before King could react. "Look, I know what you told Simon was bullshit, and you don't have to tell me either, but these people are ruthless. Whoever is behind this has either hired at least two separate hit teams, or there is more than one person with one angle involved."

King trusted Rashid with his life and had done so many times before. But he hadn't made it into his forties in such a dangerous career by not listening to his gut instincts, and right now, he had to think about Caroline and her safety. He could take on whatever was coming his way – in a way part of him always expected blowback from operations and he had even accepted it – but Caroline was out. She had made her choice and left MI5 behind. King had been taking a sabbatical and had yet to decide his future. "She's safe up in Scotland," he lied. He had checked their email accounts; found her alteration to the message in the draft folder on his third attempt. She had done all he had told her. Taken a devious, less obvious route and swapped the number plates at the first opportunity. Her aunt's cottage was near Scafell Pike, and Caroline would be able to disappear hill walking for most of the days around the Lake District and catching up with her aunt in quaint tearooms and cosy pubs with log fires. It sounded more favourable to King than being shot at, but he had to admit that he was more than a little curious about who was behind this.

"How did you find out about the contract?" King asked. The helicopter's engine fired up and the rotor blades began to turn slowly, gaining momentum as the engine revs built. "If you don't know who's behind it..."

"A man named Reno. A French-Spaniard." Rashid paused. "He's a former Basque Separatist. Used to be a big name in ETA but left for political reasons. Like ETA don't have the fight in them anymore. ETA had training and financial support funnelled to them from the IRA, but with the peace agreement that revenue and resource stream died out. The Arab Spring saw many of the North African training camps shut up shop, so Reno decided to go as a gun-for-hire. He's good at what he does. Interpol and both the French DGSE and the Spanish NIC have open files on him."

King nodded. He had worked in partnership with the French General Directorate for External Security, or the *Direction générale de la sécurité extérieure*, but he knew very little of the Spanish National Intelligence Centre, despite their work against both ETA and Islamic extremism. "Open files, as in, actively investigating him?"

"Yes."

"And?"

"His conversation was intercepted with an arms dealer with links to the Russian Bratva," said Rashid. "They have very little on this Reno guy, but he was pinged through voice recognition held on file from a few years ago. The arms dealer was under surveillance, not this guy Reno. From the conversation a location for Reno was discovered and raided, but Reno got away. It was close. The man was unable to fully destroy details of the hit, but that hit was you."

"And this guy, Reno, he was here tonight?"

Rashid shook his head. "No. And he wasn't behind this." Rashid shrugged. "He's disappeared into thin air, but whoever hired Reno for the contract hedged their bets and put the contract up for grabs. Police, Interpol and intelligence services across Europe have intercepted various communications and they're all mentioning one man. Or two..."

King looked at him, his eyes narrowing. "Go on..."

"The name on the underworld's hit list is Alex King," Rashid replied, then shrugged and said, "And Mark Thomas Jeffries..."

King said nothing. His spine felt like ice. Even his heart felt cold, and he was aware of his pulse thudding in his ears. It wasn't a name he had heard in many years, but so few had known that he knew where the source of treachery would have come from. A sealed file in a seldom visited basement at MI6. He doubted it had been uploaded to a computer file – just one of hundreds of manilla envelopes holding the dirty little secrets of the country that nobody was ever meant to open again.

"You know this guy?"

King nodded. The helicopter was taking off vertically and Flymo being Flymo, was making Simon Mereweather wish he'd taken a ride in a car instead by banking at an impossible angle as he pulled into a steep climb. "I do," he said quietly, the helicopter further away and its engine and rotor noise almost a distant hum. "We have to go to Southampton first." He paused. "I need to check on someone."

"Who?"

"My sister," replied King.

"But you don't have a sister."

"I never mentioned her."

Rashid shook his head. "No, you *don't* have a sister..."

"Been checking my file?" King asked sharply.

"Just being thorough."

King said tersely. "I'm Mark Jeffries." He paused. "Now, let's get going. I just hope it's not too late..."

FOUR

The police boat cruised slowly out through the boats in St. Mawes harbour and back towards Falmouth, a twinkling of lights a mile across the mouth of the Carrick Roads. Only a few fishing boats remained in the natural harbour sound, the pleasure craft would be out of the water until late March or early April. Ramsay had been here before in the summer months and the entire inlet had been littered with all manner of pleasure craft from rowing boats and dinghies through to motor yachts worth millions of pounds. Located on the tip of The Roseland – a peninsular jutting off the peninsular of Cornwall – an affluent area of second homes that was quiet in the winter months and overrun with tourists throughout the summer.

"They must know we're onto them…"

"I doubt it. They will be relieved just not to get nicked," Sally-Anne Thorpe replied, her right eye close to the infrared monocular. "They've gone from being arrested on suspicion of having illegal weapons and being involved in a shooting to getting a ticking off for night fishing without the proper use of running lights. They won't be thinking that many moves ahead." Ramsay shrugged and turned back to the laptop balancing on top of his knees. He had activated the tracking device that Thorpe had slipped under the suspects' car once the police had ascertained which vehicle was theirs. Thorpe adjusted the reticule and said, "They've moored the boat. The last man is climbing the ladder to the quay now." She paused. "Most hobby fishermen would probably grab a pint in the local pub to warm up and discuss their trip, but these guys are just heading for the car." She held out the monocular for Ramsay.

"They've got a couple of rods, but no tackle," he said, his tone suspicious.

"You're a fisherman on the quiet?"

"No. But I did a bit when the kids were younger. Those aren't boat rods, either. They're too long. They look more like beach casters to me."

"And the difference is?"

"You don't cast your line far on a boat because you're already out there. You drop your line, hence the shorter rod. From the beach, you cast as far as you can, or at least into the surf where the green waves break into white water." He paused, passing the monocular back to Thorpe. "And most fishermen wouldn't leave their tackle on the boat for fear of theft. These men have rods but no equipment. They are just props."

"That pretty much confirms it, then." Sally-Anne paused, looking at the laptop. "Is that thing ready?"

"It is."

Thorpe started the car, but kept the headlights switched off. Many modern comfort features largely seen as standard within the car industry had been addressed by the car-pool at MI5. There were no courtesy lights, no follow-you-home headlights to remain on or come on before you wanted them. The vehicles made no sound and nor did their lights flash upon locking or unlocking and could be driven without fasten seatbelt lights and alarms if wearing a seatbelt was not practical, and the vehicles could also engage gear and drive with the doors open, whereupon many modern vehicles simply wouldn't move or go into drive. Like many vehicles within the car-pool the car – a BMW 335i had been fitted with a larger fuel tank, enhanced run-flat tyres and had three-hundred-and-sixty-degree camera recording from front and rear-mounted cameras and a camera in each front wing, looking just like a parking sensor – an alteration made after King had once knocked off both wing mirror-mounted cameras on a previous mission. These frontline vehicles were also fitted with ballistic enhanced glass, Kevlar sheets between the panels and door cards, a filtration system to operate during a chemical or biological attack, and a master override switch that could be operated before an EMP – electromagnetic pulse – the phenomenon that happens during the detonation of a nuclear warhead that renders most electronic devices and microchips useless. If the EMP override is operated before the pulse, then the system could be started back up and the vehicle would still be able to function. The system had been devised for the possibility of an EMP machine being created for financial fraud. Many attempts had been made to hack financial institutions and deploy EMP to cover the money trail, but as yet the EMP devices were by no means powerful enough and all attempts had been thwarted with little disruption. MI5 intelligence had shown that the likelihood of terrorists attempting to source a nuclear warhead for the purposes of their cause was infinitesimal compared to organised crime willing to set off a warhead to get away with unprecedented financial fraud. The tools were out there – Russia was still unwilling (or unable) to confirm a full manifest of their nuclear weapons after the fall of the Soviet Union, and Russia was being as belligerent as ever with the West, almost daring NATO to make a move over the invasion of Ukraine. A leadership with nothing but lies and retribution on their agenda.

"Don't get too close," said Ramsay.

"Thanks, but I *do* know what I'm doing…"

"I know. I'm just saying, the tracking device will do the work for us. It's a long road out of The Roseland and we'll likely be the only other car on the road this late in the evening. No sense in giving ourselves away when the technology can do the work for us."

Thorpe tutted. She hated relying upon tracking devices when a visual confirmed all was well. It was always disconcerting to follow suspects and yet be completely blind. Two of the men could leap out of the car at slow speeds and they would be none the wiser. "Fine," she said eventually and replaced the monocular in its soft velvet bag. She watched as the vehicle pulled out of the parking space and performed a three-point-turn before taking off rapidly and passing the quaint pub and luxury hotel, now quiet after the recent Christmas and New Year visitors had left their second homes empty for the remainder of winter. Some empty houses even had Christmas or 'winter festival' lights of reindeer and Father Christmas and snowmen, or religious Christmas decorations with nativity scenes and wise men atop camels, the owners obviously leaving in a hurry and promising themselves to take them down 'one weekend', that never came. But it was evident that the majority of quaint cottages were shadowed in darkness, the owners either skiing or in London (or 'town' as they referred to the capital) for winter. As the dot on the screen of the laptop started to gain in distance from them, Thorpe put her foot down and the silky-smooth straight six engine took them effortlessly north of eighty-miles-per-hour.

"Easy," Ramsay warned her. "You're gaining too quickly. And it's just likely that a local copper will be sat parked up down a quiet lane waiting for drunk drivers going too fast and with too many drinks inside them." Thorpe eased back on the accelerator, knowing that Ramsay was right, and angry at herself for being too eager and having her judgement called. "That's better," Ramsay commented without looking up from the screen, or seeing the scathing look upon her face in the gloom of the cabin. He clicked on an email notification that popped up on the corner of the screen. After he'd finished reading, he said, "They've set off back to London. Using the convoy as bait."

"Is King with them?"

"Yes."

"And Caroline...?"

"No. She left before they got there. She's lying low somewhere."

"Right..."

"Still not her biggest fan?"

Thorpe thought about how she had thought they had started to warm to each other a little, how she had been taken in by her and ultimately betrayed. Of course, Caroline wouldn't see it like that. She would have seen Thorpe as an interloper, the face of the law amid the team's flagrant disregard for the rules and international law. She would have seen her as the enemy, because in Caroline's mind, if she wasn't part of the solution then she was part of the problem. Caroline had broken the law, killed a man when the operation had been to arrest him and hand him to Interpol. Caroline had manged to play Thorpe enough to incriminate her if she needed to. As far as Sally-Anne Thorpe was concerned, her ten years exemplary service with the Metropolitan Police had been the reason she was now working with MI5, but she had been played and incriminated by one of the people she had been working to ultimately protect. A man had been killed when due process should have put him behind bars. And if she ever voiced it publicly, there was CCTV footage in the Italian town and post office incriminating Thorpe, fingerprints on the weapon and Caroline had even hidden her hair under a hat for the CCTV that she knew would capture her at the victim's villa. No one thing could incriminate Thorpe, but Caroline held all the cards because collectively it painted a picture of Thorpe that would be difficult for the former detective to disprove. No, Thorpe was not a fan of Caroline Darby. "I think the feeling is mutual..." she replied quietly.

"You should give her a chance. She's loyal and dependable."

"So was my Labrador before it went under a bus."

Ramsay shrugged. Most people would have expressed sympathy or sorrow, perhaps a word of comfort upon hearing what the woman had just said, but Ramsay was more than a little on the spectrum, although it was his autism that made him a brilliant planner and analyst, if not terrible as a confidante or shoulder to cry on. "She has been an essential part of every operation since I came aboard. I can't think of anyone I could depend on more."

Thorpe frowned. "You know I have your back, don't you?"

"Unproven. We'll see."

"Say it like you see it..."

"Is there any other way?"

"I suppose not," Thorpe replied.

She was starting to get used to Neil Ramsay and his idiosyncrasies, but she couldn't help thinking that she had not been free to work so exclusively with the other members of the team and would therefore never bond with them in the same way that Caroline had. Although she knew that Dave Lomu had only recently returned from Berlin at Simon Mereweather's request, and King had been on an unofficial break, referred to by the others as a sabbatical. It did not look as if she would work with Caroline again, as she had formally left MI5, although Thorpe was not privy to all the details, it concerned the outcome of their last mission and what she had done in Italy. However, if she was going to truly blend into the team, she would have to be more than Ramsay's police advisor and oversee part of an operation on her own.

"Slow down," Ramsay said, frowning at the screen in front of him. Thorpe took her foot off the accelerator but the BMW – denoted by a flashing blue dot on the screen, which was taking its bearings from the vehicle's unique GPS signal - was still gaining on the static red dot. "Slow down! I mean it!"

Thorpe planted her foot on the brake pedal, but the car nosed around the corner before it came to an abrupt halt, and the suspects' vehicle was pulled across the road. Two men stood behind the vehicle with their pistols drawn.

Time seemed to stand still.

"Down!" Thorpe shouted and slammed the gearbox into reverse. Ramsay ducked his head as the bullets slammed into the windscreen, the muzzle flashes lighting up the night sky enough to see the men's faces clearly behind the weapons. The BMW's rear wheels span briefly before the traction control activated and the vehicle surged back around the corner. Thorpe swung the steering wheel around and as the car span around in the road, she slammed the gearbox into first and floored the accelerator before finding second and almost instantly third gear.

"Crickey!" Ramsay managed to say, before looking into the wing mirror, and then down at the laptop, which had landed screen down in the footwell. He picked up the device and groaned. "Damn and blast…"

"What?"

"The screen is buggered…"

"We've got bigger problems!" She screamed. "We've got headlights behind us…"

Ramsay turned around in his seat and stared at the headlights. "Is it them?"

"I can't tell," Thorpe replied testily. "But the road is quiet, I doubt it's anybody else."

Ramsay took out his phone and started to dial. He looked in the wing mirror, dazzled by the lights, then spoke quickly giving a brief explanation and their location. He ended the call but kept firmly hold of his phone. "Turn off here," he said.

"What? It leads to the beach. It's a dead end!" Thorpe slowed the car but seemed to have second thoughts. Her instincts telling her it was all kinds of wrong. She was about to steer back through the bend when Ramsay caught hold of the wheel and yanked it hard to the right, the car veering across the solid white line and down the narrow lane. "Shit! What are you doing…?"

Ramsay checked his phone, but only to use the clock. He had released his grip on the wheel and Thorpe was now tackling the narrow country road, their headlights cutting through the pitch-black night, but the high-sided hedges giving the effect of travelling through a tunnel. "Ruan High

Lanes," he commented. "The place certainly lives up to the name..."

Thorpe wasn't listening. She was scathing. They had left the main road and even if the road ended back in St. Mawes, at least there were alternative roads and a loop that would put them back on track for Truro or St. Austell. This road, however, led only to a quiet cove and once they reached it, then their pursuers held both the high ground and the only route to escape. The road narrowed even further, but the headlights behind them were incessantly bright and gaining on them, despite Thorpe driving for all she was worth. Ahead of them, their headlights glinted upon the ocean and the road opened out onto a concrete launch slip and a large, gravelled carpark. The BMW slewed on the loose surface and their lights cut a swath across the empty carpark.

Ramsay checked his phone, then said, "Drive right up to the end..."

"The police will be miles away they'll never get here in time!" she protested but followed his instruction all the same, turning the BMW around so they could at least face their enemy. A hundred metres in front them the vehicle reached the carpark and slowed down considerably. "Jesus... they'll pick us off with their guns..."

Ramsay tapped the windscreen. There were a few spider's webs of cracked glass from the earlier gunfire, but the ballistic glass had held. "We're okay," he said. "Bullet resistant."

"But it won't hold for long..." There were muzzle flashes ahead of them. In the flashes of light, they could see that two of the men had got out of the vehicle and were walking slowly towards them, taking their time and their bullets coming onto target as they closed the gap. The driver and their vehicle remained parked blocking the only exit. It was now a killing zone. Sally-Anne screamed as several bullets ricocheted off the windscreen. "How soon before it breaks?"

Ramsay checked his phone again and smiled. A bright light filled the sky and the beam terminated on the two men and their vehicle. The 'whump' of rotor blades filled their ears and neither Ramsay nor Thorpe needed to look to know that the helicopter was hovering perilously close to them, the BMW buffeting from side to side from the rotor wash. The two men aimed at an unseen point above them and started to fire. Return gunfire erupted almost instantly, drowning out the sound of the men's pistols and in rapid bursts that both men were unable to either match or contend with. Empty shell casings rained down on the BMW's roof and clattered onto the gravel. Both men went down and rested still. The vehicle started to reverse out of the carpark and attempted to turn around on the launch slip, but the driver aimed and fired his weapon out of the open passenger window and sealed his fate. Rapid bursts of gunfire peppered the door and went through the open window. With the driver slumped over the steering wheel the vehicle continued to travel backwards all the way down the launch slip and into the calm water. The rear of the vehicle started to sink, the bonnet rising into the air, then amid a flurry of air bubbles it sank quickly, its headlights soon underwater and the beams flickering and fading until it was lost to the depths.

"Timing is everything," Ramsay commented, looking at Thorpe beside him. "As is a team you can truly count on..."

The two watched the helicopter land at the far end of the carpark and King leapt out and checked both bodies before he walked towards them, followed by a nervous-looking Simon Mereweather. King cradled the AR-15 and tapped on the driver's window. Thorpe lowered it and looked blankly up at him.

"Well, I'll be blowed. Plod decided to stay on to police the Security Service..."

"Someone has to hold you lot accountable," she replied quietly.

"You're welcome, by the way," said King. He bent down, looked at Ramsay and said, "Alright Neil?"

"Fine. Thanks."

"This is terrible! Absolutely terrible!" Simon Mereweather exclaimed as he stood beside King. "Bodies here, bodies at your property... And a car that will need dragging out of the sea with a crane at low tide... I don't know where to start..." He breathed out a long sigh and for a moment the silence was all-encompassing as nobody knew quite how to respond.

King smirked. "This place is a bit of a lover's lane with the local youths and extra-marital types." King paused. "Not to mention one for the doggers when the weather is warmer. I must admit, I was surprised to see you two here..."

"Funny..." Thorpe grinned. "And now I have to explain what dogging is to Neil..."

"This isn't the time for larking about, you two. People have died, and this is a right mess," Mereweather said tersely.

"Well, you're lucky, Simon. It's nice and quiet here. Which will give you time to get a story concocted," said King. "You can get a ride back to London with Neil and Sally-Anne while Flymo drops me back to my car." He paused. "I would suggest you start by saying that two of your number were caught up in the same gang-on-gang violence they were investigating near Mylor."

Thorpe looked up at King, her expression softening

somewhat. It was the first time King had used her name. It was early days, but she suddenly felt some acceptance. "You're going back to see if you can flush out the other hit team?"

"It's the best we've got," replied King.

"And how do I explain that earlier incident?" Mereweather snapped.

"You hide behind the Official Secrets Act and the Terrorism Act. Your agent, that would be me – no names - was getting close to discovering something crucial about them and they sent a hit team to eliminate me. The rival gang followed and decided to end them right there and then. Both sides withdrew and the battle resumed here. The other gang fled the scene." King paused. "Just tell them what they need to know, or what you can afford to let them know..."

"We can't just blindside the police!" Thorpe interjected.

"You can and you bloody will!" King roared at her, noting that all three physically flinched in response to his raised voice. "We work in the shadows to keep people safe at night. We do what has to be done and we have to live with the consequences. That's the job. Sometimes, people have to be held to account. If that person is me, and it is truly in the peoples' best interest, then I will fall on my sword. But until that day, we fight, and we keep moving forward until our battles are won..."

FIVE

Nobody came for him. Nobody took a shot at the motorcade, nor attempted to run it off the road. After King re-joined the convoy at Cornwall Services, Flymo pushing the boundaries of what could be done in a helicopter at night in a service station carpark, they had stopped at Exeter Airport for the helicopter to refuel, then left the M5 motorway opting for the A303 which they had mutually agreed would be more susceptible to an ambush from their enemy. They had given any would-be attackers every possible chance, but as the rest of the motorcade joined the M3 for London, King held back and took the slip road for Southampton. He had switched off his mobile phone a few miles back – having given his pursuers every opportunity to track him - and now turned off the Motorola two-way radio that he had been using to keep in contact with Rashid and Big Dave.

King stretched the Audi's legs and thundered along in the fast lane at over a hundred and forty miles-per-hour. The motorway was quiet, and he knew from experience that there were no gantry speeding cameras along this stretch of road - and if there were, then he wasn't overly worried because he had earlier fixed the false set of number-plates to the vehicle. They wouldn't fool a police PNC check from a patrol car, but he would at least avoid a stack of fines if he passed any speed cameras that he wasn't aware of.

He was making good progress. The sudden change in direction and his ability to cruise at such speeds along the relatively traffic-free stretch of road gave him the edge over the helicopter. Or at least, it gave him a lead. Because what he had to do now was personal. Furthermore, it would mean the end to his identity, and he would be left with no choice but to erase Alex King from existence and disappear forever.

King came off the motorway at Winchester. He was heading for a suburb of Southampton, but he travelled through the town which was deserted at this time of night and past the prison, hospital and university halls, then headed out through the hamlets of Standon and Hursley, bypassing Chandler's Ford and on towards Knightswood.

He knew the address. He had memorised it many years ago after purchasing the property after the black-market sale of a Congo conflict diamond. His mentor Peter Stewart had facilitated the sale through a trusted lawyer and the property had been registered in the name of Leanne Jeffries. King's sister had been spiralling the drain. With his other siblings integrated with loving families after the death of their mother, just like King, Leanne had not been an easy fit. A series of foster homes had done little to channel her, and she had found herself back on the same tower block estate in South London mixing with the same types her own mother had before her fall into drug and substance addic-tion, and prostitution to make ends meet and sustain her habit. King had made his own mistakes but had been handed a lifeline by Peter Stewart and MI6 and had left Mark Jeffries behind in favour of Alex King and a new life and backstory, which was commonly referred to by MI6 as a legend. The legend of Alex King had been easy to slip into. Both parents estranged from small families had been killed in a traffic accident and Alex himself had gone missing travelling in Asia, having believed to have attempted a drug deal in Thailand's notorious Golden Triangle to sustain his middleclass gap year. The man had no friends and social media was still a decade or more away, so King had slipped easily into a ready-made life. He had inherited a modest sum and started his training in MI6's highly secretive special operations wing. King had managed to let go of his old life, but while saying goodbye to his sister from afar, he had realised that she was vulnerable and needed a way out. A modest legacy and an even more modest house had made its way to Leanne Jeffries, and the young woman had taken a leap of faith and left her old life behind. King had never seen his sister again, but with this one gesture, he had been able to travel a new road without looking back.

And now all that was going to come to an end.

King did a drive past. The estate had changed over the years. Most of the properties had undergone renovations adding conservatories and decking, and he noted that the driveways were home to many new cars with some of them being premium brands. He guessed the area suited professionals, with many of them working in London with good train links nearby and just over an hour's commute to better salaries and the chance to keep their fingers on the pulse. He found Leanne's address and noted that it looked to have been kept in good condition. King turned around at the end of the cul-de-sac and pulled up just short of his sister's driveway. He killed the lights and watched the street. There were a few lights on inside the houses, but mainly the blueish glow from television sets and he imagined many of them wall mounted and oversized, taking pride of place as the home's year-round focal point, just like his own wood-burning stove at home. King preferred to read on the worn leather chair in the corner of the kitchen these days, or sometimes just stare at the flames or dying embers for hours as he thought about old friends and dead enemies, and whether the things he had been asked to do for his country had made a difference in the grand scheme of things.

He hoped it had.

King got out of the Audi and closed the door quietly behind him. He stepped backwards into the shadows and locked the door with the key fob, his eyes on the line of vehicles that were lining the kerb. No lights flashed and no interior light had illuminated the car as he watched. It had taken him a while to achieve - painstakingly snipping and splicing wires and removing fuses - but the Audi was now as stealthy as the MI5 watcher unit vehicles.

King subconsciously felt for the Sig Sauer in his jacket pocket. He decided to leave the AR-15 in the boot. Every fibre of his being told him it was a mistake. His old mentor Peter Stewart had always said, *"Never gun down when you can gun up..."* and King had lived his life to the mantra. Why compromise? But he had to be careful. He was in a cul-de-sac surrounded by houses. The infrequent street-lamps had given the street a dull hue of light, and ambient glow that would easily identify a man with a rifle to anyone casually drawing their curtains for the night or glancing out the landing window as they made their way back to bed from the bathroom in the darkness. That stumbling, lethargic walk where a person is half asleep, yet still retains the ability to be wide awake if they see or hear something out of the ordinary. No, the rifle was a step too far. The pistol was concealed and gave him a firepower if he walked into something that his fists couldn't handle. And what was he realistically going to find? Were there people waiting for him here on the off chance? He seriously doubted that. But he was here because whoever wanted him dead had discovered his birth name. And if they had tortured and killed Margaret Stewart on the infinitesimal chance that she had remembered something that her husband had once told her, then they wouldn't hesitate in harming a member of King's estranged family.

King walked past the house without losing pace. He took in the driveway, the parked hatchback and the front door. Down the side of the house a narrow pathway led to the back door. He supposed it would lead to the kitchen door and rear entrance. There were no exterior lights, but he could not assume that there wouldn't be a passive infrared security light. In fact, the chances were high with hardware stores offering relatively inexpensive solar powered lights that required no wiring and at just a fraction of the cost of mains wired installations. King didn't turn back, but he darted into the neighbouring property and made his way down the edge of a flower bed with a thick boundary hedge of privet on his right and a relatively cluttered driveway on his left that was a mass of children's ride-on toys and abandoned bicycles. King wondered how long the toys would have lasted left outside the tower block where he had grown up. He was pleased that Leanne lived in a place where her children would not think of such things. Although it pained him that he realised that he had no idea whether she even had children of her own, or whether he was in fact an uncle. No lights illuminated and he was past the house and into the rear garden, convincing himself that the man who may or may not have nieces or nephews had died long ago escaping Dartmoor Prison, drowning in a bog on a savagely cold night a few miles from Princetown. King knew that he was not the sum of his parts. He had pushed aside his former life as best he could, but it had never truly left him. Just as memories of past events often made it into dreams, his old life often caught up within his subconsciousness, and now that he had decided to protect his sister, he was remembering more and more of his past life pre-MI6 and thinking little of the days afterwards. King was now a changed man. He had been trained and educated, gone to great pains to self-educate further and had shown remorse for the events that had ultimately led his former self to prison. He had made a difference, or at least hoped that he had, and he always approached his missions with an open mind and the knowledge that he could decide if the trigger should be pulled or not.

King slipped over the fence separating the two properties and dropped lightly onto the grass. He remained crouched as he surveyed the rear of the house. There were no lights within. King peered in through the kitchen window, the ambient light from the streetlights giving him enough light to make out objects inside. The cooker was a modern electric range, but King could not see a timer or clock. He was familiar with such models, and they never worked unless the time was set. A power cut could have been responsible, but the timer was always left flashing 12:00 afterwards. The rest of the street seemed unaffected, so perhaps the power had tripped out on the circuit board. King looked around him. He did not want to knock on the door, risk waking the inhabitants, but he needed to get in and talk to Leanne if she was in. The car on the driveway would suggest she was. King reached behind him and whipped out the KA-Bar knife he had secured in a sheath horizontally attached to his belt. He worked the tip of the blade between the lock and the wooden frame, then jimmied, twisted and drove the blade deeper as he caught hold of the doorhandle and eased his shoulder against the door. The wood crumbled and splintered, and his fourteen stone of muscle and well-honed core flexed the door enough for it to give and he stumbled into the kitchen, then froze in his tracks. He still had the knife in his right hand but swapped it instantly to his left and reached for his pistol, his eyes still on the blood covering most of one half of the floor.

SIX

She had returned to the car breathless and silent, and she had tossed the latex gloves in the carrier bag on her seat and used the wet wipes to clean the blood off her face and forearms. She stripped quickly and Reno averted his eyes as her small breasts swayed and bounced with the movement. She shivered against the cold as she stripped off her jeans, underwear and socks and wiped herself all over with the wet wipes. He glanced back briefly catching a flash of trimmed red pubic hair, highlighted by her smooth porcelain skin. It stirred him within, but he looked away and cursed himself for feeling such emotion. She had been just a child when she had first come into his life and the thought that he should feel such stirrings now, however brief, disgusted him and left him feeling cold inside. She stuffed the used wet wipes into the bag, piled in the bundle of clothing, then wiped her hands once more before nodding for Reno to tie the handles of the bag together while she pulled on clean underwear, leggings and a thick Kashmir sweater. Lastly, she put the trainers into a separate bag and pulled on socks and a new pair of trainers. Reno took the bag with the soiled trainers inside and stuffed them behind his seat. Natasha had already got back into the car and silently continued to load ammunition into the magazine, just as she had been before the hit.

"How many rounds have you put in there?" he asked, starting the engine and pulling back onto the road. The weapon was a Valmet M71S – a Finnish copy of an AK-47 and chambered in 5.56mm NATO and was on the backseat covered with a tartan blanket. It had been a popular weapon in the US and Europe during the nineteen-eighties when civilian shooters wanted what the countries behind the Iron Curtain would not give them. The Finnish company had copied the Kalashnikov and seized a commercial opportunity. Reno found that the solid, somewhat dated design and smaller cartridge gave the weapon unparalleled performance because of its minimal recoil. Reno had brought it to Britain, along with the rest of his weapons and equipment, in a fishing boat using the winding waters of the Norfolk Broads to land the illegal haul at a quiet, dilapidated dock once used for the export of peat. That had been ten years ago, and he had stashed the contents around the country for contracts such as this.

"Twenty-nine," she replied. "Just like you taught me to."

Reno nodded approvingly. "For us, every shot counts and what does one less round in the magazine mean to people like us?"

"Reliability. Less tension on the magazine springs. A higher chance of success."

"Correct." He paused. "You find yourself in a situation where you need ammunition for a pistol. A forty-five ACP. What else will work if the correct ammunition is unavailable?"

"Point three-oh-eight or point thirty-oh-six rifle cases.

Cut the casings down to twenty-two point eight millimetres. Thirty-three millimetres for a forty-four Auto Mag."

"Good. Back to the forty-five, any other considerations?"

"Military seven-point-six-two uses a thicker shell casing than civilian three-oh-eight or thirty-oh-six, so that means less powder once trimmed. Around ten-percent less power than a factory loaded pistol round."

Reno nodded and smiled. "Well remembered."

Natasha looked pleased with herself. She brushed a lock of her red hair out of her eyes. She had an innocent smile, but that innocence would not last long. Not if she was determined to finish her training with him. It would be interesting to see if tonight's hit affected her in the coming months. Only time would tell. When Reno had found her, she was just fourteen years of age. She had been at a critical turning point. The daughter of both a wealthy Russian mafia kingpin and a former Miss World finalist, Natasha had been orphaned after both parents had been assassinated in a power struggle in France and had subsequently spent three months homeless on the streets of Paris. Drugs and prostitution beckoned her, a life on the streets unavoidable. But he had given her another road to travel down. He had paid for her to spend two years at a Swiss boarding school. Another two years in a Swiss college, and three years at Oxford university followed. He had paid for it all. But still when they met again after her graduation, she had wanted to know more about what he did, how the enigmatic French-Spaniard paid his bills, paid for her to be safe. Why he returned from overseas trips with bruises and stitches and often with a limp. One night after too much vodka, he had told her, and she had been captivated. Now she was twenty-one. Often mistaken for his daughter, more often viewed with disgust at partnering an older man, but their detractors would be wrong on both counts. Theirs was a relationship of mentor and protégé. Reno needed a successor for his employers and Natasha needed revenge on her parents' killers. Perhaps she would go the rest of her life without retribution, but her focus at least provided her with the closure of her grief and what Reno would call her *raison d'être.*

"Can shotguns use rifle bullets?" he asked as he took the slip road for the M3 motorway north to London.

"Only as a last resort," Natasha replied. "Point three-oh-three British will work in a four-ten shotgun. Point fifty will work in a twelve gauge, but only in a pump-action or auto chambered for three-and-a-half-inch-magnum and then again, perhaps only once or twice before the weapon breaks in half..."

"Tell me about patching," Reno said, then added, "And keep loading the magazines. You should always be able to do two things at once..."

"You fire a bullet from a person's weapon into water. Pistols only need around three feet of water to halt a bullet, six or seven feet for most rifles. After you have retrieved the bullet, you crimp it into a casing that uses a larger calibre bullet. So, seven-point-six-five works well with nine-millimetre, nine-millimetre with a point-forty and so on." She paused. "Typically, the next calibre up the ballistic chart. You then use non-vegetarian collagen supplement powder with a few drops of water to create a paste, brush over the bullet and leave to dry to a film. When fired, the bullet retains the rifling grooves of the previous weapon. Most of the collagen is burned off at the muzzle with the flash that engulfs it, any remaining traces will dissolve in the victim's blood. Hence non-vegetarian, and certainly not marine collagen. The patching process allows you fire a bullet with another weapon's signature."

Reno nodded. "Considerations?"

Natasha shrugged. "You have to get access to the initial weapon..."

"And?"

"Range is affected. It is best used in a close-range scenario."

"Best scenario?"

"When we want it to look like a suicide," she replied, then looked thoughtfully at him and added, "Or murder suicide..." She paused. "So, the real target is the person murdered in that scenario and the patsy is the suicide."

"Exactly," he smiled. "Always give the police and authorities an open and shut case whenever possible." He paused, glancing at her as she finished loading and put the magazine in the glovebox. "So, how did it go in there?"

Natasha shrugged. "You got what you needed to know. It was just a straightforward exercise."

He nodded. It had been essential for her training and both mentally and practically, would have provided her with a range of experience. "But you sent a message, nevertheless?"

"Yes."

"You're sure?"

"Positive," she replied emphatically. "When you set the trap, I guarantee that he'll go to the ends of the earth to find you..."

SEVEN

King shone the red-filtered torch beam on the floor and stared at the body. Its throat had been sliced cleanly. The hair around the wound was matted with blood and he knew that death would have been quick. Less than a minute, and by the signs, the killer would have held him in place to avoid a struggle and further complications. King had no idea what sort of dog it was, but he thought labradoodle would be in the right ballpark. Certainly, a young dog given its build, condition and the colour of its coat around its chin and muzzle. No grey hairs.

There was no good going to come of this now. The house was in a state of total silence. King wondered how the killer had done it. Kill the lights, take out the dog and head inside. But the power would have to have been cut at the circuit board and not at the junction box, otherwise other houses would have been affected. Circuit boards were generally located near the front door for ease of access to meter readings. King kept the pistol aimed in front of him as he worked his way out of the kitchen and down the hallway.

He could smell death. He couldn't describe the sweet, fetid, sickliness of the smell in any tangible way, but he had been around it enough to know what he was going to find. When people died and their muscles finally relaxed the body would begin to leak. People who had passed in a violent manner smelled worse than someone who had drifted off peacefully in bed. Fear, tension and release did things to the gut and bowels. Of course, the bodies would smell worse in time, but right now, King knew he was near a recent crime and that he would not be seeing his sister again, nor offering her sanctuary.

He flicked on the master trip switch and listened intently. The fridge rattled back into life in the kitchen and broadband routers and satellite tv boxes whirled into start-up and configuration procedures, and the landline telephone beeped and announced *no new messages*. But King wasn't listening for any of these things. He was listening for a killer who would soon realise that they were now trapped in their own crime scene.

King's heart raced, his mouth dry and his hands clammy. It was always this way. He had lost count of the times he had held a weapon with damp hands and his throat as dry as sand as bullets had pinged around him. But tonight, it was fearful anticipation of the unknown, the dread of the suspected that made him feel this way. He licked his lips and swallowed, took a deep breath to calm his nerves, then eased forwards. He had done this enough to realise he had entered a state of calm. Controlled it, even. His hands were becoming less clammy now, also. The lounge door was open and a few of the upstairs lights were on, which provided enough light for him to see by. King could see that the room was empty, but he still needed to see behind the door and the sofas. He eased inside the room, could already see in the reflection of the mirror above the gas fireplace that nobody was lurking behind the door. With the pistol trained on the sofa, the weapon's sight picture slightly above the headrest, he side-stepped until he could see clearly behind it and the chair next to it. King backed up to the wall, took a breath and headed back outside to the hallway.

The inevitable ever closer.

King took the stairs, the pistol aimed in front of him. He kept looking up towards the landing, the weapon trained between what he assumed were two bedroom doors. Both were closed, but this gave King containment while he checked on the open bedroom door and the open bathroom door. The bedroom was empty. King felt an indescribable, unfamiliar pang of emotion as he realised that he had indeed become an uncle. Bunk beds, Manchester United posters on one wall, Liverpool on another. It must have been fun in the household when the two teams met on the pitch. The toys scattered on the floor were superhero dolls and cars. King figured that the boys would be somewhere between six and nine. He wasn't sure what he based that assumption on, but older boys favoured computer consoles and sporting equipment, skateboards and models. Younger boys tended to play with more tactile toys. That was King's understanding. He only had a few toys as a child, didn't really remember many things from his early childhood.

The bathroom door swung open freely, but the light had been switched off. King pulled the cord. But wished he hadn't. He wished he'd stayed at his home in Cornwall. Or even died fighting his attackers in his garden. Anything but be here at this moment in time. He bowed his head, sheathed the knife and closed the door behind him. It shouldn't have meant anything to him. He'd seen worse for sure. When ISIS had first taken hold in Syria and Iraq, they had been brutal. The scenes still haunted him, but he already knew that what he had just seen would be with him forever. They had been his flesh and blood, despite never knowing them, their deaths meant everything to him. King opened the next bedroom door. Not tentatively. There was no point in that any longer. He'd seen the worse he could have expected. But then he realised he hadn't.

Leanne had been tied to the bed before she had been killed. He glanced at her hands, noticed the wedding and engagement ring on her left ring finger. No other jewellery, but he noticed a thin gold chain on her bedside table. The last time King had seen her she had half of the *H. Samuel* and *Argos* nine carat gold selection around her neck and on every digit. She had learned more about refinery over the years. King stared at her, his eyes watering for the first time in years. He'd always loved Leanne. She was closer in age to him than his other siblings and by the time they were walking King was out the flat day and night trying to earn enough for them to eat. But he remembered playing with Leanne as a child and her accompanying him to get chips, sometimes running a diversion so he could get the chips back to the flat before the older kids on the estate stole them and scoffed the lot around the back beside the bins.

King did not know the man lying next to her, but it was clear that he had put up a fight before dying. It would have needed at least two people because the man was well-muscled and a sizeable opponent. The cable ties and rope had cut deep into the man's flesh, and he would have bucked and contorted and fought against what they had done to him. King noted Leanne's right hand had held onto his left hand right up until the end, and despite their wounds, they both looked peaceful in death.

"Jesus... Allah... Buddha..."

King swung around, but he had already registered the voice. Rashid. Perhaps the only person who could have made the walk up the stairs so silently. King turned back and looked at his sister. "Someone's going to pay..."

"I hear you, mate."

"I was an uncle..." King said quietly. Rashid winced, glanced down the landing at the closed bathroom door. "They drowned them in the bath..."

There was a heavy pounding up the stairs and Big Dave stepped onto the landing, cracking his head on the light fitting and cursing loudly. Rashid was grateful for the distraction, not knowing what to say or what to do next. He had never seen King so distant, so adrift. "Shit," said Big Dave as he looked at the two bodies on the bed, then quickly added, "Ramsay and Thorpe are on the way." He walked past Rashid and snatched the 9mm out of King's hand, then put his other hand around King's shoulder, and guided him away. "This place needs to be contained. Thorpe will liaise with the police, that's what she does." King started to resist but it was only a half-hearted attempt and Lomu's eighteen stone of muscle swept him along and out of the room. King was unsteady on his feet and the big Fijian half-lifted half-supported him down the stairs and into the lounge. "Get a brew on Rashid," Big Dave said, helping King into a chair. "Strong and sweet, mate." He paused. "And mind what you step in..."

King stared at the floor and said, "They killed her kids..."

Lomu nodded. "Listen. You're not quite at the slap across the cheek state, but I'm warning you, you're getting pretty damned close. Snap out of it, soldier. Get your head in the fucking game…" King looked up at him, his eyes like glacier ice. Cold, blue-grey and the unnerving hint of danger behind them. "That's more like it," said the big Fijian. "Somebody's out to get you, and they will if you let them. They're fucking with you. Coming here to find out something you know from your past is a reach at best. So, what else was it?"

King frowned at him. "I…"

"It was to wound you!" Lomu snapped. "You fight a pro with a knife, what do you do? Do you wait for an opening and the opportunity of a killer strike? Or do you parry and slash and stab them until they are weak and disoriented?" He stared intently at King. "Exactly! You wear them down… you make them bleed!"

King nodded and sat back in the chair, clasping his head with both hands. "Shit!"

"No idea who it could be?"

"No." King leaned forward when he saw Rashid enter with a mug. King noticed he was wearing a pair of latex surgical gloves. He took the mug and sipped. It wasn't very hot. Rashid had rushed the boil. But he drank it down quickly, the extra sugar probably being nothing more than an old wives' tale.

"Where's mine?" Big Dave asked.

"Your family weren't just slaughtered…" Rashid looked at King and shrugged, "Sorry…"

"And no fucking biscuits, either." Big Dave commented flatly.

"We'd better be getting out of here," said Rashid. "Sally-Anne will likely tell the police that she got a tip off from a protected informer, so we really don't want to be here to complicate things."

"Where are we going?" King asked quietly.

"Somewhere safe until we can work out what to do next." Rashid paused. "You go with Big Dave in the Disco, I'll follow in the Audi."

"They know the Audi belongs to me."

"You get your head together in the passenger seat for a while. I know the risks, and I'm willing to take them."

"You'll be a target..."

"You're not listening. We need to get to London, regroup and get our heads down for a bit," Rashid replied, glancing at his watch. He got up and gathered up the cups and ran a sink full of water to wash them. "Look, it's late. Things will look better in the morning." Rashid found the bleach and dropped a large amount in the hot water. Bleach could strip DNA from a crime scene as effectively as not being there in the first place.

"My sister and her husband were tortured and killed; their children drowned..." King said quietly. "Things aren't going to look any better in the morning." He paused shaking his head. "And I haven't got a clue who is doing this, who would be behind it, or what secret they want silenced."

Big Dave got out of his chair and patted King on the shoulder. "In Fiji it is widely believed that a serpent called Degei created all of Fiji's Islands. More than three-hundred and thirty, plus a further five hundred rocks in the ocean. Degei judges newly dead souls after they pass through one of two caves: Cibaciba or Drakulu. He sends a few paradise Burotu. Most others are thrown into a lake, where they will eventually sink to the bottom to the underworld called Murimuria..."

"Fuck me, is this going somewhere?" King asked tetchily.

"In my culture, bad men are not only judged, but it is

pre-ordained that they feel the agony of their off-spring as eternal punishment." Big Dave paused, giving King's shoulder a squeeze. "Brother, I'll tell you now, when we finish with these animals, their ancestors will be screaming for mercy..."

EIGHT

The river was still and mirrored the scudding clouds above. Out in the middle of the body of water, a thin disruption of current broke the otherwise serene stillness of the water close to the riverbanks on either side. The sun was low, and the late winter air was frigid. One of those days in March where the shade felt like winter and yet the patches of sun kissed light gave some promise of approaching spring. In the summer months kayakers and paddle-boarders often intersected the path of both pleasure craft and tourist boats alike, but for now just a few committed rowers were on the water. The Oxford-Cambridge Boat Race would run as usual in just a few weeks' time and as he watched he wondered whether any of the dedicated rowers on the water today would be taking part. It was a curious location, but he'd used it before. In fact, he had used it several times in recent months, preferring not to conduct these sorts of meetings anywhere near Whitehall. The ground backed onto waste ground and a derelict malthouse and was ripe for development and would likely soon be riverside apartments with a private dock for pleasure craft.

He looked up as the man made his way over to join him on the park bench. Behind him, his two bodyguards leaned against the wooden fence, one looking at the water, the other looking back at his charge, both men wearing dark sunglasses and trying and achieving to look as tough as hell. In the otherwise deserted gravelled carpark, fenced off by developers and with wheel clamping signs to dissuade parking, his government Jaguar and a Land Rover Discovery were parked nose out and another bodyguard paced around deliberately, his eyes glancing between the road beyond the rickety fence, and the few people who had parked were all dressed in running gear and performing some warm-up stretches before their early morning run along the riverbank.

"You're late, Reno," he remarked as the man joined him. "But finally, it's good to put a face to the name... and voice."

"I've been here for a while, watching the dawn breaking," Reno replied quietly, his accent laced with a curious mix of French and Spanish that the man couldn't quite put his finger on. "I like to see what I'm walking into, and how to get out quickly if I have to."

"I have five men with me. All serving police officers with the Diplomatic Protection Command's Royalty and Specialist Protection," he replied. "I hear you're good, but not nobody's *that* good..."

"You're paying me a great deal of money." Reno paused, taking out a cigar and lighting it with a gun-metal grey gas Dunhill lighter. He snapped the lid of the lighter shut and slipped it back into his pocket. "I have someone with a gun on you and your men as we speak."

"Just one person?" the man replied incredulously, but he looked visibly shaken.

"It's enough." Reno paused, blowing smoke into the

man's face. "If things don't look right, then they have instructions to take you down first..."

The man coughed and waved the smoke out of his face. "I don't like people who play games!" he snapped.

"You've spent your life playing games. Chess with real peoples' lives. Sometimes, not even chess. A reckless game of checkers at best." The man shrugged, and took a deep pull on the cigar, blowing out a smoke ring and appreciating everything about the Cuban cigar. "You have paid the deposit as agreed. Now, you will call off these amateurs you have been using. When King has given up the information your employers require..." He looked the man in the eyes. "...and after I have killed him, you will pay the remainder."

"That is what we agreed, yes."

"Yes, I have had experience of what men like you – politicians, that is - agree to then decide to conveniently forget." Reno paused. "You have already hedged your bets and employed ex-soldiers and criminals who are doing no more than playing at being assassins. You either call them off, or I will kill every last one of them and leave the evidence at your door..."

The man regarded Reno for a moment and noted that he appeared decidedly average. Average height, average weight and entirely forgettable. Which was exactly why the man had lived so long doing what he did for a living. He knew him only as Reno. It was thought that he was of French origin, but some had said he was in fact from Spain – but he had certainly served in the French Foreign Legion, although many men on the run had found sanctuary in that old institution – and GCHQ's top vocal specialist had detected anomalies that suggested Basque Spanish.

"This is important to me. You were not making progress, so I employed some people I have used in the past." He paused. "They have always proven successful in my endeavours."

"I was not making progress?" Reno replied, feigning a look of confusion. "And why do you think I was not making progress?"

"Because King is still alive!"

Reno laughed bitterly. "I have my methods and I will not have those methods questioned. When it is time for King to be killed, then he will be killed. But until then, there are many things to be done, information to be gleaned, traps to be laid..." He paused. "One cannot just go blindly up to a man like King and ask questions and force him to answer." He sighed, blowing out a plume of cigar smoke. "As any of your surviving amateurs will concur..." The man frowned at him, his eyes belaying uncertainty. How could he know about last night's debacle? Reno smiled, knowing exactly what the man was thinking. "Call off your dogs. Let me do what you have hired me to do. I have already made... *inquiries.*" He smiled, picturing King's sister, her dying breaths. There was something about the moment a person passed that had drawn him into his chosen profession. When he was close enough to a victim to hear the death rattle, to see the sudden stillness in their eyes, he felt empowered. He would swear at that moment, he could see their soul leave their bodies. The Jeffries woman had been no different. And nor had her family. Reno's smile faded and his expression became darker. Almost as if the colour of his eyes changed. Pure evil personified. "Don't ever question my judgement again. And for your sake, for your family's sake, do not even think about double crossing me..."

"Alright, it's done. I will call them off." The man paused, looking furtively around him, more to avoid looking into the man's ever darkening eyes. They reminded him of the eyes of a shark. Black, soulless. "And rest assured, I won't double cross you."

Reno shrugged. "People try. They try all the time. They pay the deposit, then decide in a moment of madness that they will renegotiate the terms once the job has been done. Such foolishness. But they have never lived long enough to regret it. Not even after they have apologised and paid the agreed amount with interest."

The man nodded. He was outside his normal comfort zone and something about the man shook his usual confidence. He had only previously hired these ex-soldiers and criminal elements to have people beaten or coerced, or to take a photograph of a colleague in a compromising position, or steal information. He had seen a way to force King's hand and he had taken it, not imagining how ineffective they would prove to be. He passed Reno an envelope, which the man promptly took without so much as glancing at it and placed it in his jacket pocket. "You already have the file on him from his days at the Secret Intelligence Service, but in that envelope are all the further details I could get hold of from his time with the Security Service. Offices of work, his colleagues' details as well as their families. Enough to find him."

"And his partner?" Reno sneered. "His *fiancée*..."

"The last intel I had was that she had gone to ground..."

"Intel from these amateurs?" Reno interrupted.

"Well, yes..."

Reno shrugged. "It doesn't matter. I will find her."

"I doubt she'll know anything of value. The word is the two started a relationship after King went to work for the Security Service, but keep each other in the dark regarding anything classified, or if they are working separately on a matter of national security. I gather it's the only way it can work."

Reno shook his head. "If they fuck, then they talk. If they do the talk on the pillow..."

"Pillow talk," he ventured.

"*Oui*, the pillow talk... then she could know. And if she knows, then she will tell Reno, because everybody talks to Reno when he asks them questions with a sharp knife and a hot iron..."

He looked at Reno and smiled nervously. "What about friendlies?" He paused. "Family members and such..."

"I am a gun for hire. There are no friendlies. That's why you hired me." Reno paused. "When I first spoke to you, you said that you almost had King at the end of his last operation. That your men were getting close, but he disappeared. This will not happen with Reno working for you. I will get to King, I will find out what your... *employers* want to know, and I will kill him. That is why people use Reno, because he gets the job done."

"You'd better not fail," the man replied.

"I don't fail," Reno replied tersely and blew another lungful of smoke into the man's face.

The man waved the smoke away from him as he stood up. Reno did not move. The man glanced at his security detail and both bodyguards stood straighter and looked his way expectantly. "If you fail..."

"I won't fail."

"If you take the money and run..."

"Don't make idle threats to me."

The man sighed. "Idle threats. Idle threats like you when you first sat down?" he sneered. He looked around him, something theatrical in the act, as he scanned the opposite riverbank, the bridge and the disused buildings once used for storing goods ready to be steered down river. "Where's your gunman, Mister Reno? Where's your back-up?" He paused, shaking his head. "I hope I haven't made a mistake hiring you. All bullshit and nothing to back it up while you take my money and run!"

"Tell me," Reno smiled. "Do you smoke?"

The man looked at the cigar in Reno's hand. Personally, he couldn't abide second-hand smoke of any kind. Many of his colleagues now vaped and with such a heady variety of flavours and equipment, he found the practice utterly ludicrous. However, as much as he may have baulked at the second-hand smoke, he *was* partial to a cigar after a formal dinner. Port or brandy and cigars. There was something about the opulent ceremony. The occasion. That's when the real deals were done. "I do," he replied. "When the time or social situation calls for it." Reno smiled, reached inside his jacket pocket and retrieved a thick cigar tube around five inches long. A Romeo Y Julieta, Romeo No.2. one of Cuba's finest. He handed it to him. "Thank you. I'll smoke it later," he said, seeing the gift as a sign of humility from the man he had paid with his own money to kill someone, albeit upon someone else's orders.

"Smoke it now," said Reno sharply, but his expression softened with an unnerving quickness and ease. "I insist. To show that there are no hard feelings between us..." The man shrugged. He unscrewed the cap off the tube and tipped the cigar out. Reno retrieved his lighter and the man, more used to after dinner cigars with formality and ceremony heisted in lieu of a cigar cutter. Deciding one wasn't to be an option, he nipped off a vee with his teeth. Reno smiled as he lit the man's cigar, but he took the cigar tube from his hand and stepped backwards a pace, holding the cigar tube between his thumb and forefinger. "I think perhaps a demonstration is in order, just to remind you what I do, and why you should think twice before double crossing me, or taking matters into your own hands again, as with the likes of those amateurs…" There was no noise, no muzzle flash anywhere to be seen, but a hole punched through the tube. A clean in and out. Non-expanding bullets only made a large exit hole through flesh. The cigar tube did not offer sufficient material or resistance to create a pressure vacuum often associated with hydrostatic shock and traumatic exit holes. Just a thin sliver of metal remained on either side of the tube. Reno held the tube up to his eye and peered at the man through the hole. "Peekaboo…" he smiled and tossed him the tube. "Keep this as a souvenir and reminder of what is at stake…" The man fumbled the catch, almost dropped his own cigar as Reno walked past him and headed back across the grass to the road, got into a non-descript silver hatchback parked on the verge and drove away.

The man looked back at the hole in the cigar tube, his hand shaking and his heart hammering against his chest, and there was an uneasy, nagging feeling in his gut that he had made a mistake. The European assassin was an entirely different entity to the underworld that he had occasionally been forced to encounter and exploit. He had given up control in the hope for deniability and distance. But he couldn't help thinking he had unleashed nothing but trouble.

NINE

"Quite a house of horrors..." the detective said adjusting the hood on his white over-suit. "What did you touch?"

"Nothing," replied Thorpe.

The man frowned. "Alright, then what did your agents touch?"

Sally-Anne Thorpe opened her phone and thumbed until she found a QR code. "Take a photo of this," she told him. "It will take you to a portal and three sets of finger-prints, all correlating with their DNA profiles. All three are agents of the Security Service and that is all you need to know, and all you'll get to know. Use this information to eliminate them from your enquiries." She held the phone out and the detective took a picture on his smartphone. "I can't emphasise enough how important it is that the service is kept out of this investigation."

"That's all well and good," the detective said as his slipped the phone back into his pocket. "But I won't cut corners or sit on information. My superiors can decide whether or not the police service can turn a blind eye to aspects of the investigation."

Thorpe nodded. "I expect no less, DI Miller. However, there is a detail that could prove problematic in the course of this investigation."

The detective smirked. "Of course, there is..."

Thorpe shrugged. "Look, I get it. I was a DCI in the Met. I haven't been with the Security Service long, so I know what I'm asking of you. But there is a mighty big elephant in the room, and it's not going away anytime soon. Furthermore, if this elephant gets out, then there is going to be a shitstorm of epic proportions." She shrugged. "It just takes one person with a sense of the bigger picture to decide whether it is in the public's best interest or not."

"And that is?"

"One of the agents will have DNA matching the dead woman and her children."

"I see."

"Well, to be frank, you won't..."

The detective smiled. "And was this move to the secret squirrels worth the trade-off in ethics?"

She shrugged, as honest a gesture as he was going to get. "It's complicated. Police work is blissfully straight forward. You put your efforts into getting justice for a victim by catching the perpetrator. Whether it's vandalism, theft, rape or murder, it all boils down to the same fact. It may not be easy, but the objective is constant." She paused. "But in intelligence work, the picture changes along with the political and social landscape and the result you start off working towards may not be in the country's best interest in the long run."

"So, if this DNA matches, it could be an issue," he commented flatly. "How so?"

Thorpe looked warily around her. Forensic officers were organising equipment in the back of a van and a uniformed police officer was standing guard at a police cordon. She looked back at the detective and said, "The DNA and fingerprints of one of the agents will come back as someone who died more than fifteen years ago..."

"Oh..."

"This is a man who has done more for his country than anyone both you and I will know." She was in it now, there was no going back. But if they had found King's DNA and ran it blindly through the PNC database, and she had not given the officer the heads up, then the tightly wound ball of wool that was King's legend would soon be unravelled to a single thread. And threads had two ends and a middle that could be cut. "Please bear this in mind when collating the evidence..."

Detective Inspector Miller nodded. "Okay. Maybe I can." He paused thoughtfully, then said, "But first, get into coveralls and walk the crime scene with me." He paused, looking at her intently. "And when you've seen it in detail, you'll understand whether or not I can in good conscience sit on anything at the cost of finding the monster who did this." He waited for her to get into her coveralls and put on the over socks and gloves, then leaned forward and tucked a lock of her hair under her hood. She looked at him and smiled and he looked embarrassed that his action could have been misconstrued. "Sorry, shouldn't have done that. The *Me Too* movement has a lot to answer for."

"Which can only be a good thing."

"I didn't mean..."

"Forget it," she shrugged. "But always best to look and not touch. No offence taken, though."

"Anyway, wouldn't want to contaminate the crime scene further." He paused. "Considering three people of yours have been riding rough shod over the crime scene."

"I've seen things like this before," Sally-Anne said. "If wanting me to see this is some sort of payback for sticking my nose in..."

DI Miller scoffed. "It's nothing like that," he replied. "But this is the worse I've seen, and I've been on the job for fifteen years."

"In Hampshire..." she smirked.

Miller pulled a face. "I know we don't get the frequency of nasty crimes that the Met does, but we're not short of a few horrors down here, either."

She nodded. "Fair enough. So, if I do this, you give me quid-pro-quo regarding our agent?"

"Perhaps," Miller replied. "It depends on how much you can help me."

"Help you?"

He shrugged benignly. "Okay, so we get a few horrors down here. But nothing like this. And to be frank, I don't know where to start. I could do with some input. And if there is any hope of protecting your agent..."

Thorpe could get an MIT sent down. A specialist team of homicide detectives could lend real experience and depth to the investigation, but if she did, then she wouldn't hold her breath and wait and see where the DNA link went. There would be no chance keeping aspects of the investigation quiet. Miller knew this, but what else would he want from her if he could keep up to his end of the bargain? Thorpe nodded and said, "Naturally. Only too glad to be of help."

Miller nodded and led the way into the house. SOCO were working every aspect, of every room. In the kitchen, the body of the family pet lay macabrely still while one technician dusted the surfaces for prints, and another meticulously photographed the scene. "The dog was stabbed in the heart and had its throat cut," said DI Miller. "Forensics have swabbed the animal's mouth and claws for DNA on the off chance it managed to have a go at its killer."

Thorpe looked at the scene. It was a strange phenomenon that the death of an animal could sometimes be more upsetting than that of a human, and she hadn't worked out why in all her years on the job. She supposed it was an animal's lack of understanding, its innocence. It had never made any sense to her, but she recalled how she had felt early on in her career when someone had been torturing and killing cats in the most macabre and violent of ways. Her senior investigating officer had taken the case seriously as she had felt it was only a matter of time before the killer progressed to humans and a potential serial killer could be halted before they made the transition. Thorpe had been greatly affected by the killings, but the cat killer had never been found. The killings had merely stopped, and it was assumed the killer had succumbed to fate themselves. Illness, accident or death was sometimes the only thing to stop a killer in their tracks.

"Doggy person?" Miller asked as they left the kitchen and headed towards the stairs. "Or could that question be seen as ambiguous and pushing the boundaries of *Me Too*?"

"Yes, and yes," she replied with the faintest hint of a smile.

Miller shrugged as he paused at the top of the stairs. "Bathroom next."

"Not saving the worse 'til last?" she asked tersely.

"I'll let you be the judge of that..." He paused as he swept his hand towards the bathroom in a polite, yet partly theatrical gesture. "Ladies first..."

"There are courses for men like you. I suggest you take one soon," she said bustling past him. "I feel for your wife."

"Divorced."

"You surprise me..." Thorpe pushed open the bathroom door and stopped in her tracks. She had been expecting far worse. But then it suddenly hit her that the killer had merely been practical. An icy coldness, a detachedness that somehow seem altogether more sinister in its application. The bath had been run until it was full. Both boys had their hands bound behind their backs with black duct tape. Positioned on their knees, they seemed to have been placed evenly apart, likely with room for their killer to kneel between them as they had held their heads under the water. Only the front portion of the boys' hair was wet, and both their faces were still under the surface, their hair wafting imperceivably like fine seaweed in a rockpool. Only the infrequent drip from the tap disturbed the surface of the water enough for the outward ripple to animate the strands of hair. Thorpe stared, the scene as macabre as she had ever witnessed, yet somehow calming, and it proved difficult to avert her eyes. "Oh my god..." she said quietly, the words barely spilling over her lips.

"It's quite something," Miller almost whispered. "But this is where I need help. I've called in a criminal phycologist to lend an opinion."

"It's a drowning," Thorpe replied. "Horrid, reprehensible, even. But it's still just a drowning."

Miller nodded. "Very well," he said and stepped outside the bathroom. Thorpe followed and Miller led the way to the master bedroom. "But if someone can kill two boys, almost simply put them down with the same dispassionate practical manner as one would a sick pet... I'm not talking method, merely the process... then why in hell would they do this?" He pushed the door to the bedroom open and stood back for Thorpe to enter first. Inside, two forensic officers were photographing and sampling the scene. Miller had asked for the bodies not to be moved until he gave the order and both officers stepped back knowing that Miller and Thorpe would be scrutinising the scene. "Get a coffee," he said to them. "We need ten minutes here, then the coroner can take them away." He turned back to Thorpe as the two officers left the room. "What do you make of this?"

Sally-Anne Thorpe felt her insides shift and her legs go weak. She had seen dozens of bodies. Over-dosed whores, teenage stab victims, death by massive head trauma, shootings and gang violence. She had established death by misadventure, accidental deaths, murders and suicides. But all of those paled into insignificance with these two poor souls. She steeled herself by taking a deep breath and said, "Well, there's intent."

"I know. But it's establishing the intent that's going to be the problem." He paused, looking at her intently, only his eyes visible behind the mask with the hood covering most of his forehead. "Tell me the connection to your agent so I may better understand the intent."

Thorpe hesitated for a moment, but the man was right. Without some background for him to work on, they had less chance of him sitting on a DNA link at the crime scene. Quid-pro-quo the man had said. A favour or advantage granted in return for something. "It is believed that the agent in question knows something. What, we don't know. And it's unlikely that Leanne Jeffries..."

"Armitage," he corrected her. "The couple were married three years ago. Arse about face, but these are the times we live in. Nick Armitage has this address listed as his residence from nine years ago." He paused. "The boys were eight and six years old..."

"And this is Nick Armitage?" Thorpe shrugged.

"Wouldn't be the first time a husband kills his wife and their lover. They then kill the kids, then go off to top themselves..."

"No, we found the man's passport. There's no doubt about it, his face matches the photograph..." He paused. "At least they left his face in relatively one piece..."

Thorpe nodded. Whoever had done this had bound the man's wrists and ankles tightly to the wooden headboard and the foot of the bed. Leanne Armitage as she would now be known had been tethered with the same method. Thorpe could see that she had managed to hold her partner's hand and had died squeezing tightly. The man would have died first. There was no doubt about that because Thorpe knew that the man would not have been able to hold onto her hand at the end. Nobody could have.

"I wonder what your agent knows," he said quietly. "Because it must have been bloody important. There was no doubt that this was torture. And if this poor bloke knew, then he would have told his killer anything and everything." He grimaced. "But why the focus on the genitalia? Do you think it was some sort of sexual deviance?"

"Perhaps. Or it could be that human genitalia are so very sensitive. There is also the humiliation element, as well." She looked up as the door opened and a woman hovered in the doorway.

"I feel we should remove the boys," the woman said through her mask.

"Absolutely," DI Miller replied. "And what would be your initial thoughts be here?"

"I'd prefer it if you didn't quote me. As far as I'm concerned, I won't know any more than you and I have already speculated until I've got them both on the slab."

Miller shrugged. "Alright. But how about a quick talk

through now and if you decide it's not conclusive, I'll strike your findings through."

The pathologist sighed. "I would conclude that both victims were tortured, but there is sign of clotting on the female's lacerations. Impossible to tell with the male as the removal of the large portions of skin on the shins, thighs and stomach make it difficult to tell at present. The female was tortured in front of the male, but his ordeal was to a higher degree of viciousness, no doubt to either intimidate the female, or perhaps simply for the killer's own enjoyment. The decimation of the female's genitalia was absolute. Simply put, there's nothing external left and I would bet that internally I will find an obscene degree of damage. The removal of the male's sexual organs would denote perversion, and if not perversion... although there is going to be a degree of sexual perversion to perform such an act... then a torturous act to persuade the female to talk, or simply to make her suffer. The removal of both the female's areola, again perversion or torture..."

"And the boys?"

The pathologist nodded. "So far removed that it beggars belief."

"Clinical?"

"Absolutely. No perversion there. Impossible to tell without an internal examination, but I'm ninety-nine-point-nine percent positive neither child was interfered with." She paused. "No, I feel it is so clinical that it could not have possibly been the same killer..."

"Two killers?" Miller exclaimed. "That really changes things..."

"For you, yes." She paused. "But it may help your investigation because the killer of the boys was performing a process. They did it calmly and calculatedly and when all is said and done, they would have gone together, not known of the other's fate and after a minute, maybe two, I suspect they would have both passed out. Children have smaller lungs, after all. Compared to the bloodbath happening in here, I know how I'd rather go…"

"And what kind of person are we looking for?" Miller asked, staring at the scene from an abattoir on the blood-soaked bed, the walls and the ceiling.

"For these? Oh my… well, somewhere between cold and calculated and a damned frenzy. Not helpful, I know, but this killer scares the crap out of me." She sighed, her shoulders sagging. "Because I think they *really* enjoyed it…"

TEN

Mayfair, London

KING HADN'T SLEPT. He had rested fully clothed on the bed and stared at the ceiling in the gloom, hoping to get at least a couple of hours, but it wasn't to be. How could he sleep? His sister and her family had been slaughtered, but the sad fact was, he had compartmentalised his life, drawn a line under his former existence. He had lain awake wondering why it was that he could not grieve and that in itself had been counterproductive. There was no sense to it, because he had an overwhelming desire to avenge her death, and yet he could not turn that anger into sorrow. Frustrated, he got down on the floor and started a series of press-ups and sit-ups in reps of twenty, alternating between the two until he was breathless, and his forearms and biceps ached from the burn, and he then forced himself to do another three sets of each.

A hot shower made up for some of the lack of sleep and soothed his aching muscles, and after he had soaped all over, even using the bar of hand soap instead of shampoo on his hair, he ran the shower to cold and forced himself to stay in place as the icy jets invigorated him, repaired the muscle tissue and raised his heartbeat and breathing. King changed quickly and stepped outside, greeted by the smell of cooked bacon and coffee.

Downstairs Big Dave was in the kitchen manning the stove. Rashid sat at the breakfast bar nursing a black coffee and a stack of toast and butter. King nodded a silent greeting and made himself a cup of tea.

"Here, get that down 'ya..." Big Dave said, sliding a plate of heart attack across the polished granite surface. King nodded, but he wasn't feeling hungry. He sipped his tea and after a few more sips, he picked up a sausage and ate distractedly. Big Dave sat down with a plate piled high with bacon, sausages, fried eggs and toast. It was quite a feat to pile a plate so high without spillage. "Not hungry, 'bro?"

King shrugged. "I'm getting there," he replied and picked up a slice of toast. He watched the big Fijian make much of his meal into a three-inch-thick sandwich and consume with the hunger and pleasure of a man who hadn't eaten in days. But knowing Big Dave, he had probably eaten a few sausages while he finished cooking everything else. "You're something else, mate," King said drily.

"Never know when it will be your last meal."

"Carry on like that and it may well be," Rashid quipped.

"This is good stuff," Big Dave replied. "I grew up eating shit, so this can only be better." He shovelled in another huge forkful and chewed industrially.

"What, freshly caught lobsters and fish from your own lagoon?" Rashid laughed, then added, "Coconuts from the trees and ripe mangos?"

"Ah, you know nothing!" Big Dave retorted, speaking

with a large mouthful of sausage and egg. He chewed quickly, wanting to respond without the risk of choking. When he swallowed it took a real effort because he hadn't chewed it enough. "You know all those companies that make tinned corned beef and spam and all that kind of luncheon meat? Well, when they made batches with too much fat content that would be rejected out of hand by Australia, the US and Europe, they sent it all out to Oceania. But not before making the regular canned meat more expensive and difficult to import." He paused, for once not looking to replace his mouthful. "We island nations got the shit nobody else wanted. Then, some bright spark at one of the canning companies thinks - *Do you know who likes eating fat? Samoans, Tahitians and Fijians, that's who. Let's make it even fattier. Hell let's make it almost all fat and maximise our profits! Fuck the natives and their health. Fuck their need for meat because the Chinese factory fishing vessels are emptying the oceans of fish at a critical level.* Pretty soon all the canning companies follow suit, and the island nations no longer have a choice." He paused. "Except for high cholesterol and fatty liver disease..."

"Holy shit, mate. Where the fuck did that come from?" Rashid glanced at King, then looked back at Lomu and shrugged. "I had no idea..."

Lomu shovelled in another mouthful and said nothing.

King pushed the fruit bowl slowly towards him and grinned.

"Fuck off," Big Dave grinned.

"I've never heard you talk about your home before," King commented. He'd now found his appetite and dipped some toast into his egg.

Big Dave shrugged. "I don't," he replied. "I haven't even thought about it much over the years. My dad died suddenly and my mother remarried. I didn't like the guy and sort of fell out with everyone around me. We have family in Fiji, but many communities are like one big open family. Sometimes you'd feed a kid and they'd sleep over, then they're gone the next day and turn up a few weeks later. Well, I kind of fell out with all those extended families over it all, too. The British recruitment ship sailed in one day like something out of the fucking slave trade two hundred years before, and five of us left for a new life. The army trained me and fed me, and it was a pretty good life. Clearing out the stragglers in the caves of the Tora Bora using just knives and night vision goggles was a bit of a low moment, but other than that it all worked out well enough until the army dumped me on my arse. Cutbacks and shit. Many regiments went that way, and many NCOs in other units." He took out his mobile phone to check a text that had just alerted, then shook his head and put the phone back in his pocket. "Shit..." he commented quietly.

"Girl trouble?" Rashid ventured.

"Something like that..." Lomu replied, then pushed his plate aside.

King looked up. He'd never seen the man-mountain leave food on his plate before. Or other people's plates for that matter. "Everything okay?"

"Fine."

King shrugged, pushed his plate aside, too. He was thinking about last night. But more than that, he was thinking about his inability to grieve. Had his work finally stripped him of human emotion? "So, what's the problem?"

Big Dave looked at him as he picked up his own cup. "What?"

King shrugged. "Well, we all meet up, get given a mission, kill some bad guys and get the job done, then we disperse until the next time." King paused. "So, what's troubling you?"

Lomu sighed. "Some family shit, that's all..."

"Yeah, I have family shit all the time," Rashid commented. *"Why are you no longer eating halal? When are you going to marry a nice Muslim girl and make us all proud?"* He chuckled. "I thought a chest full of medals might have gone some way towards making them proud, but..."

"Oh boo-hoo, your mother cares," King said mockingly. "If we're all caring and sharing, then my mother was a crack whore who OD'd and left us all to go into care. But that was easy because I'd already left school at fourteen or fifteen to work, steal or scam to buy groceries so that my siblings could eat..."

"This kind of chat is more fun," said Lomu, clearing away his plate. "You had me worried for a moment, I thought we were going deep or something there. I missed basically taking the piss out of each other when I was in Berlin." He looked up as Neil Ramsay walked in folding his overcoat and looking for somewhere to put it. He handed it to Rashid who took it before he realised what he was doing, then simply tossed it onto the floor as Ramsay pulled out the stool and sat at the breakfast bar. He hung his leather laptop case on the back of the stool. Ramsay was never more than six feet from his laptop. "Care to share a glimpse of your childhood, Neil?" Big Dave asked. "We're all getting in touch with some shit here..."

Ramsay helped himself to coffee from the pot. "I enjoyed solving puzzles and constructing trainset dioramas in a blissfully unaware home of a long line of middleclass Tory voters. We took a holiday to Polzeath and Rock every summer and to the South of France or Tuscany every autumn. Do I win?" He sipped the black coffee and said, "I'm sorry about your sister, King."

King had never heard the man speak with such sincerity before. Neil Ramsay wasn't intentionally obtuse. The rest of the team had worked out that he must have been autistic on some level. For an intelligence officer being unable to lie should have been debilitating on some level, but for the people he worked with, it was a transparent quality. He was on the level. There was no bullshit. King supposed that his childhood spent solving puzzles also went towards making him an excellent planner and analyst. "Thanks, Neil."

"That was quite a bloodbath last night. Do you need therapy or anything?"

"And he's back..." Rashid said quietly.

"No. I'm OK." King would hate to admit to the fact that he had seen worse in his time. It made him sad, too. He should be grieving Leanne, but all he wanted was to put a bullet in her killer's forehead.

"Any breakfast going?" Ramsay asked. "My wife has me on a high-fibre, low fat diet and it's been hell..."

"Egg banjo?" Big Dave offered

"A what?"

"A fried egg sandwich," he replied, but was already cracking two eggs into the frying pan. "The pan's still warm..."

Ramsay shrugged and turned to King. "Sally-Anne is still at the crime scene liaising with the police." He paused, taking a flash drive out from his pocket. "This is our data-base on contract killers. It's an interesting read at the best of times, but I'm hoping that we can find something that links to your sister's murder..." He paused, straightening an imaginary kink in his tie. "Or her family." He looked up as Big Dave set down a plate with a sandwich on it. The white bread was sliced thickly, and the sandwich had been sliced in half. "Why on earth do you call it an egg banjo?" Ramsay asked Big Dave as he caught hold of one half and took a bite.

"That's quite a reach," said Rashid. "And quite a lot of reading, I would imagine."

Ramsay nodded and a rivulet of egg yolk trickled down his chin and onto his tie. "Bugger!" he exclaimed, holding the sandwich away from him in one hand and trying frantically to remove the yolk stain with the other. It looked like he was playing air guitar.

"Because of that," Big Dave grinned. "Duelling fucking banjos, right there," he laughed.

Ramsay put down the sandwich and used a square of kitchen towel on a nearby dispenser to attack the egg yolk on his tie. "Very funny..." He looked back at King and said, "Sally-Anne phoned and told me that she had a theory that it was two killers. And two very different murders. I thought it may spark something. Maybe there's an MO that will stand out on that file." He paused. "The intercepted transmission named this character Reno, but as far as I can make out, he's never worked with an accomplice, and they seem convinced that there were two entirely different killers down in Southampton."

"Well, there's no time like the present," said King. "Here, let me take a look."

ELEVEN

St. Petersburg, Russia

"AND HE HAS BEEN good to his word?"

"He has."

"Scared, greedy or committed to our cause?"

Viktor Sokolov shrugged. "I would say a little of all three."

"A little?"

"Maybe greed is the highest motivator of the three." Sokolov paused, a sneer of disdain on his top lip. "But he is a Western politician, what more can we expect?"

Arkady Volkov stared out at the frozen waters of the Moyka River, his back to his second in command. It had been mild this year and the river had not completely frozen to solid ice, but it still carried sizeable slabs in its flow. The rooftops glistened white with snow, but the streets below had been cleared and people walked confidently on the salted and gritted pavements carrying meagre bags of shopping where before the sanctions imposed by most of the world, where only a matter of a month or more before, they had been laden with Christmas shopping and groceries for the feasts. Traditionally Christmas was celebrated on January 7th in line with the Orthodox Church, but many people were now 'westernising' and Father Frost and the Snow Maiden, Russia's traditional injection of colour and cheer in the bleak mid-winter, were slowly being superseded by Santa Claus and the commercial trappings of the West. Although Volkov was now confident that Russia would look inwards once more, and it was all the West's doing. Imposing sanctions on a country who was only protecting its neighbours from Nazism. Where the rest of the world saw madness in the Russian President's methods, men like Volkov saw only genius. "Fear is always the most effective motivator of all," he mused. "And what of his belief in our cause?"

Sokolov hesitated. Volkov liked his answers to be definitive. He could take bad news, but he could not abide indecision or redirection. "He's not a traitor to his country. He has none of the ideals that saw his fellow countrymen defect to us as was common in the sixties, but then again, we don't have the same ideals now. Our cause is a world apart and our direction is one that other countries are too scared, to gutless to take. But he recognises Russia's influences in investment and does not want to continue this witch hunt the British have against us with property, sports and entertainment, investment and construction." He paused, trying to gauge the man's reaction, but it was impossible with his back to him. Even the smoked glass window did not show enough reflection. "He has many business interests which align with our own, and we need to work with him to control the breadth of sanctions."

"Indeed."

"He will come good on our investment."

"And so, he should!" Volkov snapped. "We have funded him for too long. We paid for his university degree, his Master's at Yale. We set him up in business and funded his interest in politics until it became a career in politics. All the while playing the long game. We paid off his indiscretions, his affairs, and so far, he has given us little in return."

"The timings haven't been right."

"The timing is perfect!"

Sokolov looked at the man's back, grateful he did not have to stare him in the face. He had dealt with Volkov's predecessors and although they had commanded respect – and it would have ultimately been foolhardy to ignore this - there was something about the man that made him nervous, and for a man like Sokolov, who had worked in Russian intelligence for almost two decades, that was quite an admission. Volkov had held a seat at the family's table for twenty years, operating in Georgia, Ukraine and Azerbaijan. Recent events had seen him take control of the family's interests, and he now used St. Petersburg as his base, inheriting not only the family's assets, but also their enemies. "He has never baulked at maintaining Russian business interests..."

"And nor do half the Tory party!" Volkov interjected sharply. "Or many of them, at least. And the unwitting ones are all too stupid or too greedy to follow the money and find the root of their investment."

"But the majority are all for the process of Russian sanctions and taxation penalties for ambiguous investment," Sokolov replied, making certain that his tone could only be taken for deference. "The Prime Minister is one of these such people. Hence the difficulty in moving forward with our plans."

"With our asset in the chair, Britain will truly be a satellite state for a new Union expanding covertly, but with eyes everywhere and a hand in governments and their financial institutions around the world..." Volkov turned around, a sneer on his face. "But we need commitment," he said, walking to his desk and sitting down heavily in the leather chair. "We need our asset to prove he is committed to our cause. When Russia expands her reach, it will be money, not nuclear weapons nor armies that shows her strength. Our asset is not working hard enough influencing the British Prime Minister to drop the prejudice against our investments, not getting enough support in the back rooms and bars of parliament to see that our money creates jobs and business." He paused. "And now, we need a swift end to the Ukraine fiasco, and a leadership coup to reverse blanket sanctions over the war."

Sokolov did not point out that Russian tax evasion meant that nothing tangible was filtering into Britain's health service, police and public services, schools and education. On the face of it, their investments sometimes created jobs and business for employment agencies. Even after Brexit, many of these agencies still largely employed East-European workers who sent much of their money home. "Our asset is strategically placed. I have every confidence that he will be both useful and valuable." He paused. "Besides, we are testing him. Testing his commitment, while settling old scores for the Bratva. I have word that he is holding up his end of the bargain."

"He wants money and power. I can give him this. I can give him the cream off a billion pounds of investment, but I don't work with people who aren't fully committed."

"Then, what will you have me do?"

"Make him understand what fear truly is..."

TWELVE

Virginia, USA

NEWMAN LOOKED out across the frozen lake. The surrounding trees were sparse and grey and moribund. The last time he had been here it had been summertime and the trout had been rising to feed on midges and dragonflies in the late evening sun that had cast a hue of gold across the water, and Robert Lefkowitz had offered him bourbon. There was no bourbon on offer this afternoon, but the CIA director's wife had bought Newman a coffee and a green macrobiotic protein shake for her husband.

Lefkowitz was hooked up to a series of tubes and wires and his nurse sat beside him watching the monitor and checking her notes.

"Chemotherapy," Lefkowitz explained with a shrug.

Robert Lefkowitz had cancer but downplayed it to the rest of Langley. He was head of the CIA and used to keeping secrets. And he wasn't leaving until he was in a box. Only the nurse, his oncologist and his wife knew what type of cancer it was, along with the prognosis.

"Does it hurt?" Newman asked, although he wasn't entirely sure why.

"Uncomfortable and tiring," Lefkowitz replied. "But don't worry about me, I'll be right as rain after this next course."

"Yes, Sir." Newman glanced at the nurse, but she remained impassive as she checked her notes. If she played poker she would likely win. Newman knew that she had signed her life away with not only the *Defense Secrets Act* and the *Espionage Act,* but knowing Lefkowitz, she would have signed a damned sight more than that and he would likely own her soul if she so much as thought about divulging what she overheard whilst he was in her care.

"Thanks for asking," Lefkowitz said. "But you don't have to. People don't know how to act around someone who has the spectre of death hovering near them. But I do not fear death. I have been surrounded by it my entire adult life. What I fear, is dying before I get the job done, and I have a dozen files that need a satisfactory and just conclusion."

"If I can help in any way..."

Lefkowitz looked at the young man. Barely thirty, tall with tousled sandy hair and the build of a man able to lend himself effectively to most events on the track and field, he looked almost preppy and entitled, but the old spymaster knew that behind the kind-looking face a killer lurked with frightening ability. Lefkowitz had used Newman to great effectiveness in the field, but his ultimate goal was to get him settled as a department head before the man eroded on the inside. Lefkowitz's great conundrum, though, was the fact Newman was just so damned effective in the field and the list of jobs needing clearing before he could let go was growing rather than shrinking. Such was the nature of intelligence work. Every time a leak was plugged, another sprung up in its place.

"I have a task for you," he said quietly. The nurse didn't falter, merely kept checking the flow rate against her chart and the man's vitals on the monitor. Lefkowitz's blood pressure rose slightly as he said, "In England." Newman nodded. He had operated there before. "I'm hoping this will end all animosity between us once and for all. But there's more than a good chance that it won't."

Newman had cleaned up there as part of the fallout from an unsanctioned operation that had caused betrayal and mistrust between MI5 and the CIA. Tensions were nowhere near as high, but so long as there was apprehension between the two intelligence agencies, they could not fight common enemies and threats as effectively as they had always done so in the past. Newman knew that the former President's commercial and private interests had overlapped his presidential duties and had started the animosity. Hopefully this assignment would draw a satisfactory conclusion on both sides.

"The international crime desk has been in a joint surveillance operation with the NSA for some time. They have something. Something solid. It's all in the file," he said, tapping his fingers on a manilla folder on the bed beside him. "I want you to investigate, then terminate with extreme prejudice."

THIRTEEN

Mayfair, London

KING STARED AT THE SCREEN, Ramsay impatiently re-reading, mouthing silently with his lips and the odd exhale of breath. "Do you have to do that?" King asked impatiently. "How fast do you read, anyway?"

"I was going to say you're an extremely slow reader."

"I read just fine."

"Where are you, then?"

King sighed. *"...a threat unlike anything preceding. A threat not only to the perceived freedom of the West, but one that will incite violence and discord as swiftly as the Nazi Party and Adolf Hitler during the mid-thirties..."* He paused. "A bit melodramatic, isn't it?"

The file on contract killers had yielded nothing. Ramsay had then presented a report on Russian hacking that had come through from GCHQ, part of a taskforce against electronic interference spearheaded by MI5.

"You're a hammer, King. A blunt and violent tool. And to a man with a hammer, every problem is a nail…"

"Did he just call you a tool?" Big Dave smirked.

"Do you know, Dave, I think he just did." King stared at Ramsay and said, "I have been known to bring the finesse and intelligence to a mission, and not just the brawn…"

Ramsay shrugged. "Very well. But this direction the Russians are taking is a far greater threat than ever before."

"Brainwashing teenagers on social media and hacking stock markets isn't quite in the same league as detonating a nuclear device on UK soil."

"Agreed," Ramsay conceded. "But Russia has the means to switch off the gas and oil, drive alternative means of energy through the roof, flatline the British pound, destroy economic growth and turn our citizens into an unquestioning herd that fail to question anything and accept what happens underneath their noses." He paused, shaking his head in despair. "Look at the recent phenomena we've seen with Covid deniers and anti-vaxers. Okay, so it's your choice and I get that. But the misinformation being spread is frankly laughable and even when scientists get involved in the argument, they spend their time deflecting utter nonsense. How does a person living in abject poverty with no qualifications and no work experience come up with argument and counterargument on a subject they should never understand? Because of interference. Name a subject, a socio-political angle and Russia is behind the conspiracy theory. You see, conspiracy theories make the uneducated feel very educated indeed. We saw this with US election results, not only with Russian-backed votes, but with conspiracy theories when that administration failed to get re-elected. Everyone is at it. China and North Korea are more of a threat to us now that they have hacked into cryptocurrency. North Korea made four-hundred million dollars last year alone. They are creaming off the top and sending businesses in the West into bankruptcy." Ramsay paused. "They have cottoned onto the fact that after years of plotting to destroy the West, we are worth more alive. And if in the pursuit of wealth, they send us on a course to destruction, then so much the better."

"We've always known about Russian hackers," said King. "So, how does this affect my situation?" He paused. "Because with the best will in the world, I'm only here to find out who is trying to kill me, and who the hell just slaughtered my family."

"Patience," Ramsay said as he scrolled down the document. "GCHQ have tagged two of these hackers. A discreet, yet thoroughly innovative piece of code that has allowed them, and by default us, to gain screen access to their terminals..."

"And what?" King asked impatiently. "You've found the assassin?"

"Oh, dear Lord, no," Ramsay cracked a mirthless, uningratiating grin. "I'm afraid it's not going to be as easy as that. But what we do have is a connection. As hackers, you'll see that GCHQ refer to them as Rasputin and Romanov. You see, in Russia in the middle of the First World War the peasant preacher and mystical figure Rasputin was instrumental in the fall of the Romanov empire because an already dissatisfied population saw his influence over Empress Alexandra take a turn after Emperor Nicholas left to oversee troops. Rasputin was assassinated by conservatives and not long afterwards the Russian revolution removed the house of Romanov..."

"I feel I speak for all of us when I say, what the fuck has

this got to do with King's situation," said Big Dave. "In short, Neil, get to the bloody point."

"It is widely believed that British intelligence agents assassinated Rasputin because he was pushing for the Romanovs to make peace with Germany and therefore Germany would be free to concentrate on fighting on just one front and the rest of the West." King said, staring at Ramsay and finding the man's surprise and annoyance pleasing to say the least. "But as Big Dave said, get to the bloody point..."

"Indeed," Ramsay conceded and scrolled down the screen. "Romanov is a hacker that has given us the most interest, but it's Rasputin's influence that has given us the opening. For a hacker he... or she... was sloppy. Which was how the GCHQ techies got their coding in place."

"I know little about computers, Neil," said King. "But I'm surprised that they got close enough to Russian hackers."

Neil Ramsay smiled. It was a rare event, and the other's took interest despite the man's ramblings and potted history account. "They didn't. They found the link quite by chance." He paused, clearing his throat. "They were hacking the Foreign Secretary..."

FOURTEEN

Surrey

HE DELETED the text message and slipped the phone back into his pocket. Natasha lay at his feet. She was on her stomach, her legs spread slightly, her right leg pivoted slightly.

"There is a difference, my dear, between creating the *perception* of a monstrous crime, and committing one."

"Dead is dead."

"Spread your right leg more," Reno told her. He watched, satisfied she was in a good position. "You said that you made it look like torture and dispatch."

"No, I said, when you set the trap, I guarantee that he'll go to the ends of the earth to find you..." She looked up at him and he pressed her head back down to the scope on top of the rifle. "Anyway, like I said, dead is dead..."

"It sounds like you enjoyed it."

"I did," she replied breezily. "I enjoyed every sweet second..."

"It becomes dangerous if you live out your fantasies."

"You didn't enjoy killing those two boys? What with their snivelling and crying for their parents?" She paused, eased the bolt of the rifle forwards, chambering the .308 cartridge and resighted her right eye to the 3.8x60mm rifle-scope. She allowed three inches of gap between her eye and the reticule so that she would not get 'scoped' – taking the full recoil of the rifle through the scope to her eye. She had done so once, and she would never allow it to happen again. "Did it not give you a thrill? The sense of power alone is difficult not to revel in. For me, it's a bit like coming. The tension, the build-up and then the glorious release..."

Reno felt awkward at the sexual connotations. He had never felt sexualised by killing, but he had enjoyed being the last man standing, of the victor enjoying the spoils, and in every case, the spoils had been hanging onto his life. He looked up at the target some six-hundred metres distant. The target was a twelve-inch-wide plank of wood, seven feet in length and buried a foot deep in the soft earth. Paper targets had been placed at three levels. The largest target was a red circle the diameter of a football and placed at the top. Below that two circles, one sat atop the other and each approximately eight inches in diameter. The bottom target consisted of four circles, each just four inches in diameter. From this distance he could not see any of the circles, and he knew that Natasha would struggle to see the bottom four even with the magnification of the scope.

Did it give him a thrill? No. Perhaps it would have once, but he had seen a lot since then and he had lived two lives. A drunken life without remorse at the time and with little consequence, and the life he now led. Professional. Respect-ful. That was why he had drowned the two boys together. That was why he had let them both come up for air but had pushed them both down before they could snatch another breath. To speed up their drowning, to make the whole process smooth, rapid and without drama. Both boys had died well within the three-minute timeframe that was normal for drowning. He had shushed them soothingly the entire time. Natasha had watched, taking in the process and after it was quiet once more, and the water in the bath had calmed to an eerie stillness, she had asked questions and he had answered them, mentor to student.

"The rule of three, is it true?" she asked, keeping her right eye on the reticule of the scope, hovering the T-post hairs over the top third of the largest circle. "The boys, for example. Did it take the full three minutes?" She paused. "Three weeks without food, three days without water, three minutes without air and three seconds for the brain to shut down from bullet trauma or a severed throat..."

"It's a guide," he replied. "It is a general rule, not gospel."

"But from what I have seen of it, the three-minute rule is true. Like a message from God. Like a Fibonacci number. A mathematical code found in nature from the distance of veins on a leaf to the spiral of a snail's shell. A perfect equation..."

Reno thought about the boys. They had drowned well inside the three-minute rule. The Armenian he had killed twelve years ago who had needed three 9mm bullets to his brain before he had stopped moving, and even then, had taken a full minute or more of groaning and muttering before he had rested still. He remembered the Canadian businessman who had survived for six days without food or water in a barn when he had been delayed returning with the ransom money. The drop-off had gone like clockwork, but Reno had been run off the road by a drunk driver and had woken in hospital five days later. It had taken him another day to drive out to Alberta, his leg in plaster and his wrist bandaged with thirty stitches from the compound fracture. At first the hospital would not allow him to discharge himself, but he had managed to get away and had hired a truck to make the journey. Despite giving the man water and biscuits, he had died on the drive back and Reno had left him in the woods. For some reason that he could not understand, even in the early hours when dark thoughts and regret came to him, and despite the many lives he had taken without remorse, the man's death still troubled him.

"It's a guide," he said tersely. "Now, three shots to establish a grouping, then make the sight adjustments."

"Always three?"

"Always three," he replied. "Every time you adjust, you take three shots to establish a group."

"See?" she said smugly. "The rule of three…"

FIFTEEN

"Steve Moore is a bodyguard with diplomatic protection. He served for seven years in the British army before joining the police service eleven years ago. He was an experienced infantryman with the Household Calvary and served in Afghanistan. He also did a two-year attachment with military intelligence."

"And he contacted GCHQ?" King asked.

Ramsay shook his head. "No. He was unsure what to do and so contacted a Major Houghton of the military intelligence detachment he served with. He did not want to ruin his reputation with diplomatic protection..." Ramsay shrugged. "Bodyguards often have a misguided loyalty to their VIPs. That's how some private individuals end up working for a despot or organised crime boss. In the police, it's no different. Protection officers are there to do a job, not report the things they see, but Moore was concerned that some of the meetings his VIP was attending were simply not on the level. When the Foreign Secretary met with what he described as a *shady-looking Russian* a few months ago, DS Moore made a call and met with his former commander. Major Houghton has many points of contact with the Security Service, me included, and together we met with GCHQ and decided that we would very much like to know a little more about the Foreign Secretary and his *shady* meetings."

"Considering how British politics is these days," said Rashid.

"Exactly," Ramsay replied.

"And this bodyguard saw what, exactly?" King asked. "He's a politician. Shady meetings are second nature to that shower of shit."

"We left our bodyguard in play. But this morning he contacted me to say that he had just observed a meeting beside the Thames in a quiet carpark frequented by joggers and rowers parking their cars. A strange place for a politician to meet, don't you think?"

"His protection detail has what? Four or five men? A driver and BG in his vehicle. Two, maybe three in the support vehicle?" King mused. "All DPG. So, all serving police officers. None of these other men saw this as strange?"

"They do their job, keep their head down, I suppose," replied Ramsay.

"Right..." King shrugged. "Mind you, this government seem to do whatever the hell they like in plain view of everyone. I suppose arrogance or confidence is an overriding factor."

"Indeed."

"So, what did he see that got his attention?"

"It was the man himself," Ramsay said quietly. "Our man was a serving solider who went to war twice..."

"We refer to it as tours," Rashid corrected him. "So, if he went twice, he did two tours."

Ramsay ignored him and continued, "…and was a police officer of vast experience. But he said it was the person he met, rather than the meeting. He said he could tell that the man was a killer. Through and through, no doubt about it."

"Interesting," said King. "I think I should meet this man, Moore."

"You think it's linked?" asked Big Dave. "That's a hell of a stretch…"

"Is it?" King asked. "You took down some Russian mobsters and smuggled the informer into Finland. I have crossed swords with the Russian mob, the Albanians, too. Rashid and his gang of mercenaries waged war on the Albanian and Russian mafia."

"But the hackers work for Russian intelligence, not the mafia," Big Dave argued. "And if there is a link with the Foreign Secretary and Russian hackers, then that's a completely different line of investigation."

King shook his head. "The sooner we all accept that the Russian mafia families own the Russian intelligence services, the sooner we'll be able to fight them more effi-ciently." He paused, looking at Ramsay. "Set a meeting for the bodyguard. I want to talk to him within the hour…"

SIXTEEN

Detective Inspector Miller had given Sally-Anne Thorpe a lift to Southampton Central, and she had taken the train to London Waterloo. Two hours after she left Southampton she was seated at her desk in Thames House where she had full access to the Police National Computer database and had got straight to work in her third-floor corner office overlooking both the River Thames and Lambeth Bridge, with glimpses of Victoria Tower Gardens. She had a large black coffee in a go-cup on her desk and for the first time in months, she did not feel tempted to reach for one of several packets of biscuits she kept in the third drawer down in her desk. Snacking was a problem in her job, and she rarely ate regular meals at anything like a proper mealtime. Since taking on her role with MI5 she had risen early, worked late and often found herself ordering takeout meals from delivery services around eleven pm. But she doubted she would tonight. It was hard to believe she would feel like eating anything again after what she had seen that morning. She had seen some sights in her time with the Met, but nothing like the shop of horrors in that quiet cul-de-sac.

Nothing had prepared her for that. The two methods of murder had been poles apart. Two separate acts. One had shown a sadistic barbarity and if not carried out in rage, showed a complexity and brutality that frightened her. A monstrous act. However, the drowning of the boys had been so dispassionate, so clinical that she could hardly believe that it could have been carried out by the same killer. The torture and murder of Leanne Armitage – nee Jeffries – and her husband had left her feeling queasy, while the murder of the two boys had left her cold. So cold, she feared she would never recover from the experience.

SEVENTEEN

Hyde Park, London

"I DON'T GO in for theatrics, Mr Ramsay. We could have done this anywhere." He sighed. "Walking anonymously around the park and discussing matters of state security is a bit like something out of a *Le Carre* novel."

"Because that is how it is done," said Ramsay shaking his head. "Rooms are too easily bugged, and records of meetings are recorded in government buildings. My men are out there looking out for parabolic microphones. This is a far easier, and safer way to talk."

"And who are *you?*" Moore asked looking at King.

"King."

"King works with my team... *is* the core of the team, I suppose," Ramsay explained in a rare, albeit indirect compliment.

"Fine," Moore muttered, looking around him. "Anyway, what have you got?"

"Got?" Ramsay asked. He started to walk, his feet crunching on the frost-kissed grass.

"What do you want me to do?"

Ramsay shrugged. "Nothing, old man. We're grateful for your observations."

"You don't want me to find out more?"

"Do you?" Ramsay asked, stopping and looking at him.

"I just thought..."

"This isn't a recruitment drive," King said quietly, watching the rest of the park. The sun was low, the sky clear and he was wearing a pair of *Ray Bans* against the glare of the sun. Patches of grass were steaming from the touch of the sun, the shady areas still white and crisp.

"What?"

King shrugged. "Undercover work is the arsehole of intelligence work," he replied. "A sweaty arsehole. You just don't want to go near it if you can avoid it."

"I'm happy to go undercover," Moore replied quickly. "I want to serve my country."

"You've already done that," said King.

"We thank you for your service," Ramsay said as sincerely as Neil Ramsay could ever say anything.

King shrugged. "Well, I don't..."

"What?" Moore stared at him disapprovingly.

"It's your career choice. There isn't a draft."

"Have you ever served in the armed forces, King?"

"No."

"Then you wouldn't understand."

King smiled at the irony and continued to walk. "What did the man look like?"

Moore shrugged. "I don't know if you know anything about killers, Mr King. But there are men who have seen it all. I'm not talking about soldiers, per se. It's true, men change after a tour. It's the stress, the missing of loved ones, the rations, the catering, the endless heat. Avoiding land-mines and IEDs takes its toll. Many soldiers kill, but largely it's a protracted affair with multiple soldiers claiming the kill because the contact was three-hundred yards away and all that was seen was a Taliwanker falling behind a wall. Of course, we see some heavy shit, but PTSD aside, the majority of soldiers come back at least *almost* whole." He paused. "But occasionally you'll come across a soldier of real experience. A long-serving member of the SAS or SBS, or a US Navy SEAL. Some of those guys have the real thousand-yard stare. Some of those men have seen it all. And within those groups of men, there's the one who's done that little bit more. Gone the extra mile. Those guys have *the look*."

King nodded. They had reached the Serpentine Water-fall. It was King's favourite part of the park and he had once picnicked there with his wife Jane on a glorious afternoon in June, turning the picnic blanket into a giant poncho which they wrapped around them when the evening air chilled and the champagne had run out, neither one wanting to leave. That was the day their steady stream of dates had flourished into a relationship. "And this guy had the look?" he ventured.

"With bells on."

"Alright, supposing we asked you to have a snoop around?" Ramsay asked. He never liked to ask a person to turn spy, especially when that person was so close to the subject, but Moore had already intimated that he was willing to do so. He sensed a real 'Queen and Country' element to the man's character, perhaps a little too arro-gant, but that was always better than someone requesting financial gain. "Nothing too brazen. What we especially want is a notification should your charge meet this man again."

"He will," Moore said authoritatively. "Campbell is the most arrogant person in the cabinet. And I've protected a few. He won't suspect a thing. He carries on his private ventures with impunity. Half the time we are out I suspect it is for his own personal gain."

Edward Campbell was one of the political elite. Attending Eton, Oxford and the somewhat ridiculous and thoroughly reprehensible Bullingdon Club at the same time as the current serving Prime Minister, the Home Secretary and the Chancellor of the Exchequer, except Campbell completed his Master's, as so many did in Yale to get the American college experience of unlimited funds, *nouvou aristocracy* and guest speakers earning a million dollars a time on the 'speaker circuit'. The four men were often referred to by the press as the *Fantastic Four*, the *Four Toffs, Four Horsemen of the Apocalypse* or the *Pudding Club*, depending upon the political leaning of the newspaper. Campbell was from a long line of bankers, shipping merchants and traders who had been handed a convenient family fortune made at the height of the slave trade and later helped through good old fashioned Victorian servitude and exploitation. Two world wars helped top up the coffers because the Campbells had subsidiary companies and Swiss holdings that benefitted from both sides, until they finally went all in with the allies and bought up German factories and early investments in a car company that would soon buy out British control. By the fifties the Campbells were out of the automotive industry and into pharmaceuticals, tobacco products and sugar. It had been notably said that if you had illnesses from smoking or poor diet, then a Campbell product would likely to have been both the cause and the potential cure.

"It's a tough one, this," Ramsay commented. "The company the man keeps, the alliance made with his peers when he was at school. These aren't normal people. The four of them, sat up in their dorms late at night discussing how they will one day run the country. Then university, local politics, getting elected and being back benchers, getting to the fore and into the cabinet. One of them getting the top job, the other three landing the next best roles..."

"Nothing tough about it," said King. "If one of them, or all of them are being influenced by the Russians, then we'll take them down. I don't care if it goes all the way to the top..."

Ramsay nodded, under no doubt to the lengths King would go. Although he doubted that he would ever be able to prove it, he knew that King had the blood of two world leaders on his hands. "But we have to be careful. Campbell could be on the level, and then we jeopardise the service's integrity."

"Bollocks. He's bent," King retorted. "They probably all are."

"It could have been a legitimate meeting with this mystery man," Ramsay countered. "Away from the prying eyes of Whitehall, Westminster Palace and the press."

"No." Moore cast a hand around the park. "Is this legitimate, on the level?" He scoffed. "Legitimate meetings are done in a warm office with a cup of coffee. The man Campbell met was a killer. The worst kind. I'd bet my life on it."

A bank of clouds had drifted ominously close, and the park was cast in a dull, grey hue. King removed his sunglasses and tucked them into the inside pocket of his bomber jacket. "You're sure about this?" he asked, staring intently at Moore.

"I..." Moore hesitated for a moment, then nodded. "Absolutely."

King turned to Ramsay. "That's good enough for me," he said. "I'll meet you back at the house, there's somewhere I have to go first."

Both men watched King make his way past the waterfall and head back the same way they had come alongside the edge of the lake. Ramsay sighed and looked at Moore. "And you are sure about this man?"

Moore continued to stare at King's back as he walked briskly among the joggers and dog walkers, and said, "I'm certain of it," he replied. "Just as certain as I am that man King is exactly the same." He paused. "No military service my arse. He's a cold-blooded killer."

Ramsay didn't respond, merely checked his watch and started to walk back the same way.

EIGHTEEN

On first appearances there was no apparent reason that the street should be so quiet given its central London location. On the face of it the buildings were in good condition and the road it branched off was a busy thoroughfare. However, King knew that not only had the former brewery been purchased using MI6 money, but the surrounding buildings had been snapped up as well. The four large buildings that had once been used for the storage of barley and hops would be worth millions today for development into apartments, but they had been purchased inexpensively years before and now served as the perfect cover for what the brewery building was now being used for.

King parked the Audi in the quiet street and got out. There were signs everywhere warning of vehicle clamping, but he knew it was all part of the façade. He glanced up at the eaves of the buildings, noticing a few more CCTV cameras than had been there before on his last visit. On the third floor, high above the steel door to the street, there was a ledge and a loading arm that he knew from experience would take a block and tackle and rope. King checked both ways before crossing the road, the eeriness of such a quiet street in the centre of London seeming more threatening than if he had been walking around a high-rise estate. By now he knew that the man would know he was here, but he pressed the intercom and stood back awaiting a reply.

"Come in." The door clicked open as quickly as the instruction had been issued.

King stepped in and closed the door behind him. There was another steel door six feet ahead of him and the walls of the 'foyer' were steel lined. There were two holes cut into the steel at waist height, and at adjacent angles. King knew that behind each hole was the barrel of a semi-automatic shotgun loaded with no.6 birdshot, both controlled by an electronic trigger unit. King knew that they worked and noted that the steel walls had been replaced since his last visit, too. That time there had been an interruption to their meeting, and the 'killing room' had repelled hostile forces.

The second door clicked open, and King walked through. He headed up the stairs, turned left at the top and made his way across the walkway, noting that the loading bay below was full floor to ceiling with M16 and M4 rifles. All in various configurations and most with ACOG rifle-scopes and some with M203 grenade launchers fitted underneath. King had no idea how many weapons there were, but it would be in the thousands.

"Quite a sight, isn't it?" said the man.

King didn't know the man's name. Had never asked. All he knew was the man had served in Iraq and Afghanistan, lost his leg during his final tour when he had stepped on an IED and had later become a 'Section 5' firearms dealer in his civilian life, aided greatly by his training and qualifying as an armourer and fabricator during his army service. He had dealt with the foreign office on a contract and had later undertaken work with MI6. That had been over ten years ago and even though King wasn't sure how the man made his money with MI6, he knew that the government was haemorrhaging money and that a few people were growing very rich indeed.

"The withdrawal?" King ventured.

"Oh yes. America pulled out in a hurry, left tons... and I mean fucking tons... of kit behind. I got this lot out before the Taliban got their hands on it all. The Americans left it all for the Afghan forces to use, but they had it away on their toes pretty lively, and security contractors working for yours truly... and your old employers, of course... got several containers out before the Taliban could get their hands on them."

"That was lucky."

"There's tons of kit that's been left behind. If there was one thing that we had over them in that war, it was the fact every allied soldier had a weapon system with optics. The ragheads had open sights. You don't often see a scope on an AK. That's why we won every battle we engaged in, or at least sent them packing. If we go out there again, the advantage will have disappeared. We'll be going up against an enemy completely at ease in their surroundings, who now have M4 rifles and scopes, as well as Humvees and artillery." The man paused, leading King into another room. When they stepped inside, the man waved a hand around the production line. There were piles of weapons, boxes filled with riflescopes – or what was commonly referred to as 'optics' – wooden crates with M203 grenade launchers, crates stacked with magazines and crates of the rifles in all their variants. A forty-five-gallon oil drum served as a dip tank and King could see that there were several – some filled with chemicals and others filled with oil. The man pulled a rifle out of the chemical bath using a pair of long-handled grips. He dipped the weapon into an oil drum, then fished it out and laid the weapon beside approximately ten others on a table topped with waxed paper. "First, they're dipped to removed powder residue and half the desert, then they get an oil bath. I have to run through them, check the working parts and then they get another oil dip, get gift wrapped in waxed paper, then boxed and sold on."

"Where are you selling them?"

"Anywhere there's a profit." The man paused. "And where Britain PLC want their next coup or society vision upheld..."

"You should burn the fucking lot..." King said coldly.

"Undoubtedly. But where would that leave your career prospects," he grinned. "Or mine, for that matter."

"Right..."

The man shrugged. "Anyway, there are six thousand rifles here, an estimate because it was all done by weight. There's a half a million rounds of five-five-six ammunition as well. This is all bound for Ukraine and to thwart Russia's invasion and vision of installing another puppet government like in Belarus. Certainly, a just cause and better than the Taliban getting their hands on them to use against us next time round." He paused. "Same shit, different day, eh?"

King nodded. "Who gets paid?"

The man smiled. "Some goes to the *Firm*," he said, referring to the Secret Intelligence Service by the name many insiders tended to use. "Some will go to a government department to cook the books, the security contractors who liberated it get a cut, then the rest goes to little old me."

"And who pays?"

Still smiling, the man said, "The British Government

pays. Largely it is redirecting funds to aid the budget, but the merchandise is all donated as lethal aid. This is all heading to Ukraine. If they survive the Russian overthrow, then Britain PLC gets a strong ally and no doubt, some oil, gas and lithium from their reserves. All tickety-boo..." He shrugged. "I tend to sell to countries where Britain's interests are best served."

"Helps one sleep at night."

The man laughed wryly. "Well, you're not here for anything less lethal, are you?"

"I suppose not."

"What are you after?"

"Something like last time," King replied. He hadn't needed the weapon and had tossed it in the Thames, but MI5 was an unarmed civilian service and even the way the team had evolved through necessity, being routinely armed was not an option, and nor was being caught with a weapon by the police. And certain weapons were illegal in any British service in any situation. "A silenced pistol," he said quietly.

The man nodded. "I'm out of Glocks," he said. "Using the barrel from the Glock seventeen in a shorter Glock nineteen proved popular. The extra barrel length gave something really solid to thread and screw a suppressor to." He walked over to a well-used chest of drawers that was cluttered with tools and stained with oil. He pulled out the middle of three drawers and rummaged about for close to a minute. When he had finished, he had a medium-sized pistol in his hand and some assorted pieces of metal. "Ruger mark-four. Ok, I know it's a twenty-two, but this is as silent as a sparrow's fart, and I can run you up a suppressor while you wait."

King nodded. A .22 was low on power, but accurate and

certainly quieter than anything else. His only reservation was that being a rimfire cartridge instead of centrefire, reliability was an issue. A .22 could misfire one in a hundred times when centrefire rounds that used a dedicated primer cap in the centre of the seat of the bullet case could be expected to suffer a misfire rate closer to one in a thousand. A .22 round has primer around the rim of the shell casing and instead of a firing pin shaped like the tip of a nail, the firing pin was squared off like a flatheaded screwdriver.

The man handed King the pistol and he looked it over. Without asking, King dry fired it a few times, then stripped it down and used a cloth and oil to clean the weapon thoroughly. He used a cleaning rod that the man had been using to clean the barrels of the rifles. The 5.56mm military ammunition was hugely powerful but used a bottle-necked casing so the bullet was the same diameter as the tiny .22 pistol despite the size of the charge and casing behind it, and the bronze cleaning brush fitted perfectly. As King reassembled the pistol, the man was already pressing out a tube on a steel press and had stamped out a series of baffles that he would stack inside the tube after he had inserted a sheet of fire-retardant welding drape, which he measured by rolling the tube over it with one revolution. After the sheet had been fitted inside around the edge of the tube and trimmed, the baffles held it in place and stacked together tightly. As the bullet travelled through each baffle the gases following would veer off and be absorbed by the sheet of fire blanket. By the time the bullet left the muzzle almost all the gases that were associated with the noise of a gunshot were dissipated and the gunshot would be virtually silent. King watched as the man threaded the end of the tube and applied a threaded cap with a hole only marginally larger in diameter than point-twenty-two of an inch. He put the other end in the press and threader. The man tossed the suppressor in the air and caught it like a baton, before wiping it all over with an oiled cloth.

"Never pays to leave one's prints on something like that."

"I agree."

"Want to test it?"

King nodded. Now was the time. The man could fine-tune the weapon system if there were any issues. King took the suppressor and threaded it onto the end of the threaded barrel and the man handed him two magazines and a box of .22 subsonic bullets. Anything with more velocity would make too much noise, even with the suppressor. King noticed that the sights had been raised to compensate for the suppressor, and he made a mental note to aim a little low at close range, figuring the line of sight would balance out at ranges over ten metres. Not that he would use the weapon over twenty-five metres from the target. There was a world of difference in what it was possible to hit on the range, and the lethal effectiveness of such a small round.

The man opened a door at the back of the room to reveal another room that was just three paces wide, but that was over fifty metres in length. The room stretched for almost half the building's width and was lined in carpet and more lengths of carpet was draped in half over a steel girder at the end of the room. Ballistics was a strange science where bullets could penetrate multiple people or travel through twelve inches of concrete and yet a few folds of carpet with gaps in between could slow and stop projectiles capable of travelling several miles.

King saw the targets leaning against the wall. They were military figure 11 type with a life-sized soldier brandishing a rifle and bayonet and in full charge. The bullseye centre mass was the size of a tennis ball and the V-bull inside that was no bigger than a fifty pence coin. The man picked one up. It was pasted onto plywood and two posts lined up on either side of the target which were slotted into two equidistant metal holders bolted to the floor. When he had secured the target, he walked back a few paces and nodded for King to continue.

King had loaded the ten-round magazines while the man had made the range ready. He slotted one in and pulled back the slide. He brought the weapon up slowly, allowing for the extra weight of the suppressor. If anything, it provided a decent counterweight and King fired off a round as a marker. Left and low. He had over-compensated. He raised his aim until he had settled the V and pin sights on the centre of the V-bull. He fired and was still a little to the left. Instead of moving to the right, he allowed the weapon's weight to shift in his hand and he used a little less finger, and little more fingertip on the trigger. The next shot hit the bull and the next three shots peppered the bullseye with one in the V-bull. King fired the next five and only one bullet went outside the bullseye. He backed away another few paces as he changed magazines. There was no score marker on the target's forehead, but he fired a series of double taps, and all ten shots went in an area the size of his own fist.

"That's some skills you've got there," the man said quietly, not hiding his enthusiasm.

"Likewise," said King, looking at the weapon and feeling the weight and balance of it in his hand. "This is no louder than an air pistol."

"Glad you like it. Not cheap, though."

"I'd certainly like to have your retirement plan," he said, but for the first time in his life King was now financially independent. That is, if they managed to hold onto the mafia funds Caroline had liberated. MI5 had no claim to it and the last thing she was going to do was send the money back to the surviving relatives of the former Italian crime boss she had set up. Perhaps if the couple were inexperienced and less world-weary, they would have handed the million euros back. Life was different now.

"Eight-hundred quid, mate."

King nodded. "Call it two grand." He paused. "But I'll take one of those M4s with a two-oh-three launcher and a few grenades..."

The man shrugged. It wasn't like he was low on stock. "Get the kettle on and I'll sort some kit out for you."

King smiled. "And I believe you did a custom order for my partner recently..."

"Can't talk about my clients," the man said curtly.

King said nothing. He was pleased with the man's response. He had known him for many years and had dealt with him whilst working for MI6. King had later returned to precure a firearm a few years ago and the man had never questioned whether he was still with the firm. After all these years, neither man even knew the other's name. Ask no questions and you'll be told no lies...

While the man unwrapped a cleaned and checked M4 rifle and selected several magazines and plain brown cardboard boxes of ammunition, King made the tea. White and one sugar. Just how many ex-soldiers took it. By the time King had finished brewing the tea, the man had attached an M203 grenade launcher and put aside five grenades. Looking like fat bullets, the size of a tall 'slim Jim' glass, the weapon system gave the user the ability to use a projectile with the explosive power of an L2A2 hand grenade but with a range of three hundred metres. Additionally, a set of pop-up sights in increments of fifty metres was fixed to the rifle to use with the grenade launcher. The man was an experienced armourer and gunsmith, and the system was complete when King handed the man his tea.

The man raised his mug in a toast. "Here's to doing some good in a world full of bad."

King raised his mug, too. He wasn't sure if he had always done good. He wasn't even sure if many of his operations had made a difference in the long run. Today's friends could very well be tomorrow's enemies on the whim of Downing Street. But King had always used his judgement and thought his actions were right at the time. He had chosen not to kill many times before, even suffered reprimands and career doldrums because of it, but he had always slept better for it. "To carrying a big stick but knowing when to use it." Ten minutes later, King had the M4 stashed in the boot of his car and the silenced Ruger in the door pocket beside him as he pulled out into the street and made his way back to the Mayfair safehouse.

NINETEEN

Reno read the email a second time to commit it to memory. He had used the hacker before. He had performed many assignments for the Russians. He wasn't sure whether it was for the FSB of the GRU or the Mafia. They were all connected these days. But what he did know was he had world-class, possibly the world-leaders in computer hacking at his disposal when on an official assignment for the Russians. Reno had been an 'auditor' for many Russian mafia bosses. The last man a crocked employee would ever see when he had been sent to square the account. Men with their sticky fingers in the mafia's pies. Men who thought they could skim off the top, whether it was a hundred dollars or a hundred million. The auditor would close the account with a bullet to the man's brain and the business would go to the next man deemed suitable to succeed. It was good work, because people made mistakes, grew greedy and over-confident. It was the human condition. And Reno would never be short of work.

"What have you got there?" Natasha asked breathily,

looking over his shoulder at the screen of the laptop. She was dressed in active wear and had just performed an hour workout after her five-mile run.

"The next phase," Reno replied.

She poured a tall glass of water from the dispenser and drank it down in one. She was perspiring and her face glowed red. Reno had always told her to run at the same pace as if she was escaping a volcano. There was no point jogging at a walking pace. Running from trouble was something that their work would undoubtedly give them cause to do and they needed to condition their bodies accordingly. Reno always concentrated on running, stretching and core work. He focused on workouts that involved pull-ups, press-ups, dips and climbing. It was important to be able to climb. Either up to a target's window, or for their own means of escape. In conditioning themselves for these scenarios, they seldom lifted weights and sparred daily with each other in boxing, karate and ju-jitsu techniques. Both now favoured Krav Maga, the Israeli art of fighting invented and perfected by Israeli commandos.

"We are no closer to finding King," she said tersely.

Reno smiled. "We do not need to find King," he said quietly, looking at the picture of the woman that had been attached in the email. "When the time to kill King comes, he will come straight to us."

"You think so?"

"I *know* so."

"We slaughtered his family. You don't think that is enough to provoke him?"

Reno chuckled. "We haven't yet begun to hurt him," he told her. "But we will."

"Who is Caroline Darby?" Natasha asked, reading over

his shoulder. "His lover?" Reno nodded. "Then we kill her next?"

"That is my plan."

"Can I do it," she asked, staring at the face of the woman on the screen. Mid-thirties, mousy blonde hair, good features with an aquiline nose. Natasha smiled. "She is a very beautiful woman. I would like to sleep with her." She smiled. "That would be good, no? To sleep with someone whom you knew you were going to kill." She sucked in her breath and bit her bottom lip, clearly aroused by the thought. "I like the thought of that very much..."

Reno smiled. "Well, my dear, I cannot promise that she would succumb to your feminine advances, but I *can* promise you the chance to kill her." He paused. "It is essential now to split our forces, if you will. I will be in London to keep close to our contact and to King, and you will do what now needs to be done."

"And what will that involve?"

Reno smiled. "Caroline Darby is, by all accounts, a worthy opponent. She served with the army in their intelligence corps. She was awarded a medal when her patrol was ambushed, and she held off thirty Taliban insurgents singlehandedly while injured members of her patrol could be safely evacuated. As well as this, she has been involved in numerous dangerous operations in the security service. Do not underestimate her. However, if she is unbalanced, grieving and desperate, then she will be weaker. She will make mistakes and when she does; you will strike."

Reno tapped away at the keyboard of his laptop and sent her an email. They used several accounts, all created using false details and only ever connected by a dongle and a pay-as-you-go, or burner, mobile phone. Never through a landline and wireless routers. He watched as Natasha picked up her iPhone and scrolled through her email account. The phone was the latest model and somewhere in size between a conventional smartphone and a small tablet.

"Her family?"

Reno nodded. "You know what to do..."

TWENTY

"I think I have something," Sally-Anne Thorpe announced, looking up from her laptop screen as King walked in. She smiled somewhat awkwardly and nodded a greeting, and King returned a non-committal nod.

Ramsay's eyes did not leave the screen. They were both seated at the breakfast bar with a pot of coffee on the go and laptops open. "We think it will prove significant," he said, nodding for Thorpe to continue.

King looked behind him as Rashid came in. "I've got something for you, too," he said. "All the bells and whistles."

Rashid nodded as he headed for the coffee pot. "Is that where you went?"

King shrugged. "Sorry, thought it best I shook you off." He paused, looking at Ramsay. "And nice try, Neil, but I can spot a tail by now."

"Bastard. Just following orders." Rashid picked up a cup and reached for the coffee pot. "What's all this, then?"

"Thorpe was about to give us some news by the sounds of it," King replied. He hadn't made any secret of not wanting the ex-police detective on board, and he wasn't one to warm quickly. "Where's the big man?"

"Lomu is on security," Ramsay replied. "He's outside keeping tabs."

"A static guard?" King did not hide his annoyance. "You're not utilising his skills effectively. Get him in here and have a couple of service guards keep a lookout."

"Thank you, King. I'll take it under advisement," Ramsay replied tersely.

"Actually Alex, what Neil hasn't told you, is that there are no service resources for this," Thorpe said somewhat defensively. "Nobody here is getting paid, and we're all shown as *on sabbatical* on our files." She paused. "Your team is here because they want to help you resolve this. Whatever the *hell* this is."

"Oh..." King said solemnly. He had not thought about it; hadn't for a moment questioned the response and support. Caroline had left the service and King's own future had been in doubt. He poured himself a rare coffee, not just for the caffeine hit, but because to stand there stubbornly making a cup of protest tea among these coffee drinkers seemed trite and pedantic in the face of what Sally-Anne had just said. "Well, thanks. I mean it. Thank you." If King had ever felt that he had never truly had real friendships over the years, he was in no doubt about who had his back now.

"I found this," Thorpe said, cutting through the silence like an axe. "I looked at the killings of... your sister and her family..." She paused. "I'm sorry for your loss, by the way..."

King shrugged. "Estranged," he said. "Another life. I didn't even know she had got married, let alone that she had two boys, or what their names even are..."

"Mark and Thomas," she said softly. "Mark was the oldest."

King nodded. Inside his stomach was turning somersaults and his chest tightened. They were both his names from another life. Mark Thomas Jeffries. A bum who died escaping Dartmoor Prison and who he felt nobody would mourn. How wrong he had been. Leanne had obviously cared and mourned and given him a way to live on in her own children. King sipped some coffee for a distraction, and to hide the emotion on his face. He willed himself not to fold, not to yield to the emotion welling up inside him. He drank more coffee and did not look anybody in the eye. He had seen death hundreds of times, delivered it more times than he cared to remember. And yet, he was left feeling raw and vulnerable not by the deaths in that blissfully normal cul-de-sac, but by the simple fact that both dead boys had borne his name. He was aware that Rashid was looking at him, and he took another sip of the strong, black coffee, and when he took the cup away from his mouth, his poker face was resolute and there was no emotion in his cold, grey eyes.

"The violence and sadism of the deaths was shocking. The PNC and Interpol databases were full of horrendous crimes. There are some evil people out there, but you don't need to be told this. We've all met or heard of demons in the guise of people. They walk among us." She paused. "But it was the killing of the boys that was more shocking for me. It was, so cold. So, calculated." She scrolled on her laptop until she found what she was looking for. "I found a case where one man drowned two children aged seven and nine, after he had assassinated their parents."

"Tortured and mutilated?" King asked.

"No. Not at all. A point-thirty-two calibre bullet to the head and heart on both counts."

"Right..."

"Wait. It gets better. Because the same man was found guilty of killing a man and drowning the man's fifteen-year-old daughter. Same MO." She paused. "The first instance was in Spain, the other was in Switzerland. He was a fledgling assassin named Manuel Renault. French-Spanish parentage, lived in Bayonne, France."

"I fail to see the connection," said Rashid. "If the police knew his name and he was sentenced... I take it that's what you meant by *found guilty*?"

"Absolutely," Sally-Anne nodded. She hesitated as she checked a text. She smiled, tapped out a swift reply, then put the phone back on the table, screen down.

"Private call?" asked Ramsay.

"Business," she replied, blushing.

"Yeah, right," Rashid grinned. "Sally-Anne's on a promise..."

"It's business," she said a little too emphatically. "Maybe pleasure afterwards. But only when we're done here."

"I was right," Rashid said, still grinning.

Sally-Anne Thorpe had not had a relationship in over a year, and she had never been the type of person to have a one-night stand. She had 'bonded' with DI Miller. Enough to use his first name by the end of her walk-through the crime scene. Enough to share a smile over a coffee and enough to share a look when he had dropped her off at the train station in Southampton. That was the most contact she had had with a man in a year, enough to feel stirrings inside her and enough to lay it on the line and ask if he would like to meet up. Of course, they would remain in contact throughout the case. She had agreed to liaise with him and would soon redact some of her findings and send the bare bones to his email. DI Miller had text messaged her on the train and she had felt like a teenager texting on the journey back to London.

She glanced at Ramsay, but his expression said it all. Ramsay must have been born middle-aged and married with children. "Sorry, I digress," she said, her cheeks flushed and her lips quivering slightly, embarrassed at the attention. "He was tried in the European Court because of his crimes in two countries and sentenced to life in La Santé Prison, Paris. Renault had dual citizenship of both France and Spain but was living in France at the time of the murders." She paused. "But he promptly escaped. There have been, however, unsolved cases around the world fitting the same MO. Always children drowned after the murder of an adult. These are contract killings, no doubt about it. But the person behind them, the person drowning these children, have criminal phycologists all arriving at the same conclusion – that he sees the process of drowning them as a less violent end than a number of other methods he could use. There is a paradox to drowning in that after the brief, initial panic, it is a dreamlike experience. Certainly, many survivors of drowning, those brought back from the brink by resuscitation agree that it was a calm ending..."

"There's also plenty who won't see it quite like that," replied King. He had resuscitated Caroline after she had fallen through the ice on an operation in Lapland and but for his CPR expertise and an adrenalin shot to the heart, she would not be alive today. She had shared what she had experienced, and it had been far from a calm ending.

"I agree," Thorpe nodded and squinted at her screen as she brought up a page. "I think it's a perception some people have, and in this case, the killer of these children. This is an excerpt from Sebastian Junger's *The Perfect*

Storm: A True Story of Men Against the Sea." She paused. "*The instinct not to breathe underwater is so strong that it overcomes the agony of running out of air. No matter how desperate the drowning person is, he doesn't inhale until he's on the verge of losing consciousness. At that point there's so much carbon dioxide in the blood, and so little oxygen, that chemical sensors in the brain trigger an involuntary breath whether he's underwater or not. That is called the 'break point.' Laboratory experiments have shown the break point to come after 87 seconds. It's sort of a neurological optimism, as if the body were saying, Holding our breath is killing us, and breathing in might not kill us, so we might as well breathe in.*

When the first involuntary breath occurs most people are still conscious, which is unfortunate, because the only thing more unpleasant than running out of air is breathing in water. At this point the person goes from voluntary to involuntary apnea, and the drowning begins in earnest. A spasmodic breath drags water into the mouth and windpipe, and then one of two things happens. In about ten percent of people, water—anything—touching the vocal cords triggers an immediate contraction in the muscles around the larynx. In effect, the central nervous system judges something in the voice box to be more of a threat than low oxygen levels in the blood, and acts accordingly. This is called laryngospasm. It's so powerful that it overcomes the breathing reflex and eventually suffocates the person. A person with laryngospasm drowns without any water in his lungs.

In the other ninety percent of people, water floods the lungs and ends any waning transfer of oxygen to the blood. The clock is running down now; half-conscious and enfeebled by oxygen depletion, the person is in no position to fight his way back up to the surface. The very process of drowning makes it harder and harder not to drown, an exponential disaster curve similar to that of a sinking boat." Sally-Anne paused, letting the words sink in. "It doesn't sound a great way to go, does it..." she stated flatly.

"The bastard..." Rashid said quietly. "Those poor kids..."

"And this Manuel Renault," King said. "What happened to him?"

"He escaped La Santé Prison fifteen years ago," she said and turned the laptop screen towards him. "This is a seventeen-year-old photograph of him when he was convicted. But I'm certain the person who murdered your nephews and this man are one and the same."

King stared at the photograph of the man on the screen. His features were gaunt and there was black around his eyes. And then there were those eyes. Cold and emotionless. Not the worse King had seen, but if the drownings tied in, then the man had been killing ever since. There was no telling what the man had seen. "Get Steve Moore to have a look at this photo, and any others you can get hold of. If we have access to it, then some ageing software might be a good idea."

Ramsay picked up his phone and looked at a text. He frowned and looked up at King. "You're going to love this," he said.

"What?"

Ramsay stood up. "Come with me."

TWENTY-ONE

Thames House, London

"THIS SEEMS to have escalated to a little more than off the record," King commented as he rode the lift to the third floor. "But still not to the top of the food chain," he said, knowing where most of the briefing rooms were in MI5 headquarters.

"Simon will be there. The room's been swept and sealed. This is still off the record."

"But you're all on the payroll again," King stated flatly.

"We are."

"Good. But thanks for the sentiment," he said. "It was appreciated, and…" King trailed off when he saw who was standing beside Simon Mereweather. He hadn't brought a weapon with him to Thames House – would never have got past security in the first place – but he would gladly have taken a pistol out and shot the man in the forehead. He had missed his opportunity in Svalbard.

"King, you know Mr Newman, I hear."

"I've come across him."

"We bump into one another from time to time." Newman extended his hand, but King measuredly put both hands inside his leather bomber jacket. Newman glanced mockingly at his own hand as if it was filthy, then smiled and said, "Shall we go in?"

Simon Mereweather said, "Certainly," and opened the sealed door, breaking the security seal tape. "Refreshments are on the way, gentlemen." He waited for the other three men to enter, then closed the door behind him. "I have a great deal of time for Robert Lefkowitz, my opposite number with the CIA. Not that we deal with him a great deal these days... how is he?"

"He's holding on in there," Newman replied, his Virginia drawl sounding as smooth and silky as pancake syrup. He sat down and placed a thin, leather document holder on the desk in front of him. "He wants to clear his desk, if you get what I mean..."

Mereweather looked at King and said by way of explanation, "Director Lefkowitz has cancer."

King nodded. He knew all about cancer, had watched it kill his wife, Jane. Well, almost. She had finished the job herself. As understanding as he could be, he was light on sympathy in this case. He remembered his old mentor Peter Stewart telling him that if he ever wanted to find sympathy then, *"it's in the dictionary somewhere between shit and syphilis..."* The tough Scotsman certainly had a way with words.

"So, what does Uncle Sam want with us?" King asked irritably.

Newman smiled. "Just building bridges," he said lightly. "That business with the rogue NSA agent was put to bed."

King shrugged. "An innocent Secret Service agent was killed."

"I couldn't possibly comment on that," the American replied.

King knew that the man was responsible, but there was nothing recorded. Somewhat annoyingly, he knew that Newman had helped him in Svalbard, too. "I'm sure you can't..."

Newman smiled, but it did not go with the man's façade and King knew in that moment that he had underestimated the man. He had him down as a high school jock, a preppy, clean-cut quarterback who dated a cheerleader and beauty pageant winner in college, but he suspected the man was far darker underneath, and would have to have been from what he had done. But through Newman, Robert Lefkowitz had acted to end the tit-for-tat war between the CIA and MI5, and King knew that he had been at fault and accepted his role in it.

King turned to Mereweather. "What is all this about?"

Mereweather leaned forwards, resting his elbows on the table. The tabletop was made from Formica and the chairs were straight-backed and plastic. The room was a ten by twenty box with much of the far wall taken up by a flatscreen television which was accessed through a router with cable connection, as MI5's security protocols meant there was no wireless connectivity in the building. He looked up at the sharp knock on the door. "Enter," he said sternly and waited for the secretary to bring in the tray. She smiled, placed it down before them and retreated silently. "Three coffees and one tea," he said, passing Newman his coffee first, then handing the mug of tea to King. There was milk and sugar on the tray and four teaspoons. Mereweather waited for everyone to help themselves.

King took a sip of his tea and wondered whether he had a reputation for being difficult. He noted the others had cups and saucers, but his own mug was twice the size and already sweetened with one sugar. He had lost count of the times the previous director had asked him to wear a suit, and yet he turned up to meetings in jeans or cargoes and sweatshirts or his old, scuffed leather jacket. He glanced across at Newman. The young CIA operative wore an expensive grey suit and King could only guess the price tag of his tan leather brogues. Naturally both Mereweather and Ramsay wore suits, although Simon Mereweather's suit would have cost twice the national average monthly wage. Mereweather was old money and would one day take over the family's Hampshire estate. However, the Mereweathers were not an idle family and Simon's brother was a surgeon, and his sister was a human rights lawyer. His mother wrote children's picture books, and she illustrated them as well. The family's patriarch was Sir Galahad Mereweather who had an illustrious naval career in intelligence before serving in MI5 and later in GCHQ.

"Hell, I'll get the ball rolling," said Newman. "Russian hacking."

"The greatest threat we have today," Ramsay agreed. "The public see Russian troops on the Ukrainian border or their jets straying into UK airspace as unacceptable, but they're sleepwalking towards oblivion. Believing the lies on social media is the thin edge of the wedge, because they are being unwittingly recruited to a way of thinking, an indoc-trination that starts with pictures of grumpy cats and ends with putting a president in office..." He held up a hand. "Sorry, I have strong feelings on the subject."

King stared at him. It was the only time he'd seen a flare of passion in the man's face, a determination in his voice.

He reasoned that it was probably because it was true and Ramsay felt like he was in the lifeboat while the rest of the passengers denied the ship was sinking. Normally Ramsay was such a closed book, but this was the first time that King had been given an insight into what made the man tick. King looked back at Newman and said, "We know about Russian hacking, thanks." He sipped some of his tea. The secretary had got it just right. Well-brewed, a splash of milk and a confidently scooped teaspoon of sugar. Not shy. King made a note to thank her on the way out.

"The world knows," replied Newman. "But the information isn't joined up. I have information that could prove useful."

"Then spill," King told him somewhat tersely.

Newman smiled. "You've been cracking heads too long."

"What?" King glared back at him.

"No offence..."

"Just what people say when they think they're about to cause it," King interrupted him. "If you're going to offend, sunshine, then have the balls to do it without playing a bullshit get out of fucking jail free card first..."

Newman shrugged. "Very well. The intelligence game is like a poker marathon. It isn't just about playing your cards but it's about playing the other players' cards as well."

"No," said King. "That's not what this is. You have something we want, but by the very fact that you're here means we have something you want, too. But we need what you have more. This is a straight up case of you're going to fuck us, but this time you're going to be polite enough to give us a little rub first..."

"King..." Mereweather said firmly. "Please be courteous enough to listen to our CIA friend."

"Friend?"

"Last time I checked; a rogue NSA agent was trying to kill you." Newman paused. "You're welcome, by the way."

"Thought you couldn't comment on that?" King stared hard at the American then his lips cracked into a mirthless grin. "That would have served you guys, too. You de-escalated a problem that would otherwise have left you tarnished."

"Alright, Mr King, if you insist, I'll take it down a level for you."

"No need for that," King replied coldly. "I just like to say it as I see it. It tends to save a lot of time and misunderstanding. Don't feel that you have to take it *down* a level, just be *on* the level."

Newman sipped his coffee unhurriedly, then replaced it to the saucer and leaned back in his chair. "We intercepted something. Well, two things, actually. The first is a Russian directorate to cause havoc within your government."

"British politics," said King. "Doesn't matter what party is in power, they manage quite well to create havoc all on their own."

"Quite." Newman agreed, trying not to smile when he noticed the flare in King's expression. Newman could see that King thought he could criticise, but he wasn't having an American do it in front of him. "Believe me, it's the same stateside," he added tactfully. "But here's the thing. They have been working on this for decades. The project was referred to as the Paradigm Shift."

King tensed. The last time he had heard the word *paradigm* it had been a cover for a CIA black ops operation using mercenaries as security contractors. He had to hand it to the world powers for their originality. Although he knew that the American opposite him had something to do with shutting that down, too.

"We are aware of Russia's intentions," said Ramsay. "But anything you have will be gratefully accepted and assessed. I'll send your findings to GCHQ."

The American shrugged, leaned forwards conspiratorially and said quietly, "I think that under the circumstances, discretion would be of the utmost importance here." He opened the leather folder and took out a file. "You see, we have two pieces of information. One may very well link to the other, but in any case, I think it would be best to continue in the vein of, what is it you Brits say, Mum's the word?" He held a finger to his lips and grinned.

"We *are* the Security Service," Simon Mereweather said sternly. "Mum's the word is what we do."

"Yeah, very cloak and dagger," King commented uninterestedly. "You going to let us look in that file, or what?"

Newman shrugged. "You know you're on a hit list?" he asked, staring at King.

"Same shit, different day."

"You know who the assassin is?"

"No," Ramsay said, glancing at King and looking back at Newman. "We have a name but the man's a ghost." He paused, not mentioning that Sally-Anne and himself may have found a possible connection to their killer. "We would naturally be grateful for any leads that you may have." He turned back to King and said, "Isn't that, right?"

King kept staring at Newman as he answered Ramsay. "That depends on what he wants."

"We want to rebuild bridges," Newman replied. "I think, when all's said and done, that's what all of us want, right?"

"Absolutely," replied Mereweather. "But you must also know that we will always cooperate with America, that is to say, America's intelligence agencies. Obviously, as long as our interests align."

"We're not in any doubt about common interests. It's not like either of us are going to come down on Russia or China's side anytime soon. And certainly not in spite." He paused. "I'm here only because Director Lefkowitz wants to help." He opened the file and slid a pile of papers across the table, where Ramsay picked it up and started to peruse casually.

Ramsay wasn't being disrespectful to the Director General of the Security Service. He was cleared to Top Secret security clearance, but he had the ability to scan read and could finish full transcripts of A4 paper in just a few seconds, and certainly ten-times quicker than the average person, and Mereweather both knew and respected this. Ramsay regularly read documents ahead of Simon Mereweather, especially in meetings such as this. He slid the sheet across to Mereweather. "What is this going to cost us?"

Newman waved a hand in much the same manner a patriarch would at a meal where he was picking up the bill for the entire family. "Nothing," he replied. "Just a courtesy."

King did not hide his annoyance at still being in the dark. "Well, what is it?"

"A name," Ramsay replied. "A transcript mentioning a contract on you, and the name of the assassin."

"Nice for you both to read it first."

"We've heard it's this Reno character, but we need to know more about him," Ramsay said.

"Oh, for fuck's sake!" King snapped and snatched the sheaf of papers out of Simon Mereweather's hand. He caught Newman's expression and could see that the man would never have dreamed of doing the same thing with Director Robert Lefkowitz. That could either tell him something of Lefkowitz's character, or that of Newman's, but he had never seen Simon Mereweather as a pushover, so it said far more about King. "Reno..." *Who the hell was this Reno?* thought King. "You've come along way if this is all you have, pal," said King belligerently. He thought about Sally-Anne Thorpe's revelation about the killings, the man who had drowned the children of the people he had assassinated. *Manuel Renault.* Reno. The pronunciations were identical, especially when imagined with a French accent.

"Just a name," replied Newman. "The IP address changed, the software corrupted our trace, and we lost the rest of the transcript. Discovering snippets of emails and various IP addresses is easier than tracing and identifying the hackers. They use all sorts of rolling addresses and bounce connections off corporate accounts all over the world."

"A name..." King mused. But if Sally-Anne was correct in her assumption that the *modus operandi* was the same, then they now had a solid confirmation of the name, as well as a face. He wasn't about to share that with the American, but he was certainly glad the man had made the journey across the Atlantic. He turned to Ramsay and asked, "What's happening with the bodyguard?"

"He's on his way over to Crescent Park," he replied, referring to the town house they were using in Mayfair.

"Send Sally-Anne a text and confirm the name."

Newman watched Ramsay as he typed out the text. "You have something else on this assassin?"

"A possible phot..."

"What else have you got in there?" King interrupted. Ramsay caught on quickly and kept his eyes down as he typed and sent the text. "You said that there were two things."

Newman hesitated, then took hold of the file and eased most of it out of the leather document folder. "This, gentlemen, is where we have a little quid-pro-quo..."

"Naturally," King commented flatly.

"Before I give you this, I want to make it clear that we're done with it. We want nothing more to do with the situation. However, by giving you this, we will require a favour."

"And what *is* it that you require, exactly?" asked Mereweather.

"There will come a time when we may require you to look the other way."

"That's vague, mate," King said gruffly.

Newman shrugged.

"We couldn't possibly agree to anything without knowing what you have for us, or what it is you want from us," Ramsay said tersely.

Newman nodded. "OK. So, I'll tell you that this document provides a definitive link to the hackers."

"You said that you could only find a name for the assassin, and that you couldn't trace the hackers," King glared at him. "So, what the hell are you playing at?"

Newman held up a hand. "I did say that. However, we know that you have a source that will allow this to be viewed with clarity." He paused, standing up. "Gentlemen, I have another engagement..." He left the transcript on the table and closed the leather holder. "There's a name in there. Use it wisely..."

"That's it?" Mereweather asked. "We haven't agreed to anything."

"But you will," Newman replied. "It's a favour, and you'll repay it. Director Lefkowitz was certain you could all be trusted to keep your word. After all, without being true to our word, what else do we have?" He smiled. "Don't worry, I'll see myself out, if you'd be good enough to call ahead and tell security I'm leaving."

The American did not shake hands or linger. He'd done his boss's bidding and his job was done. Mereweather waited for the door to close behind him, and Ramsay made the call to the outer office and instructed the secretary to see him through security on the ground floor.

King opened the file and read silently. When he looked up, his face was pale. He downed the remainder of his tea and stood up, tossing the file across the table to Ramsay and Mereweather.

"What is it?" Mereweather asked, picking up the sheets of paper.

"Just a name," replied King. "But it's whose bloody name it is that you're not going to like..." He paused, shaking his head. "Ramsay, give Rashid a call and tell them to meet me at City Airport. Then get hold of Flymo and tell him to be fuelled and ready to fly..." He took a small Moleskin notepad out of his pocket that had a half-length of pencil jammed down its spine. He scribbled a few notes down, tore it off and handed it to Mereweather. "That's what I need." He paused. "And be ready to deny all involvement. This is on me." He handed another scribbled sheet to Ramsay, who took it off him in bewilderment, still yet to read Newman's second file. "Tell Flymo that's where we're headed. I'll call you when I know my final travel arrangements."

Mereweather hastily read the file, then looked up. Jesus Chri..." He stopped himself in time. Simon Mereweather was never one for expletives, especially blasphemy. "What on earth are you going to do?"

King was already heading for the door when he turned to him and said, "What needs to be done..."

TWENTY-TWO

Crescent Park, Mayfair

SALLY-ANNE THORPE HAD CONTINUED to search using the photograph of the escaped prisoner Manuel Renault. She did not yet have a positive identification, but Ramsay had text messaged her confirmation of the name Reno and after she had double-checked online on the pronunciation and origin of the name, she had a strong gut-feeling that the two men would indeed be one and the same. Renault. Reno. It sounded identical, especially if pronounced in a French accent. She checked her slim Cartier watch – a present from her former fiancé, and her only true love – and tutted. Steve Moore, the diplomatic protection officer was almost an hour late. Ramsay had informed her that the police officer was coming straight over.

Her phone buzzed, and like a teenager her heart fluttered at the notion. She had childishly given DI Miller - or Nathan as she had entered him into her phone's address book - his own message alert and ringtone. She could see that it was a call and she told herself to get her head in the game because the detective was likely calling regarding his multiple murder case.

She answered the call. "Hi," she said breezily.

"Hey..."

Sally-Anne smiled. She barely knew the man, but she could tell that he was trying a little too hard to be casual. "Something you can't say in a text?" she asked, cursing herself. Her tone wasn't as warm as she'd intended. God, she was out of practice.

"Just to thank you for your help, and as soon as you have it verified, I would really appreciate that name and photograph."

Sally-Anne's heart sank. It was too much to hope that the man was interested in her, too much to hope for a glimmer of pleasure and happiness in her life. She checked her watch again, angry that the diplomatic protection officer was holding her up; angry with herself for thinking this could be more than the professional association it was. "Any minute now," she said sharply.

"Great," he replied.

"Anything else?"

There was an awkward pause, and then Miller said, "Look, I'm forty years old, have an ex-wife who's draining my finances and a son I barely see because I seem to be working twenty-four-seven, and who I'm convinced my ex-wife is poisoning his mind against me, but I know we shared a look. And even though I never had a mobile phone in my teens, we were texting like a couple of teenagers on your journey back to London..." He paused. "Shit, I thought I knew where this was going..."

"I think I do," she replied. "I haven't been in a relationship for well over a year, and well, to be honest, haven't been with anybody since... But yes, I *did* feel something, too."

"What's wrong with us?" he laughed.

"Talk about meeting in the worst possible environment..."

"I know!" Miller paused. "Perhaps that's why coppers should only ever go out with coppers. Or, I guess in your case, ex-coppers."

"Don't remind me..."

"Really? I thought working with the secret service would be exciting."

"Security Service," she corrected him. She thought about her run-ins with Caroline Darby, King not hiding his disdain for bringing an ex-police officer in to keep their operations within the law – for what good it had done – and of the wildly contradicting remit of this team that operated in the shadows, and she missed the clarity of her role as a police officer. *Those were the days*, she thought. "And no, it hasn't been exciting, so much as challenging..." She looked up as the doorbell sounded twice. "Sorry, I have to go. It looks as if that confirmation is a little closer..."

"Great. Dinner one night?"

"In Southampton?"

"Either. I'll nip up. It's only a ninety-minute drive."

The doorbell sounded again. Thorpe cursed under her breath. "Sound's great, got to go, bye-bye." She ended the call feeling a little giddy and flushed. She had not felt the pang of anticipation in too long. She smoothed down her dress as she got off the stool at the breakfast bar and walked to the front door, her heels clipping the parquet flooring and echoing off the cavernous hallway that had stairs both sides leading to a mezzanine with sofas and indoor palms in terracotta pots. The Security Service had many grand properties in its portfolio – not including their more utilitarian safe houses - and she knew that they had been bought many years ago with a view to free up funds for unofficial operations if the need arose. Rising London property prices had returned investments twenty-fold.

She checked the security monitor beside the door. The man staring back at her was six-feet tall, broad with an athletic build and with sandy-coloured short hair. He looked pensive, his eyes sunken in their sockets and so dark that he looked to be wearing eyeliner. She supposed working undercover had already affected the man. She had seen it before. Deep cover police officers usually turned into a bag of nerves.

Sally-Anne opened the door and greeted him hesitantly. "Yes?"

"Steve Moore, he said. I was asked to come here by Neil Ramsay."

"Come in," she said opening the door fully and allowing him to step inside. "Through there..." She pointed. "Left and into the kitchen." He looked around as he walked. The townhouse was impressive by anybody's standards but in Mayfair, doubly so. "Coffee?"

"Please."

"White? Sugar?"

"Black."

She took the pot off its heated base and poured two cups. Moore walked slowly around the kitchen and peered out of the window onto the small garden behind. It had been paved over years ago and was merely a place for people to smoke and talk and drink coffee in the fresh air. Or as fresh as the London air ever got. An established array of plants made it look less like an exercise yard. Sally-Anne looked up at the man as she poured, but the cup overflowed, and she continued to stare. Not at him, but at the large kitchen knife he had taken out of the knife block and which he gripped firmly in his hand.

"I'm sorry," he said.

"Please..."

"Turn around and don't struggle," he said quietly. "It won't hurt that way..."

TWENTY-THREE

Scotland

KING HAD FORGOTTEN QUITE how short the days were in the Scottish Highlands. It was only two-thirty, and the sky only promised another hour and a half of daylight. The rain-laden cloud seemed to hem in his surroundings and offer nothing of promise on the horizon.

He had lived here once. All too briefly. A tiny cottage on a loch with no neighbours for miles. Leaving behind the world of MI6 but soon dragged into the blur that had been his life with MI5. Charles Forrester had seen the writing on the wall and had wanted King to skirt the law, take the fight to their enemies. Forrester had not lived to see King's role fulfilled, nor along with his agent Caroline Darby, what they had achieved. Was the world a better place? King doubted it. But their enemies were certainly fewer in number.

Castle Tay was a private house. Somewhere inside those stark grey stone walls were a hundred rooms. Some were reception rooms; others were bedrooms, and some were prison cells. The world condemned the United States for operating secret prisons and using Guantanamo Bay as a holding area without trial – a true beacon for the practice of withholding human rights, but nobody knew what Britain had done with her enemies. The men and women who had known the secrets of Islamic State, Al Qaeda and any number of terrorist organisations who posed a threat. Many of these people were presumed dead in the barrens of Iraq or Syria or Afghanistan. Some were in the process of being turned, some still held out, but most would never leave this place. King had been here before. There were fewer prisoners then. Simon Mereweather had told him that there were now just twenty-seven inmates. Twenty-seven souls that posed a problem. A question of morality in a civilised country. The intelligence services had wanted to interrogate them, and now nobody knew what to do with them. Despite men like King having killed for their country, nobody was going to come forward to do the deed, and nor was anybody going to ask.

The sign on the front gate said that the property was a private clinic strictly by appointment only and referred to a website and telephone number. A uniformed guard was positioned behind the gate in a guard hut. He was reading a magazine and sipping from a thermos of coffee, but King was in no doubt that the man in the rent-a-cop uniform had training that belied his appearance and somewhere in the hut and close to hand would be a weapon ready to use if he was forced to. King had spotted the cameras in the trees on his drive in, and they would have seen him coming from a mile away. The guard would have been told that the facility was expecting a visitor from Thames House and would have had his car registration – which King had phoned through to Ramsay after collecting the hire car - and King's physical details on their daily manifest. Even so, the guard stepped out of his hut and came out through a locked pedestrian gate to the side of the vehicle access and stopped at the driver's door. The guard wore an NCO's moustache and had the manner to go with it. King figured him for an ex-guardsman. Most likely a sergeant.

"King, with the Security Service..."

The guard perused an extremely short list and checked the vehicle's numberplate against his own records. "And the daily word, Sir?" the guard asked in a broad Welsh accent, which went further towards King's assumption of his former military service.

"Penguin..." King replied, feeling a little foolish. The word changed daily, as too did the degree of embarrassment.

"Very good, Sir," he replied, taking out his mobile phone. "Retina scan now, if you will..."

"You could have done that first..."

"We don't get many visitors out here, Sir. Got to have our fun." He took a picture of King's right eye and an audible text alert confirmed King's identity. The guard nodded. "Through the gate and all the way up the drive. Park in the visitor bay and somebody will be there to meet and greet." The guard turned on his heel and swiped his lanyard fob to open the pedestrian gate. A few seconds after entering the hut the vehicle access gate slid open and King drove steadily through. He glanced to his right and saw a Heckler and Koch UMP .45 carbine with a compact scope attached. The weapon was resting on its buttstock beside the guard's chair. King realised to maintain the charade, the guard couldn't be seen to be armed by the outside world, but the weapon was close at hand should friends of the inmates ever discover the location.

King looked right and left as he drove. There was a perimeter wall of granite topped with wire. It wasn't the most difficult of defences to break, but the wire would be alarmed for sure, if not electrified, and if the facility had cameras installed on the drive in, then they would cover the perimeter for certain. He looked back at the castle, saw a woman standing at the top of the steps. Either side of her, life-sized stags carved from stone and replete with eight-point antlers stood atop polished granite bases. King had seen them before, but they had not looked in such good condition as they did now. One had half its antler missing and the other had lost a front leg when he had last seen them, and he wondered in the age of post-austerity, Covid debt and financial uncertainty, who would have seen fit to get funding to restore two statues standing resplendent outside a government-owned, government-funded secret prison. When King had last visited, a groundsman had told him that the story was US servicemen had shot the stags, along with the weathervane that sat on top of the eastern turret, before leaving for the D-Day landings.

King parked the hired Vauxhall and got out. The air was colder here too. He looked up at the woman as he made his way across the gravelled drive. She was serious looking, her brunette hair pulled back in a tight bun and the skirt of her grey business suit pulled tightly against well-muscled thighs and trim waist, showing off a build King would associate with competitive horse riding. He was no expert, but he had noticed that many horse riders filled their jodh-purs where they touched.

"Mister King, I am Layla Hardcastle," the woman said as he reached the second to last step. "I will be your guide today." King already knew her to be the facility director. He was getting the VIP treatment, despite the facility's flat-out refusal to give MI5 full access to their prisoner at another location. King wasn't surprised, the last time they had the CIA had forgotten to give him back.

King shrugged. "Just a straight in and out. I want to talk to the subject privately, though."

"We have a few procedures in place," she replied. "I gather you've been here before, but things have changed. New procedures and protocols." She paused. "I'm sure you'll understand."

"Sure. Paperwork for paperwork's sake," he said as she led the way through the open doorway. Inside was a glass door and behind that, an armed guard stood easy, but his hand was on his weapon, his finger near the trigger. King noted the marking on the glass and realised it was ballistic resistant. "We have upped our security protocols since your last visit. Primarily for just one prisoner..."

"You must get all sorts in here."

"That's putting it mildly," she agreed. "But not for a long time now."

King nodded. "But you don't know what to do with them all now..."

"It *is* a quandary. No Prime Minister wants to be the one to release them, because then they'll be the one who has to explain that we've kept them here neglecting their human rights while the world changed."

"It hasn't changed."

"No?"

"No."

"But the theatre of operation has. We left Afghanistan. We only have a handful of military advisers in Iraq, no presence on the ground in Syria. Simply put, no more prisoners caught in the thick of the violence that can provide us with valuable intelligence." She swiped them both through the door and beckoned King to walk through the metal detector. King took out his car keys and a small wad of ten-pound notes and put them in the tray. He stepped through with no drama but even so, another guard worked a metal detector wand over him while the man with the rifle watched him intently. "You'll get your things back later," she assured him. She led him past the guard's desk and down a long stone corridor. The guard who had used the metal detector wand placed it down on the desk and followed them. King noted that he wasn't armed. Standard operating procedure in maximum security facilities. It never paid to give prisoners access to your own weapon. "So, after a term of absence, your man is in favour again," she observed flatly.

"What?"

"Your prisoner. He has friends."

"You must be joking," King retorted.

"No. I only wish I was. Your prisoner now accounts for half our budget. Our security became routinely armed as a result, and we have had to quadruple personnel." She paused. "A nice, handy coronary would put us back within a reasonable budget."

"I don't think you'll get that lucky somehow."

She stopped at a solid oak door and nodded. "I don't think we will, either." She opened the door to reveal a pair of polished steel elevator doors. She swiped her fob, then pressed her thumb to the keypad for a reading. The keypad unlocked and the digits, backlit in blue, performed a brief light display, then remained illuminated for her to key-in a code. The doors opened and they stepped into a lift that was rated to five-hundred kilos. King thought that to be about six or seven average people. Or three and half Big Daves. King had to think what he himself weighed in kilos and worked it out as ninety-two. Layla Hardcastle stood next to him. She was five-eight in heels and despite her well-muscled thighs and ample, though shapely backside, she probably weighed no more than sixty kilos. They stood a pace apart and King could smell her perfume. He wasn't one for mental arithmetic, but it had served as a distraction standing so close to an attractive woman. He found himself feeling aroused, a familiar scent that reminded him of Caroline. But as soon as he thought about her, the feeling diminished and he wondered if she was remaining off-grid and taking her personal security seriously. And then he wondered no more, because of course she would.

"He's kept in lower two," she said, stepping closer to King to allow the guard inside the lift.

The doors closed and the three of them stood spaced apart like points on a triangle, with the normal awkward silence that is always so prevalent in lifts.

"No daylight?" King asked, breaking the void.

"Not feeling sorry for him, are you?" she asked mockingly.

"Never," replied King as the lift settled, the doors opened, and they stepped out and walked down the corridor. The walls were the same stone as above ground, only they seemed damp and much colder down here. The steel doors on either side of the corridor looked like they belonged to nuclear reactors. There were four cells but only one was occupied and King only knew this because of the glass window taking up much of the width of the cell.

Vladimir Zukovsky sat in a leather recliner reading an edited magazine. King could see it had been edited because multiple sections had been cut out with scissors and the magazine looked a tattered mess. Beside him a cot bed was fixed directly to the wall. A pedestal sink and toilet took up two corners. Both looked to be made from stainless steel and a stainless-steel sheet affixed to the wall served as a mirror. A single dome light high above in the plastic sheet ceiling was the only light and it did not look as if it could be controlled from the inside.

"Very homely," King said sardonically.

"He had the means to detonate a nuclear device." She paused. "One can never forget that. Apparently, it was only seconds from going off."

"You don't say..." King replied quietly, glancing at the palm of his own hand, scarred and burned from where he had shielded the implosion mechanism from the RDX detonator, the clock reaching zero.

Layla Hardcastle nodded. "The man is a threat to our nation. I don't feel sorry for him because of a lack of view." She paused. "Don't worry, this is one way glass and the same thickness that aquariums use. He can't see us, and he certainly can't break out."

King nodded. "The door looks heavy duty, too."

"It's probably overkill, but given that the Russians want this man back, we're taking no chances."

King nodded. He hadn't been made aware of any Russian intent, and he felt sure that Simon Mereweather would have read him in. King stared at the man behind the glass, his file indelibly etched on King's mind. General Vladimir Zukovsky. Former KGB officer under the Soviet Union. Commander of Helmand Province for three years when the Soviets occupied Afghanistan. Narrowly escaped war crimes in Chechnya because the UN investigating team disappeared after submitting their report, which was later claimed to be forged, yet vehemently denied by the Russian Federation. Stole a nuclear device from Latvia and transported it to Britain to destroy GCHQ along with many military bases within the blast radius. Later captured by MI5 agents (REDACTED). Known associates: Dimitri Zukovsky AKA *Uri Droznedov* (son) Alesha Mikailovitch (partner/lover) both killed by agents (REDACTED) of MI5. Vladimir Zukovsky later interrogated by CIA. (REDACTED). (REDACTED). (REDACTED).

King smiled at the thought of the last entry. Redacted seemed to cover a multitude of sins. King had sprung the man from a CIA and NSA secret prison in South Dakota to get back a UK asset the Americans had so blatantly abducted. Was it worth it? King thought of the tit-for-tat on both sides that had followed. One of their own team members and her family dying in such terrible fashion, the rift that reprisal had caused between himself and Rashid. No. In the grand scheme of things, snatching the man back from the Americans had been nothing more than standing their ground in an ever-changing landscape. He supposed the diplomats had failed and what had transpired next had been because of bruised egos in Downing Street.

"Do you know him?" Layla Hardcastle asked.

King said nothing. Redacted was redacted. The omission covered himself as much as it did the Security Service. This facility was a joint intelligence project and Layla Hardcastle was nothing more than a warden in a tight-fitting skirt and with an expensive taste in perfume. "I need him to talk," said King. "Is he locked up down here twenty-four-seven?"

"Yes."

"No exercise?"

Hardcastle shrugged. "He's in his mid-seventies and never leaving this place. Considering the Russian threat, nobody cares about his fitness levels and whether he gets his ten-thousand steps in each day."

King stared at the man behind the glass. Zukovsky was a

lion. He may be an enemy of the West, but King respected him and knew what it was to be incarcerated. "Why not just cut his rations and be done with it?" he said, then added sarcastically, "You could always forget to check on him for a week or two. That ought to do it. Job done, back within budget..."

"That's not the same."

"Bollocks!" King shook his head. "The man is rotting down here!"

"Take it up with your superiors," she replied curtly. "But there are more forces at work here than *'Box* or *The Firm,* so good luck with that!" She paused. "He's here for political agenda. He's a hot potato and nobody wants to get burned."

King nodded. "Alright, I get it. But I want to talk to him and believe me, what I have to say can't be recorded... either visually or audibly." He paused. "A leisurely stroll around the grounds will open him up to me. Otherwise, I'm going to have to interrogate him thoroughly and at his age..."

"Like you said, problem solved."

"Don't be so sure," King said coldly. "It's on your watch, and despite your budgetary concerns, he's *your* hot potato, too."

"Meaning?"

"Meaning that he still holds valuable information on a whole range of things useful not only to all three civilian intelligence agencies, but to military intelligence and the government alike." King shrugged. "I wouldn't want to be the person who lost such a valuable asset, despite an over-spend on budget."

"I can't allow him up top."

"I thought you were in charge?"

"I am."

"I have been granted access to the prisoner."

"And you have it."

King sighed. "Look, it will go a long way to softening him up. When he sees me, he's not going to want to talk. But if he has the chance for some fresh air and a stroll in the grounds, then it might well make all the difference."

"So, you *do* know him."

King shrugged. "I put him here."

"You snatched him back from the Americans?"

"Yes." He paused. "Well, not just me. It took a few of us."

"My god!"

King stared at them both. "This is all highly confidential."

"Of course," Layla Hardcastle replied, then turned and looked at the guard expectantly. "Right?"

The guard nodded, but he didn't seem fazed. King thought the man couldn't have cared less, and that suited him, too.

Layla Hardcastle's expression softened. "I will have to make some surface security arrangements," she said. "Just a loop of the grounds. That's all I'm willing to allow."

"And a quiet sit."

"Very well." She turned to the guard. "Please allow our visitor entry. Usual security protocols to stand at all times."

"Yes, ma'am." The guard unlocked the door with two separate keys on his bunch. King noted they had a marker on each of them. One red and one yellow. King always studied, always remembered. It was what had kept him alive for so long in the field. The guard pressed the intercom button. "Prisoner will stand!"

King watched as Zukovsky tossed the magazine onto the bed and slowly got to his feet. He wondered how much both age and lack of physical exercise attributed to the slow movement, or whether it was obstinance.

"Prisoner will place his hands behind his back!"

Zukovsky did so.

"Prisoner will back towards the door!"

The Russian complied, yet slowly and with a sneer on his craggy face. King noted how much greyer the man's hair seemed, how emaciated he had become. He had a hard time believing he was working for a democracy, the government of a so-called civilised country. But then again, if that really were the case, then men like King would not exist.

The guard opened a flap in the door. Large enough to slide a tray of food through, or a roll of toilet paper. King realised that the man probably never left the cell. The promise of a walk around the grounds may be all that he needed to get the man talking.

The guard took a pair of handcuffs off his belt and secured them to Zukovsky's wrists. "Prisoner will make his way back cross the room!"

Zukovsky moved stiffly back across his cell, then turned and looked at the door.

"He's all yours," the guard said to King. "I'll be outside. And just to warn you, if you give him the opportunity, he bites and kicks and spits..."

TWENTY-FOUR

Mayfair, London

"YOU DON'T HAVE to do this…"

"But I do."

Thorpe had managed to put the breakfast bar longwise between herself and Moore. She clutched the edge of the counter with both hands and the moment Moore moved either one way of the other, she countered. The bar was three metres long and one and a half metres wide. There was a good deal of solid granite between them, but the standoff wouldn't last long.

"Why?" she asked desperately. "We know who you are!" She shook her head in bemusement. "There's CCTV on the front door and the street. Ramsay knows your identity, your military service. You won't get away with it!"

Moore shook his head. For a moment he even squinted his eyes shut, so much so that the gentle crow's feet around his eyes wrinkled deeply. "I *have* to do it!" He opened his eyes wide and tested Thorpe's reactions feigning an attack.

Thorpe reacted well and the length of the table remained between them. "He has my wife and son..." He darted around the table and Thorpe dodged the other way. When the distance narrowed between them, Moore slashed with the knife and caught her across the shoulder. The house had been furnished expensively and in keeping with the opulent décor, the knife was a Japanese Global and sharpened to a razor's edge. The blade ran deep and with little resistance and she glanced at the flap of skin and blouse that was turning dark red. She hadn't screamed, hadn't felt the blade as it passed through. But she felt it now and she groaned and started to sob.

"Please..."

"I said to turn around and not to resist." He told her, looking at the wound and the stream of blood making its way to the floor. "I saw hostages killed in Iraq," he said quietly. "They didn't suffer, didn't feel a thing. This knife is sharp, it will be over in seconds. You'll just close your eyes and won't know anything else about it..."

"Please..." she sobbed.

Moore feigned another move, but this time he vaulted the width of the bar as she darted and landed just feet away from her. Sally-Anne swiped the coffeepot behind her, and it hit him in the stomach, spilling hot liquid all over his torso that was soaked up quickly by his shirt and suit jacket. He cursed and screamed and slipped on the spilt coffee on the floor, but he regained his balance and lunged with the knife, and it stabbed her in the back before she could get away. Sally-Anne fell forwards and crashed down hard onto her knees. She tried to scramble to her feet, but Moore was on her and caught hold of her hair and pulled her neck backwards, the knife raised high above his head.

TWENTY-FIVE

"How's tricks?"

Zukovsky looked at King, studying his features intently and taking in every detail. King could sense the rage within the man but could also see that he kept it contained. "You..."

"Surprised?"

The Russian stared at him for several seconds before saying, "I have thought about you much this past year and a half." Zukovsky smiled. "Thought how good it would be for you to be in this cell with me. But only so I could kill you..."

"Well, that's gratitude for you." King shrugged. "This *has* to be better than that hell-hole in South Dakota."

Zukovsky sneered. "Solitude is overrated."

"And freedom is underrated until you no longer have it."

"Indeed."

"How are they treating you?" asked King. Zukovsky glanced at the guard hovering in the doorway, and King turned around and said, "Shut the door and fuck off, pal..." He looked back at the Russian expectantly, the door closing behind him.

"You care?" Zukovsky chuckled. "Now *you* can be the one to fuck off."

King nodded. "I get it," he replied. "And yeah, really I do." He shrugged. "I don't like you, and naturally I'm glad I put a halt to your plans. But I suppose people like you and I are flipsides of the same coin. You have your ideals, and I have mine. But at the end of the day, we are both wolves."

"Perhaps you are the sheepdog," said Zukovsky. "I am the wolf, you are the sheepdog – herding the sheep to safety, while barking at the wolf..."

King shrugged. "I can live with that," he replied. "But either way, neither of us are sheep. And if that makes us both predators..." He looked around the room, then back at Zukovsky. "... then neither of us would want to end up locked up somewhere like this."

"Better to die fighting, than to live slowly dying," Zukovsky mused.

"Precisely."

"It is not easy to live with losing."

"I wouldn't know, I've never lost."

"Such bravado! Such bullshit!" Zukovsky chuckled. "You have lost much," he ventured. "Many times, in fact. I can see it in your eyes. Like me, you have lost in love. Loved ones who are no longer here." He paused, staring King in the eyes. He thought how similar they were to his own. Cold, indifferent and almost impossible to read. Except that he recognised the eyes of a killer, and the eyes of somebody who had been taken to the edge. "And then there are the decisions you regret, the things you may not have needed to do."

King smiled. "From the man who would have murdered millions?" King walked across the cell and stood a pace from him. "I sleep well at night," he lied.

"Well, you know what they say?" The Russian paused. "Don't do anything by day that will forever keep sleep at bay."

"Then *you* must not sleep at all," King replied quickly. "Or maybe you're just evil and have no conscience."

"What I did, I did for my country!"

"Bullshit! You continued with the ideals of relics!"

"Not so different to today's Russian leadership," he said. "Perhaps with Ukraine as an example of what direction Russia wants to go in, I will be in favour once more, no?"

"Because of one ageing egomaniac. The rest of your country just wants capitalism. Plain and simple."

"Never!" Zukovsky spat at him. "The Russian President is a Trojan Horse! You are all fools, and particularly your snowflake, fully inclusive younger generation who know nothing of the threat of war or what it is to suffer even minor discomfort, only makes the task easier! All the Russian government wants is the destruction of the West, but it is done with cybercrime and Russian financial interference. Or control of gas and oil. I was simply speeding up the task. I had orders; I was to spearhead a new offensive! And now, perhaps the old ways will be used once more as Russia expands its borders. Who knows, perhaps Poland and Georgia will be next?" He laughed. "I hope so!"

"Nothing really changes. The Cold War never ended, it just got more difficult to read," King shrugged. "So, I'll get to it. You have contacts and I want a name." He paused. "And I'm here to tell you that I'll get the information I want from you by any means necessary. The easy way, or the hard way."

Zukovsky sat down heavily in the chair. "The CIA, the NSA and your own intelligence services took all I have," he said weakly. "There's really nothing left..."

"I don't believe that for a moment."

"They assaulted me. Humiliated me. Body *and* mind. I have you to thank for that."

"You're welcome."

"Whore's bastard, that's what you are," Zukovsky muttered under his breath.

King had heard it before. The truth hurt. Or at least it used to. "I want to ask you some questions," he said.

"Ask all you like. You won't get the answer you are hoping for."

King nodded. He knew the man's hatred for the West, his own hatred for King. Zukovsky's plan had failed, but he had escaped arrest. King had caught up with him in Majorca and from that day onwards he had not only been a prisoner of various intelligence agencies, but he had owed King his life. Snatching him away from a Russian-sanctioned hit, King had later saved him from a CIA and NSA operated secret prison. A place where some prisoners – undesirable and of no further use to the intelligence agencies - had met their end with a bullet to the back of the head and an unmarked grave out on the Great Plains. It must have eaten Zukovsky up inside to know that he lived and breathed because of King, and that the same man who he owed his life to had also killed his only son. "You don't get out much," King stated flatly.

"I can cope."

"Walk with me," said King. "I've cleared it for you to have some fresh air."

"So that a colleague can pick me off from a thousand metres with a sniper rifle?"

King smiled. A job for Rashid, he thought. No, too obvious. "Could be one of your countrymen," King replied lightly. "The word is they want you. I'm guessing from the way two men were about to kill you in Majorca that you are still persona-non-grata."

"My operation was sanctioned." Zukovsky paused. "And with current Russian affairs, I'd bet I have more friends out there than enemies."

"Maybe just some fool who is living in the past," said King. "Or by fools who saw the political tide about to turn. Either way, they tried to kill you. You being locked up here is all that is keeping you safe. And trust me, it won't be long before the Russian President gets a bullet or some poison in his breakfast. It's Russia's last hope before World War Three."

"So, you want me to thank you for holding me here?" the Russian raised an eyebrow, his cold, grey-blue eye surrounded by a dark socket, his eyebrow white and unkempt. King thought the man had aged rapidly during his incarceration. "It will be a cold day in hell before that happens."

"Nothing like that."

Zukovsky laughed heartily. "Then you must want to turn me!" He paused, still chuckling to himself. "Thank you," he said. "That's the first time I have laughed in so long. The last time was when my team killed your former boss, Charles Forrester."

King smiled. "I don't lose my temper, Vladimir. It's a waste of effort to even try. You could talk about my whore of a mother all day, my dead colleagues, my lover. It won't enrage me. If I wanted to kill you, I'd walk right over there and tear out your throat." King paused. "And there's not a damned thing you could do about it."

"Ah, the arrogance of youth." Zukovsky glared. "The feeling of invincibility a fool has because he has been lucky to win all his fights. There is always the chance of outrunning your own luck."

King stared at him. Long and hard. He knew then that Zukovsky wanted out. Not simply from his confines, but of life itself. There was nothing for Zukovsky now. No people on the outside to free him, to help him in any way. An enemy of the West and an enemy of his own state. He was merely a dead man walking.

TWENTY-SIX

Mayfair, London

THE BLADE PLUNGED DOWN, but she pulled out of his grasp, leaving him holding the knife in one hand and a clump of her hair in the other. She felt no pain, driven only by fear and the will to survive. Moore dropped the tuft of hair on the floor and followed her as she staggered out into the hallway and for the front door. He was quicker than her and stabbed again, driving the blade downwards and gashing her shoulder. She fell and rolled onto her back, kicking out and driving her heel into the man's crotch. He dropped the knife and it clattered onto the parquet flooring. Sally-Anne kicked again, this time catching his knee and sending him off balance. He fell to the side, but to her horror he landed right beside the knife, and he reached for it as she got up and dived for it as well. They both got their hands on it at the same time. Thorpe's hand clasping the pitted stainless-steel handle, and Moore's hand clasping her own. Moore had the strength, but Sally-Anne wasn't letting go anytime soon, and remembering her training from when she was a police recruit, she locked her arm out straight and with just one hand on hers and the other hand taking his weight, Moore could not get control of the weapon.

"Let... go... you... bitch..." he growled, sucking breath through his clenched teeth. "I have to do this!"

"Please... whatever is happening, we can help..." Moore adjusted his weight and got up onto his knees. With his weight supported, he punched her in the face with his left hand and when she did not succumb, he punched repeatedly and eventually, she lost her strength and her grip on the knife. Sally-Anne stared up at him, her vision blurred and the fight leaving her body. "No... don't... please don't..." she begged.

Moore plunged the blade into her chest, and she let out a long, slow breath. "I'm sorry," he said, choking back tears. "Really, I am so very sorry..." He stared into her eyes, but looked away, not wanting to see the life leaving them, but heard the lock and saw the front door opening. Still clasping the knife, the blade driven into the hilt he stared at the black man in the doorway. Six-four and eighteen-stone. With a black, military-style jacket and several layers underneath to combat the cold, he filled the doorway almost as effectively as the door.

Big Dave stared for a second, but not much longer. He dropped the shopping bag and rushed forwards. Moore pulled the knife out of Sally-Anne's chest, and she arched her back and groaned, a wave of blood flooding her blouse and turning it crimson. Moore staggered to his feet and challenged Big Dave, but the man never stood a chance. Lomu swiped the knife aside with his left hand and drove a pile driver of a straight punch into the man's sternum with his right, dropping his right knee to transfer his considerable weight, his fist indenting several inches as the bone splintered and cracked. The punch drove all the air out of the man's lungs and his heart had already started to go into cardiac arrest. Big Dave caught hold of the man around the back of his head with his left hand, grabbed the entire package of his crotch with his right and upended him, then smashed him down on his back on the bottom stair to the sickening sound of the man's spine shattering, and Lomu's guttural scream of both victory and anger. And despair.

Lomu turned to Sally-Anne and knelt beside her. He caught hold of her hand, clasping it gently between his big paws. Her skin felt cold, and her wrist was limp.

"He... he... said he didn't have a choice.... Someone has his family..." she managed weakly, but there was blood at her lips, and she struggled to breath. "We need to get someone round to check on them..." The brightness of her eyes seemed to fade in front of Lomu and she simply let out a breath and said, "Oh, Christ..."

Lomu squeezed her hand.

"I'm scared," she said, her voice barely a whisper.

"It's OK," he lied. He stroked her brow tenderly. "It's all going to be OK..."

TWENTY-SEVEN

"You are a fool to think I will talk to you."

"Just enjoy the fresh air, then."

Vladimir Zukovsky looked at the snow-capped peaks. King noticed him take a deep breath and it was clear that the man was indeed enjoying the air, the view and the temperature. To feel the chill on your skin was a welcome relief to recirculated air at a constant 23°c. "Your sniper is up there somewhere, I'd imagine."

King said nothing. Twenty metres behind him two armed guards looked bored and uninterested in their conversation. Even so, King kept his voice barely above a whisper. "I can get you out of here," he said.

"To go and be humiliated by the Americans again? Fuck you."

"The last time I checked, I stole you away from the Americans. My service wants to build relations with the Yanks again, I don't think doing a deal with you would be wise. I don't think even mentioning your name would be the way forward."

Zukovsky scoffed, but there was the sliver of a smile at his lips as he considered this. "You are a crazy bastard." He paused. "It hasn't been so bad here."

"Can't beat British hospitality."

Zukovsky sighed. "When you first caught up with me, that was the worse. Your colleagues from the SIS were, let's say, thorough. Then there were the European agencies, but all the time both your service and the SIS supervised." He paused, studying the ridge of snow in the distance. "And then there were the CIA and NSA. Bastards, all of them. Guantanamo Bay was nothing compared to that secret prison." He turned back to King and said, "I despise you and your agents. You killed my son, and my beautiful Alesha. She was disfigured by that bitch of yours, then died horribly."

"If you want to dance, you've got to pay the band."

"You will pay the band one day, my friend."

"Friend?" King chuckled. "See? We're making progress!"

"No, I despise you. I always will. But I will concede that you had me locked away somewhere better than the Americans."

"I'll look out for the review on Trip Advisor."

"Get on with it," Zukovsky said irritably. "The sooner you tell me what you wish to know, the sooner I can tell you to go fuck yourself again."

King shrugged. "Russian state-funded computer hacking."

"Go fuck yourself."

King laughed and kept walking. He glanced back at the guards. Layla Hardcastle had joined them and was talking conspiratorially with them. King was sure that the guards hadn't heard them talking. "The world has moved on. Dinosaurs like us will soon be extinct. I mean, you're an old, out-dated fuck but even I have to admit that my methods are frowned upon by the very people who are still alive because of them. We have bad PR, you and I. Apparently, it's not the done thing to try to smuggle a nuclear device into a country with hostile intentions. It breaks all kinds of proto-cols. And apparently, waterboarding or stabbing someone in the leg for information and shooting the enemy in the fore-head isn't something the younger generation, the snowflakes or the Woke are prepared to tolerate. It's all tech nowadays. I might have to get an IT diploma before too long." King grinned. "It's all bullshit, of course. Because so long as there are still people like you, there will be people like me to try and stop you."

"Hurts, doesn't it?" Zukovsky said quietly, then look at King intently and said, "It's frightening, too."

King couldn't think what the man meant by him hurt-ing. Zukovsky knew nothing of what was happening in King's life. "What's frightening?"

"The spectre of death." Zukovsky paused, taking in his surroundings. The snow-capped mountains, the ridge of heather and grass with just a few stubborn gorse bushes refusing to bow to the wind. "To be hunted. For a man like you, a man who usually does the hunting, it must feel as though the tables have turned."

"What do you know?"

"Nothing. I have been incarcerated for two years. How can I know anything current? Alright, the magazine editing sometimes isn't as thorough as it should be. I got my hands on an unadulterated copy of *National Geographic* last week, so I'm up to date on Ukraine." He paused. "But you are here to talk about more than hacking and electronic manipulation."

King shrugged. "You are right. Someone is trying to kill me."

"Good."

"They want something I know, or they want to silence me."

"It goes with the territory." Zukovsky smiled mirthlessly, then shrugged. "What do you know?"

King chuckled. "Everything and nothing."

"Secrets and lies."

"It's the same for all of us, I guess. You end up knowing so much that you forget what is important and what is not."

"They are close?"

"They have been. They killed the widow of my mentor. Tortured her." King paused. "And they killed my sister and her family. I haven't seen my sister in years. I changed my identity when I went to work for the SIS."

"How did they die?"

King thought how Zukovsky could use the information. And he was damned if he was going to allow himself to be rubbed up the wrong way by the Russian. "Forget it."

"No, I am interested," he replied with a shrug. "I will not be flippant."

"My sister was brutalised. Her husband was skinned in places, stabbed in others. His penis was removed and stuffed into his mouth. Before he died." King closed his eyes as he thought about the boys. When he opened them again, they were moist and sore-looking. "Both of her sons were bound, then drowned in the bathtub."

"Were there signs of a struggle? With the boys?"

"Thankfully, no."

"Sounds familiar. But not the mutilation."

"We think there were two killers. A double act."

Zukovsky shrugged. "I wouldn't know about that. But we had a man work for us from time to time. We called him *Vodyanoy Chelovek*, or the *Water Man*, on account of his penchant for drowning the children of the people he was sent to kill."

"It sounds like the same man."

"Then you are already as good as dead." Zukovsky paused. "He was caught once. But he escaped, changed his identity and nobody has got close to catching him since. His name is Reno." King felt his neck tingle. An old woman on his estate used to say someone has walked over your grave when that happened. King had never known what the old woman had meant, but it felt apt now. Zukovsky smiled at him. "This killer doesn't want information," he said. "He wants to unsettle you. That's his method. To flush you out like feathered game in front of the shotguns. Why else would he torture and kill a woman and her family? A woman that you cut all ties with before you changed your name. What could she possibly know?" King thought about this. It made sense. He had not seen the wood for the trees. "But your biggest problem is how they found out about your former identity."

"And that's where you come in."

"Me?"

"Absolutely," King shrugged. "I think that a Russian intelligence agency has hacked into the British intelligence services."

"We have done so before."

"You were very quickly detected," he replied.

"Oh, come now. It's nothing you haven't already done to us."

"I wouldn't know," King replied, mindful not to

mention GCHQ's coding hack of Russian intelligence and their hackers.

"You're good," Zukovsky observed, smiling wryly.

King sighed. "My problems aside, there are people in your country who are using financial manipulation, misinformation and conspiracy theories to harm the West."

"Wasn't it always thus?" Zukovsky smirked. "Propaganda was always a tool for both sides of the Iron Curtain, it's only the delivery system that has changed." He shrugged. "Computers and smartphones mean more people see the fruits of our labours, that is all."

King knew that the man had a point. Social media was a constant and ever-evolving delivery system for content and advertising, so why not propaganda? The Russians got to work using it on day one. "The Russian intelligence services want you dead."

"Maybe. The political landscape changed, and I was a loose cannon. I imagine things have changed again. That's how Russian politics works. I'm probably an unsung hero by now."

"No. They want you dead." King paused. "You know too much. You're right, the politics changed but now you know far more than anyone wants you to. You started the hacker program."

Zukovsky nodded, looking at the snow-capped mountains again. "I didn't start the hacking program. That was started the moment the internet was invented. But I did start the social media program." He smiled wryly. "We called it the Paradigm..."

"Shift..." King interrupted. "The Paradigm Shift. Like moving from the Old Testament to the New Testament in the Bible. From being commanded by God, to being shaped by one's surroundings and teachings into the type of person God wants you to be."

"Guided by a higher power, but answerable ultimately to yourself." Zukovsky nodded. "We drip-fed the masses and when the few were successfully targeted, we turned up the flow of disinformation. The unintelligent and ill-informed soon felt the flush of power, the superiority that they knew something their peers did not. Soon, the people become prophets and the word is spread faster than we could ever anticipate. Tell these people something for long enough with links to verify the *facts* and you could very well convince them that the moon is made from cheese."

King had seen the shift not only in the publics' views, but the unwillingness to accept presented fact. There was no smoking gun anymore, always the belief that the facts presented were the least likely answers of all.

"The ultimate get-out." King paused. "Manipulate beliefs and behaviour to create entire movements without any recourse. Even if the majority believed Russia was manipulating the facts, they would soon believe the next lie you put out there." He looked over at Layla Hardcastle, who was trying to act casual with the two guards but failing. She wanted to know what they were talking about. Zukovsky had not been interrogated for some time and if she got to divulge anything new to her superiors, then funding and maintaining her position would not be a problem. He looked back at Zukovsky and said, "You are a stateless person. Your own intelligence services want you dead, and the Americans would like nothing more than to get you back off the grid and have another round of questioning. Electrodes and waterboarding. White noise and beatings." King paused, catching a glimpse of unease in the man's eyes. King admitted he admired the man's toughness. Most people would fold at the prospect, especially if they had experienced it first-hand. "But I can give you an out. The offer is time sensitive, I'm afraid," he said, glancing at his vintage Rolex. "You help me learn more about this Paradigm Shift program and I can give you your freedom."

"You'll learn what you want to know and then you'll give me a bullet. I know how this works."

"I'm a man of my word, Zukovsky. I am offering you a new life." King paused, turning to look at the grassy ridge behind him. He looked back at Zukovsky and then to the snow-capped ridge beyond. His eyes dropped to the two guards and Layla Hardcastle standing in an uneasy triangle some twenty-metres distant. The two guards carried Heckler and Koch UMP carbines. King could see from the straight magazines that they were the more powerful .45 ACP versions. Good for short distances with tremendous stopping power. Sixty-five metres. Eighty tops. But one shot one kill. Its less powerful 9mm variant was good for a hundred metres, perhaps twenty more, but lacked stopping power. Ballistics was a complicated science. King could see that both weapons were on 'safe'. "If you're on the level, you will not be mistreated. When we're done, there's a bungalow with a garden and a small pension for you. Naturally, we'll keep tabs on you, but that also works in your favour should two GRU heavies stop by for a cup of Novichok and a chat about the motherland or brass rubbing in Salisbury Cathedral. We'll afford you an element of protection."

"How time sensitive?" Zukovsky asked, his gaze still on the mountains.

"I'd say roundabout now…"

"Why?" the Russian asked, somewhat perplexed.

King didn't know what to say. He had gone up against

the man and won. Zukovsky had been put through hell with an endless round of interrogations, and yet he was still standing. King did not regret anything. But he did know that he felt something on his albeit limited emotional scale, much the same way as he felt sorrow when he saw a lion in captivity pacing around its enclosure. Strong, powerful and utterly humiliated. King always thought it would be kinder to put a bullet through a lion's brain than to keep it in a cage. "I want what you know," he said. "You have no friends, but plenty of enemies. Do this thing, and there's a liveable, workable future for you."

Zukovsky scoffed. "You would kill me as soon as look at me!"

"Fuck with me and that could happen," King said coldly. "But tell me, what have you got to lose? Nobody is coming to rescue you, and you will rot inside that castle until you die from old age. One day, someone may even grow a pair of balls and shoot you in the head and bury you up on the moors. Take a chance and agree to help me."

The Russian's mind was whirring, his eyes darting between King and the castle and his guards. He sighed deeply. "Very well."

King ran both hands deliberately through his short hair and scratched while he yawned. As signals went, it wasn't much, but it would do. It had been agreed upon with all parties earlier. The reverberation of the helicopter's engine and rotors was instantly audible. The two guards and Layla Hardcastle turned towards the snow-capped mountain ridge and cupped their hands against the pinkish-grey light. When one of the guards turned, King was already upon him, and he snapped his fist into the man's throat. His weapon was attached to the harness around his chest and shoulders by a webbing strap that would allow the weapon to dangle with both hands free. King kept hold of the weapon nonetheless and directed his elbow to the second guard's temple. He hadn't counted on Layla getting in between them to thwart his attack and his blow was merely a glancing one. Unable to free the guard's weapon and still needing control of it, he hammered a backfist into choking guard's jaw and dropped the weapon hoping it was enough. It was, and the guard was unconscious before he hit the ground. Layla was hammering King in the face with both fists, and he caught hold of her by the lapels and cannoned her into the other guard who was fumbling for his weapon. She gasped, the wind driven out of her, and she looked at King with an expression of both fear and disappointment. Still holding onto her, he swept her feet off the ground with his right foot, and she landed heavily on her back. There was too much ground between himself and the guard for a regular, safe attack, so King took a leap with his left foot, pivoted and drove his right foot deep into the man's stomach. Not generally a fan of complex spinning kicks, it worked this time, and the man staggered backwards as he fell, allowing King enough time to crouch and drive a right cross into the man's jaw. The engine and rotors of the helicopter were loud and as King glanced up, the aircraft was already over the grounds and banking hard. King looked down and saw Zukovsky holding the carbine, the strap unclipped and dangling. King glanced up at the grassy ridge and held up his hand.

"My man has a rifle on you! Drop it!" he said without looking at him. "I've never known him to miss…"

Zukovsky hesitated. There was no cover for a hundred metres. He'd been around the block enough to know a suicidal move when he saw it. He dropped the weapon and smiled. "Once a fox…"

The helicopter hovered less than three feet off the ground as King caught hold of Zukovsky and raced him towards it. He snatched open the door and bundled the Russian inside, shoving him into a backwards-facing seat. King climbed in, pausing briefly to look back at Layla Hardcastle. She stood belligerently, her hands on her hips. Her skirt had split at the seam and her blouse was untucked; her jacket torn. At her feet the two guards were moving and attempting to stand. The helicopter lifted quickly and banked, rotating in one of Flymo's trademark bugouts. There were so many directions of G-force, that King could barely work out where they were going and if either guard fired upon them, and then he was unaware of what was happening and which direction they were heading in, because they were soon two-hundred metres clear of the castle grounds and several hundred feet high and climbing rapidly. Well out of range of .45 carbines.

"Welcome aboard Highly Illegal Airlines where safe and level flying is a thing for other carriers and your life expectancy just took a turn for the worse..." The intercom buzzed through their headsets. *"Your pilot today is Leroy Wilkinson, but you can call me Flymo, because nothing hovers lower..."*

King chuckled and the aircraft dropped in height, just clearing the ridge before Flymo settled into a hover just two feet above the heather. Rashid did the 'helicopter run' and King opened the door to let him in. He settled into the spare seat beside Zukovsky and faced King. He carried a bundle of camouflage netting and a large pair of Zeiss binoculars. He was clearly unarmed, and especially with the sniper rifle King had warned Zukovsky about.

King glanced at Zukovsky. "Whoops. I might have exaggerated my man's lethality. It would appear he was just equipped for bird watching."

"Bastard," Zukovsky sneered.

"No argument there," King smiled briefly, then the smile faded, and he stared at him icily. "But that was your last chance, Zukovsky. Try something like that shit with the gun again, however slight, and I'll choke you to death with my bare hands."

TWENTY-EIGHT

Hursley, Hampshire

NATASHA BALANCED THE CLIPBOARD. The pen was clamped to the paper and the pistol was underneath the clipboard in her right hand, her finger close to the trigger and she kept the clipboard at enough of an angle that the woman couldn't see it.

"Sorry, we had Caroline Darby down as living here."

The woman shook her head. "No, not for some time now," she replied helpfully.

Natasha looked out across the fields, then turned back to the woman and said, "You have a lovely place here." She paused. "How many hectares?"

The woman shrugged. "I don't work in hectares, not sure what they equate to," she replied. "Thirty acres, I think."

"A farm?"

The woman shook her head. "No, nothing like that. We

sold off most of the land years ago. Just a few of our own pigs for the freezer, and a few horses." She paused. "Not to eat, you understand! Caroline was a keen rider as a child."

"And you are...?"

"Hilary Darby, Caroline's mother," she smiled helpfully. "I'm sorry, but who are you?"

"Equity Assurance," she replied. "Caroline took out a policy years ago and it has matured. Unfortunately, she did not update us with her new address, and we do not know where to send the money."

Hilary Darby nodded. "But she continued to pay the policy?"

"Of course."

"By standing order?"

Natasha hesitated, unfamiliar with the term. She frowned, a little flustered, but continued to bluff her way through. "Pardon me, I am Polish," she smiled. "Standing order?"

"A monthly payment."

"Yes," Natasha nodded.

Hilary Darby frowned, easing the door until there was only half the gap. "Then, you already have her banking record." She paused. "Wills Morgan?" Natasha glanced at the clipboard and nodded. "Well, I don't think that's correct. Her uncle had to foreclose on his farm and Wills Morgan treated him terribly. He committed suicide. Despite being a local, independent and long-standing bank popular in the agricultural fraternity, the family agreed never to use them again." She paused as an old Land Rover Defender swung off the quiet road and bounced its way down the lane. "Ah, Gerald's back now. He can answer any questions you still have."

Natasha nodded and stood back from the top step. Her hands were moist with perspiration and her mouth was dry. It was so often the way. Even slaughtering an unarmed couple in their late sixties called for the same emotions. Her adrenalin level was soaring, and her heart began to race. Naturally, she would take out the man first. Equality aside, men generally made for the bigger threat or greater adversary. Reno had taught her so, and even if she was confident there was not a man alive that she could not kill, she knew the fundamentals and respected Reno's experience and training.

The Land Rover swung in, its tyres crunching on the loose gravel, and parked twenty metres from Natasha's hired Hyundai SUV. The man who she knew to be Caroline Darby's father got out and walked around to the back of the vehicle. He was dressed in olive trousers, a country checked shirt and a waxed Gillet. He emerged from behind the Land Rover carrying several braces of pheasant hanging from a noose of bailer twine and a double-barrelled shotgun broken over his arm. Natasha stared at the gun and dropped the clipboard. The pistol was a small semi-automatic with a bulbous suppressor fixed on the muzzle. Hillary screamed a warning and slammed the heavy oak door shut. Gerald saw the pistol and somewhat bizarrely, threw the bundle of feathered game at her. The dead birds arced through the air, all feathers and wings and long tails and Natasha dodged the bundle, but by the time she found her footing and aimed the pistol, Gerald Darby had darted behind the Land Rover and when he emerged from the front of the vehicle, he had loaded both barrels and let them go at her. Two deafening booms echoed off the façade of the farmhouse and heavy no. 5 shot peppered his own front door and the side of his house. He ducked back down, used his thumb on the lever to brake both barrels open, and both empty shells ejected over his shoulder and clattered on the gravel. He delved into his game pocket and fished out two more cartridges, slotted them both home in the breech and closed the barrels, flicking the safety forward with the natural affinity gained from a lifetime controlling pests and joining the local pheasant shoot seven or eight times a season. He peered out from behind the front of the Land Rover and three bullets peppered the bodywork. Two punched through, but one hit the welded and riveted seam and ricocheted off with a whine into the sky. Gerald Darby, former captain in the Parachute Regiment and a veteran of the Falklands Conflict didn't duck down. Instead, he moved forwards firing at first one shot to harass his enemy, and the second to find the target at his convenience. Natasha yelped as shot peppered her arm, but Darby knew the strengths and weaknesses of a shotgun and he reloaded on the march, his weapon becoming more effective with every pace the distance short-ened. He fired another shot at the running figure and as she fell, he marched onwards, reloading the used barrel and snapping the weapon closed.

"Let's be having you!" he screamed as a Sergeant Major would on the parade ground. He fired again, this time peppering the windscreen of her vehicle as she clambered hastily inside.

The SUV raced forwards, and Gerald fired again. Natasha returned fire and there was a melee of gunfire, the quiet suppressed shots making more noise as they struck the wall and planters behind him than the actual discharge. As the vehicle passed within twenty-feet, Natasha fired for all she was worth, and Gerald let her have the second barrel. There was another gunshot as Hillary Darby staggered in the doorway with her grandfather's old .416 Rigby African game rifle in her hands, the barrel smoking from the tremendous discharge. The rear window of the SUV shattered, and steam or smoke worked out from under the bonnet and the vehicle slowed and entered the road without turning and stopped on the far verge. Gerald took a few paces, then wobbled and fell heavily to the ground.

TWENTY-NINE

Hemel Hampstead

"WE NEED SOME BACKUP."

"There is no backup." King took the silenced Ruger out from his jacket pocket and made it ready. "Not until we know what's going on. Plod will only get in the way." He thought how he'd seen Sally-Anne only as a police obstruction. He knew, of course, that she had been an asset to the team, but his stubbornness had got in the way, as it so often did. And now he would never get the chance to show her that he valued her as a member of the team. "The man said his family were at risk."

"And if they're in there with a gun to their heads, then we need a tactical firearms unit," Rashid replied, referring to SCO-19, the Metropolitan Police Service's team of specially trained firearms officers. "And we need to get eyes-on first."

King opened the glovebox of the car and took out his Sig

Sauer P226 9mm pistol and handed it to him. "Front or back?"

"Oh, for fuck's sake…"

King opened the door of the Audi. "And we're just wasting time sat here…"

Rashid got out and looked at him over the roof. The streetlights were distanced every two or three houses, and King's face was barely visible in the gloom. "And you still owe me for the car," he said gruffly.

"It's got a rattle…"

"That's because you ripped all the satnav out."

"Relax, I'm good for it." King paused, looking at the house. Situated in a quiet tree-lined road on the edge of town, the four-bedroomed property sat in a quarter acre of gardens. "This isn't a copper's pad," he said quietly.

Rashid shrugged. "Inheritance perhaps? And some people just bought at the right time."

"You still living above that corner shop?"

"Fuck off…"

King smiled. "Open the boot, there's a little something in there for you."

Rashid walked around the vehicle and opened the boot. He stared inside for a moment, then closed it again. "Seriously? For a stop and look?"

"Oh, you know when trouble is coming, do you?"

"Yes, I do. And it's usually every time I work with you…"

"I get you a belated Christmas present like that, and this is how you treat me?" King closed the door as quietly as he could and started to cross the street. "I even got you some grenades for it. Like stocking fillers…"

"Oh, we're actually doing this are we?" Rashid shook his head as he quickly checked the pistol and tucked it into his pocket. He followed King across the road and said, "Front. I'll take the front."

"Great."

"And we want this bastard alive if he's still here." Rashid shrugged. "Just saying. Don't tap him in the forehead as soon as you see him."

"He isn't going to be here," King replied. "He's too cunning for that. And watch for booby traps or IEDs. The man's a sadistic bastard."

King took a deep breath as made his way down the side of the building. This time, not merely to steady his nerves, but because the banter between Rashid and himself had merely been a coping mechanism for the tragedy of Sally-Anne's death. He was feeling it. And he knew it was because he had never really given her a chance, and the guilt he now carried was both heavy and constant. King had been around death his entire adult life, and each time it touched someone he was close to – whether a loved one, a friend or a colleague – the emotion was different, as if death did not allow the survivors to build a resistance or stoicism to the loss.

As with Leanne's house, there were no lights on inside. Again, not even the oven clock. He took out his red-filtered pen torch and a set of picklocks, clasped the torch between his teeth and set to work with the two picks. He had the lock open within a minute, replaced the picks in the leather case and shone the torch beam through the glass and around the doorframe. He tested the handle. It moved smoothly and without any noise or resistance. King eased it inwards and looked around the kitchen. He saw a red beam ahead of him. Bugger. Should have come up with a codeword. He raised the pistol and said, "Rashid..."

"Who else? This guy is long gone. Have you seen the trip box?"

In King's experience they were generally situated at the front of the property to allow for meter readings. Smart meters did the work now, but this house was old enough to pre-date them. He shone the torch around the kitchen, found the circuit breaker directly above the back door. He shone the torch around it, then tentatively lifted the trip switch flap. He knew that the man had cut the power at Leanne's house, but he also may seize the opportunity to use that MO as a trap. King retrieved a rubber-handled multi-head screwdriver from his picklock case and used it to carefully flick up the power switch. The lights flickered on, and various wireless devices searched for a connection with a series of beeps and clicks.

"Well, nothing went boom," Rashid commented.

"He's playing with us," King replied. He picked his pistol up off the counter and nodded to Rashid. "Get behind me, this is my shout."

Rashid shrugged. Nobody ever wanted point. He held his pistol ready, finger just off the trigger. "I've got your back."

King led the way into the hall and up the stairs. Rashid would not have bypassed the lounge for the kitchen, so he knew he was clear to continue. At the top of the stairs, he heard the dripping tap in the bathroom. The rest of the house was ominously silent. "Check the bedroom first," he said. "Whatever's in there can wait."

The two men checked the bedrooms, but there was nothing and nobody to be found. The beds were made and the two of the spare bedrooms had the smell of rooms infrequently used. The other spare bedroom had been turned into a playroom. King already know that Steve Moore and his wife Charlotte had an eleven-year-old boy, and the toys and football memorabilia reminded King of his own nephews' room. The feeling of loss and grief welled within him, and he took a deep calming breath to quell the emotion. He had never met the two boys, never even knew they existed until he had seen their bodies. And yet there was the sense of loss as though he had known them all their lives.

"I'll check the bathroom," said Rashid.

"No, it's OK. Like I said, this is on me. My shout." King walked past him and pushed open the bathroom door. He hesitated a moment, scanned the room, then stepped back onto the landing and closed the door a touch. He nodded and said, "The bastard has done it again. The wife and son."

"Ramsay wants some photographs so that he can pick up where Sally-Anne left off," Rashid said, taking out his phone. He eased past King and stepped into the bathroom. There was the sound of several photographs being captured, and for good measure, a couple of bright flashes in case the exposure or lighting wasn't right. Rashid stepped back out. "I want that bastard more than ever now."

King nodded. "Get in line."

THIRTY

The house was a four-storey townhouse in Holland Park. Simon Mereweather sat in the kitchen at the head of a large glass table with ornate wrought iron legs and seating for twelve, sipping herbal tea. His personal bodyguard-come-driver was in the lounge with a cup of tea and a plate of biscuits. His name was Abbott, and men like Abbott who had served in the army for ten years before training in close protection always ate and rested at every opportunity. Neil Ramsay sat at the table with Thorpe's laptop and his own, both open and syncing. Big Dave sat at the far end of the table beside Vladimir Zukovsky. Behind him, Zukovsky was flanked by two security officers in cheap suits and worn shoes. They were 'strongarms', used for interrogations and transporting defectors, foreign agents or terrorists. One of the men had once infiltrated white supremacists and fought against the police to retain his cover. Both men were in their late twenties, well-built and physically fit. Young enough to not ask many questions, old enough to know not to.

"They're here," said Ramsay, looking at a pop-up display in the bottom right corner of his screen.

"I'll see them in," said Mereweather, heading for the front door. His bodyguard intercepted him and stood in front of him still chewing a biscuit. Mereweather allowed him to do his duty and the man checked the security display above the keypad and intercom. He opened the door and stood aside for King and Rashid to enter. "Ramsay's called the police and they're on their way over to Hemel Hampstead. Clearly, Moore was acting to save his family, the poor bastard..."

"With respect, Simon. I'm short on sympathy for that bastard," Rashid replied.

"He's got a point. We lost one of our own," said King.

"You didn't exactly get on with her," Mereweather retorted.

"That's for me to square away." King glared at him, his eyes cold and grey and predatory. "But this bastard Reno will pay."

"I trust we can keep things professional," Mereweather replied, but King had already pushed past him and was heading for the kitchen.

It had taken just two and a half hours to return from Scotland to London by helicopter. They had refuelled at Edinburgh Airport where King had hired his car, before Rashid and Flymo had flown on to Castle Tay. Flymo had dropped Rashid two miles short of Castle Tay, where he had made his way across the moorland and lain up on the ridge overlooking the estate. He had watched King arrive and from then on, it was down to timings and signals. Given that Zukovsky was wanted by the Russians, and the CIA still had use for him, Rashid would have felt better viewing the grounds through the sight of a powerful sniper rifle, but King had been adamant that they should not be armed. The castle was run by joint intelligence and security, and everyone should be classed as 'friendly', even though they were all going to get royally shafted. *If you carry a gun, you'll end up using it,* King had said. And he had reflected on the journey back to London, just how different the result would have been had Rashid been armed with a rifle when Zukovsky had grabbed the guard's weapon and held it on King.

The Augusta 109s helicopter had just over sixty miles of fuel time left upon landing at City Airport in the heart of London near Canary Wharf. Mereweather had a car waiting for them, but they had not expected the change of venue, or the terrible news. Big Dave had told them what had happened, and they had barely time to process it as both King and Rashid had headed out to check on Moore's family.

King looked at the coffee pot. Normally a tea drinker, he needed a serious hit of caffeine. He had not eaten since breakfast and was running on empty. He poured a cupful and spooned in four sugars. Rashid nodded at him, and he poured the man a cup and slid the sugar bowl and spoon across the breakfast bar to him.

"We need some answers," said King.

"We're not waterboarding and torturing this man," said Mereweather, looking at the Russian. "There's nothing that can't be found out with money and security that can be found out through force. Personally, I deplore all methods of torture."

"Agreed," replied King.

"Really?"

"The man's a fucking lion," he replied quietly, out of Zukovsky's earshot. "He's been in a cage for too long, he won't want to go back there and he's tough enough to give us sod all under interrogation. He's given us enough to stay alive, that's all." King looked at Zukovsky and said loudly. "I want you to tell Ramsay here everything you know about the Paradigm Shift program, or *directorate* as you lot would say." He paused. "And everything about this man called Reno. You admitted that the Russians have used him from time to time and did so during your service with the FSB. The man is being used by a brotherhood of the Bratva, or what we call the Russian mafia. I want to know about this man."

"So, you can kill him?"

"Yes."

"Forget it, he's too good for you."

King ignored the jibe. Someone was always tougher. King just hadn't met him yet. Or perhaps Reno hadn't.

"It will have to wait for a moment. There's been another development," Mereweather said, ushering King with him as he walked out of the kitchen. The two men stood in the hallway, Mereweather noting just how tired and drawn King looked. "An attempt was made on the lives of Caroline's parents..."

"Oh, shit..."

Mereweather held up a hand. "They are fine. Well, not fine, Mr Darby was shot in the hip, but otherwise he's in good health." He paused. "Mrs Darby was approached at their home by a woman. Mr Darby arrived home from his fortnightly pheasant shoot and invariably changed the outcome. He returned fire and from what the police are reporting, there was a lively exchange of gunfire in which Mr Darby was hit. But get this, as the woman was driving away, Mrs Darby fired with what the police termed *an elephant rifle*, and it went through the rear window, the front passenger seat, the dashboard and out through the front grille, taking the entire engine block out. The car conked out and the woman escaped, but there was blood in the vehicle and on the front garden of the house, so she was definitely wounded in the exchange."

"I wonder where Caroline gets it from?" King smiled, but it was more from adrenalin and shock.

"Mrs Darby said that the woman told her that she was from Poland, but they have employed Polish labourers before they sold off a large piece of farmland for their retirement. She knew that the woman's accent was off. But as both Sally-Anne and DI Miller suggested of your sister's crime scene... sorry to be so pragmatic... it is likely we are dealing with two killers." He paused. "It's a lot to take in, I know, but this can't be seen as a coincidence. There *are* two killers, and one of them just tried to get to Caroline's parents to get to you, or more worryingly, get to her. And I don't mean any disrespect by that, it's just that you are here with a team around you and Caroline is Lord only knows where, and on her own."

King nodded. "I'll take care of it."

"Meaning?"

"I'll give Caroline the heads up. But I'm not having anything committed to any record. This hacking program, the Paradigm Shift are all over us. Somehow, they found out where Caroline and I live. They found out about my old mentor Peter Stewart, and they tortured and killed his wife. They found out about my real identity, and they traced my sister. I can only assume that adoption, and name changes have kept my other siblings safe. For now." King paused. "And it's all been part of a plan to get to me. To force my hand and bring me out into the open. This killer, backed by the best hackers in the world and a filthy government with intelligence services operating in partnership with organised crime, is playing with me."

"So, what's the play?"

"Zukovsky knows about the hacking program. He helped set it up. Look, it's old intel, but Russia has always been slow to adapt its infrastructure. They are a belligerent nation. They have the best hackers in the world, but I'd bet they never changed where they operated from, or where their servers were located."

"You'd bet this on a seventy-year-old fanatic who tried to detonate a nuclear device just a hundred miles from here?" Mereweather shook his head. "You're as crazy as he is!"

"He is convinced that the hacking program will still be operated from a former weather station in the Republic of Karelia that Russians used all through the Cold War."

"You'll never get in," Mereweather replied tersely.

King shrugged. "Getting in will certainly be easier than getting out," he said. "But I can make it happen."

"If you go into a Russian facility, they'll swamp the area with soldiers. That's a remote and wild area. We'll never know what happened to you."

"Thanks for the vote of confidence."

Mereweather stared at him. "You need rest. When did you last sleep?"

King didn't answer because he really wasn't sure. He was starving, too. "I need to shut down this hacking program. The Russians are controlling the man likely to take over as Prime Minister, and in any event, he is in one of the three top jobs in government with access to highly classified information and attends every cabinet and COBRA meeting."

"We'll take care of that," Mereweather said calmly. "We're already deciding how best to play him. He can only feed back the information that he is given. I've spoken with my opposite number in MI6 and we're of the same thinking. He has now become a disinformation asset. The Russians will only know what we want them to know."

King shook his head. "You can't be sure of that unless he is brought into line and read the riot act. He needs to know that you will be listening to every conversation he has, read every email he sends and be his constant shadow."

Mereweather nodded. "Rest assured; life will soon become very uncomfortable for Campbell. But if we close down their operation, they may suspect something isn't quite right in Campbell's reports."

"They'll certainly suspect something if there are any changes, so we need to control the narrative and let the odd gem of information through as a sacrifice," King replied. "But he's their asset and they will be reluctant to give up on their investment. Sure, they'll test him, and we need to be ready for that. But the Paradigm Shift program needs ending. Every second of every day, hackers are using algorithms to spin and re-spin society's thinking. Their conspiracy theories are put in front of people who think they have worked it all out for themselves. The people who pride themselves on calling other people 'sheeple' because they go along with the wider debate, the party line. The people who do their research on social media instead of a medical textbook or an encyclopaedia." King paused. "Russian hackers have mocked up entire newspapers online to get their disinformation in front of people who have commented on previous posts from The Sun, The Daily Mail or The Mirror. Nobody is checking the URL. This needs to stop."

"We'll only pause it for a while."

"Long enough for you and your opposite number to get Campbell in order and sniff out anyone else in government or opposition who have links to Russian intelligence or the Bratva." King paused. "Russia will have hackers all over, but the ones behind the Paradigm Shift operation will have specific tasks and for security reasons, they will be in a dedicated facility capable of enough storage for their mainframe and with enough equipment to cool the servers and circuitry. Hell, they probably only have to open the bloody doors for six months of the year to keep that lot cool."

"No, you're right. This program can't be allowed to exist." Mereweather paused. "When they re-emerge, we'll be ready."

"With their servers and information wiped, we'll knock them back ten years."

"But there is still the problem of the killer."

"Who is being fed God knows what information from leaks in our seals. Regardless of what transpires in Russia and running Campbell as a double agent, both services need a security circuit breaker – so we can go forward with a clean sheet. We need to root out the security breach, be it electronic tampering from Russian coding, or a physical traitor in our camp. But there isn't any point doing that until the Russian hackers lose their connection and hold on our database and a member of our government."

Mereweather nodded. "Are you going to tell me where Caroline is?" He paused. "She needs protection."

"No." King shook his head.

"You don't trust me?"

"I don't trust your position."

"Meaning?"

"I'll send Big Dave to bring her back. I'll tell him where she is. No electronic communication and no way for him to get intercepted." King paused. "But he will remain deniable, as will anything he has to do to bring her back safely. If you know nothing about it, then you won't have to lie about it later."

Mereweather regarded him for a moment, then said, "Alright, I understand. But you're sure you don't want to go yourself?"

"This Russian thing needs to be done first. I trust Big Dave with my life, and he's worked with Caroline before..." he trailed off, knowing that the last time the two had worked together Caroline assassinated an Italian mafia leader right under the team's nose and Big Dave bailed out and spent six months lying low in Berlin. The matter had caused great consternation and Caroline had effectively quit MI5 with the small matter of a million euros going missing. MI5 had no claim over the money and neither did the family of the mafia don. After the way she had been treated, Caroline had considered the found money as compensation and a chance for the couple to leave MI5 and start a new life. King suspected they would never get a clean break and the past thirty-six hours had proven that.

"OK, what's the plan?" asked Mereweather.

"Well, I'll need Rashid and Zukovsky," he replied.

"You're taking Zukovsky?" he asked incredulously. "The man can't be trusted."

"And he has no friends left in Russia. They tried to assassinate him in Majorca before I snatched him back. He won't try to escape; he is my insurance. He knows he's owed no favours by the current government or intelligence services. His last act almost sparked a leadership coup and could have started another world war."

"But he's right on point with Russia's current foreign policies. You may well find that Zukovsky has more friends than ever. The Russian President would certainly use a man like him, now that he has shown his commitment to expanding Russia's borders."

"I didn't paint that picture for him."

"What have you promised him?"

King shrugged. "A bungalow or cottage someplace. Tabs kept on him, naturally. And some money to live frugally."

"Out of the question!" Mereweather snapped. "You had no authority to do that! Lord knows we're in enough trouble seizing him and I'm hiding behind the latest terrorism act and a lot of previous favours to a lot of influential people to stop this escalating further."

King said nothing. He walked to the hall table and scribbled down an address, then walked to the kitchen and got Big Dave's attention. The big man had been on his mobile phone, reading something and frowning.

"What's up?" he asked casually, crossing the room in just a few lengthy strides.

"Caroline is in danger..."

"I figured as much. Ramsay said her parents were attacked but are OK."

"Are *you* OK?" King asked. "You seem pre-occupied."

"Family shit," the man shrugged.

"Back in Fiji?"

He shrugged again. "I'll handle it, 'bro."

"If you need help..."

"I think you have your hands full."

"Can you bring Caroline back for me?"

"Sure." Big Dave shrugged. "I'll do it for you, for her, for all of us."

King handed him the torn sheet of paper. "Eyes only. And there's a little something in the boot of my car for you."

"Hey, I thought that was *my* belated Christmas

present!" Rashid shouted, a steaming cup of coffee in one hand and a hastily folded cheese sandwich in the other.

"You're getting socks now..." King grinned. "Anyway, I've got you something far more exciting. Think of it as a *gift experience...*"

"Oh shit, that sounds ominous..." Rashid went back to his sandwich.

Big Dave looked at the piece of paper, then stuffed it into his pocket. "I'll get my shit together and get going now. Give us your keys and I'll get my *present*." He glanced at Rashid and smirked. "Enjoy your socks, dickhead!"

Mereweather looked uncomfortable amid the banter, but he also knew it was how people like these – men of action – dealt with death. They saw it, lived it, and all of them would be thinking of Sally-Anne and every one of them wanting vengeance for one of their own. He looked at King and said, "What are you going to do?"

"I'll write you a list and you need to have completed it in the time it takes for Flymo to fly us to Hereford," said King. "But first, I need to speak with the RAF top brass and GCHQ. I take it *Boris the Bear* still makes regular jaunts over UK airspace?"

"Belligerently, yes. And with a no-fly ban on Russian commercial airlines, a provocative and insane action, almost daring us to shoot it down and start World War Three."

King nodded. "It's what they want." He paused. "But let's give them something they would never suspect..."

THIRTY-ONE

22 Special Air Service Regiment
   Stirling Lines
   Creden Hill, Herefordshire

THEY HAD ARRIVED SHORTLY after midnight and been barracked in one of many new T-shaped buildings with decent amenities. King hadn't expected a room to himself, and all four rooms were in a row with views over a newly developed housing estate. King had asked for a guard to be stationed outside Zukovsky's room and the adjutant had reluctantly agreed, posting a member of the military police -who usually secured the perimeter of the barracks - in the corridor.

King had showered, grateful for the five hours' sleep he had been afforded. He was dressed and could see figures moving below him in the darkness. Soldiers personally maintaining their levels of fitness before the day's tasks. King made his way out into the corridor and knocked on both Rashid's and Flymo's doors. He dismissed the guard and opened Zukovsky's door.

"We wanted to get an agent inside here for years," he said, staring out at the lights of the housing estate. "This place thrives on the mythology of the unit. And in reality, it's just twenty or so buildings with neatly trimmed grass and well-maintained paths and residential housing just metres from the double fence." He shrugged. "Only the British would keep their most elite fighting force in the heart of suburbia and just a short walk from a supermarket."

"I think it's Asda."

"We got someone into the original Stirling Lines in Hereford. Back before ninety-nine when the SAS moved here."

"I don't think we were bothered about your lot. We already knew our guys were the best," King shrugged. "Unless he was going to set an explosive device, he wouldn't have gone away with much more than you already know. It's the men that count."

"You don't think we have tough men?"

"Tougher, possibly. But it's conditioning. Mental and physical."

"You have been up against our Spetsnaz?" Zukovsky laughed. "You will see tough..."

"Like your son?" King shrugged, watching the pain in the man's otherwise unreadable eyes. "I've killed many men purported to be Spetsnaz." He paused. "And I've seen the toughest SAS troopers imaginable fall to a few men wearing robes and carrying fifty-year-old rifles." He checked his watch and looked up as Rashid craned his head around the doorjamb.

"Breakfast?"

"Yeah. Is Flymo up?"

"He's at the end of the corridor. He's famished."

They headed downstairs and across the road to the canteen. The aroma of sausages and bacon and eggs was heavy on the air, as well as tea and coffee. A few men were heading in and out, but it was still early, even by SAS standards for breakfast. Most men tended to run around the track and grounds and head to the canteen after a shower.

King heaped some scrambled eggs onto some wholemeal toast. They had been greeted with sandwiches and soft-drinks last night and having been famished from not eating anything since breakfast, he had cleared most of the tray. He was only eating now because of the old soldiers' adage. You ate and rested at every opportunity. Flymo, who had worked with the SAS on several attachments to its elite 658 Squadron of helicopter support pilots, was at home in the canteen and had chatted with the chef overseeing the serving trays on the hotplate. He had got the man to make him a bacon and egg sandwich and returned to the table in good spirits.

"I can't believe I'm here and Colonel Fuckhead is still head shed," Rashid said, sitting down with a bowl of porridge. "He's going to know it's me."

Flymo frowned and King grinned. "Rashid escorted the Colonel's eighteen-year-old daughter to a ball. Gave her the contents of two of his own, by all accounts."

"You make it sound worse than it was, I was twenty-seven at the time. It *was* age appropriate," Rashid said somewhat defensively.

"The Colonel didn't see it quite like that."

Rashid shrugged. "I don't play the racist card," he said. "But that fucker was racist. Didn't want his little debutante sullied by a Paki..."

"No man wants his daughter sullied, regardless of race,"

Zukovsky shrugged. He ate slowly from his bowl of yogurt and fruit and granola.

Rashid shook his head. "I can't believe we're doing this," he said, pointing his spoon at the Russian, then looking back at King. "We're sat here like friends, with this son of bitch eating and joining the conversation."

King shrugged. "Alliances come and go in this game," he said uninterestedly. "For the time being, this man has information we need. I don't trust him enough to take his word for it, so he's coming with us. If it's bullshit, then he'll die there. And if it's a trap, he'll get caught up in it, too. He's only part of our exfiltration plan if he delivers the goods."

"I will deliver," Zukovsky said, looking at a picture of sheep between the canteen and the bar, which was shuttered closed. "What does this mean?" he asked, frowning at the picture and the writing underneath.

King had been here many times over the years, but he had never been a true a part of it, and never a soldier. He looked at Rashid, the youngest non-white British captain in the history of the SAS, and said, "Are you going to tell him?"

Rashid shrugged. "Lead, follow or get the hell out of the way," he said quietly. "Unlike the Soviet and Russian special forces, the SAS often use a Chinese parliament system. We usually deploy in eight-man teams with a team commander. Usually a senior sergeant, sometimes an officer, although the officer will generally be responsible for multiple teams and overall command of the operation. You guys are strict on the chain of command. Your soldiers are grunts that take orders. That picture is a reminder that even if you are in charge, you should be a big enough person to step back and let the people with the ideas get on with it. You lead or you step back and assist, or you just get the hell out of the way. You don't waste time procrastinating over the situation and you don't bitch about still being in charge when others have better ideas."

Zukovsky considered this for a moment, then said, "Surely this will bring chaos?"

"It's not every decision. It's just when things have gone wrong, or in the heat of battle. And it's not mutiny. It's just getting on with what's decided and making it work." Rashid paused. "That picture is a reminder to leave your ego behind."

The Russian nodded, but he did not seem convinced.

"You boys have a leisurely one, don't worry that we've all lost a fucking lie-in today..." A short and slightly built man with a *bandit* moustache and full of nervous energy walked over like a fighting cock and stood in front of them, hands on hips and staring at each man in turn. "I'm Sergeant Rawlings, but you can call me Stan. Eat up and meet me outside in five. The Colonel wants a word before we get started. We've only got helicopter pads and a short runway for rolling take-offs, so we're going to RAF Brize Norton to run through the op." He turned on his heel but stopped and glanced back at King. "You're fucking crazy, by the way."

King watched the man strut back across the mess hall and barge out through the doors. Two men stood aside for him, and King sensed he was clearly feared or respected by most people he encountered. He looked at Rashid and said, "Well, looks like you're going to get reacquainted with the Colonel." He paused. "Ever met him before?"

King shook his head. "I was sent here for assessment and training when I was with the *Firm*. People like me were kept away from anyone who mattered."

"Well, he's got Russian heritage, strangely enough. The

family name is Oskopy, related to the last Tsar by all accounts."

Zukovsky frowned but remained silent. He scraped his bowl clean and finished his orange juice. As the rest of the men stood, he checked his pocket and King could see that the man had stuffed a bread roll and a sachet of butter and jam away for later. He wondered how well the man had been treated at Castle Tay, locked away in his ten-by-ten-foot box and fed through a slot in the door.

Outside it was pitch black and dawn was still another two hours away. There were three open-topped Land Rover Defenders with men and kit piled high. Stan waited beside the lead vehicle talking to a man who could not be mistaken for anybody else than the Colonel, or head shed as people referred to him. He looked up as the four of them approached.

"Which one of you is King?" he asked gruffly.

"I am," King replied. "Good to meet you Colonel Oskopy."

Rashid did his best to stifle a laugh but failed miserably. Beside the Colonel, Stan bit his lip and walked away. The two men in the front of the lead Land Rover looked as if they were going to explode with laughter, physically biting cheeks and fingers to avoid breaking the silence.

The Colonel let out a noise, something like a 'humph', then looked at Rashid and said, "You…" He paused, looking between him and King. "A couple of fucking jokers who are going to get my boys killed."

King shook his head. "I didn't mean to offend you with the colonoscopy thing. Everyone likes a joke, eh? But your lads signed up for this kind of shit, so don't try putting a fucking guilt trip on me and my team. They get the pay packet, and they take the risks. We all do. Right now, this is the job they're needed on, but rest assured, we're all in this together and if it kicks off, we all face the same risks."

"Bloody spies," the Colonel muttered as he turned on his heel.

They all watched the man walk briskly into the darkness, then turned to Stan who had started to laugh, quickly joined by the two men in the lead vehicle.

"You absolute fucking legends!" he chuckled. "Colonel Oskopy... which one of you came up with that?"

"Guilty," Rashid smiled.

"I remember you," Stan said. "Captain Casanova. D Squadron. Handy sniper."

Rashid shrugged. "For a while. The top brass doesn't like officer snipers. It's like giving them a day off from the daily bullshit."

King climbed into the lead vehicle and indicated for Zukovsky to sit next to him. There was no way he was going to let the man out of his sight. Rashid got into the middle Land Rover and some of the men made room for Flymo in the third. They took off into the night, rapidly threading through the circuitous route with a few grinding gear changes and noisy diesel engines. On the helicopter runway, usually reserved for laden Chinook helicopters that saved fuel with rolling take-offs, three *Dauphin 2* helicopters with glossy blue paintwork fired up their engines, their rotors starting to turn slowly.

"Right, kit out and loaded, bodies on board," Stan shouted over the building noise of the engines. He looked up as a tall, lean figure got out of a Porsche 911 parked on the grass verge of the road and strolled over. "Ready to go, Sir."

"Thanks for that, Stan," the man said casually. He turned to King and said, "I gather you're the man in charge?" King nodded. "Major Scott MacPherson," he said. "Thought I'd come along for the ride. It sounded... interesting."

"It's going to be a challenge, but I think it's doable."

"It's fucking madness," MacPherson replied. "But I'm always up for a bit of that." He looked at Zukovsky and said, "So, that makes you the Russian..." Zukovsky ignored the new arrival, watching the trio of helicopters which were now running at full chat. "What is this, then? Day release?"

"Insurance," replied King. "Now, are we going or what?"

THIRTY-TWO

RAF Brize Norton, Oxfordshire

THE FLIGHT to the Royal Air Force's largest airbase took just twenty-five minutes to cover the sixty-four miles including a circuit of the airfield. The helicopters touched down outside a large hangar with a Lockheed C130 Hercules outside. The SAS troopers unloaded their kit and stored it in the hangar while four RAF personnel dressed in overalls smoked and chatted beside an old Bedford lorry.

A tall man with hawk-like features and a handlebar moustache walked out of the hangar along with a stocky woman with her frizzy ginger hair tamed by a peaked officer's cap and a severe expression upon her face. "Group Captain Amis, Intelligence Branch. This is Wing Commander Harrison," he said, gesturing to the woman.

"King. Security Service." He paused. "This is Soldier 'B'," he said, gesturing to Captain MacPherson, who smirked at the introduction."

Both officers smiled wryly. "This is all a bit beyond *Box's* remit," Amis commented.

"Tell that to my union," King said flatly. "Have you got the kit?"

"They've just finished installing it. While you're briefing and organising your kit, the pilots will take the one-thirty up for a test flight. Your pilot will join them." Wing Commander Harrison paused, a touch of the Home Counties to her voice. "Your pilot's record shows that he hasn't flown fixed wing for a while, he should get behind the one-thirty and put in a bit of airtime."

King looked at Flymo, who was staring at the Hercules, while Rashid was standing beside Zukovsky beside the hangar door. "I'll tell him," King replied. "But he needs to be in the briefing, as do both your pilots."

"We'll work through the timings." Amis paused. "Have you had breakfast?"

"Yes, thanks," King replied. "But flasks of tea and coffee, some bottled water and a shed-load of biscuits would be most welcome." He paused. "Other than that, we had better be getting on with it."

"We'll organise packed lunches, but you can dine in the officers' mess tonight," said Amis casually. "It's curry night."

MacPherson shook his head. "For security reasons, we'll take what you can give us here. Zed-beds and field rations will be fine. Once we're in that hangar, we're in there until zero-seven-hundred tomorrow."

King nodded. "Agreed. And that goes for you, too."

"This is highly irregular!" Amis retorted.

"Make the arrangements for refreshments now, get what you need for the briefing, and we'll meet you inside in half an hour," said King. "But once we start briefing, you're in for a night in the hangar and a plane ride in the morning."

The two men watched the RAF intelligence officers walk to a nearby Land Rover and MacPherson chuckled. "Bloody RAF," he said. "Always know when the tea breaks are."

"And whether they're over their flying hours for the day," replied King.

"Give me Royal Navy and Army Air Corps pilots any day, especially if you're pinned down on the top of a mountain waiting to evac with the Taliban swarming below. I've known RAF pilots turn back for fear of the paperwork and reprimands they'll face flying over their hours." MacPherson shook his head. "The Royal Air Force is a self-consuming monster made of paperwork and procedure and tradition." King smiled. He'd been on those same mountains. Of course, he'd been thankful to the pilots of the RAF, especially fighter-jet pilots raining down airstrikes around him when things had got too hairy, but there was something about the Royal Air Force, an intrinsic feel, that felt as if there were parts of the establishment that were still in 1942. Amis fit the bill entirely with his handlebar moustache. "Look, I don't normally get to find out how an operation pans out for me and the lads." MacPherson paused. "But that Russian chap was behind a coup that saw me and some of the lads here performing a hostage rescue on a boat in the middle of the North Sea."

King smiled. "You did some good work."

MacPherson nodded. "Thanks." He shrugged. "So how come he's here? Box did a deal with him?"

"It's complicated."

"It so often is." MacPherson shrugged and walked back to his men.

"Yes," King said quietly to himself. "It so often is."

THIRTY-THREE

Scafell Pike, The Lake District

SHE HAD PUSHED IT. Pushed her body, her mental strength and her fitness. It had been too soon to take on such a peak – England's highest – and too soon after sustaining such traumatic injuries. She had not intended to reach the summit, some three-thousand-two-hundred-feet in height, but in typical fashion, Caroline had not known when to stop. Only when the icy ground became dangerous under foot and the wind became dangerously cold, the windchill bringing down the temperature by a factor of five, had she allowed herself pause to reflect and make a tactical retreat. These factors could not be ignored but admitting to defeat through stamina and endurance and pain was not in her psyche. She had always been tenacious, but she had never been stupid. After slipping for the third time, and this time perilously close to a steep and icy slope to rocks several hundred feet below, she had called it for what it was – a fool's errand – and turned around and headed back down the path. As she did so, she was pleased with the decision. The Peaks and moors of the Lake District claimed many lives each year. Spring days became like mid-winter within minutes with snow and sleet and ice creating white outs, when just minutes before people would have removed layers of clothing and complained about the heat during their hike.

Three hundred metres further down the mountain a lone figure strode the same path. Caroline had made it to Y-Junction, two-thirds of the way. She was now approaching Lingmell Gill Crossing. The person was wrapped in a blue waterproof windcheater and green waterproof hiking trousers. Caroline had set out in active wear, but she had brought emergency kit in a small daysack and stopped to pull out her windcheater. The descent was far easier than the ascent and she was cooling down quickly. Her legs were hurting. She had been told by the surgeon that the metal could ache in the cold, but she knew it was less to do with the weather and more to do with the exertion. She had only got rid of her crutches two months ago. *Straight, level walks and ease into a slow jog, but only when walking five miles regularly is completely pain free* – that had been the advice. And now she had overdone it. She cursed herself. Not many people would be tackling such demanding walks this early today. It was barely above zero and the windchill was painfully frigid. The figure grew closer, and Caroline could see by the gait that it was a woman. Red hair poking from under her hood, a strong and determined pace tackling the incline. A woman who was both physically and mentally fit.

At no more than twenty-five metres between them, the woman stopped and reached into her pocket. Caroline could not see the woman's face, obscured by her hood, but when she pulled her hand out of her pocket, she knew...

"What the hell are you doing, girl?"

Caroline laughed as she closed the gap between them. "What are *you* doing, more like?" She kissed her aunt on the cheek. "For me?" she asked, looking at the painkillers in her aunt's hand. She took them from her, opened the bottle and took out one. It was a morphine-based painkiller, and she was still taking two a day, although she was thinking about dropping the night-time dose. She swallowed the tablet and slipped the bottle into her pocket, linked her arm around her aunt's and started down the hillside with her for as long as the path would allow, which was only fifty metres or so before the rocky steps forced them into single file. "Thanks," she said. "And yes, before you chastise me like a silly little schoolgirl, I am aware that it was too much, too soon."

"Just like your mother," she replied flatly. "Stubborn and won't be criticised."

"Aunty Kate! Now I've told you, I don't know what you have both fallen out over, but I am completely impartial, so I won't be taking sides!"

Kate laughed. "Good!" She pulled Caroline close to her as they reached the bottom of the rocky steps and the path widened enough to walk two-abreast once more. "Anyway, having you here these past couple of days has compelled me to make the first move. Lord only knows, Hilary won't..."

"Aunty Kate..." Caroline pulled a face.

"OK, I get it. You're Switzerland on this."

Caroline shrugged. "Life's short. I'm only too glad you want to make the first move, I'm only sorry that mother hasn't."

"It's nothing to do with you, dear. But time is a great healer, and I think perhaps it's time. For me, at least." She paused. "I just hope your mother feels the same."

Caroline nodded, then looked at her aunt and frowned. "How did you know where to find me?"

"You're you," she said kindly. "It's England's highest peak, so what else were you going to do? Where else were you going to try?" She smiled at her niece. "I'm extremely proud of you. I don't know much about your work with the secret service, but I'm sure we all sleep safer at night because of you."

Caroline smiled. She didn't correct her use of the term *secret service*, technically it didn't exist, but her aunt's praise meant a great deal to her. Kate had never had children and had not been lucky in love, either. But she was happy, maintained a decent career illustrating and writing children's books. Despite never becoming a mother, she had always been maternal with Caroline and had even based a character on her. Kate enjoyed her life in the Lake District, inspired by her literary hero Beatrix Potter who had both lived, worked and set many of her stories here.

The temperature increased and the windchill became less harsh as they descended, but it was Cumbria in late winter, and the Lake District was still high above sea level and barely above freezing where they had left the cars in one of several small laybys near the foot of the mountain. Caroline was grateful for the heater in her Mini as she followed her aunt home, looking out for the typically suicidal sheep on the sides of the single lane road. They passed England's deepest lake, Wast Water, three miles long, yet just a few hundred metres wide, the narrow lake looking cold and black against the grey skies, hemmed in by vast slopes on all sides. Caroline's aunt owned a small farm cottage near the southern end of Wast Water and supplemented her modest literary income with a self-service stall with an honesty box selling homemade cakes, bread, fudge,

Kendal mint cake and free-range eggs from her own hens, from spring through to autumn. When they arrived home, she was pleased that Kate had restoked last night's fire before she had set out after her, and two large logs were teasing out flames in the wood burning stove, the flames licking at the glass and making the open-plan kitchen and lounge a welcoming place to be after the bracing moorland wind.

Caroline stripped off her windcheater and put on a baggy sweater. Kate had brewed some tea and in typical fashion, served it in a pot with a matching jug of milk and cups and saucers. Caroline hung her daysack on the back of her chair. It only contained Kendal mint cake, a survival blanket, a torch and a bottle of water, but something as trivial as a twisted ankle could quickly escalate to a life-or-death situation out on the peaks. She sat down heavily, the fire sending a wall of heat her way as she sipped her tea and warmed her hands on the cup. She would have preferred a mug, but Kate had her ways and she accepted her hospitality with the humility in which it had been given. She stared at the fire, losing herself in the flames. She was only aware that Kate had opened the door when she heard her start speaking.

Caroline looked behind her, saw Kate on the doorstep, the open door blocking the visitor from view. There was no sign of confrontation, no raised voices and certainly Kate did not react. But one minute Caroline was looking at her aunt, the next she saw the flash of blade across her throat, the blood gushing out impossibly quickly, impossibly final. Caroline leapt up, but the woman kicked Kate in the stomach, and she fell backwards clutching her throat, her eyes wide in not so much terror, but surprise and disbelief. The woman stepped in, the knife in her left hand and the pistol in her right. Caroline, still holding her cup splashed the woman in the face and she screamed loudly as the hot tea found her eyes. She dropped the pistol as she clawed at her scalded face but kept hold of the knife and at the last minute, she slashed at Caroline as she darted forwards to tackle her. Caroline felt the wind behind the blade as it sliced through the air, just an inch in front of her face. She powered a punch into the woman's sternum, and she gasped and doubled over, but swept upwards with the knife, the blade perilously close to Caroline's chin. Caroline flung herself backwards, then lost her footing and fell. To her horror, she realised that she had slipped in her aunt's blood, and she was covered in it, sticky and warm and dark. She risked a glance at her aunt, her eyes wide as she clutched her throat with both hands and struggled to breathe. Caroline went for the pistol, but the woman had recovered enough from her scalding to kick the weapon away. It clattered across the floor to the Aga at the end of the kitchen and the woman immediately put herself between Caroline and the pistol, warily keeping the blade in front of her.

Caroline advanced, her hands ready to block or grab at the woman's arms. She breathed heavily, never once taking her eyes off the woman's own. It only took a flicker to see what they intended – people who won fights never took their eyes off their opponent's eyes and used their peripheral vision to spot everything else.

"After I have killed you, your lover will be next..." the woman said, but she was clearly in pain from Caroline's well-targeted punch, and her already pale skin looked somewhat paler from the shock of Caroline's rapid attack.

Caroline didn't respond. She knew enough about fights to know that breath was precious, and breathing was all she was concentrating on right now. Breathing and spotting an opening.

"I'll make him bleed like his sister and her husband." The woman could see that Caroline was oblivious and she smiled. She took time to sweep a lock of her red hair out of her eyes and glared back at her. "And I'll show him pictures of your mutilated body before he dies."

Caroline edged forwards. Surprisingly, the woman was defensive, taking a pace backwards. But with every inch she moved backwards, she got closer to the pistol. Caroline calmly picked up Kate's mobile phone from the counter and flicked left with her thumb, opening the camera without the need for a pin.

"Put it down!" Natasha snapped at her. Caroline aimed it at her and kept her thumb on the button, taking a dozen pictures of the woman. "What is the point? I will only take it with me after I have gutted you."

In a snap move, Caroline turned and raced for the stairs. She took them two at a time and bounded across the landing to her room. The Sig Sauer 9mm was in her bedside table and it was made ready and gripped firmly in her right hand and aiming at the doorway a second after she opened the drawer. She listened intently.

Nothing.

Not a sound.

Caroline knew that tactically she would be at a disadvantage heading back down the stairs. The woman could use the furniture if not for cover, then to present herself as a smaller target. She could shelter behind the centre worktop and cupboard unit and catch Caroline in her line of fire as she rounded the bend in the stairs. Caroline headed into Kate's bedroom, opened the window and climbed out onto the flat roof of the kitchen extension. She could hear a vehicle, and she caught a flash of a silver hatchback as it slewed out of the driveway and onto the road. She aimed and fired half-a-dozen shots at the car, more out of rage than to stop it, and she could have squealed in delight when the rear window shattered, had it not been for what she knew she would find downstairs.

The vehicle was almost around the bend when a tractor and trailer blocked the road. It backed up for the tractor, but the farmer hopped out to open a gate and left his rig in the road. The silver hatchback reversed back towards the house. The road was too narrow to U-turn in, and a three-point turn would likely turn into double figures. The car veered from side to side, almost clipping the four-foot-high grass verge on both sides as the driver struggled for control reversing at such a high speed, the gearbox whining.

Caroline looked up as a black Jaguar saloon pulled into the driveway. She recognised it as one of MI5's luxury vehicles and her heart raced when she saw Big Dave at the wheel. She waved urgently at him, and he paused, frowning at her on the roof with a pistol in her hand, but he caught on quickly and spun the vehicle around on the gravel, putting the vehicle between himself and the house as he got out, ducked down and retrieved the M4 rifle out of the boot. He took aim at the house, using the vehicle as cover.

"No! Behind you!" Caroline shouted, pointing at the road as the silver hatchback reached the gateway and spun around in a J-turn, now that there was room to do so. "One X-Ray!" She saw Lomu's indecision, but to be fair the man had just driven in. "She's an assassin! She's just killed my aunty!"

Big Dave turned around, aimed at the moving vehicle and fired two rounds. He stood up and took aim again, firing another three rounds, but the car was now two-hundred metres away and accelerating rapidly. He stopped, pulled up the sight for the M203 grenade launcher, shouldered the weapon and wrapped his finger around the forward trigger of the grenade system. He adjusted the sight to 300m and squeezed the trigger. There was a 'plop' and a 'whoosh' and the 203mm grenade took to the air in an unseeable arc, dropping just in front of the vehicle and detonating instantly. There was smoke and flame and the hatchback pivoted into the air and turned end over end in a cannonade of noise and sparks as it smashed into the tarmac.

"Oh shit! Where the hell did you get that?" Caroline sat down on the flat roof, then lifted herself off and dropped down onto the ground some eight feet below. She winced at the impact, started to limp across the gravel but the pain wore off quickly and she was walking normally by the time she flung her arms around Big Dave.

"From King," he replied with a shrug. "Who else?"

Caroline smiled. But only from the thought of King and the release of adrenalin. The thought of Kate wiped the smile off her face, and she turned and ran back into the house. Big Dave looked at the smouldering wreck in the road and he jogged out of the driveway and down the road towards it, the rifle held lazily between his hands but easily brought to bear.

She was quite still. Peaceful. Caroline ignored the blood and cradled her aunt's head, sliding her back down the side of the kitchen counter and sitting on the floor, sobbing loudly as she stroked Kate's hair. Big Dave hovered in the doorway surveying the scene. He stepped back outside and sat down on a garden bench seat and rested the rifle beside him. In the distance the car still smouldered.

Caroline came out after ten minutes. She had washed

her face under the cold tap, and she slumped down beside him and rested her head on his shoulder.

"I'm sorry for your loss, luv."

Caroline didn't respond, but she patted his knee twice in acknowledgment.

"There was nobody in the car," he said.

"What?" she sat up straight and stared at him.

"A motorcyclist stopped to assist, but the woman promptly kneed him in the balls and stole his bike. He's called the police. The bike was a Honda Fireblade, so she's long gone. It's a myriad of lanes and tracks down that way, I got lost twice coming here..."

"The woman said something about killing Alex's sister and her family. That can't be right, Alex is an only child."

"It's complicated," Big Dave replied.

"I've worked out that much."

"King has a past. You two need a chat when you get time."

"It certainly looks that way," she agreed. "Call Mereweather. We're going to need him to run some interference here, or we'll both be in jail within the hour." She paused. "I can't leave Aunty Kate here," she said tearfully. "Not like this..."

Big Dave nodded and took out his phone. "We're going to need the police. They'll organise a doctor to confirm the death and of course the coroner for the death certificate. But they'll start a murder investigation and that could be a problem for us, especially as I've just used a military weapon to take out a hatchback." He paused. "All the people who need to know will be told. But not before I've gotten you out of here. I promised King I would bring you back, and that's exactly what I'm going to do. Get in your car and follow me."

THIRTY-FOUR

Carlton Gardens, London

EVERY DAY, the Foreign Secretary drove from his official residence at No. 1 Carlton Gardens to the Foreign Office in Whitehall, and every day he did so in a two-car convoy. His official Jaguar with himself, driver and lead bodyguard, a Range Rover Vogue with a driver and two security officers. However, due to the death of one of their own – although no details had been released regarding Steve Moore's death – and the murder of his wife and child, the Foreign Secretary's security had been stepped up with the addition of a Land Rover Discovery which was often chosen by diplomatic protection as a 'ram' car because of its sheer weight and size and the fact they were less expensive than Range Rovers. The vehicle added another three bodies in the form of a driver and two security officers on board. All personnel were serving police officers with diplomatic protection.

The Foreign Secretary ran every day, too. He would cross The Mall and run a lap of St. James's Park, cross into

Green Park and then back to Carlton Gardens which had also been home to such dignitaries and institutions as Prime Minister Earl Grey, Prime Minister Lord Palmerston, Lord Cardigan – leader of the Charge of the Light Brigade, Prime Minister William Gladstone, and was the official headquarters of MI6's Y-section shortly after the Second World War. Banks, political parties and embassies had all held residence or offices at the prestigious address, as well as Viceroys of India and somewhat notoriously, Ashraf Marwan – the Egyptian billionaire arms dealer and former spy, who died after somehow falling from his flat in the terrace. He was believed to work for Israeli Mossad and Egyptian intelligence as a double agent. Or triple, if you counted his documented work for Britain. Accidents happen.

Campbell always warmed down in the gardens opposite his residence. He used one of the park benches to lean against and stretch out his hamstrings, his glutes and calf muscles. Campbell was fit, but he was in his mid-forties and muscles needed looking after. He always warmed down for ten minutes and would often talk to his bodyguards about using a foam roller once he was inside and had even taken tips from some of them, advocating ice baths or at the very least, cold showers. Campbell sat on the bench and leaned forward, touching the grass with his fingertips. His two running companions for the morning hovered in the gateway of the gated garden. Both men wore bum-bags and inside each was a Glock 19 pistol. Neither man paid much attention to their VIP in the otherwise empty garden. They did not warm down either. Both men were fit enough to have considered this morning's run a mere warm-up. When Campbell had finished, he walked over and was already on his Bluetooth taking a call. The two bodyguards fell in behind him, escorted him across the road and up the steps to his home. Inside, the two bodyguards headed left to a small flat where they could shower and fix snacks and hot drinks, even watch some TV in any downtime between events. Principals only needed protecting when they were on the move. The life of a bodyguard was made up mostly of sitting around waiting for meetings to come to an end.

Across the road in the gated garden. A woman from MI5's watcher unit was lying prone, deep in the belt of bushes behind camouflaged netting with natural foliage weaved into it with great care and attention to detail. A survey had been completed beforehand and plants had been selected and fixed to the netting and the netting had been sprayed with water to keep the cuttings of foliage fresh. The hide had been erected through the previous night and this had been the second watch. The woman wore a ghillie suit, similar to that which military snipers wore, named after the ghillies of the Scottish Highlands - the deer stalking guides and gamekeepers who lent their name to the suit during the First World War. She had video and audio recording capabilities as well as a top of the range SLR digital camera, and somewhat less glamorously, she wore a pair of adult incontinence pants should she not be able to make it through her shift without a call of nature.

On the street a BT Openreach liveried works van had fenced off a broadband box, and two engineers were working on it inside a three-sided work-tent. Only these men were not telecommunications engineers. They were both part of MI5's surveillance unit, or 'watchers'. To negate interception from electronic counter surveillance equipment, the watchers had not used wireless or radio frequency communication intercept methods, relying on what Ramsay had ordered to be 'old school' techniques. The Foreign Secretary's phonelines had been bugged and MI5 were now in complete control of the man's mobile phone account as well. His phone screen was displayed on a screen in the Thames House basement and Ramsay was receiving updates on his own phone, as well as recordings of conversations that were sent to Ramsay's voicemail. Next to this screen was another showing Campbell's laptop screen. Everything the politician looked at would be seen on the screen in the basement of MI5.

The men retrieved the flash drive from the digital receiving unit and replaced it with another. To any casual observer, they were merely two engineers trying to sort out somebody's broadband connection, but they were both acting as back-up to the woman across the road in the gated community garden.

"Bravo Three Nine, this is Alpha Two Seven, Birdcage, Over."

One of the men crouched deeper into the work-shelter and replied through his throat-mic, "Alpha Two Seven, have that. Birdcage. Wait-out." He turned to his colleague and said, "Get Ramsay on the phone. Tell him we've had both a visual and intercept."

THIRTY-FIVE

She had ditched the motorcycle soon after stealing it. Five miles or less at a layby popular with hikers near Santon Bridge. She could not go on without wearing a motorcycle helmet without attracting negative attention. The Honda Fireblade was an all-out racer with a race-tuned engine the size of most city cars. With its exhaust the bore of a field artillery gun, it attracted enough attention on its own without a helmetless woman riding it with a mane of blazing-red hair flowing behind in the wind. Besides, she had taken a massive beating inside the car and had been lucky to escape without broken bones, or worse. Already nursing a pebble-dashed stomach and leg from her earlier encounter with Gerald Darby's shotgun, she had been in great discomfort before her attempted hit on Caroline, but because of the attack on her parents, she had rushed her next attempt on their daughter. She had only patched the wounds with hastily purchased first aid supplies from a filling station, lying down in the backseat of the hatchback she had stolen and squeezing out much of the shot the way a teenager would with breakout of spots. Only these were infinitely more painful to exorcise. She still had plenty of shot under her skin, but as far as she could tell, there had been no deeper penetration. Her clothing and muscled torso slowed the shot, which had already travelled towards the end of its effective range. Distance was everything with a shotgun. Distance and luck.

Natasha had stolen a ten-year-old Vauxhall Astra from the layby and driven to Barrow-in-Furness, where she had ditched it in a grotty-looking council estate and walked into town, taking an equally old and well-used Peugeot Estate from a side street near the town centre. Reno had taught her how to boost cars, and she always targeted older cars with an actual physical ignition key, when she did not have more specialist equipment at her disposal. Older cars that were not classics, nor premium marques never had trackers in them either. Nobody was going to pay a subscription to a security company when they didn't want to pay finance for a better vehicle. Old cars were Reno and Natasha's bread and butter. They travelled all over Europe in boosted cars on stolen number plates.

She had not yet told Reno of her two failed attempts and didn't know where to start. Caroline Darby had a military career and worked for one of the best intelligence services in the world. The intelligence gleaned on both King and Darby by Reno's Russian contacts and their hacker program would point at them being world-class operatives, and with some background on King's previous employment with MI6 and their deniable operations wing – so secretive that it didn't even have a name - the two assassins had known that they could not afford to underestimate their quarry. However, she had done just that. If Natasha was brutally honest with herself, she was taken aback at how the woman had apparently ignored the killing of her own aunt and fought her off. First with the hot drink, and then with the punch. Powerful, accurate and fast. Caroline had then advanced on her, and to her chagrin, she had backed away. Caroline had then bolted for the stairs, and Natasha had just known that the woman had been heading for a weapon. She had lost the element of surprise, and she had panicked.

And then there was Caroline Darby's back-up. Natasha had not known how it had been arranged, but she had driven right past the large black man in the Jaguar. Moments later, she had been blown off the road by an IED or a rocket, or God only knew what else. She had crawled from the wreckage, bruised and winded and bleeding, and had it not been for the motorcyclist travelling the other way, then she would surely have been confronted at the scene of the crash, and by then she would have been outnumbered two to one. As confident as she had become, she cringed as she thought how different the outcome could have been.

Live to fight another day... that was what Reno had taught her, and that was how they had lived through their contracts. Reno, caught once before and incarcerated until he had managed to escape, had since kept Interpol and the police services of most of Europe, America and Asia at bay. But she could already see that Caroline Darby had a different mantra, that might well have read; *fight to live another day...* Natasha had underestimated her quarry, perhaps over-estimated her own abilities, but she would not do so again. She would kill the woman simply to weaken King, and she would enjoy doing it.

THIRTY-SIX

RAF Brize Norton

KING DRANK THIRSTILY, draining the bottle of water quickly, then tossed it into the bin and sat down heavily in the director's style camp chair. Rashid had simply slid down the wall and rested with his legs sprawled out, breathing heavily and wiping his brow. Stan had put them all through their paces from stretching and calisthenics through to an insane workout focusing on upper-body strength, before the rope work. Several of the SAS troopers had rigged the walls and ceiling with ropes and each section had a specific task to complete, while testing confidence, will and endurance. The session focused on both teamwork and independent endurance, and when the first had finished – King and MacPherson racing to the last when they realised that they were in fact direct competition to each other – Stan had joined in to benefit from the training exercise, rather than glide through in his instructor's role. Flymo had trained, too. Although he did not possess the same fitness levels or experience as his SAS soldier counterparts, he needed to train like everybody else. After a quick lunch of sandwiches, Flymo would join the RAF pilots for the next training phase. Stan had called for sandbags and a range had been set up at the far end of the hangar and drills and weapons testing with the Heckler and Koch HK416 carbines and Glock 17 9mm pistols would start soon. They also had a spare SCAR-H battle rifle chambered in 7.62mm with a 3.9x50 scope and two Remington 12-gauge pump-action shotguns with Hatton rounds for breaching doors. This slug of compressed zinc filings disintegrated when fired at point-blank range at door locks, deadbolts and hinges. In a pinch, it could be used at close range as a weapon, the Hatton round remaining intact until it struck an enemy target. Recovery from a million zinc filings was slim, which was why it was meant only for breaching doors.

MacPherson pulled out one of the canvas director's chairs and sat down opposite King. He had finished his water and tossed it into the bin. He seemed satisfied with the shot. "The Russian is too old for this," he commented.

"He gets the easy bit," King replied.

"As easy as gravity," Rashid added.

"He's baggage," MacPherson replied. "Baggage can't be relied upon when the bullets start to fly."

"Let me worry about him," said King.

"I don't know why we can't just go in off his intel."

"There's a lot you don't know," King got up and stretched, then looked down at the SAS Major. "And a lot you don't get to know." His phone vibrated in his pocket, and he took it out, checking the number before answering, then stalked off without another word.

MacPherson turned to Rashid and shrugged. "He gets to the point, doesn't he?"

"Won't use ten words when two will do."

"Worked with him much?"

"Once or twice."

MacPherson nodded. "Good man in a crisis?"

Rashid stretched, stood up and looked down at him. "There's nobody I'd trust more with my life."

"You were in D squadron, weren't you?" Rashid nodded. "So, you've worked with plenty of good men," MacPherson stated flatly.

"I'll stop you there, Major. King is a machine. He's got unlimited endurance and resolve. He will do anything, and I mean, anything to survive and win."

"He may well have to on this mission," the SAS Major replied curtly.

"He'll go first." He waved a hand around the hangar. "All this shit we're doing here... he'll go first. I guarantee it. And he'll be the last man out. And if you take a bullet, he'll carry you until his legs fall off. And then he'll make a sledge out of those legs and keep on fucking going..." Rashid walked a few paces before turning around and saying, "But make an enemy out of him, and you're done..." Rashid shook his head. "You might just as well end it all right there."

MacPherson smiled. "None of my enemies have been left alive either, sunshine."

Rashid smirked, shaking his head. "You've had enemy engagements and followed orders. Yes, you've killed and returned from missions, but like all soldiers you return to base and wait for your next order, because you're not paid to think about the last job. King has had proper enemies. A list of them. People coming after him for retribution. It's a different matter entirely," he said and headed outside and found King leaning against the bonnet of a Land Rover and rotating his phone in the palm of his hand somewhat thoughtfully. "What's up?" he asked, looking at King's expression.

"I sent Big Dave to look after Caroline."

"Crikey, don't ever let her hear you say that!"

"Right..." King grinned. "To aid her in any way required... how's that?"

"Better."

"Well, it looks as if he got there just in time. Somebody tried to kill her. The description matches the woman who attempted to kill her parents." King paused. "But the bitch killed her aunt."

"Shit..." Rashid replied, wishing he'd chosen a better response. "You've spoken to her?"

"Yes. She and Big Dave were getting a coffee in a motorway service station. They're heading back to London. Caroline wants to be front and centre with the investigation. She's hunting down the assassins, and something tells me she's never going to stop." King paused. "Christ, I'm done with all this."

Rashid patted him on the shoulder and perched on the front bumper of the old Land Rover. The bumper resembled a steel girder. The vehicle barely moved as Rashid sat down, such was its lack of suspension. "It's certainly not easy."

"How many more?" asked King. "How many more lives? My sister, her husband and their two children. Sally-Anne, for Christ's sake. I don't give a shit about Steve Moore, but there's his wife and child. And now Caroline's aunt, her father getting shot and injured at his age. All because of somebody's grievance with me." He shook his head, scuffed his foot on the ground as he kicked a stone away. "And not just now, before. Look at Marnie, and her parents."

Rashid looked away. He and Marnie had a casual thing going – certainly blossoming to more - but when she had been killed to provoke a response from King and the team, it had almost ended King and Rashid's friendship.

"No, I'm done." He said decisively. "I'll do what I can to cut this link to the hackers and Russian cyber-attacks, and I'll go after this bastard Reno and the bitch working with him, and then I'm out."

"You'll get the job done," Rashid agreed. "And then you'll get bored, agitated and you'll end up wanting to do the right thing. But most of all, you'll miss the action. You'll be back inside a year."

"Bollocks."

"So, what will you do?"

King shrugged. He and Caroline had talked about sailing around the world. "A bit of travel," he replied.

"I'll give it six months," Rashid laughed. "That MacPherson's asking questions about you."

"A man with his experience should know better."

"He's OK. Just a Rupert, that's all."

"*You* were a bloody Rupert." King reminded him, using the nickname SAS troopers gave to officers.

"Yes, but I'm just an immigrant whose dad owned an off-licence and newsagents. I don't think even the roughest knuckle-dragger was calling me Rupert behind my back."

"Ignorance is bliss." King paused. "I don't think MacPherson is a classic officer, either. What's his story?"

"I'm not sure."

"Fat lot of good you are."

"I saw him around back in the day, but I never worked with him. He's clearly been invited back."

The Special Air Service took its recruits from privates and NCOs, or Non-Commissioned Officers such as corporals and sergeants. Upon selection, each man was paid one rank above. Officers could only come in for a four-year secondment, where they returned to their unit and passed on their experience to the men under their command. It strengthened the British Army immeasurably. Occasionally an officer would be invited to a second term, and they would then stay on indefinitely. The other way to a commission was to work up the ranks, which happened rarely.

King shrugged. "He mentioned that he was on the hostage rescue that got the security service agents back in the North Sea. Part of Zukovsky's plan when we were chasing around radical imams and getting caught in a mosque."

"Yeah, I remember. That was another fine mess you got me into. I should have learned then." Rashid frowned. "But how does he know about Zukovsky?"

"That's my point. He was never up against Zukovsky. He had an operation come in... hijackers unknown. No intelligence on how many terrorists, or X-Rays as you green army lot call them. There was never any mention of Zukovsky, because he was never making his escape that way." King paused. "Keep your eye on him. And the men closest to him. When we get there, we're on our own. You're the only man I trust."

THIRTY-SEVEN

Whitehall

SIMON MEREWEATHER'S two bodyguards peeled off and took the leather sofa opposite the secretary's desk in the anteroom. Their job was done until the director of MI5 reappeared. Like most bodyguards, they would chat up the secretary for a tea or coffee while they waited. Neither man would expect a cup and saucer or biscuits – that would be reserved for their boss – but they took refreshments when they could get them and made the most of the comfortable seating.

Simon Mereweather and Neil Ramsay entered the Foreign Secretary's office. Campbell was seated behind an expansive mahogany desk, a large in-tray to his left, an ominously empty out tray to his right. Behind him, two civil servants were leaning each side of him, guiding him through a particular issue that judging from their expressions, looked to be of critical importance and of little understanding to the Foreign Secretary.

"Quite irregular, Simon," Campbell said without looking up. "There's the COBRA meeting regarding Russian cyber-attacks scheduled for tomorrow morning you could have caught up with me then."

"I'll remind you that the content and pretext of tomorrow's meeting is not for the ears of your aides." Mereweather paused. "And nor is what I have to say, so..." He looked at the two civil servants, who had stopped working long enough to prove that people were always listening. "Make yourselves scarce," he said. The two men hesitated, and Mereweather added, "Actually, busy yourself for the rest of the day."

Campbell looked set to protest, but something changed in his attitude, and he sat back in his leather chair, regarding the two men from MI5 closely. "I think I may give the PM a call..."

"Or a lawyer," said Ramsay.

"What?"

"But I'm not sure you want it to go that far, just yet," Ramsay said pointedly.

Campbell waited for his two aides to close the door behind them, then asked, "What is this about?"

"I think you know," Mereweather said dispassionately.

Campbell sighed. "I'm a busy man, Mereweather. I don't have time to play games."

Mereweather noted how the Foreign Secretary had switched from his Christian name to surname, trying to garner some authority in the situation. He also noted that the man had started to perspire. People tended to do so under duress, regardless of the temperature. The office, like most government places of work was heated to twenty degrees, not enough to have beads of sweat on his brow but enough to stop employees from complaining about being cold. "There's been a question raised about how you undertake certain meetings."

Campbell frowned. The cogs were turning, but the man was going to bluff his hand for all he was worth. "They are minuted, as are all ministerial meetings in Whitehall and at the Foreign and Commonwealth Office." Campbell shrugged. "If you have an issue with me, then please direct it through the appropriate parliamentary channels. Anything else?"

"What about outside business interests?" Ramsay inquired.

"We *all* have outside business interests. How do you think we all live on the pittance we're paid?"

"You're on over a hundred-thousand pounds a year," Ramsay persisted. "Hardly a pittance."

"And cabinet ministers all took a five-thousand pound a year pay cut to appease the Daily Mail readers!" He shook his head. "Everybody has a private entity. That's how we remain votable! We bring expertise and experience from our lives and use it in the business of running the country."

"Not everyone," Ramsay commented. "Only a small percentage of the opposition party members have a considerable income outside of politics."

"I rest my case," Campbell replied smugly. "Inept, unambitious and unappealing. Except to the lower working classes." He smirked. "And northerners..." He looked at Mereweather and said, "Isn't that right, Simon? Someone like you, someone from your background would agree, right? Your family own half of the Home Counties, doesn't it?"

Mereweather smiled. "Founded on slavery, colonialism and working-class suffering, I'm afraid. That's why the last four generations of Mereweather men have invested their time in public service, military service or the country's security. Personally, I have never voted. I hold no political ideals or persuasion, and nor did my father or grandfather." He paused. "I think we'd better get back on track. And I suspect, you'll be glad that we are not minuting this meeting. For the sake of votes, that is."

"My financial records and Company House details are there for anybody to scrutinise." He glanced at his watch and added, "Look, is this going to take long? It's just that I have important things to do like running the country."

"No, that's the Prime Minister's job," Ramsay interjected. "Or do you Bullingdon Club lot do it all together behind closed doors?"

Campbell smirked. "I'm sensing a little class animosity, am I right?" He paused. "Middle-aged, lower middle-class, poor-fitting suit from a chain store... bought the one with the thickest material so it would last. Always too hot in the summer, though. Generally bored with his lot, but too financially constrained or unmotivated to strike out for something new and revitalising. Bored of his semi in suburbia, his two-point-four kids shut away in their rooms studying for a university that is little more than a college or polytechnic in a drab midland town, his wife who stayed at home but now has no career to return to, his hours spent at a desk keeping the country safe by sitting in front of a screen day in and day out..."

Ramsay knew the man was right, of course. But the man didn't know about his brief excursions into the field – as much as he would protest to the rest of the team at the time – and he didn't know that Ramsay had once killed a man in Albania using nothing more than a pen. And he didn't know that as much as it had repulsed him and given him countless sleepless nights ever since, he had never felt so alive as when he recalled the time when it was either him or the other man.

"I'll stop you right there, Campbell. Lord knows your own mother should have years ago," Mereweather said cuttingly. "We're here because of our belief that you are communicating clandestinely with people who you shouldn't be. We can minute this now, if you prefer?"

Campbell swallowed, his pallor fading. Mereweather had noted that the man's perspiration had gone, but his colour had changed. It was out there now, and the man was feeling nothing more than dread. "Tell me what you know," he said meekly.

"No," said Ramsay. "You tell us what we should know."

"You're enjoying this, aren't you? Must be the class thing..."

"It's nothing to do with class," Ramsay replied. "You don't possess a shred of it. You're an elitist. And that guides your judgement, which sails the population down the river. Slogans and lies on buses, the promise of things unattainable to the NHS. Your own business agenda that means you no longer pay taxes in Europe and that your competitors do. That was your sole reason for backing Brexit – your tax affairs. But right now, it's far more important issues that bring us to your door. And if you don't start talking, then someone is going to leak this to the press and you'll sit in an inquiry with the cameras on you, and by the time they've finished asking the questions, your political career will not only be over, but your shareholders will have voted with their stock bonds and shares, and your companies will be worthless. Less than the value of the benefits your so-called lower classes collect each week."

"I want my lawyer." Campbell picked up his phone and started to dial.

"That's fine," said Mereweather. "If that's the road that you want to go down, then yes, it would be smart to lawyer-up." He paused. "Let your lawyer know that you are defending a charge of high-treason from the outset, though. See what he advises. Or whether he'll even want to get involved. Wouldn't look good for his knighthood, would it? Defending the biggest traitor since the Cambridge Five."

Campbell paused mid-dial. "High treason?" Mereweather nodded. "What do you mean?"

"Tell me who your contact is." Campbell shook his head. Mereweather pressed on. "It will be better for you in the long run."

"It *is* quite a quandary, isn't it?" Ramsay commented. "To be up to your eyes in it to the degree that you can't possibly consider admitting to wrong-doing until you have an idea what wrong-doing we are referring to. That's quite a thing. Right about now a criminal suspect would be asking for other crimes to be taken into account, so they wouldn't be charged and tried twice."

"You are a couple of smug bastards, aren't you?" Campbell sighed.

"What about the other Bullingdon Club members? You had quite a year, didn't you? The four men at the top all in the same year at school, the same house no less. And then the same university, and the same elitist club." Ramsay paused, shaking his head somewhat despondently. "Is the Prime Minister involved in your little venture?"

"Certainly not!"

"I trust that your heart-felt denial is more of a case that you consider yourself to be more worthy than he is, rather than through loyalty to him." Mereweather commented flatly. "It's no secret that you have your eyes on the top job.

So, does your outside indiscretion aid you to power, or is it merely financial?"

Campbell regarded him steadily. "It's more than that."

"Then what?"

"You wouldn't understand."

Mereweather leaned forward in his chair. "Try Me."

THIRTY-EIGHT

Latitude: 54.658506 Longitude: 1.011077
North Sea, 27,000 feet

THEY HAD FLOWN the same route three times a week
for fifteen years. A demonstration in Russian belligerence.
Every time they had flown the route two RAF Tornadoes
flew in from RAF Coningsby to intercept. Only now, years
later, it was two Typhoons that made the intercept. Technology moved with the times. There had been thinking in
the Ministry of Defence that if the Russians could see that
their forty-year-old aircraft was indeed old technology, then
they may well cease the thrice-weekly flight through
embarassment, if nothing else. The aircraft had met an array
of intercept craft from Britain's arsenal including a
Hercules gunship and a brace of F-35s, but the games
stopped abruptly when six Mikoyan MiG-35s flew in
escort. Missile lock-on tactics and close flying formations
had never been so tense. Boris the Bear as the Antonov AN-
24 was known to both civilian air-traffic control and military

installations monitoring the east coast airspace had next been met simply by two Typhoons and after a few tense weeks, the old aircraft flew down the east coast of Britain without an escort once more.

The aircraft would break UK airspace off the coast of the English-Scottish border and fly down the coast until it got a little too close for comfort – and even Russian belligerence – to RAF Marham in Norfolk, home to a squadron of cutting-edge F-35B Lightning fighter jets. From there, Boris the Bear would head east and fly a somewhat provocative route between Denmark and Sweden, then cross the Baltic Sea, skirt Lithuanian airspace and cross its ally Belarus until it was back over Russian airspace and would then head north to its base in Archangel, in northern Russia.

The Hercules was flying a parallel route to Boris the Bear and at an altitude of twenty-eight-thousand feet. The two aircraft were separated by eleven miles and one-thousand feet when the co-pilot switched on the device. They were passing over Newcastle, while the AN-24 twin-prop workhorse was nine miles out to sea. The two Typhoons had scrambled and were ready to intercept in seven minutes.

The co-pilot switched on the red light and the men in the cargo bay switched to the aircraft's oxygen supply just before the aircraft started to decompress. A green light flashed twice then remained on when the aircraft had reached neutral compression and the rear cargo door lowered slowly. There were eight SAS soldiers and they remained seated until Stan got up and told them to 'make ready'. MacPherson and a thirty-something sergeant called Peters were checking a map, and a quiet corporal known as Chubs was readying the other men. King figured it was a nickname based on reverse humour as Chubs looked to be made of nothing more than skin and bone, but the way he swung his Bergen onto his back told King he was deceptively strong.

Flymo and Zukovsky both looked as nervous as each other, and for a man like Flymo, a supremely skilled helicopter pilot, the fact that he was looking so worried didn't sit well with King now they were so close to the crucial part of their mission.

"Get a load of Flymo," said Rashid, seemingly reading King's thoughts.

"If a black man could ever look pale, then this is it," replied King. "Now he knows how we all feel when he's doing his thing with the ground racing just feet below us at a hundred and fifty miles per hour. Remember Albania?"

"I'm still trying to forget."

King stood up, and Rashid helped him to his feet to ease the weight of his equipment. "This is crazy..."

"*This* is *your* idea!"

"Right."

"You can call it."

King glanced across at Group Captain Amis and Wing Commander Harrison sitting in backward-facing fold-down seats and staring daggers at him whenever the opportunity arose for eye-contact. The pair wore fur-lined bomber jackets over their uniforms, and he suspected neither officer had been in the air for a while. King suspected he would feel their wrath through formal channels soon, but he couldn't care less. His insistence upon them accompanying them on the flight meant that the only person who knew the *wheres, the whys and the whens* of the operation was Simon Mereweather. King ignored them and looked back at his friend. "Never," he replied adamantly.

Rashid looked at the sky outside the open loading doors

just in time to see two RAF Typhoons fly past in a blur. "Great. The calvary's here."

"It's time." King made his way past the SAS troopers to the hinge of the ramp. He clipped on the rope, and Stan made sure the carabiner was flipped and screwed tightly to the mount. "Time to see if this device is working," he said to the cockpit over his throat-mic. "Get into position and let me know when altitude and distance has been achieved."

"Roger that," came the pilot's reply. *"Gaining rapidly on the target, no change of course and no radio communication intercepted."*

"That's promising," King said to Rashid.

"Boris the Bear is now altering course. Bearing east, height and speed unaltered. Six more minutes and the Typhoons will peel off as it leaves UK airspace," the pilot announced.

King checked his watch, then reeled out the slack and gathered the coil of rope in loops beside him. It was all hypothetical. The calculations had been done. Now it was down to him. And of course, luck.

THIRTY-NINE

Whitehall

"IT WAS the usual things at first," Campbell said wearily. Mereweather had seen it before, a mix of relief, stress and emotion leaving the mind, body and soul. Curiously, when a traitor is caught out, there was always the sense of relief. "Trading tips. Insider information. Season tickets to Chelsea, private box of course."

"Of course," Ramsay commented emotionlessly.

"And then cold, hard cash," Mereweather filled in the gap. "For what?"

The Foreign Secretary sighed. "Information on our policies dealing with Russian cyber-crime and terrorism." Campbell looked at the expressions on the other men's faces and said somewhat defensively, "Nothing with too much detail, nothing more than."

"Keeping the bastards one step ahead," Mereweather interjected.

Campbell shrugged. "I suppose."

"You suppose correctly," Mereweather chided. "And the money?"

Campbell shrugged. "Gold, property and stock options."

Nothing as crass as a briefcase full of banknotes. That's not what the rich wanted. They wanted assets and investments. Mereweather stared at the man across the desk from him. "Tell me what you know about the hacking."

"Gentlemen, I believe it's time to speak to my lawyer."

"Alright, as I said earlier, if that's the road you want to go down." Mereweather stood up and buttoned his suit. "Special Branch will be here within thirty minutes, and in the meantime, I will be seeing that my bodyguards block your access to all tech and communications. You'll get your call when you've been arrested, not before. Neil, call the boys in here, will you?"

Ramsay got up without a word and headed for the door.

"Wait! Wait!" Campbell shook his head. "What's another option? There must *be* another option?"

Ramsay hovered by the door.

"There is always another option," Mereweather replied.

FORTY

Latitude: 56.490015 Longitude: 4.961865
Midway between Norfolk and Denmark
25,000 feet

BORIS THE BEAR had made its regular altitude and height adjustments and the Hercules now flew two thousand feet above the Antonov AN-24 and a thousand feet ahead. From their position below them, and from the enclosed cockpit, the Russian pilots could not see the aircraft above them. They had lost their RAF escort, and as far as the pilots were concerned, they would see the RAF in two days' time. They had no idea that the latest weapon in Britain's arsenal was directed at them, jamming their radar with passive infrared and black light. With the two RAF fighters returned to base, the Russian pilots had no reason to doubt their radar, but it would not last for long. Commercial airliners flew routes above them, typically at thirty to forty thousand feet, and if they did not pick up another aircraft soon, then they could become suspicious and check their instruments and navigation system or may well change their heading or altitude. Nobody knew what the Russian protocol would be in such an event.

King took a deep breath, steadying his nerves. He was using his own oxygen supply to combat altitude sickness and the sterile oxygen was like breathing nectar. He did not look back as he made the jump and released the coil of rope to his side. Immediately, he felt the rope tug at him and as he spun around in the air like a top, he caught sight of the Antonov below, appearing far larger than he had antici-pated. He made corrections with his arms and after a few more spins, he had worked out how to right himself and enter a steady plane as the rope played out on the spool inside the Hercules' loading bay.

He was operating on an open mic and could hear the co-pilot calling out directional instructions to the pilot as he charted King's progress from the ramp, fastened to a webbing safety strap. The sound of the C-130's four giant turbo props and engines was reverberating inside his chest as King was fed out with the winch and within ten seconds, he was less than six feet above the AN-24, directly above the mid-section of fuselage.

King readied the two suction cups. Each cup had a five-inch handle with a button operated by his thumb and their normal application was by glaziers installing heavy sheets of glass or mirrors. He drew ever nearer, then almost at once he was flung high in the air and slammed down heavily onto the top of the fuselage. He missed his opportunity, taken by surprise at the airstream running over the plane like an invisible current. The rope tightened, the co-pilot instructed the pilot of the correction, and he was spooled out further. The airstream caught him again. Again, he was flung high, like a fisherman casting off his bait, and he instantly plummeted back down, this time engaging both suction cups which were strapped around his wrists. He worked the button to release and secure him, working hand over hand to make his way down the spine of the plane and towards the side door. The windspeed was close to two-hundred and fifty-miles per hour, but the tautness of the rope kept most of the weight off his arms, as he eased himself down the side of the plane, now catching propeller wash as well as windspeed.

Stan and Peters had made the charges. It had been decided that magnetic fixings could not be trusted. Nobody was entirely sure of the material used on the aircraft nor its magnetic properties. The two demolition experts had made charges of PE4 plastic explosive in six 2oz flat rectangles with a peel-off adhesive patch on the back, with an extra-large tongue to aid King in pulling the paper off. Each charge had a detonator and det-cord attached and a manual trigger on a length of det-cord. King used just one suction cup and the taut rope to maintain his position, as he battled with the wind and getting the first charge in place. When he finally made it stick it was a little off-line with the door frame, but he figured he had a better chance now that he no longer feared dropping the length of charges. The next charge stuck straight and true, but King's left arm was aching from taking the weight.

"How's progress?" MacPherson asked, echoing in King's earpiece.

"Slow. Windspeed is a bitch."

"Can't help you, but just telling you to get things speeded up down there."

"Fuck off."

King got the next charge in place. The diagram he had studied back in RAF Brize Norton had shown the placement of the hinges and locks. He just hoped that Peters and Stan had got the charge right. Too little and they were done. The pilots would feel the explosion and come and investigate. Too much, and they could take the plane down. Like many military aircraft, the Antonov was unpressurised, the pilots used a central air supply and switched to their own personal supply when moving around inside the plane. Military planes remained unpressurised in case they caught a bullet. Total decompression – likely leading to structural break up or crashing – because of a single bullet hole was not a scenario the military could afford. So, the aircraft could cope with its door blowing off its hinges, but if the explosion was too large, then the structural integrity of the plane could be affected, and it may well split into pieces.

King could hear the change in propellor pitch, felt the plane change course as the aircraft banked hard to starboard. A second later he was torn from the suction cup by the rope and swung out a hundred metres from the AN-24 like a pendulum and started to spin. He had let go of the length of explosive charges and could only hope that the first two charges had held the length in place, but the thought was short-lived, and he spread his arms and attempted to right himself. He could only hope that the Russians had not seen the Hercules or the length of rope, and that the RAF's infrared and black light system was still working. Someone was screaming in his ear, and he could not make out a word as he fought the G-forces of his spin and concentrated on steadying himself.

Unbeknown and unheard to him from above, the Hercules pilot fought to maintain the same distance from the Antonov as it followed the aircraft's new course. However, the Hercules could not reposition King as he continued to spin like a top. In a bid to aid King, the co-pilot reeled the winch in at maximum RPM and shortened the distance by a hundred metres, then played it out slowly. King not only fought the rotation, but the acceleration of the retracting rope, but as the rope played out more slowly, he managed to right himself on the edge of unconsciousness. The moment he maintained his position, the Hercules edged above and in front of the Antonov and the rope played out once more. King barely had time to adjust as he was dangled onto the spine of the aircraft and instinctively slammed down the suction cup and pressed the button on the end of the handle to secure it. There was little slack in the length of rope and King was dragged forwards, twisted around and pulled between the Hercules and the suction cup like a tug of war. He managed to tell anyone listening what was happening, and felt the rope loosen.

King knew that he was running out of time. He checked his watch. There was only another ten minutes of air remaining. Without delay, he worked his way back down the fuselage and asked for an additional twenty feet of rope. He just hoped that the string of explosive charges was still in place.

FORTY-ONE

Whitehall

"IT'S NOT JUST FINANCIAL, or indeed political. I don't share Russia's political ideals, but I do feel they are unjustly punished financially. Take Ukraine and Crimea aggression. We respond by freezing assets, when we should have waved a big stick militarily," Campbell rolled his eyes.

"That's because Russia has one of the largest, if not the largest nuclear arsenals in the world, and we are never quite certain whether they would indeed use them in the event of a military response," Mereweather said curtly. "When two people each draw a gun, both should be able to back away. Honour intact. But you would never know if Russia would shoot, and simply chance being shot." Mereweather paused. "You've heard the story of the frog and the scorpion, surely?"

"No," said Campbell. "I don't believe I have."

Mereweather nodded. "Well, one day a frog and a scorpion are standing on the bank of a river. The frog is about to cross, when the scorpion asks for a ride on his back. The frog considers this for a moment, then says, *Okay, but don't sting me, or we'll both die in the river*. The scorpion hops on the frog's back and the frog swims them out. Just past half-way, the scorpion stings the frog. *You've stung me! yells the frog. Now we're both going to die! You're going to drown! Why did you do that?* Well, the scorpion thinks for a moment, and just as the frog starts to sink underwater, he says, *Because I'm a scorpion...*" Mereweather paused. "It's in their nature. I know we're all meant to be inclusive of sexual identification, of religion, colour and creed... but Russians are different. There are still enough of them alive who know first-hand of starvation and torture and false imprisonment, and men in trench coats dragging off their neighbours in the dead of night, never to be seen again. They know what it is to queue for frozen bread and potatoes in the snow. Life is both nature and nurture, and they haven't yet been nurtured enough to change."

"Your authority as an anthropologist beguiles me."

Mereweather stared at him, then looked at Ramsay. "Check on legal and surveillance. We need to get this wrapped up."

Ramsay nodded, took out his phone and walked over to the window. He spoke quietly, while Campbell craned his neck and strained his ears to hear.

"What's he doing?"

Mereweather sighed. "You work for us now. You can protest, as is your legal right, but let's face it, you and your family will be dragged through hell and back. Red banner newspapers don't like traitors. And wait until the Daily Mail gets hold of you. They're still touting conspiracy theories with Diana and the tunnel, so God help the man with the Prime Minister's ear when they are given the data trail leading back to Russia..." Mereweather examined his finger-nail as he added, "Your accounts will be frozen, and your assets will be put on hold. The world and his dog will know every part of your private life and, let's be honest, the Government won't survive this."

"Those are the breaks," Campbell said arrogantly.

"They are. However, your Russian backers may also have something to say about it. You're an investment that clearly won't have paid off. They aren't renowned for rewarding incompetence and disloyalty." Mereweather paused. "And they will be worried about what you tell us. Expect some Novichok on your doorhandle at the very least. That's a gift the whole family could end up receiving by mistake."

"Alright, alright!" Campbell looked truly flustered for the first time. He was visibly shaken and had once again started to perspire. "What do you want me to do?"

"They're on the way up," said Ramsay. "Another team is at Carlton Gardens on the pretext of a security threat analysis."

"What?!" Campbell seethed, standing up suddenly and knocking his chair back. He launched across the room, but both Mereweather and Ramsay remained where they were.

"I have two men out there who will have you back in here with or without your front teeth, Campbell. The choice is yours." Mereweather watched the man hesitate, his hand hovering over the doorhandle. "Another step and it's Special Branch, anti-terror laws, lawyers, the press, bankruptcy and most likely divorce. Nobody would blame your wife for leaving a traitor. You'll spend years getting custody, too. But I imagine the children will be grown by the time you see your freedom again. If you ever do."

"And then there's the contract," said Ramsay. "That's the tipping point. You hired a killer. What was it, a test?"

Campbell looked like he was going to crumple. "I..."

"The target is still alive, Campbell. However, they have killed seven innocent people. That rather changes everything if you walk through that door. Hiring an assassin who kills, carries the same sentence as if you had pulled the trigger yourself."

"You can make this go away?"

"Only if we catch the assassin. Otherwise, no dice," said Mereweather. "I'm not condoning what you have done, but if we get the killer then we can get things back on an even keel."

"I didn't know he was going to go *Apocalypse Now* on this," Campbell said meekly as he practically staggered back to his chair. He sat down heavily, not even bothering to drag it back to his desk. He looked feeble and weak and defeated. "I was given an email account to sign into. The dealings with the assassin were made through a draft folder, meaning..."

"Meaning nobody could intercept the email." Ramsay said quietly.

"But somebody must have found something," Campbell mused. "Otherwise, you wouldn't be here."

Mereweather thought about Newman giving them the transcripts of an email that the CIA had intercepted. Not a mistake by the assassin, but by his Russian mafia contact to the FSB officer that the CIA were keeping under electronic surveillance. Links in the chain. Goodwill by the CIA. Mereweather didn't think so. In fact, he knew that this had never been the case at all.

There was a knock at the door, but it opened instantly, and three serious-looking people all wearing dark grey suits walked in. Two men and a woman. Not big on humour by the looks of them, although they probably shared MS-DOS puns on their coffee break. Without waiting for instruction, they took Campbell's laptop off the desk and plugged in a cable to another laptop. The woman plugged an electronic box into the router and the man started taking one of the three telephones apart on Campbell's desk. Mereweather ushered a bemused Campbell to a cluster of low chairs surrounding a glass coffee table near the window.

"There's no element of your life that we will not look into," said Mereweather matter-of-factly as he sat down. "So, what you tell us now will help you, rather than hinder you later."

Campbell shrugged. "What do I do? Do I still go to work, the COBRA meetings?" He shook his head. "I don't get how this works, or what the terms are."

"To be fair, our terms are all there is. You serve us, and you pass on the information we deem suitable. We control the narrative now. You are in the unenviable position of having the FSB on one side, the CIA on the other and us in the middle."

Campbell frowned. "The CIA?"

Ramsay placed his own laptop on the coffee table and opened a folder. He moved the device so that Campbell could see. "You went to Yale," he said. "Is that where they recruited you?"

"We've already traced payments to your account," Mereweather added. "Or rather, your wife's account. I imagine you've convinced her that it's some form of tax write-off from a numbered and nameless account. Unless, of course, a former party-planner turned PR consultant with a rather bland further education, a two-two – a Desmond, no less! - from the University of Leicester, is in the employ of the Central Intelligence Agency. But I rather think not."

Campbell stared at the screen. He did not know the man in the video clip, but he entered the garden confidently, although as he watched, he could see that the man was using his peripheral vision to survey the entire area. He took a moment, checked the entrance to the gated garden, then sat on the park bench and took something out from his pocket and slipped it underneath the bench. Upon closer inspection, the MI5 watcher team had reported that a ledge had been constructed from wooden slats and held in place by screws. When the man had planted the envelope, he got up, casually checking his mobile phone as he made his way out of the garden.

Campbell waited silently for Ramsay to open the next mpeg, but he already knew what he was going to see. Like when most people saw themselves on TV or on a CCTV monitor, Campbell didn't seem convinced at first that the man in the footage was indeed himself. But it was. The security detail hovered in the gateway to the garden, chatting and scrolling on their phones to check for messages or updates now that they had stopped running. Campbell had it down. He looked well-practised. He had the envelope out from under the seat and inside his tracksuit top in a swift motion between stretches. It was far from his first time.

FORTY-TWO

**Latitude: 56.944974 Longitude: 6.785829
Midway between Norway and Denmark
24,000 feet**

HE WAS DOWN to mere minutes with his own oxygen
supply. The chain of explosive charges had held, and this
time King positioned himself so that his body sheltered the
doorframe and charges from the slipstream. The adhesive
pads were difficult to feel in his gloved hands, but he did not
risk peeling off his gloves to aid his grip as the windchill
factor was close to - 20°c.

Finally, with all eight charges in place, he used the
suction cups to climb back onto the top of the fuselage and
set about connecting the control device to the end of the
det-cord.

"Charges set!" King rasped. "Give me ten feet of slack!"
He paused, watching the rope spool out and whip wildly in
the C-130's propellor wash. "And get ready to give me
another twenty feet of slack the moment I breach the door!"

he shouted but was barely able to hear his own voice above the wind and noise of the two aircraft.

King flipped the switch, then twisted it a half turn clockwise. The detonation was clearly audible, and he moved instantly, pulling himself hand over hand to the edge and kicked his feet over. He had barely started to slide, when his legs caught in the new slipstream, and he was sucked clean in through the door hatch. He landed heavily and coiled a handful of rope. It was imperative that he unclipped and secured the line before the pilot made any adjustments to the altitude or attitude of the aircraft. He found the ring on the starboard side of the plane, which was used along with multiple others for securing freight with webbing straps.

"Give me another ten feet of rope!" he shouted. He fought with the air channelling in through the door hatch, and the movement of the rope which was whipping wildly in the wind. When he clipped on, he shouted, "Secured! Send the first man, then Flymo!"

King headed for the door, but before he got there one of the crew was already there to meet him, one hand on the doorhandle, the other steadying himself on the frame. The plan had been to secure all the crew, but if the man closed and locked the door, they would be finished. An emergency communication would be made, and the operation would not only be over, but there would be no way out of an international incident. Russian submarines attacked the trans-Atlantic fibre-optic cables daily. Russia gathered its military on Ukraine's border for the world to speculate until one day, they simply invaded. But if King and his team were to be discovered hijacking a Russian aircraft, then all bets were off. There would be no recovery from this, and King knew it. He drew the silenced Ruger from his shoulder holster and held it steady on the man's forehead.

"Niet..." King said, his eyes not leaving the other man's own. To back this up, he shook his head. But there was something in the other man's expression. "Don't..." King warned him.

The man made his move and put all his force into closing the door but had underestimated his position. As he tried to move his body out of the way, King fired and the man slumped to the floor with a small hole between his eyes and a lazy trickle of blood running down his face, the shocked expression still in place, like a snapshot of both realisation and regret.

King stepped over the body and into a small anteroom with an empty seat and a bank of radar and monitors with a doorless hatch leading into the cockpit. He pressed on and jammed the hot suppressor into the pilot's neck. "Ne dvigaysya!" he said, warning the pilot not to move. "Ne menyay kurs!" It was crucial that the pilot did not alter their course with Stan and Flymo taking the zipline route to the aircraft. King glanced at the co-pilot, but the man was already unfastening the flap on what looked like a World War Two issue holster. King moved the pistol, but the pilot started to move, and the aircraft veered to port. "Ne menyay kurs! Do not change course!" King caught sight of the Hercules dropping in height over the pilot's shoulder and two hundred metres of loose rope billowing in the air with a man hanging helplessly midway between the two aircraft. He pistol-whipped the pilot and the man slumped back in his seat, his harness hanging loose. King jammed the suppressor into the co-pilot's chest, but the man had the Makarov in his hand and King cursed loudly as he fired four shots into the co-pilot, the man convulsing with every shot until the fourth when he slumped and dropped the pistol between his feet where it clattered between the pedals.

King put the hot suppressor back against the pilot's neck and grit his teeth as he ripped the pilot's mic and headphones off his head and tossed them onto the floor of the cockpit. "Ne menyay kurs..." he said coldly, telling him not to change course. The pilot did as he was told and corrected the attitude of the aircraft, its altitude barely affected. It was only then that King could hear the shouting in his earpiece. "We're stable here now," he said matter-of-factly. "Adjust your position and send the rest of the men across..." He stared directly at the pilot; the barrel pressed deep into the man's flesh. "Do you speak English?" The man nodded hesitantly. "We have spare parachutes," King said. "We're borrowing your plane. The plan was to set all three of you out over land when we reached our objective, you stubborn bastards..."

The man sneered at King, then stared directly ahead, his hands firmly on the controls. "They were brave Russian men. Proud to serve their country," he said quietly.

"Fucking idiots!" Peters said, barging past King and tearing at the pilot's harness. "He nearly fucking killed Stan!"

MacPherson bundled Flymo into the cockpit, nudging King off balance and onto the dead co-pilot. "Get that twat out of there and get behind the bloody controls!"

King glared at Macpherson as he regained his balance. "Alright, pal. You had the fucking easy bit..."

Peters half dragged, half lifted the protesting pilot out of his seat as Flymo steadied the yoke and slipped into position. He bundled him into MacPherson, who frog-marched him to the back of the plane. King waited while Flymo steadied the aircraft and took out his laminated cards which labelled the controls. The Russian Cyrillic accompanying every control was unreadable to King, despite him having conversational skills in the Russian language.

"Are you okay up here?" King asked.

"Fine. I've got throttles, yoke and pedals. Plenty of fuel and I'll do the rest with compass headings and my pocket GPS," Flymo replied. "Oh, but you can get rid of that guy," he said, nodding towards the body of the co-pilot. "He's creeping me out."

"I'll send two blokes up here to take him away," said King as he patted him on the back and made his way back to the cargo bay. When he got there the Russian pilot was lying dead on the floor. Rashid was unclipping Zukovsky's harness and King did a quick headcount. All men accounted for. "What happened to him?" King asked, pointing to the dead Russian pilot.

"He went for Stan's weapon," MacPherson said without paying King much attention. "So, I slotted him. Is that okay with you, or were you coming back here to have a cosy chat with him?" He paused. "Not to worry, your other Russian friend is here now."

King unfastened his harness and tossed it at MacPherson's feet. "Get your men to remove the co-pilot's body." He turned to Rashid and nodded for him to follow him further up the cargo bay. "Did you see that?"

Rashid shook his head. "No. The guy was dead when I got here. I was last man over, followed Zukovsky down the line."

King nodded. "Who got the wild ride?"

"MacPherson," Rashid replied. "It looked touch and go for a moment. The thing is, you were attached, but if the rope snapped or came loose, he would have just unthreaded and ended up in the North Sea, twenty-odd-thousand feet below." He paused. "The RAF pilot was close to ordering the rope to be cut. He thought the Russians were going to bring us down with that rope still attached."

King nodded. "So, MacPherson would have been terrified. Moments later, the Russian pilot is dead," he mused. "I don't like this one bit."

Rashid shook his head. "I doubt it was out of spite. He's a long-serving member of the regiment, and a major at that."

"We had a plan for the pilots. The parachutes."

"Where are the rest of the crew?"

"Dead," replied King. "It didn't go well."

"So, let me get this straight... you killed two, and MacPherson killed one, and now you're suspicious of MacPherson?" King nodded and Rashid shrugged. "Sounds like shit happens to me."

King looked over Rashid's shoulder at the Major, who was staring right back at him. "I suppose so." He paused. "But I don't like coincidences..."

FORTY-THREE

"How often do they make contact?" Mereweather asked.

Campbell sighed. "Not often."

"You're going to have to do better than that," Ramsay said scornfully.

"First Tuesday of the month and then the third Thursday," Campbell replied.

"And that's it?" Ramsay asked. "No phone or electronic communication?"

"No."

"And your reply?"

"The next day."

"Do you see your handler?"

Campbell shrugged. "I used to look out for them, but I never saw them and soon gave up trying."

"And do you ever meet anyone?" Mereweather interjected.

"It has happened. But not often." Campbell paused. "About four times over fifteen-years. A different person each time."

"Fifteen-years..." Mereweather commented somewhat despondently.

"They paid me for five years without asking anything of me."

"They were watching your career path. So, how did they make first contact?"

"At a lecture in Yale. I got talking to someone and we had the same political beliefs. Or so I thought."

"You were a willing recruit?" Mereweather asked.

Campbell shrugged. "I thought it would come in handy."

"Come in handy?" Ramsay asked incredulously. "A handkerchief comes in handy. A bank account you don't touch comes in handy."

"I thought it was an opportunity," Campbell replied defensively. "But I eventually forgot about it. They contacted me again when I became an MP. I had just won my seat and suddenly a man was seated opposite me in my surgery and showing me photographs of things."

"Things?"

"I did a few lines of coke from time to time. There were some photographs. And some, er, lingerie..."

"Lingerie?" Ramsay queried.

Campbell shrugged. "On me," he replied, looking at Ramsay's expression. "Yes, I was bloody well wearing it! And no, I'm not a pervert or gay or a cross-dresser! It was just a bit of a rowdy party, but dressed in Victoria's Secret stockings and suspenders and snorting lines of cocaine off a whore's shaved fanny wasn't going to do my new career much good on three consecutive pages of The Sun." He paused, shaking his head. "Just student stuff, but enough to scupper me and before I knew it, the money was coming in and I was told that contact arrangements would be made shortly."

"Politics is a dirty game. Not because of the business of politics, but because of whom it attracts." Mereweather mused. "Power, responsibility, and for some, the promise of impunity."

"Who said that? Oscar Wilde?" Campbell asked cynically.

"No. I did. Just now," Mereweather replied stoically. "So, the question is: For whom are you working. The CIA or the FSB?" He paused wistfully. "Or both?"

FORTY-FOUR

Latitude: 59.524964 Longitude: 22.961656
12,500 feet above the Baltic Sea

THE HERCULES HAD SHARPLY ALTERED its course
and was heading back to RAF Brize Norton before they had
reached the jagged coast of Northern Denmark. Flymo had
used the regular flightpath of Boris the Bear's route between
Denmark and Sweden into the Baltic Sea, but had shaved
ten-thousand feet off their altitude to allow for the open
door-hatch and enable the men to come off their depleting
oxygen supply. They had been intercepted by a Swedish
Airforce Saab JAS 39 Gripen fighter jet that had escorted
them through Swedish airspace, but Flymo had ignored the
pilot's interaction, radio contact and brief, yet tense missile
lock-on just as the Russians did thrice weekly with the
RAF. The Gripen pilot broke away once they had cleared
Swedish airspace and they continued on their course
through the middle of the Baltic Sea. The Swedish pilot
would have seen the hatch where the missing door should

be and the change in altitude would account for this. All they could do now was hope that the Swedes did not reach out to the Russian government, and that they could get to their objective before half the Russian Airforce intercepted them.

The harnesses had been piled next to the three Russian bodies and the men were all checking their parachutes and weapons. They would not make the jump with loaded rifles or carbines so each man had removed the magazine of their weapon and the chambered round. The 'longs' as they referred to their rifles, were fastened securely to their bodies with Velcro straps. The same helmets and goggles used for the zipline transfer between aircraft were all fastened, and the men wore the goggles on top of their helmets, just waiting for the word to go and pull them down over their eyes before they jumped.

King sat with Rashid and Zukovsky across from the other men. The wind buffeted the cargo bay and Stan had lowered the rear ramp a few feet to allow the wind to blow clear through and eliminate drag. MacPherson, Chubs and Peters sat in a three with Stan and the other four troopers nearest the ramp. King and MacPherson hadn't spoken since the killing of the pilot, and there was a marked air of tension within the group.

"This is a foolhardy operation," said Zukovsky. "The Republic of Karelia will be frozen, troops will be near to the hacker's base and even if you succeed, then what? Escape into the Finnish part of Karelia with their colourfully painted houses and the men and women dressed like dolls? They are trapped in the past, like in a fairy tale story. You will stick out like, how you say?"

"A bulldog's bollocks?" King offered.

"No, like the sore thumb," Zukovsky thought for a

moment, then smiled. "Yes, like the balls of a bulldog..." He paused, enjoying the description. "Even then, you will have to get into Finland and there is a hard border. The fence will be smaller, and the guards will be scattered, but they will know if you try to climb it."

"Let me worry about that."

Zukovsky shrugged. "You and the commander do not get on?"

King looked up at MacPherson, then back at the Russian. "We had a disagreement."

"I heard. So, you killed two of my countrymen, but you have a problem with him killing one?"

King shook his head. "Forget it."

"I am interested, that is all. Why does the death of one man mean more than the others?"

"It doesn't," King replied tersely. "We were meant to subdue the crew and drop them by parachute."

"But you killed two of them."

King shrugged. "They did not give me a choice. Unfortunately."

"And this man of the SAS, he just killed the pilot?"

"I believe so."

"This is bad," Zukovsky mused. "But good for me, no?"

"How so?"

"You will be less inclined to shoot me once you get what you want." Zukovsky smiled. "Or perhaps, even let me go."

"I could happily kill you."

"I'm not so sure. You killed my son, and you disrupted my plans. You are the one who has remained on top. And what else can I possibly give you? You are keeping me with you for insurance. Or assurance. But either way, what further use can a man of my age be to you? My government will want me dead. So, I said that the President would appreciate my ideals, but let's face it, his days are numbered. And I have told you about Russian assets in your government, of assassins that both the FSB and Bratva use, of a hacking program implemented under my time with the KGB and FSB. So, there's no going back to Russia for me." He paused, rubbing some life into his gloved, but freezing hands. "I'm of no further use to you, but at least I know that you are fundamentally a moral man. A man less inclined to kill me unless I am a threat to you, and more inclined to stick to your word."

FORTY-FIVE

Whitehall, London

"I DON'T KNOW who that is."

"You've never met?"

Campbell shook his head. "No. Why should I know him?"

"He left you the message that you collected in the gated community garden at Carlton Gardens," Mereweather said, looking at the paused video and clear image of the man he knew as Newman.

"No. I've never seen him before," Campbell replied adamantly.

"What did he give you?"

Campbell hesitated. He looked Mereweather in the eyes and said, "Information to give to my Russian contact. I was supposed to say that I came across it at the NATO alliance conference in Canada in the New Year."

Mereweather frowned. "And do your Russian handlers give you information to pass back?"

"No."

"Then why?"

Campbell shrugged. "A sense of duty, I suppose." Ramsay scoffed, then turned his eyes back to the laptop as Campbell continued. "I pass disinformation to the Russians from the Americans, and I clear the path in Britain for Russian investment. It's just commerce in the free world. I have never told the Russians anything that can hurt Britain's defences," he said rather pompously. "But that isn't to say that they haven't asked. In fact, they have been making gilded-edged threats of late."

"The Russians do not make gilded-edged threats," Mereweather said pointedly. "They ask for whatever they want and eventually, if you fail to deliver, they send someone to rape your daughter or cut your wife's wrists in the bath. You may well deal with Russian intelligence, but you'll be met with enforcers of the Russian mafia, and they don't mess about. If you've had the slightest threat, gilded-edged or not, then now is the time to tell us and get on board. You no longer work for the Americans and the Russians. You work for me, and you will pass on what I want you to, and you will show me everything they give you. If you're lucky, you'll get out of this with your family alive and intact. You'll never be truly free, because trust me, any successor to my position will be made aware of what you have done. But there is a glimmer of freedom and relative normality on your horizon."

"And if I refuse?"

"It really isn't an option, is it?" Mereweather replied condescendingly. "We've already gone over special branch and anti-terrorism officers invading every possible part of your life, as well as that of your family's. Then there is your career, the tabloids, the inevitable charges that I'll make damned certain are brought against you, and your inevitable incarceration at Her Majesty's pleasure. And don't think you'll be able to pull a Jeffrey Archer and write memoirs of your prison days, either. He wasn't imprisoned for Terrorism, and he's also a damned sight more talented and personable than you." Mereweather paused. "Of course, then there's the Russians. They don't like being taken for a ride. The CIA aren't the good guys, either. If somebody doesn't kill you in prison, you'll soon be assassinated upon your release."

"So, you say so..."

Mereweather sighed. "Very well. I can't say I'm surprised. It takes tremendous self-belief to become a politician. And then to make it into parliament. I think at that point, the self-belief is pure arrogance. And when an MP makes it into cabinet, that's when the arrogance truly sticks. So, why wouldn't you think that you're beyond reproach, that you can paint a different picture and right an alternative narrative?" Mereweather closed the lid of the laptop and stood up. "The ball isn't in your court, old boy. It's in ours. We can only do it with your cooperation, but if we don't have that, then we must act in our country's best interests." He looked at Ramsay and said, "Freeze the man's assets, inform special branch and release our statement to the press and Sky News. *Foreign Secretary Edward Campbell has been found passing official secrets to Russia and has been in the employ of the CIA for fifteen years after being recruited whilst he studied for his Master's at Yale. The suspected double agent will be arrested at his Whitehall office within the hour...* I will call the Prime Minister and put him in the picture before we go live with our statement. Of course, given the close and historical relationship between the *Bullingdon Four*, then I think it will not only be expected, but necessary to bring in the Prime Minister and the rest of the cabinet for questioning and a deep-dive investigation into their personal and financial affairs."

"Wait! Just fucking well wait!" Campbell rested his head in his hands and sighed. When he looked up, he had tears in his eyes. "Alright. I'll cooperate..."

FORTY-SIX

London

SHE HAD TREATED her wounds as best she could, but now that she had returned to the house they had rented through an intermediary in Surbiton, Reno had gone out to fetch all he would need and set about treating her injuries. Co-codamol and Ibuprofen for the pain relief and swelling and hydrogen peroxide, tweezers and gauze and micropore tape to clean, remove debris and dress the wounds. When he returned, Natasha had taken two of the co-codamol with a large vodka before lying down on the bed in the spare room, striped to her underwear while he had doused the pock-marked shot pattern with hydrogen peroxide, and she had done her best not to scream. The pocks of broken skin fizzed and bubbled white and Reno had sterilised the tweezers with the peroxide before going in to remove the shot. He dropped each piece of lead in a bowl beside the bed, offering no consolation or sympathy to his protégé as she grimaced and tried her best to control her breathing like he had taught her, to meditate and ignore the pain, to draw upon it and focus into channelling it as nothing more than weakness leaving the body. For the best part, she achieved this, but annoyed with her double failure and silently cursing her for putting their operation at risk, he occasionally dug the tines of the tweezers a little deeper than was necessary, as if to sadistically teach her a lesson. Just like he had fought with her full contact when he had taught her ju-jitsu, karate and kick boxing, and later the krav maga fighting system. Full contact taught the desire to block and dodge and parry. Full contact taught you to take punishment and what happened when you were too slow to react. You could only win fights consistently if you knew what it was to be beaten.

"Take me through it again," said Reno.

"When?"

"The Darby woman's parents."

Natasha winced as a particularly stubborn pellet was gouged out. The skin had already started to heel, and the peroxide had softened it, the tweezers breaking the scarring as Reno dug out each pellet. "He arrived as I made my move, but he had a gun with him. He had been shooting pheasants."

"But he would not have carried a loaded shotgun. This is England. Pheasant shoots frown upon pump-action or automatic shotguns. They use traditional double-barrelled shotguns." He paused, dropping a piece of lead shot into the bowl with a clatter. "Nobody would walk with one loaded."

"It's hazy now," she said defensively.

"And the car. How did a shotgun stop the car? Shot would never have enough velocity or power to halt an engine. Not after penetrating the bodywork."

"It was a rifle," she replied. "I heard a terrific boom and

the seat next to me exploded and the airbag deployed, and the car juddered to a halt."

"So, you were fleeing the scene?"

"I had been shot!" She protested. "I was allowing myself time to regroup."

"One person, by its very definition, cannot regroup."

"To gather myself together, then! I needed to address the change, pull back for another attack."

Reno dug the tweezers a little deeper and hooked out a lead pellet. Natasha sucked in her breath, almost screaming. The pellet rolled off her abdomen and onto the wooden floor. "An old man with a shotgun got the better of you." He shook his head despondently. "And so, the man was injured. Which leaves two questions; where did this woman get the rifle? And how did you allow her time to take the shot?"

Natasha shook her head, but she did not reply. Instead, she tried to sit up, but Reno pushed her back down on the bed.

"We will finish this."

"So that you can punish me?!" she snapped. "I know what you are doing. I know that you could get this damned lead out of me less painfully!"

"Penance, my dear." He dug the tweezers in again and pulled out another piece of shot. "We all have to bear penance at least once in our lives. That way, we learn."

Natasha said nothing. She looked up into his eyes, then as always, she glanced away. Inwardly she cursed at not asking the question. She had wanted to for so long, but she guessed she already knew. But sometimes it was better not to upset the status quo. Why else would a man, an assassin no less, care for a stranger? A girl on the streets who was circling the drain of a life that could only lead to drink and drug abuse and prostitution. Reno had sent her to a Swiss boarding school, set up a trust fund and paid into it each month. Why else would he do that, other than for penance? She could barely remember what her parents had looked like. She possessed no photographs and could only now see the blood and macabre images of her parents bodies when she closed her eyes, not the happy times she knew they had together, but could no longer picture. Only the blood-soaked bedroom and mutilated, lifeless bodies remained in her mind's eye. She knew that Reno had robbed her of them, but she could never ask. If she did, then she knew he would kill her. And if she did not, then she would never truly be sure. Not being sure was as good as she could hope for, for now. Reno may have said penance, but she lived in purgatory.

"Something you want to say, dear?"

Natasha stared at the wall as she felt her body penetrated once more. She said nothing. The tweezers entering her wounds may just as well as been him penetrating her sexually. There was a lesson being taught, a sadistic dominance that she could only liken to rape. Plucking the shot from her should have been a healing process, yet each time the tweezers entered her body, she felt nothing but violation. She closed her eyes. Just like when she had been raped at just thirteen in a Paris back street, it would soon be over. That was the best that she could hope for.

FORTY-SEVEN

30,000 feet over the Republic of Karelia

THEY WERE all using the aircraft's oxygen supply and Flymo had climbed to thirty-thousand feet so that they could use the HALO technique – HIGH ALTITUDE, LOW OPENING – in order to attract as little attention as possible. Normal recreational freefalling generally took place at around twelve thousand feet with the canopy opening at three-thousand feet. The HALO technique used oxygen assisted altitudes with canopy opening at around eight hundred feet, although today, the team were going for five hundred. It was a half-hour from dusk and the plane would be unseen from the ground, with the parachute canopies open for just twenty-two seconds before landing.

Flymo had left the controls. He had set the automatic pilot so that the airplane flew directly towards its base at Archangel. He had estimated that it would overshoot and ditch somewhere beyond the Northern Sea Route. With any luck, the plane would not be found, and the fate of the crew left undiscovered. The Northern Sea Route, though proof of global warming if ever it were needed, was still a treacherous sea passage filled with icebergs, sheets of solid ice and a steady stream of tankers and cargo vessels year-round. The recovery of an aircraft would be a specialist operation, and despite Russia's power on the world stage, far beyond its skillset. Given that they had refused international help when the Kursk submarine became a ticking-tomb for its crew, it was safe to say they would fair no better in locating and raising an airplane with zero chance of survivors.

The nuclear-powered submarine the Kursk sank in an accident in August 2000 in the Barents Sea during the first significant Russian naval exercise in more than ten years, and all 118 personnel on board were killed. The crews of nearby ships felt the initial explosion and a second, much larger, explosion, but the Russian Navy did not realise that an accident had occurred and did not initiate a search for the sub for more than six hours. Because the submarine's emergency rescue buoy had been intentionally disabled during an earlier mission, it took more than sixteen hours to locate the sunken boat.

Over four days, the Russian Navy repeatedly failed in its attempts to attach four different diving bells and submersibles to the escape hatch of the submarine. Russia's response was criticised as slow and inept. Officials misled and manipulated the public and news media and refused help from other countries' ships nearby. The Russian President initially continued his vacation at a seaside resort; and eventually authorised the Russian Navy to accept British and Norwegian offers of assistance after five days had passed since the accident. Seven days after the sinking, British and Norwegian divers finally opened a hatch to

the escape hatch in the submarine's flooded ninth compart-
ment but found no survivors. The Russian Government and
its Navy were intensely criticised over the incident and
their responses. Some political commentators voiced that
Russia only accepted help after they had waited for the
crew to die in order to deny the other countries a victory
and thus feel no obligation for saving Russian lives.

"I've never jumped before," said Flymo.

King frowned. "Don't pilots learn how to parachute?"

Flymo shrugged. "I guess they want us to stay in the
aircraft. Passengers tend to be happier that way."

Stan made his way over and checked the altimeter on
Flymo's chute. "Don't worry, mate. It's set for four-hundred
feet. Just breathe and pull the toggle when we do. If you
don't, then the chute will open all on its own at four-
hundred." He paused. "Pull hard on the controls and land
with your feet together and knees bent, just like we prac-
tised in the hangar at Brize Norton." He paused. "Oh, and if
you see ours open, for Christ's sake give your toggle a pull
because it means the system's failed, and you'll have less
than two seconds to open manually."

"Oh, for fuck's sake..." Flymo said shakily.

King patted him on the back. "It'll be OK," he said.

"And if it's not, then we have a pretty slow complaints
department, anyway," he grinned and went back to the rest
of the men, where kit checks were being finalised.

"Great," said Flymo. "We all need a fucking comedian
today..." He checked his GPS and said, "Three minutes
until we're over the drop-zone."

King nodded and took his oxygen off the aircraft's and
onto his own replenished bottle, before making his way over
to where MacPherson was standing with Chubs and Peters.
He was buffeted by the wind blowing through the cargo bay

but regained his balance as he reached the three men. "Ready your men," he said. "We'll be over the drop-zone in..."

"Three minutes, we know," MacPherson casually interrupted, then added, "Is your pilot unwell? He looks like he needs a Valium."

King ignored him and walked back across the cargo bay, ready for the rush of air this time. He held out a hand for Zukovsky to help him to his feet. The Russian looked apprehensive, but he got lightly to his feet and checked his altimeter. King looked at it and nodded. "Pull the toggle when you get to five-hundred feet. The safety system will go off at four-hundred, but that will feel pretty bloody close, trust me."

"I can think of no reason to trust you."

"You have my word."

"And that's enough?"

"Help me, and I'll help you."

"And this device will set off my parachute?"

"It will work. It's British engineering, not Russian."

"One minute!" Stan called out. "Switch to personal oxygen supply!" He switched over to his own, then started ushering the men to the ramp, where he opened it fully with a large red button. "On me! On me! On me!"

"We'll go last," King said to Flymo and Zukovsky. "Let the super army soldiers get their kicks in first. Besides, if they all slam into the ground, then we'll know when to pull our chutes."

"Thirty seconds! Stand-by, stand-by," Stan paused, checking his watch and GPS. He then held up his right hand. Every man watched him, transfixed. Then he dropped his hand and shouted, "Go! Go! Go!"

The men filed off the ramp and into the abyss. King

pushed Zukovsky, felt some resistance, then gave him a shove and ran off the ramp with him. Flymo was given the same treatment by Rashid, and they dropped out into the void with Flymo screaming his lungs out.

King corrected Zukovsky's position and looked out for Rashid and Flymo above him. Flymo did not have the experience to accelerate his terminal velocity, and King did not want to try with Zukovsky, but the SAS were experts in this field and had streamlined their descent by dipping their heads and placing their hands on their buttocks, increasing from a steady terminal velocity of 120 mph to in excess of 150 mph. They used this technique to track across the sky and get well clear of King and Zukovsky falling above them. The men then formed a pattern which meant that when they finally broke away and pulled their chutes, they would likely land a full minute before King and Zukovsky, and Rashid and Flymo would touch down twenty-seconds behind them. That suited King. It gave him a chance to see the lay of the land and if the SAS boys met any resistance on the ground, then at least King and Zukovsky would land under some protection.

Their descent would take just two and a half minutes, but it was the longest two and a half minutes of King's life. Somewhere above him, Flymo had stopped screaming, but he was holding a good position and Rashid had guided them both away from King and Zukovsky's path. King checked his altimeter and he signalled for Zukovsky to do the same. He veered away from the Russian to find a good position, without his parachute hitting Rashid and Flymo above. He could see that Zukovsky had jumped before, and it would have been a rare thing for a Russian soldier to make General without doing paratrooper training. At six-hundred feet King grabbed his toggle and pulled exactly on five hundred.

The jerk of the chute was immense as it decelerated his fall to just 17 mph, pulling a full 4 Gs of force. Everywhere King looked, open canopies fanned out and twenty-seconds later, the ground was upon him as he heaved on the hand toggles to slow his descent further and watched as Flymo came past him, not getting to grips with the braking system. They had covered the basics in the hangar at RAF Brize Norton, but a 30,000 feet HALO jump was never going to be the best Segway into free-falling.

King landed, his ankles taking the jolt but holding up well as he tucked and rolled. He saw most of the SAS troopers landing feet apart and crouching as they took off their harnesses and gathered up their parachutes, but this was their speciality and King hadn't made a jump since his days with MI6 when he flew from Turkey to Iraq to tidy up a botched mission, and even then, that hadn't gone to plan. He looked around him and saw that Zukovsky was gathering his parachute, but Flymo was on his back and being dragged by the wind right past two SAS troopers, who ignored him and readied their weapons. King ran and dived onto Flymo's legs, the parachute billowing in the wind. Crawling over him hand over hand, he got a hold of a handful of paracord and started to gather the parachute up as Flymo rolled onto his stomach and unbuckled his harness.

"That's the last time I ever do that," Flymo panted.

"Yeah, I say that every time I fly with you," King replied as he got to his feet and repacked the parachute. "Are you good?"

Flymo stood up, testing both his ankles. "A bit of strain, but it'll loosen up. It feels like my balls are where my heart should be."

"You'd better change your height on your *Tinder* profile

when we get back as well." King grinned, then handed Flymo the hastily stuffed parachute pack and headed back to Rashid and Zukovsky. The two men were crouched low to a fallen tree, their packs pushed underneath where Rashid was putting the finishing touches to hiding them with sticks and slimy fallen leaves. King tossed his parachute pack to MacPherson, who was standing beside a hole two of the men had excavated and were stashing their packs in. He took Flymo's pack and tossed it to the SAS Major as he bent to pick up King's pack. He didn't acknowledge the man as he readied his own rifle.

Rashid checked his Accuracy International .300 Winchester Magnum rifle, paying particular attention to the 3.9x56mm scope. It all seemed to be straight and true, and he had landed well having previously spent two years with 'Air Troop' or what the SAS often referred to as the *Ice Cream Boys* because Air Troop spent most of their time where the skies were clear to train in all types of airborne entry techniques. Nevada and Cyprus being two popular training destinations for parachute and freefall training. Rashid was one of two designated snipers on this mission and both men carried the newer .300 Winchester Magnum instead of the long-serving .308, which was now outperformed by fifty percent. Rashid did not know what ammunition the other sniper had selected, but he had chosen 150gr soft-nosed bullets and 180gr armour-piercing rounds. He also had some tracer rounds that he could use for shot-placement confirmation, or even fuel cans if the opportunity presented itself.

King took in his surroundings as the other men readied themselves for the tab – or speed march to their objective. There was little colour. The trees were stark, and the grass was short and dry, rendered moribund by the cold Russian winter, but soon to be revived by spring, which was just weeks around the corner. The ground was hard and frozen, with patches of snow in the shadiest areas and at the bases of trees. There were snow-capped hills to the east and forest to the west. As planned, they had landed on target and were five miles from the nearest village and should be able to navigate a path passing no closer than two miles from one of seven villages in the region. King had studied the RAF and shared MI5/MI6 intelligence back at Brize Norton and had been surprised by how many of the houses had been painted in bright, vibrant primary colours and that many people sported clothes that made them look like they lived in a classic fairy tale book. There had been a strange vibe to the photographs he had observed, and it was clear that there had been a Finnish influence in what he had learned to be a shared province, with both Finnish Karelia and Russian Karelia on either side of a shared and disputed zone, that had surprisingly avoided military intervention, given Russia's desire to increase its borders by any means necessary.

The sun had just gone down over the distant forest and there was just a sliver of orange sky, with every shade of blue darkening to black over the mountains to the east. There were stars out already and in the short time since they had landed the temperature had dropped several degrees to just below freezing.

"We're tabbing out, get some scran on the move and make sure to hydrate," Stan said, but his orders fell on deaf ears as the men were already eating the biscuits from their ration packs and one man had even got a brew on in record time placing a chemical firelighter directly under a tin cup with water, sugar, powdered milk and instant coffee as he checked the rest of his kit and made ready for the arduous march to their LUP, or lying up place near their objective.

King took some mouthfuls of concentrated fruit squash and drank it down with plenty of water from his camel pack. He wasn't hungry and would have a sachet of beans and sausages when they reached their objective, although that close to the enemy it would be hard routine, which meant cold food, no hot brews and the unenviable task of defaecating in a plastic bag which every man would be expected to take with them in their bergens. Many operations relied on collecting intelligence and remaining undetected for days or weeks on end, and just like a successful burglary wasn't discovered until days after the break-in, a special forces soldier's objective was to complete a reconnaissance without anybody ever knowing that they had been there. And for the entire operation, which had only been planned as a swift in and out, they would leave no sign and no identifying equipment, apart from shell casings if a firefight was unavoidable, and the parachutes if they could not collect them on their return south towards the extraction point.

The pace was set, and it was predictably swift. Each man allowed approximately fifteen feet between himself and the man in front to avoid the entire group being taken down by machinegun fire. King walked behind Zukovsky. The man was in his seventies, and despite being imprisoned for the past few years, he managed to maintain a good pace. Obviously the only unarmed man, he carried little in the way of kit – just rations and water dispersed around his webbing in pockets. King not only checked ahead of Zukovsky when the terrain allowed, but to the sides and rear as well. There was no sense in just blindly following the Russian if the man had lost sight of the man in front of him, likewise he took it upon himself to check that he had not strung out too much lead on the man behind him.

King checked his watch. It was almost dark now, and progress would be slower. Each man was equipped with NVGs, or night vision goggles, but as long as there was a sliver of moon and a few stars between the sporadic clouds, King would refrain from using them, preferring to allow his eyes to adjust to the darkness and his surroundings. He estimated another hour before MacPherson called his men up for a rest and the chance to adjust their equipment, although King was checking his own GPS and route notes, and no doubt MacPherson was too because they were dead on track and time, which meant they were just hours from their LUP – lying up place - and the chance of some food and rest.

FORTY-EIGHT

Winchester

THERE WAS a killer still out there and as far as Caroline was concerned, she would not be able to live a normal existence - as normal as she could ever hope for – until that killer was dead or locked up. She pictured the woman with the flame red hair in her mind as she followed the police officer up the stairs and along the corridor to the ward where her father was waiting. She had been able to picture little else on the drive down from the Lake District. Her pale, almost porcelain skin, the mane of red hair untidily pulled back into a ponytail with tousles either side framing her face. The woman had moved quickly, shockingly so. And then there were her eyes. For reasons that escaped her, Caroline could not recall the colour, but she could see the intensity in them, and the vindictiveness when she had sliced Kate's throat. The action had been perfect in terms of technique. The knife had been a tactical folder with a clip point. The woman had driven the knife up to the hilt, three

inches or so, then swiped it with all her might until it had
pulled clear, but not before it had created a gash of three
inches deep and around the same in length, severing the
carotid artery. But it wasn't the look of intensity or vindictiveness in the woman's eyes that haunted Caroline, so
much as the look of glee as she faced off with her, knowing
that she had killed her aunt and that Caroline would be
next.

Caroline had sent the pictures to Neil Ramsay, and he
would have them run through all the databases they had –
hopefully there would be an identification soon. The sooner
they knew who she was, the sooner they could lean on the
police, foreign criminal and intelligence agencies and
Interpol.

The police officer showed Caroline to the nurse station,
where an armed police officer met her and walked her
through to a private room with another armed officer
standing post outside. Simon Mereweather had played the
national security card and both Gerald and Hilary Darby
were receiving round-the-clock protection. She imagined
her parents protesting and thought about how they had
raised her to be independent and never to make a fuss. She
never spoke about being bullied as a child or sexism and
misogyny when she joined the army, or chauvinism when
she first joined MI5. Even now, she treated her own cuts or
bruises, or taped up broken fingers when she had used poor
technique on the heavy bag or things had got out of hand
practising krav maga and ju-jitsu. The Darbys never made a
fuss, and now her father was in hospital and her mother
would no doubt be embarrassed that the whole affair had
led to this.

Caroline was let in by the second armed officer and she
peered somewhat tentatively around the edge of the door.

Her father was lying in bed with both legs underneath a blanket raiser. Just seeing her father in a state of vulnerability made her eyes well with tears, and she was crying as she rushed to the bed and hugged him closely.

"Oh, dad..." she managed, trying to choke back the tears.

"He's alright, my dear," her mother said from her chair beside him. Caroline hadn't noticed her; such was her focus on her father. She smiled at her mother, relieved that she was OK. "What happened?"

"You probably know by now, my dear," her mother answered. "I imagine you've been briefed." Caroline nodded, still hugging her father.

Her father pulled back, patting her on the back. "Your gun is digging into me," he said. "What is it? A Browning?"

She shook her head. "A little old fashioned nowadays, dad."

"Always did a pretty good job of it. A bit bulky carrying it in civvies in Northern Ireland, but I wouldn't have been without it in the Falklands." He paused, holding her so he could look into her eyes. "It's good to see you. Although, I have to admit, we both thought your work with the Security Service was a little less frontline. After Peter, that is..."

Caroline tensed, thinking about the day that had changed everything. Her first real love, former SAS officer Peter Redwood had been working with MI5 and after an operation to keep surveillance on a suspected suicide bomber had been deemed a success, a second suicide bomber had targeted civilians, police and paramedics at the scene. Peter Redwood had directly sheltered Caroline from the blast, and she had lost everything in a fraction of a second. Except for her life. Since that fateful day she had spent every day since trying to make a difference and to be worthy of his sacrifice. And she had not looked at another man until over a year and a half later, when she had met King.

"It's OK, dad," she replied solemnly. "And don't worry, my job is normally far safer," she lied.

"Is it even legal for you lot at Thames House to carry firearms?" Gerald asked. "Never was in my day, some of the spooks carried a pistol across the water, but an exception was made for the Troubles." He had never spoken to Caroline about his service, but she knew that he had done three tours of Northern Ireland with the Parachute Regiment during the worst of the Troubles, and she knew from her service with 14 Intelligence Company what was involved. Patrols in both an urban and rural environment served not only as a show of force, but to draw fire from terrorists, which in itself was a terrifying task to be given. Once they had been fired upon, then they return fire and finish the job.

"For the job I'm on, then yes," she replied. "But only because it's complicated." She paused. "So, what happened?"

"It was dreadful," Hilary answered before Gerald had the chance. "This woman, Russian or Slavic, she was questioning me about you, said she was from an insurance company, and then when Gerald arrived back from the shoot, she pulled a gun and started shooting. I got the door shut and heard your father shooting back at her, then I got your grandfather's safari rifle off the wall and shot at her as she drove away."

"Christ, I thought that was just an antique!" Caroline shook her head incredulously. "I never thought it could fire, and I certainly didn't think you had any bullets for the thing."

"Well, we did. I used them as paperweights in my study.

And your mother was bloody marvellous," Gerald said proudly. "Sent the bugger packing. Not like me, bloody old fool, took a bullet in the hip, but it's OK, only a bloody two-two and the short barrel and silencer slowed the bullet down considerably. Chipped some bone, ricocheted off and did a bit of butchery on the muscle. But they said I'll be out of here in a couple of days."

"Where have you been, darling?" Hilary asked wearily. "I know you don't like us to contact you because of work, but we would like to know where you are at least some of the time."

Caroline nodded, broke away from her father and squared up a chair, before sitting down heavily and letting out a sigh. "I needed to go off the radar..." She looked at her mother's face and realised that the woman had no idea about her world. Hilary Darby arranged flowers at church, cooked cakes and made jam for the Woman's Institute meetings, watched only period dramas and read only the classics. "I needed to hide out someplace and avoid people trying to find me. Only they did. And they hurt you to get to me. Would have done far worse if you hadn't sent her packing." She paused, tears welling up again. "I went to stay with Aunt Kate."

"Oh," Hilary replied awkwardly. "Well, no doubt she told you all about our falling out. Can't trust a bloody word she says, though."

"Hilary..." Gerald said, frowning. "I'm sure Kate didn't bad mouth you to Caro."

Caroline hadn't heard her name shortened in years, and the fact her father still thought of her as 'Little Caro' or 'Caro Duck' made her feel more than just a little nostalgic. She would have given anything to be a little girl right now. Protected, loved and sheltered from harm and the outside world. Her parents there to protect her unreservedly. She blinked away a tear. Those years were both short and, like everyone's past, beyond reach. "She's dead, mum. I'm sorry..." She sobbed, but managed to stave it off enough to continue, "That woman killed her, and tried to kill me, too..."

FORTY-NINE

Republic of Karelia

KING HAD CLOSED the gap and helped Zukovsky along for the last five miles. It made little difference to him because if somebody opened fire with a Kalashnikov, he wasn't overly concerned for the Russian's safety, but he needed to maintain pace and be sure that the man made it in once piece. Zukovsky was simply a commodity.

Flymo walked behind King, armed with just a pistol which remained holstered. Although he had undertaken basic training upon joining the army, he was a pilot and had never dusted off his infantry skills since. Rashid followed, the sniper rifle slung over his shoulder and holding his HK416. Behind him, Stan had taken over the rear, where he periodically paused and watched the ground behind them, then double-timed back to the line. He was armed with an FN Minimi, which gave them a ferocious rate of fire and the chance for the rest of them to bug out if necessary. The weapon was known as a SAW, or squad automatic weapon, and was both lightweight and manoeuvrable and fed standard NATO 5.56mm ammunition from either a two-hundred round belt housed in a detachable box, or by standard NATO STANAG magazines that were used in the other men's weapons.

King checked his GPS again, but the line had stopped and started to bunch. He pulled Zukovsky half a dozen strides to his left, pressed the man to the cold ground and crouched as he watched MacPherson work his way back down the line.

When he got to King, he said, "Patrol. Six men. Fairly alert."

"For a disused weather station?"

"My thoughts entirely." The Major paused. "Even something as important to the Russians as the Paradigm Shift program would need a degree of secrecy." He looked at Zukovsky, who merely shrugged. "These guys appear to be following a path, which would indicate that it's routine. Although it's pretty shit from an operational point of view."

"We need to check for biometrics, cameras and trembling devices," said Rashid, crouching down by King's shoulder.

"Easier said than done in the darkness. Besides, if they had that type of security then why the need for a six-man patrol?"

"It's likely that there are more patrols out there," said King. "And how technical do we expect the Russians to be? They'd use a wrecking ball to crack a nut. They may well have the intricacies to be able to hack into everything and anything, but they are hardly precise in military matters. Just look at Ukraine."

Rashid shrugged. King was his friend and neither man had any love for the SAS Major, but it was Chinese parliaments such as this that was the reason the British special forces and clandestine operation agents were at the top of their game. Nobody blindly followed orders down the rabbit hole that led to defeat or needless deaths.

"Looks suss to me," MacPherson said emphatically.

"You want me to go in first?" King asked.

"We're here because of intelligence gleaned from an enemy of the nation. I don't trust this Russian, so I'd rather not lead my men into a shitstorm on the whim of the Security Service and a man with an agenda."

King looked at the SAS Major, and then at the Russian. There wasn't much else for it. "Are you with me, Rashid?"

"You have to ask?"

King smiled. "Grab Flymo and meet me at the head of the line."

"Flymo?"

King shrugged. "He can babysit the Russian. Wouldn't want anything to happen to him while we're gone..."

Rashid nodded and jogged back to Flymo. King caught hold of Zukovsky and pulled him up to the head of the line where MacPherson was checking the GPS with his laminated map.

"We'll lay-up and wait for you to return," MacPherson announced. "The patrol troubles me. This isn't meant to be a military area and we have no intel regarding boots on the ground. Every swinging dick is needed in Ukraine."

King said nothing. He checked the side of his HK416, where he had fixed a luminous button compass and headed off into the night. He had only covered two-hundred metres when he caught the odour of foul-smelling cigarettes ahead of him. He crouched and held up his left hand to halt the others' progress. He could hear voices and laughter.

"Wait here," he said to Flymo. "If Zukovsky tries anything, put a bullet in him."

"Well, fuck you, too!" Zukovsky replied tersely. "So, you can't leave me back there for fear your own team will kill me, and then you drag me out here and order him to kill me if I try anything. I can't win..."

"Will do," Flymo said matter-of-factly, ignoring the Russian and taking out his Glock 9mm.

King nodded for Rashid to follow and broke right through scrub and frozen saplings that looked blackened and killed-off by the cold. He had been in the frozen Russian wilderness before, and into the Arctic Circle, and he knew that the trees would reanimate with growth in the spring and summer months, ready to take on a moribund appearance once more when winter returned. The ground was as hard as concrete and there was no avoiding the noise from his boots. Rashid followed at least fifty feet from him and further to his right. They made their way up a steep incline but avoided becoming silhouetted by the clear night sky by dropping down onto the ground before they reached the ridge and cautiously peered over the top.

Rashid placed his assault rifle on the ground and used his sniper rifle to survey the ground ahead through the infrared image intensifier fitted to the left-hand side of the scope. "OK," he said quietly. "I can see the patrol. Just grunts. Lazy and tactically shit. They're smoking and shooting the breeze. One of them has a bottle of something and by the way they're sharing it around, it's not water."

"There's something ahead," said King. "We're definitely on the coordinates where Zukovsky reckoned the hacking program was based. But this doesn't look right at all."

"That's because it's not."

"Meaning?"

"Here, have a look for yourself." Rashid handed him the rifle. "You see what I mean?"

"Oh, shit."

"Exactly right."

King swivelled the rifle around and watched as the patrol of six men headed back where they'd started from. He tracked right and back to the camp. "How did we miss this?"

"Look to the far right and left. There are massive pylons at all four corners. They have industrial amounts of camouflage netting strung between, like a roof."

"And that's stopped our best satellites from seeing this?"

"Forget GCHQ, if you want to see anywhere in the world right now, you just check the web. Especially after the billionaire tech giants made more satellites available after the invasion of Ukraine."

"And not one desk peeper saw this?" King asked, his eye still on the image intensifier. "It looks like they are getting ready to load."

"Fuel?"

King shrugged. "Looks that way. They're certainly the right barrels."

"But why all the way out here? Russia has enough fuel for the military to get their supplies direct from refineries." Rashid paused. "This was a weather station, and its location makes it ideal for their hacking program."

"Maybe it's got something to do with cooling the servers. I'm no expert, but I know that bitcoin mining uses so much power and creates such a high carbon footprint that it's not only an environmental issue, but you can see the heat signature from some of these outfits from space." King paused. "Zukovsky said that the temperature of this place helped to cool the servers. I mean, it's as cold as a witch's tit for all but a few months a year. This netting may not be just to hide it from prying eyes but may have thermal shielding properties a bit like a space blanket."

"This is an altogether different proposition," Rashid commented.

"How so?"

"Are you kidding me?" Rashid shook his head. "There are soldiers down there, and there are soldiers patrolling the area."

"It's not ideal."

"Ideal?"

"We've just intercepted a plane at thirty-thousand feet and performed a HALO jump into disputed Russian territory and you're going to let a few soldiers stand in our way?"

"Well, if you put it like that..."

FIFTY

Holland Park, London

CAROLINE SWILLED the ice around her glass, the remnants of gin and tonic tasting as acerbic as her mood. The news of Sally-Anne's death feeling as far from real as she could have ever imagined. Like a dream one awakes from where there is always the underlying nag of reality where doubt is a constant and acceptance remains out of reach. She simply couldn't make sense of what Ramsay was telling her, and her second gin in less than twenty minutes wasn't helping her to accept the news, but it *was* soothing her nerves.

"It's not like you cared for her," Ramsay said eventually, trying to illicit a response from her; something more emotive than mere silence and her staring into space.

"Oh, piss off, Neil..." She drained her glass and looked at Big Dave. "Why the hell didn't you tell me?"

The big man shrugged. "You two had beef. Ramsay's right, you didn't care for her. But you worked together, and that kind of relationship plays hard on the mind. A conflict of emotions. I've been there many times with guys I didn't like getting killed right beside me and they were always the hardest deaths to come to terms with because there is always a feeling of guilt. I don't know why, but there just is. You needed your head in the game and didn't need to be worrying about what can't be changed."

"I need another gin..." She looked at the two men but knew she would not have a drinking partner into the early hours. Ramsay had no vices and wore an air of patronising conceitedness around people who did. Big Dave was merely a machine and would not let down his guard until the job was done. In many ways, he was much like King in that respect. Only Big Dave would eventually release his tension and go on a bender of epic proportions that tended to end messily.

"You've got to grieve for your aunt," Big Dave told her quietly.

"I don't have time to grieve," she replied acidly.

"Then you'll implode."

"I want to kill that bitch," she managed between sips of gin.

"It won't bring her back."

"She didn't do anything wrong! She wasn't a part of this!" Caroline wiped her eyes with the back of her sleeve, annoyed that she was showing weakness, a lack of control in front of the two men. Too stubborn to know there nothing weak about her emotion.

Big Dave put down his coffee and crouched down beside her, placing his hand on her shoulder. "Let it go, girl."

"I can't."

"It's not weakness," he said, squeezing her shoulder and

letting her know that he was there. Ramsay got up and hovered awkwardly before skulking off into the kitchen and leaving the two of them alone. "It's just me here. Let it go."

"I can't believe she's dead," Caroline said quietly, shaking her head slowly and wiping her eyes again with her sleeve. "It just won't sink in..."

"It doesn't," Big Dave replied. "We can't accept it, no matter how hard we try. Time doesn't make it easier, it's just that you grow stronger and like everything tough, you rise above it and keep fighting. Truthfully, it will always hurt and always be there."

"You've lost someone close to you?"

"Plenty. But my father's death was the worse by a million miles. I remember feeling like I couldn't catch up. It just couldn't be *real* that he was no longer here. That I would never hear his voice again, never see him walking towards me, never kick a ball with him again. He died when I was young, and I don't think I ever truly adjusted." He paused, rubbing her shoulder tenderly. "And I don't think I ever will..."

Caroline nodded. "I lost someone, too. I was engaged. He died and I don't think I ever allowed myself to grieve properly."

"Why do you think that?"

"Because I threw myself into my career afterwards." She paused. "And because I can't stop thinking about him. Since Aunty Kate was killed, all I've done is think about Peter, and I'm just so sad. It's like his death has suddenly become as raw as Aunty Kate's."

Big Dave nodded. "Grief can manifest itself in different ways. I served with a guy whose mother died and he seemed to take it well. I guess we all gloss over death in this game. Men died on patrol when I was in Afghanistan, or they killed themselves after leaving the army. You might not get used to it, but you seem to accept it and move on, otherwise the armed services would just grind to a halt. Well, this guy was okay for a while, and then his cat was run over in the street. Fuck me, the guy went down hard. He lost it. It all come out because of the damned cat."

"Aunty Kate was more than a cat..." She smiled briefly through the tears. "But I get it. Thanks. Sad though I am for my aunt, this is as much about unresolved grief in my past as about what happened up in the lakes." She wiped her eyes again with her sleeve. "What a mess..."

"We can only deal with what we can deal with. Right now, we have to find these killers." He paused. "So, have another gin, get some more tears out and try to get some sleep. Because tomorrow, we're going hunting..."

FIFTY-ONE

Republic of Karelia

"THE PARADIGM SHIFT was done from bunkers outside Moscow," said Zukovsky. "I don't know how to get in there, nor how it would affect you once you know that they have broken your seals. If British intelligence know that they are being hacked, then a full circuit breaker is what you need to do, and private enterprises need to spend more on cyber security. Whatever you do to stop Russia's hacking and cyber warfare program, it will merely be like trying to hold back the tide."

"So, this is a fucking bust?" MacPherson asked, his face reddening and his eyes glaring at the Russian. "We've risked life and limb to be told this is a fucking scam?" He looked at King and said, "What the fuck?"

"What is this place, if it's not a hacking base?" asked King, ignoring MacPherson's anger.

"It's a waste of fucking time, that's what it is!" MacPherson snapped.

"I'm not speaking to you, so shut your bloody mouth so we can hear the answer," King glared at him. He did not acknowledge the Major's reaction as he stared back at the Russian. "What is this place? There are military vehicles, fuel and living quarters. What is going on here? Why have you brought us here under false pretences?"

Zukovsky smiled. "The love of my life," he said somewhat wistfully. "Alesha Mikailovitch." He looked back at King, tears in his eyes. "That bitch you were working with killed her..."

"It was a fight. There could only be one winner," King replied defensively.

"Such a terrible way to die. Horribly burned, suffocated by the swelling of her own throat."

"You didn't exactly hang around to help her..."

Zukovsky took a deep breath and closed his eyes. "The past has been written," he said. "Nothing will bring her back. But for her, I am here to help you and help her fellow countrymen, her family."

"How?" King looked at him but caught sight of MacPherson's bewildered and somewhat flabbergasted expression. The man was seething. Whatever was happening here, King needed to find out and get the operation moving forwards again. "How is this place going to help?"

"Alesha Mikailovitch..." he said, seeming to savour the name, the memory of her, "... was Ukrainian. I did not get to read much about the world during my incarceration at your hands, but guards and orderlies talk, sometimes the edited magazines are missed, or I hear a radio somewhere and I know what is happening in the world. My country's invasion of the Ukraine, for instance. I do not know the details, but I will tell you this... the Ukrainians will fight. They are a large country, and they have a third of the Russian population, but they have a strong army, a great many men of military age and the will to halt, bog down and stall a Russian invasion and it will turn into a long and bloody affair. The President cannot use nuclear weapons on a country he wants to reclaim, but the Ukrainian people cannot expect boots on the ground assistance from NATO, either. However, they will be afforded weapons and ammunition and missiles and medical supplies as NATO fights a proxy war with Russia, am I right?"

King nodded. He thought about the man in London, the man he used for his clandestine weapons. The haul of rifles and ammunition snatched before the Taliban could use them and repurposed for Ukraine in the form of lethal aid.

Zukovsky smiled. "Even if the Russian army is swift in declaring victory through their propaganda machine, the Ukrainians will fight a guerrilla war that will become protracted and dirty." The Russian paused. "This is a chemical weapons storage facility. It's completely off the books. And I'm guessing that because it's still here, the West know nothing of its existence, either."

King had certainly never heard about it, and nor by MacPherson's expression, had the head brass at Hereford. "Where are you going with this?" he asked. They needed to stick to their timings, or they would not make their exfiltration and extraction zone.

"The chemical agents here were secretly stockpiled after Soviet forces liberated Auschwitz at the end of the Second World War. It has been stored here ever since."

King frowned. "What the Nazis used to kill Jews in the holocaust, at Auschwitz?"

"Yes."

"In the gas chambers? The shower blocks?"

"Indeed."

"Zyklon-B gas?"

"Yes." Zukovsky nodded. "This was allocated in the eighties for use in Afghanistan, and then again in the late nineties for use in Chechnya. It was never used in either theatre of operation but was kept for Ukraine. It wasn't used in twenty-fourteen. However, if the Russian President cannot get the result that he wants, then he knows that this is his last resort. An ace up his sleeve. He'd get a kick out of it as well, what with so many Jews in the Ukrainian government, and the Ukrainian President losing relatives in the holocaust. In his mind Ukraine has been annexed by Nazis, even though this is far from the truth." Zukovsky paused. "Nuclear weapons are not an option, but Russia certainly would not hesitate to use them if NATO became involved in a shooting war. His only real option is to use these chemical weapons on the Ukrainian people to get a quick surrender. It worked in Iraq. The only person to control the factions within Iraq was Saddam Hussein, and he did it by gassing the Kurds and have them live under the threat of more gas to come. I know for a fact it will be used against Ukraine if they continue to resist. It's the next play of a desperate man. And the best part? The Zyklon-B doesn't come under any charters or accords like other chemical weapons, so the Russian government can lay the blame on Russian separatists. Officially, it doesn't exist. So, officially, any attack will be out of Russia's hands. The President could then withdraw his troops and look like it is a humanitarian gesture, rather than lose face."

MacPherson shook his head. "We're here to destroy a cyber warfare base. We were meant to go in, get the job done and exfil to the Baltic, where the SBS were going to meet us with civilian clothing and passports and take us to

Sweden where we all fly back on commercial airlines." He paused, looking at King incredulously. "You can't seriously be contemplating this?"

King thought for a moment. Zukovsky had mentioned Kurds and their persecution by Saddam. King had worked with Kurdish rebels, and two brothers he fought alongside were the bravest men he had ever known. Ukraine would be full of men like that; men and women who were being over-whelmed, outgunned and yet still fought for freedom and values. "I'm hearing him out," said King.

"It's not our fight. This is nothing to do with Britain!" MacPherson vehemently protested.

"We have a real chance to make a difference here!" King raged.

"It's not our fucking orders!" MacPherson snapped back. "But this is..." He reached inside his jacket and retrieved a silenced Walther PPK and fired two shots into Zukovsky's chest.

King's weapon was up and aimed at the SAS Major in a second, but four more barrels were aimed back at him just as quickly. He saw that the muzzle of Rashid's rifle was just a foot away from MacPherson's head and managed to get his weapon aimed at Sergeant Peters, whose own weapon was aiming at Rashid. Flymo hadn't been quick enough to draw his own pistol in its shoulder holster and had both hands semi-raised in the air with two guns on him.

"Easy boys..." Stan said quietly. "Nice and easy now..."

"I've got time for a shot or two," said King.

"We all have," Chubs replied.

"Rashid, see that you take MacPherson's head off when the shooting starts," said King coldly.

"On it," Rashid replied.

"Nobody's taking anybody's head off," Stan said quietly.

"Come on lads, let the blood drain from your cocks for a moment. We're all on the same side here..." He lowered his weapon and took a slow, tentative step in front of the muzzle of Sergeant Peters' SCAR. It was a show of conciliation, because the 7.62mm would cut right through Stan's flak jacket at that range. Most likely both sides and everything in the middle. "Come on boys, lower your weapons now..."

King watched the weapons start to lower, and he eased his muzzle to the ground. He glanced at Zukovsky, who was circling the drain. His breathing was shallow, and there was an ominous amount of blood on his chest and stomach.

"Like I said... orders." MacPherson paused. "Mereweather says to let you know that there's no bungalow or cottage, no monthly allowance coming out of taxpayers money for a man like Vladimir Zukovsky..." He smiled and said, "It would appear that you don't get to know everything, either."

King glared at him, seething. He could not believe that Simon Mereweather would side-step him like this. Several of the men watched on with their weapons still easily brought to bear. He looked at them, then lowered his weapon completely and turned to the Russian.

"On me!" MacPherson ordered the men. "Chubs, you're on point. Peters, tag the rear. Exfil as planned."

"Leave the ordinance," King said without turning around.

"No chance."

"What's it going to hurt?" asked King. "It will make your tab to the extraction point easier."

"We're stealing a couple of cars at the next village, so it's not a problem," MacPherson replied disagreeably.

"You've got plenty of plastic explosives. I can take this

place down with just a few kilos of the stuff," he said, knowing that if he could detonate rather than ignite the fuel in the fuel dump, then he would have enough explosive power to rival a cruise missile.

"No. We have orders and the parameters of the operation have changed." MacPherson paused. "You're not judge, jury and executioner, King. We can't pick and choose our missions. We're tools for the job."

"Oh, you're a tool, alright," Rashid said gruffly.

"And you fucked your career when you fucked the Colonel's daughter," MacPherson replied curtly. "So, I don't give a shit about your opinion."

Rashid shook his head, not bothering to engage further with the SAS Major, and walked over to Zukovsky. He crouched down, but there was nothing he could do for the man.

"Your weapons belong to Hereford," MacPherson reminded them. "Property of the SAS."

"Take them off us then. I dare you..." King said coldly.

MacPherson seemed to consider this for a moment, then said, "We're exfiltrating now. You're either in or out."

"Out," King replied. "So, hurry up and fuck off..." He bent down and looked at the dying Russian. A man he had tried to kill years ago, then saved because policy dictated so. He glanced up at Rashid. "You go, mate. Get to the evac."

"Bollocks."

King smiled. "Flymo?"

"I'm having too much fun, mate. Besides, I don't like the idea of a mini submarine piloted by *Bootnecks*. I prefer my transportation to be in the sky where you can breathe the fresh air."

Stan stood beside King and dropped a bag on the

ground beside him. "From some of the boys," he said. "Plastic explosive, det-cord and trigger switches."

"What about the Major?"

"Fuck the Major. If anyone asks, then it got lost on the jump. I'd like to have seen this through, but I have a mortgage to pay and take my orders from the top like all the other lads. Anyway, good luck, you crazy bastards."

King thanked him and looked at Zukovsky. The Russian gave him a look like it was inevitable and seemed to have accepted his fate. "Thank you," he said. "Thank you for getting me out..." He coughed and spittle and blood came out of his mouth and moistened his dried lips. When he spoke again, his voice had a raspy wetness to it. "Better to die the death of a wolf, than that of a lamb for the table," Zukovsky said weakly. King said nothing. He didn't have the words. "I set up this facility," he continued, struggling to get the words out. He coughed again, but this time the blood that met his lips was almost black. King knew that one of the bullets had severed the man's liver. "Russian security is not as great as we would want the world to believe. There are always lapses. Perhaps you will be lucky, no? There is a retina scan on the doors. I doubt they have updated the system." He coughed and King could see the life leaving him. "Right eye... do what has to be done..." Zukovsky started to shake and went pale almost at once. "This is for the people of Ukraine, for Alesha's memory and for her family. But you? *You* can rot in hell..."

King stood up looking at Zukovsky's body. Quite fitting that the man should hate him right up until the very end. King couldn't blame him. There were two sides to every war, and King had certainly done his part to claim the victory. Zukovsky stared blankly at him, his eyes glazed with the recent touch of death.

King turned and saw the last SAS trooper disappear into the trees. He glanced at both Rashid and Flymo, buoyed by the fact both men had remained, unquestioningly believing in him and that the dead Russian's cause was just. He looked back at the Russian, his eyes dull and dry and lifeless. Both eyes were open, but King would only be needing one of them.

FIFTY-TWO

Rashid had the high ground, but he knew that he would not be able to hold it for long once the enemy returned fire. However, he was east of the compound, and in a few minutes, he would have the sun on his back and the enemy would have the sun in their eyes. Details mattered. And so did having a .300 Winchester magnum at his disposal. At just three-hundred metres and an elevation of two-hundred feet, the 3.9x56mm scope would make it as easy as shooting fish in a barrel. But he could not simply get comfortable and shoot to his heart's content. More than two shots from a sniper from the same location was suicide in the theatre of war. But then again, these soldiers would have other things on their mind.

The fuel dump would be King's first port of call, and Rashid watched as he made his way around the perimeter of the camp and edged his way ever closer. It was clear that the Russians were trying to hide this camp in plain sight. There was no fence, but there were a lot of guards. Another patrol had gone out, working their way anti-clockwise from the camp. Rashid doubted that they would climb the escarpment for no good reason. The guards looked a lacklustre bunch and had sparked up cigarettes when they were a hundred metres clear of the guard post. Discipline was not their forte, and he wondered whether they knew that the war in Ukraine was still shrouded in mystery and propaganda for them, or whether they knew that their government had lied and cheated and killed in its bid to overthrow a peaceful and independent nation. Surely the soldiers would know of colleagues who had been killed. And then there were the mothers who had gone to visit their POW sons or collect their remains at the behest of the Ukrainian government in an attempt to let the Russian people know what was happening. How committed to a bloody war could soldiers be, knowing that they had not been told the truth, nor that their cause was just? Within one month of war in Ukraine, Russia had lost more men and equipment than in the ten years spent fighting in Afghanistan, and those kinds of losses would be hard to hide, even for a regime like Russia.

Rashid watched King use the dawn shadows to emerge at the fuel dump. The sun was not yet on Rashid's back and the frozen ground bit savagely at him. There was likely to be a deficit of several degrees down in the compound and a hundred metres from where King was now laying the PE4 charges, soldiers paced around stomping their feet and rubbing their gloved hands as they glanced around and took schoolboy drags on cigarettes while looking out for officers, who were no doubt still in their warm beds.

The fuel dump had been sited on a concrete plinth and there were both diesel and petrol drums in separate rows. Militaries operating in cold climates always used vehicles with either petrol or multifuel engines as diesel froze at Arctic temperatures and having two fuel options made sense militarily when operating in conflict zones where specific fuels may not be readily available. Rashid could see that there were also filling station style pumps to the side, indicating that there would be larger fuel reservoir tanks set into the ground and then he realised that the barrels had been filled from these tanks, which could only mean that even the fuel used in transporting the deadly chemical agent to Ukraine would be off the books. Whatever was going on here was escalating and with mounting tensions in Moscow over the situation in Ukraine, it certainly wasn't a reach to see this hidden horror show of a base as the answer to the Russian leader's prayers. A humiliating surrender at the hands of Russian sympathisers, yet under no *official* orders from the Kremlin.

Rashid cast his scope across the compound and steadied it on Flymo, who was now underneath a lone Mil MI-17 helicopter gunship checking it for fuel and airworthiness. It was a beast of an aircraft, but Flymo was certain that he would be able to fly it, despite the controls being in Russian. All he had said he needed was a starter and a fuel gauge, and he could wing everything else.

There were three guards smoking nearby, but Flymo had remained unseen, and Rashid watched tentatively as he eased open the cockpit door and slipped inside. When he cast the scope back to King, he was no longer by the fuel dump. In fact, as Rashid scanned the crosshairs over the entire compound, he could not see King at all.

FIFTY-THREE

King found the series of bunkers a hundred metres from the fuel dump. They were little more than semi-cylindrical lumps under the grass, with steps leading down at one end with slopping concrete reinforced ceiling and staggered walls leading to a solid steel door at a right-angle to the steps. They were blast bunkers, and everything about surviving a blast came down to gentle curves and right angles. King already knew that the door would lead to another door at a right-angle. These low, smoothly graded lumps no more than ten feet above ground and possibly thirty-feet deep would allow a blast – atomic or otherwise – to flow over, much like a vehicle in a wind tunnel test, and when the blast travelled down the steps, it would be met by twenty-feet of concrete. Explosions travelled the path of least resistance and once the energy met an immovable object, the door at the right angle would take the brunt, and so the next door within would be angled acutely away. Of course, that was the theory and King could see that these were Second World War or perhaps early Cold War struc-tures, and likely designed and constructed before the world went crazy designing larger yield and more lethal nuclear weapons. King had seen the large nuclear defence bunkers of Ukraine and Albania and by contrast, these were tiny.

There was a steady stream of men from two of these bunkers. As the doors opened, King caught the heady aromas of tea and warm bread and of body odour and was reminded of once boarding a submarine and smelling what a hundred men living together with limited amenities and personal space smelled like. There was clearly a no-smoking policy inside, as this accounted for the steady procession of men who gathered around a few empty oil drums with fires inside them fuelled by broken pallets and branches gathered near the perimeter. The men smoked in the fashion of naughty schoolboys, shielding their cigarettes and looking around them, but for what, King did not know. It struck King that these men were young conscripts and as clueless as the men who had been tasked with invading Ukraine. He imagined that they did not see newspapers nor were able to watch anything but state-controlled news.

King moved quickly down the row of bunkers and stopped at the top of the steps of one without a well-trodden pathway. He made his way down the steps and saw what he had been looking for. A digital keypad with a screen. This would be the retina identification system that Zukovsky had spoken about. The other bunkers, with their free-flow procession of men would not have this as a method of entry. Too many men, too thorough and indeed, unnecessary.

King took out the silenced Ruger pistol and tucked it into his belt for quick access. He then fished inside his jacket for the sealed plastic bag – one of many that had been intended for each man to defecate in – and held it out in front of him. The eyeball looked alive. King had splashed some water in the bag when he had done what had to be done, and he opened his pocket multitool and selected the thin, razor-sharp blade and set about opening the seal of the bag and easing the tip of the blade into the back of the eyeball. It was a grim task, but sadly not the grimmest thing King had done in his life. He looked at the keypad. There was a green button and a red button. Universally, green meant 'go', so he pressed it hopefully and the screen flickered into life displaying Russian Cyrillic alphabetised phrases. King could speak Russian, but he wasn't about to sit down with a cup of tea and read Tolstoy's *War and Peace* in the writer's native language anytime soon. He picked out words he recognised, but he had no idea what he was meant to do with them, and in desperation, he held the eye up to the lens and waited. The writing changed, and to King's elation, he recognised the name 'Vladimir Zukovsky' among them. The door clicked open somewhat undramatically, and King stuffed the eyeball back into the bag and tucked it back into his pocket before retrieving the silenced pistol.

King needn't have worried. The place was empty and the lights, which were motion-sensitive, flickered on and as he walked through the ten-metre-wide bunker, he could see that it went on for a considerable distance. All of it full of drums with the contents and hazardous symbols telling King he was in the right place. He did not know much about Zyklon-B, other than it wiped out millions of Jews, but he knew that there was enough down here to change the course of history. What on earth had the Nazis been planning to produce such quantities? What had the Soviet Union thought they would use it for when they liberated it? And why had the Soviet Union and later, the Russian Federation, sat on this stockpile for so long? The answer was clear. The Russian leadership was no better than the Nazis, and never had been. They had their own dark history with the persecution and mass murder of Jews, the forced labour camps for anyone who dared to think or acted differently from the party line. Russia was always going to use this stockpile for something, and Ukraine was now the most likely candidate.

King had no idea whether Zyklon-B was flammable in its current state, but he did know that hydrogen cyanide was, and he was sure that was what largely made up the formula. He certainly knew that it was a lethal concoction that made it a devastating pesticide and if he could cause enough damage to the barrels, then it would be highly unlikely that any remaining stock could be used, and that decontaminating the site would become a tremendous task for an army trying to keep it a secret. If he could burn the entire stockpile to the ground, then so much the better.

King attached the charges to the barrels using tape and chose the lower tier barrels and ignored the outer rows. If he was going to make use of his surroundings to aid the detonation, then he needed to work from the inside out. Placing charges on the outside may not reach the opposite side and the explosion would work its way outwards in all directions. When he was finished, he fed out the detonation cord and worked his way back to the door, pausing beside a bank of pipes and taps. He looked up at the ceiling and saw the sprinkler system, the thought occurring to him that he could take care of this if he could work out what the taps did. The Russian writing didn't help, but he turned the taps anti-clockwise, and nothing happened, so he turned them back and could hear an audible flow of highly pressurised water. He turned them back again and figured he had just stopped the flow. It was clearly a maintenance and emergency practicality to locate them by the door, and it went some way to explain the Russian psyche that could be construed as arrogance. Nobody was going to be crazy or brave enough to take on the Russian might, so the taps to the sprinkler system should be as utilitarian as possible.

King edged out of the two doors and turned to climb the stairs, staring straight into the faces of two soldiers. Both men were as shocked as King, but not as fast. King drew the pistol and fired. The second man went to raise his hands just as his companion dropped but it made no difference and the bullet hit him in the eye. He crumpled, the AK-12 assault rifle clattering down the steps and landing at King's feet.

King cursed under his breath. He put down the coil of detonation cord and caught hold of the nearest man's feet, dragging him around the blast door and into the bunker. He dropped him unceremoniously on the concrete floor and went for the other man. King realised that he could not afford to be caught here. There was no other way out and the doorway was the perfect killing ground. The enemy would have him funnelled into a tight area and they would have the high ground. It would be unlikely they would toss grenades down on him, given the contents of the bunker, but he had seen Russian soldiers do more ridiculous things than that.

The second body was lighter than the first and King wasted no time in dragging it down the steps, its head bouncing and knocking on every step. King closed the door behind him, picked up the detonation cord and climbed the stairs. He unravelled the cord all the way back to the fuel dump, then joined the two ends together and clamped them tightly with the initiation box. He armed the box by turning the key. The box had a small display on it and showed a signal bar identical to that of a mobile phone.

There were soldiers behind him, warming their hands

on the fuel drum fires and smoking, sharing jokes and from the sounds of the laughter they had been lurid ones. King knew that he only had a few minutes before the disappearance of the two soldiers would be noticed and he had a large area of ground to cover to get to the far side of the compound and the safety of the trees beyond. Running was a bad idea as it would elicit a response and frankly, would look suspicious. King walked purposefully, using the shade and shadows of the dawn, but had only taken a few steps when a shout rang out.

"Ostanovka!" the voice commanded him to stop.

King froze. He could have turned around and engaged the soldier, but he may well have faced a dozen men. But he did have God on his side. Or at least, a man on high with the ability to hand out death with his fingertip and unseen by the glare of the sun.

FIFTY-FOUR

There were two soldiers with their weapons trained on King. Rashid knew all about reflex and muscle spasms and he knew that there would be the possibility that they pulled their triggers when the bullet hit them, but he almost had the perfect shot. A two for one. He clutched the rifle closely to him and gently rolled to his left and resighted the rifle. He now had the back of the closest man's head in his sights and directly in front of the man's cranium, the other soldier stood stock-still, some six feet further in distance, the centre of his shoulder blades making a compelling option. Three hundred metres at 2,450 feet per second gave a drop of just 6.5 inches, having already taken 500 feet per second off its muzzle velocity. Rashid estimated the bullet would drop another two inches after passing through the first man's head. Probably shave off another 300 feet per second. It was largely guesswork, but that guesswork had been honed by a million bullets on the range.

Rashid steadied his breath, took up the pressure on the trigger and squeezed. The rifle recoiled violently and when he resighted, both men were down, and King was running for his life towards the treeline. Gunfire erupted and men scattered around the compound like ants. King reached the trees, then opened fire on the compound, his muzzle flashes clearly visible in Rashid's scope. Men dropped and Rashid worked the bolt and got into the fight. He looked for someone who seemed to have an idea what was happening and found a young officer giving orders and pointing towards the trees. Rashid aimed and fired. The man fell out of view of his scope, but Rashid had been careful to aim at the man's hip. They now had an officer down and in need of medical attention. It aided to create confusion and more tasks for the panicked men below. Rashid soon found a man designated as medic and put a bullet in the man's calf muscle as he reached the officer. He then rolled a few metres to his left, aided by the gradient of the hilltop and searched for King in his scope. He soon found him, firing single shots at men advancing down the treeline. King pulled back, reloading as he went, then took out a control unit and typed in the code before pressing the send button. The fuel dump went up in flames, then a secondary explosion sent the fuel and barrels sky high. There was a tremendous 'thud' behind, then black smoke billowed out of the entrance of one of the bunkers and the entire grass hump seemed to flex up and down as if breathing. The smoke gained in height and soon looked like a twister, wafting from side to side in the wind. An almighty explosion sent up concrete and scorched grass and thousands of tonnes of earth which started to rain down on the centre of the compound.

"Shit, he's overcooked it!" Rashid said to himself. Surely the earth would be contaminated with chemicals. Or perhaps the fire had burned off the toxicity. Rashid decided it would not be a good idea to wait around and find out. He rolled off the summit and ran around the hill slope, emerging a hundred metres further north of his original position. He could hear the 'whomp, whomp, whomp' of rotor blades and when he peered over the edge, he could see the Mil taking off. "Fucking hell, Flymo's only gone and done it!" he said quietly and in awe of the man's ability. He watched as the helicopter turned mid-hover, its tail rotor chewing through the camouflaged netting. For a moment, it looked as though the helicopter would be pulled back down, but Russian helicopters always had plenty of power and the great leviathan continued to climb. None of the soldiers below seemed to think anything of it, assuming that the pilot must have been saving a valuable piece of military equipment, not to mention his ride home.

Rashid watched as the Mil banked hard and overflew the camp. When it banked towards the hill, Rashid waved and started down the other side of the hill away from the chaos of the compound and towards the safety of the tundra-like open ground and trees beyond. The Mil's powerful engines and rotors roared and thudded above him, and he could feel the wind on him like a gale-force storm. Flymo put the helicopter down a hundred metres from him and Rashid sprinted for all he was worth, ducking his head instinctively, but in no way close to the spinning rotors above him. Surprisingly, the doorhandle opened differently, and Rashid heaved it upwards and got the door open. He searched for headphones to drown out the maelstrom of noise. When he was connected to the intercom he said, "I last saw King two hundred metres north-west of the compound in the treeline!" He paused breathlessly. "He has a few men on his tail!" Rashid got the sniper rifle ready, then pulled the emergency release handle, which dropped the hinges and jettisoned the door. "Get me into position!"

The Mil rose quickly and Flymo banked so that Rashid would have a clear line of sight, but he could not hold the zero on any of the men firing at King. He could see a group of three men getting a PKM general purpose machine gun ready. They had the belt out and one of the men was locking it down. The weapon had a fearsome rate of fire and an effective range of over a thousand metres. In Vietnam, the American soldiers had called it the 'meat grinder', and for good reason. Rashid attempted to hold the zero, but the Mil was banking hard, and the inertia was difficult to battle. He fired but missed. Rashid cursed and worked the bolt to chamber another round, but Flymo squared off the turn and opened up with the 12.7mm cannon. The noise was deafening through the doorless opening and when Rashid managed to gain sight of the three men and their support weapon again, it was a scene of carnage, and looked as if a tractor and plough had driven over them.

"The boy's got some toys!" Flymo shouted into the intercom, but Rashid knew that his bravado was merely a coping mechanism, and the worst images of the engagement were yet to come for the pilot. The Mil banked again and Flymo said, "There's your boy!"

Rashid saw King returning fire down the treeline. When he looked up at the Mil, he pointed to the clearing, dropped the empty rifle on the ground and sprinted out into the open. King drew his Sig Sauer 9mm and started firing at an unseen target. Flymo knew that he would almost be out of ammunition, and he pulled the helicopter up, spun around and gave two bursts of fire with the cannon. Trees splintered and men fell, and he put the aircraft down short to afford King some cover. Rashid watched King toss the pistol aside and draw the silenced .22 Ruger. He really was in trouble if he needed that, and Rashid jettisoned the other door, dropped the sniper rifle and set to work with his Heckler and Koch. He changed to a new magazine and fired at anything that moved. King dived into the aircraft and Flymo had the Mil off the ground and flying hard and fast towards the trees. They cleared the treetops by mere inches, tracer rounds zipping past them, and bullets clanking on the fuselage. The gunfire lasted just a few seconds and they were clear. Out of view and out of range.

FIFTY-FIVE

London

"ONE MINUTE SHE WAS STANDING THERE..."
Caroline sobbed. "... and the next she was on the ground
bleeding and unable to breathe." King held her closely and
soothed the back of her head tenderly with the palm of his
hand. He knew that she needed time to get it all out, to
accept the utter disbelief one gets when someone close to
you died suddenly, and move on to the sadness, the void of
emptiness that would follow. "I knew that she was going to
die," she said, pulling away and looking into his eyes. Her
eyes were red and sore from crying. "There's no first aid for
something like that. The bitch cut her throat and carotid
artery. She was dead in less than two minutes, I'd guess."
King struggled to find the right words. Or any. He looked at
her, but it was a moment too long. Too much silence when
there should have been some words of wisdom or understanding. He had never been good at small talk or sympathy.
But he didn't work in a bar or an office. They were not skills

that he had learned to develop. "Christ!" Caroline screamed and threw her mobile phone at the vanity mirror on the dresser beside the bed, the mirror shattering in a spider's web of cracks. "Say something!"

The prompt had the opposite effect and King looked bewildered, first at the smashed glass, then secondly at her. "I'm sorry," he said. "We'll get the bitch. Trust me, we'll get her..."

Caroline sobbed. It wasn't the response she wanted or needed, but it was the one she got. She should have known that King would offer a solution, rather than emotional support. She dried her eyes on a tissue and looked at him. "So, how did it go in Russia?"

King told her. He left nothing out. When he had finished, she said, "You think that Mereweather doesn't trust you?"

King shrugged. "I think he trusts me. But..." he shrugged.

"Then what?"

"I don't think he thinks he can fully control me," said King. "I think he was pissed off that I offered a way out for Zukovsky and wanted to show me who was boss."

"I am surprised you would offer a way out to a man like that. After all we went through initially, and after all that happened after we freed him from the Americans."

King shrugged. "I don't think I would have."

"No?"

"No."

Caroline smiled. "Then you're really just pissed off that Mereweather got there first. And you're doubly pissed off that he used someone out of the loop to do it."

"I suppose. But I guess we'll never know now." He paused. "Zukovsky was a lot of things, but he was a tough and formidable enemy. I hated him, and he certainly hated me, but I suppose I respected him as a warrior."

"Sounds like you miss him like Road Runner would miss Wile. E. Coyote. He was a formidable enemy and without him, there will be a void to fill."

King shrugged. "No, I think there will always be enough enemies out there. But I like to see a job through, not have the end game taken out of my hands."

"What now, then?" Caroline asked.

"Onwards, I suppose. I want this bastard Reno and his bitch dead. I suppose that's enough for a moment."

"Agreed," she said, hugging him. "Let's go downstairs and see how far Ramsay has got with Campbell." King nodded and followed her out of the room.

After clearing the Republic of Karelia, they had flown into Finland with Flymo doing what he did best. Flying fast and low to avoid Finnish radar and ditching the helicopter near Kotka. Several 'care packages' had been left at various drops in the vicinity by an MI6 agent operating in Helsinki. Just part of the 'Plan B' option King had got Ramsay to put in place. The care packages consisted of money, passports for each member of the team including the SAS troopers, who as far as King was concerned, had stuck with the only option that they knew they had, and rendezvoused with SBS commandos in a mini-sub that would take them on to Sweden with civilian clothes, passports and open tickets on various flights to various British airports, so that they did not travel as a group and arouse suspicion. King's Plan B option was to get to Helsinki and take the two-and-a-half-hour ferry to Tallin in Estonia. From there, they would get flights back to the UK. Upon confirmation of their exfiltration, the same MI6 agent would gather up the care packages and destroy the passports and tickets.

King had flown back on his own to Gatwick Airport on a Scandinavian Airlines flight, while Rashid had flown into Stanstead with Ryan Air. Flymo had flown into Heathrow with Swiss Air Lines. All three had been met by Security Service drivers in plain, grey Vauxhall Insignia saloons. King noted that he had yet to be picked up in one of the sleek, black Jaguars with tinted glass and sumptuous leather seats that the likes of Simon Mereweather travelled in.

Downstairs, Ramsay and Campbell were seated in front of Ramsay's laptop. They had accessed Campbell's email account and were working on the message to send Reno, based on copies of previous messages Campbell had sent, in order to get the language-structure correct. A message without any of the grammatical traits that Campbell had used before could spook the assassin, and as far as Campbell was concerned, he would be lucky to have Reno agree to a meeting. The man wasn't known for his amiable nature.

Big Dave was eating biscuits and dunking them in his tea, while Rashid was checking his equipment on a smaller kitchen table in the corner. King could see the rifle slip and rucksack. He nodded to King, loading 7.62mm bullets into a magazine. The ammunition was Swedish match grade with blue tips, which meant soft-nosed expanding bullets. King looked at Big Dave and said, "How's the family problems?"

The big man shrugged. "I need to go back there."

"The novelist Thomas Wolfe said, you can't go home again." King paused. "Whatever you expect from returning home after a long absence, it's never the same. Nostalgia is a bitch."

"He said that?"

"Well, no, he said the first part."

"He sounds like a dick."

"I can't argue there."

Big Dave shrugged. "Anyway, I'm not after a stroll down memory lane. There's some shit going on, and that's all I want to say on the matter."

King nodded. "Sure. Here if you need me."

"I'm heading off," said Rashid. "Let me know either way." King frowned and Rashid added, "I want to be at the meet before the meet is set."

"You're in for a cold night," King commented.

"I've had colder..." He swung the bergen over his shoulder and picked up the rifle in the canvas gun slip. "I'll be off. If the meet isn't a go, let me know pronto, like. I don't want to be out there freezing my bollocks off."

"Good hunting," said King. He wandered over to where Ramsay and Campbell were deliberating over the politician's private email account. "A word, Neil..." Ramsay frowned and followed King out through the corridor and into the spacious drawing room. The house was large and luxuriously furnished in a mix of modern and period furniture with works of art on the wall. King knew that some had been gifted to the service, but he could never understand why. Surely being gifted by people grateful for the service's work blurred the lines of favour. He tried not to think about mutual back-patting and hoped only that the cause had always been just, and in Britain's interests, although in recent years, he wasn't quite so sure. "What the hell was that out in Russia?"

Ramsay frowned. "Meaning?"

"I mean Mereweather giving that SAS major MacPherson secret orders."

"I'm not following," Ramsay replied. "Although, I might ask the same thing. You went out there to destroy a facility used for cyber terrorism. When you discovered that it was all a ruse, you went ahead and made decisions far and away above your pay-scale." He paused. "You can't just take it upon yourself to choose your missions and make decisions like that."

"You'd prefer that Russia use chemicals used in the holocaust to kill Ukrainians?"

"That's not the point. We suspect that the Russians will use chemical weapons as part of a false flag offensive. It's likely to happen anyway." He held up a hand to stop King before he could protest. "I get why you did it. And if the Russians were going to use captured, unrecorded chemical weapons as a first resort, then it does give credence to the fact that perhaps they will not escalate to using the chemical weapons they already own legitimately. Really, we don't know. The Russians have done what everybody failed to predict thus far, so who knows?"

King shrugged. "I want to know why Mereweather ordered MacPherson to kill Zukovsky."

"Because he's the head of British security and he chose to leave you out of the loop, for once." Ramsay paused. "And that, Alex, is the end of it."

"Did you know?"

"No," Ramsay replied.

King looked at the man's eyes. He also knew that being somewhat on the autistic spectrum, the man wasn't prone to untruths. "Then why?"

"Like I said, he's the head of the service and we shouldn't question such things. You know, the problem with giving a dog too much freedom, is it resents going back onto a tight leash."

"So, I'm a fucking dog now?"

"To be fair, I'm not best known for my analogies or metaphors." Ramsay shrugged. "Are we quite finished here?"

King nodded. He supposed Ramsay was right. Mereweather had his reasons, but King was the man who was sent on the dangerous missions, and if he couldn't trust the man at the top, then he needed to take stock. But right now, he had a score to settle. He had loved Leanne, but he had made mistakes and he had seen no other choice than to leave his old life behind him and take the new life on offer with MI6. He had set Leanne up with a house and with some cash and in doing so, had taken her away from a bad element and set her on a safer path. From there, her life had been her own, and she had done alright. And then Reno had used her as bait. He and his female accomplice had taken her life, her husband's and the lives of their two children, and they had used them like a chef used ingredients. Commodities. Nothing more.

And now they were going to pay.

FIFTY-SIX

Snipers stay alive by remaining unseen. They are the ultimate practitioners of fieldcraft using camouflage and concealment techniques and adhering to the five S's of shine, silhouette, shadow, sound and smell to avoid detection. In dry conditions, a sniper would wet the ground in front of the muzzle to avoid dust being displaced by the gunshot. They would use markers for distance, use otherwise ignored things such as a shredded plastic bag caught in a bush to judge wind direction, or the ever-changing shadow from an inanimate object to know when they were seated with the sun on their back and the glare of the sun in their target's eyes.

Rashid had the advantage. He had known the meeting place before the target, and he had arrived in darkness and chosen his position with the benefit of *Google Earth* and a little local knowledge. All he could do was hope that the target turned up and that his guardian angel chose a spot in Rashid's line of sight. He checked his watch. Fifteen minutes to go and he still did not have eyes on the sniper.

And then the paranoia kicked in. Was she behind him?

Was he in her sights right now, with her just waiting until the time was right? Heat prickled his neck, the tiny airs standing on end, and he shivered involuntarily at the thought of a set of crosshairs fixed onto the back of his head. No. She couldn't have gone further out. Campbell had told them about Reno's demonstration. The cigar tube and the tiny hole punched through at Reno's command. Rashid had given it a lot of thought and he deduced that the weapon would have been something like a .222 or .223 for the bullet hole to be so small. Undoubtedly silenced with a large suppressor, perhaps even subsonic ammunition, and fired from no more than two-hundred metres away for that degree of accuracy. Shooting a cigar tube was trick shot territory. So, perhaps the show of domination had already been done? Perhaps Reno's sniper was further back? Rashid had chosen a spot four-hundred metres away. That gave him a terrific line of sight and was well within the capabilities of the L129A1 Sharpshooter 7.62mm rifle that he had equipped himself with, along with its Trijicon ACOG 6x48 scope with bullet drop compensator reticule and the additional Trijicon x1 LED Rugged Miniature Reflex (RMR) sight atop the main scope for close in shooting. It was, as King told him, a serious piece of kit and capable of fast follow-up shots with its semi-auto action.

"This is eagle's nest. No visual," he said quietly, the voice-activated throat mic connecting him to the dedicated frequency they were sharing. Feeling exasperated he added, "Sorry guys..."

FIFTY-SEVEN

King grimaced. He hated wearing a shirt and tie, much less a suit, and the stiff shirt collar felt like it was slowly strangling him. He ran his finger around his collar for the tenth time in as many minutes.

"Christ, get over it!" Caroline snapped impatiently.

"It's uncomfortable."

"You've lain up in mountain crevices taking dumps in a bag and eating cold rations for weeks with the enemy just metres away, and you can't cope with a shirt?" She shook her head, then relented, "Sorry. I can't stop thinking about Aunt Kate. I want this bitch and Rashid hasn't located her yet. She's not on a rooftop and he can see virtually every place where a sniper can take a shot from. We're going in there with a sniper at large. I can't shake the feeling that they've got us cornered."

King nodded. He ran his finger around the stiff collar again and glanced at the Land Rover Discovery in his rear-view mirror, catching a glimpse of Campbell in the seat behind him. He looked ashen and was sweating profusely. King could see the fear in the man's eyes like a wounded animal. "Get it together," he ordered him tersely. "Reno will know something is wrong if you look like that." He looked back at the road ahead, still fiddling with his collar again.

Behind them Ramsay drove the Land Rover Discovery with Big Dave in the passenger seat beside him. Two MI5 security guards doubled as protection in the back seat. The entire team were dressed in dark suits and King could only hope that Reno would not look too closely and see that Campbell's protection detail were all new faces. Or indeed, that he would spot King and Caroline among them, but there was such a thing as hiding in plain sight and King just hoped that it would work. But the sniper troubled him. Without locating Reno's insurance, they were all at risk. And with a sniper capable of hitting a cigar tube first time and on demand, it would seem that Reno still had the upper hand.

Along the riverbank a few cars had parked on the grass verge and joggers, dog walkers and canoeists were beginning their early morning routines. The meeting place was one of Campbell's preferred locations for discrete assignations, and it turned out that he owned the site, along with another two thousand feet of river frontage. Clamping signs dissuaded people from parking and judging by the empty lot, nobody wanted to chance the rigmarole of private clampers and hefty fines. King slowed the Jaguar and Ramsay overtook them in the Discovery and swept around the rough ground and parked nose outwards close to the exit, just as he had been briefed.

Reno was there. Seated on a bench seat and looking as calm and casual as anyone could have been. Both hands were inside his jacket pockets.

Big Dave alighted along with the two MI5 security guards and the six-four, eighteen stone Fijian dwarfed the other two men, who were no lightweights themselves. Ramsay got out and stood a few paces from the vehicle, doing his best to look like an experienced bodyguard. The suit went a long way towards it, as did the earpiece and throat mic. He was the only one among them who was unarmed.

King started forwards, casually surveying the scene. He scanned the ground, the overgrown riverbank and the malthouse as he crawled through. "Got them," he said. "In the derelict building, second floor. No visual, but there was breath..." He paused, using his peripheral vision as he manoeuvred the Jaguar into a tight turn. "And again..."

"Got it," Caroline concurred.

"Are you sure?" Rashid replied.

"Positive. Unless a homeless person is taking up residence, there is definitely someone breathing up there, and close to the window." He looked at the vehicle display. "It's minus three degrees. I'm positive that's our shooter."

"It's too close. No more than fifty metres," Rashid protested.

"If Alex is sure, then he's sure," Caroline replied adamantly.

"What if our trick shooter was using a two-two? Almost completely silent with a suppressor and sub-sonic rounds, and virtually no drop in trajectory to consider at that range. What if it wasn't such an impressive shot, but an incredibly *close* shot?"

"Then God help you, my friend. A two-two is lethal at that range, and it would be like shooting fish in a frying pan, let alone a barrel..."

"That's helpful..." King replied.

"Oh, Jesus!" Campbell said from the back seat. "He'll see that something's wrong and his sniper will kill me!"

"Then pull yourself together," Caroline replied tersely. "Or I'll shoot you myself!"

"Feeling exposed here..." Big Dave said quietly. *"Which window?"*

"Don't make it obvious," King said, then regretted doubting the man's skills. "Second floor, second window from the left."

"Have that," Big Dave replied. *"Yeah, that's either breath or somebody's coffee."*

"You're up," said King, looking at Campbell in his rear-view mirror.

"We need his confession on the recording," Caroline instructed him. "Just act normally. He needs to think that this is just another meeting. He took on a job and right now, collateral damage is all you have to show for it." She fought back tears as she thought about her Aunt Kate and what could have happened to her parents. "Tell him that you're not satisfied with the way the contract is progressing, and he needs to know how you feel and that the contract may be revoked. He'll incriminate himself in the recording trying to justify his methods. That's what we need." She thought of what she really needed. She needed to come face to face with the red-headed bitch. And when she did, she did not want any witnesses.

"And then I'll incriminate myself, too. I have a deal with the Security Service and if I cooperate, then at least there is some light at the end of the tunnel. But if I incriminate myself on tape, then when I'm no longer useful, you lot will throw me to the wolves!"

"Call the union," said King.

"I could call my lawyer!"

"And then you'd be finished," Caroline replied. "I won't rest until you're tried and convicted as an accessory to murder. Your wife and children will be hounded by the press and your assets will be ceased in line with Russian sanctions. Your family will be destitute by the time you're being buggered for the first time, held down by the rest of the men in the queue."

"Alright!" Campbell snapped. "Oh God, when will all this be over?" He took a deep breath and reached for the doorhandle.

"Wait!" King snapped. "How do you normally debus?"

"What?"

"How do you normally exit the vehicle?"

"My BG gets the door."

Caroline nodded. She opened her door and stood with her back to the car and to Reno as she caught hold of the door with her left hand and pulled it open. She was dressed in a black trouser suit and had used a home dying kit to dye her hair a chestnut brown, and now wore it scraped back in an impossibly tight ponytail.

Hiding in plain sight.

Campbell alighted, buttoned his suit jacket and walked nervously towards Reno.

"How far from the gable end is the first window?" asked Rashid.

"Three feet," King replied, his eyes still on Campbell.

"And the gap to the second?"

"Oh, I get you..." King glanced back at the malthouse. "From the gable end it's three feet to the first window, the window is six feet wide, there's a three-foot gap and then the second window is six-feet wide. All in, from the edge of the building to the centre of the second window is approximately fifteen-feet."

"And the bottom of the window is how high from the ground?"

"Twenty-feet." King paused. "But like I said, it could just be a rough sleeper up there."

"Then I guess we have to wait for them to show their hand..."

King glanced at the window again. There was no more steam or breath or whatever the hell it had been. Rashid had positioned himself before Campbell had set the meeting and he had been in position ever since. Wrapped against the cold, using night vision and with a view of the entire area from just over four-hundred metres away, if there was a sniper in that building, then they could only have entered from a narrow blind spot directly in front of the malthouse. He cursed inwardly. They had assumed a competent sniper had commanded the area, not boxed themselves in at such close range. As King's mentor Peter Stewart had liked to say, *death was always in the details.*

FIFTY-EIGHT

Reno stared at Campbell expectantly. "Well?"

"You've made too many mistakes."

"You're cancelling the contract?" Reno scoffed. "That is most unwise. Your employers will not be happy and will likely use me to settle the score."

Campbell ignored the threat. Just wanting the entire affair to be over, he said, "The body count is too high. I went along with you wanting to smoke King out from hiding, but all we have to show for it so far are dead civilians."

"You wanted the man dead."

"I didn't want him dead, and you know that! My business partners wanted the man dead for previous transgressions and used me as an intermediary. They even supplied me with your contact details! You're all in this together! *You* get a lucrative contract, and *they* get a show of commitment from me! I'm the one out of pocket and with the blood toll rising!" Campbell sat down heavily beside him. "It's a fucking mess..."

"We are making an omelette; we must crack a few eggs before we are finished."

"You went too far with my bodyguard." Campbell paused. "You set him off to kill one of the people investigating you, coerced the poor bastard, then killed his wife and son anyway."

"He betrayed you. He went to a former colleague, who then brought in the intelligence services. We simply cut the line of investigation. I do not apologise for my methods."

"By coercing him to kill a member of the Security Service!"

Reno nodded. "Is that why they have changed your security detail?" Reno stared, frowning as he studied the man behind the wheel of the Jaguar. "La Merde! You treacherous bastard!"

King was already moving. He opened the driver's door of the Jaguar and ducked behind the Kevlar reinforced door as he pulled out his Sig pistol and aimed at Reno. The man was quick and already had a Glock in each hand. King did not hear the shots, but one of the MI5 security guards went down and a split second later, Big Dave spun like a top and sprawled heavily onto the ground.

"Sniper! Sniper! Sniper!" King yelled. He no longer had eyes on Big Dave and his ear felt like it had split in two as Caroline rested her arms on the roof of the Jaguar and fired half a dozen shots over King's head at the window. King fired at Reno, but the man was moving quickly towards the riverbank. He returned fire with well-practised precision, using the weapon in his left hand for a sustained burst of fire while aiming well-aimed shots at King with the pistol in his right hand. It was a curious technique that required compartmentalising the brain as well as eye dominance and hand-eye coordination. But it worked. The door King sheltered behind was peppered with well-grouped shots and if it wasn't for the Kevlar inserts, then King knew he would have been hit. The second MI5 security officer went down with part of the sustained burst.

From his position just over four-hundred metres away and across the river, Rashid punched rounds into the brickwork of the malthouse wall. He had twenty-rounds to play with and he fired in groups of three or four shots, changing his aim by a foot or so in both height and direction. He changed to the second magazine and fired another eight shots, then caught sight of the pandemonium below. He watched as Reno reached the riverbank and the inflatable he had arrived on at dawn. Rashid fired at the outboard engine and missed. A plume of water three-feet-high splashed Reno in the face and he skidded to a halt in time to see the second bullet punch clean through the engine and send another plume of muddy water into the air. Another three rounds sliced through the inflatable and several separate chambers started to deflate. Reno weighed his options in an instant and darted to his right as a bullet hammered into the soft earth behind him. He fired the remainder of his magazine at the vehicles, then tucked one of his pistols under his left armpit as he reloaded the other Glock with a magazine, then swapped over pistols to reload the other.

"Reloading!" Caroline shouted, as she ducked down and left the fight to switch to a new magazine.

King stepped out from behind the door and aimed at Reno as the man reached the cover of the malthouse. He fired four double-taps and the man went down and disappeared from his view.

Caroline darted out from cover and made it to the first downed MI5 security officer. He was already dead. The tiny .22 bullet had gone clean through the man's skull and the exit wound was no bigger than a five-pence coin. She could already see Big Dave behind the Land Rover Discovery. He was bleeding from his shoulder and working on the other security officer.

"Jesus, you're OK!"

Big Dave glanced back at her and said, "Hardly, but in a lot better health than this guy." He paused. "He's not breathing, but there's a faint pulse. I'll work his airway, but you've got to stop the bleed. It's…"

"I have to help Alex!" she shouted.

"No, stay with me! This guy needs us!"

"But I have to go after her!" she snapped.

"You don't. You have to do what's right."

"That bitch is up there, and she might get away!"

"She'll keep. This guy won't."

"But she shot you, too!" Caroline protested.

"It doesn't mean anything!" Big Dave snapped at her. "Now, get the trauma pack out of the Disco and get a tourniquet on this man's leg! It's an arterial bleed and we'll lose him if you don't stop the bleeding!"

Caroline grabbed the trauma pack, looking for King and Reno as she opened the passenger door, but neither man was there. She returned with the pack and set about working on the casualty. To her disgust, she realised that big Dave had been right, and she felt guilt and regret as she slowed the man's bleeding with the tourniquet and Big Dave cleared the blood and sputum from the man's mouth and throat and started mouth-to-mouth. She had been blinded by rage and vengeance and the self-loathing she was experiencing now was insurmountable. With the tourniquet holding back the tide, she called 999 on her phone, gave the location and status of the casualty and left the phone on speaker as the emergency operator talked through the procedures, gave them both encouragement and Caroline started to stem the blood flow on a bullet wound to the man's stomach using wads of gauze.

———

NATASHA MET Reno at the bottom of the broken wooden staircase, the lightweight Ruger 10/22 rifle in her hands. Blood streamed from her left thigh and the back of her head. She had taken her second shot when her world had erupted and the wall behind her had started to break up with pieces of bricks and mortar showering her. An entire brick had punched out of the wall and struck her on the head, and as she had got to her feet, a bullet had sliced through her thigh and left a gash four-inches by three-inches in her muscle. What was commonly referred to as a flesh wound but looked a whole lot worse. She had torn her blouse and stuffed a folded wad of material into the wound, binding it in place with the scarf she had been wearing against the cold. She had staggered down the staircase and almost into Reno, who looked aghast when he had seen her blood matted hair and ghostly pale complexion.

"I've been hit," he managed to say, holding onto her and using her selfishly as a crutch to aid his progress.

"Where?"

"In my ass," he replied angrily. "The bastard shot me in the ass..."

Natasha looked and could see a great deal of blood. There were four distinct bullet holes, but one of them was much higher than the man's buttocks and looked as though it had punched out his coccyx. Reno was running on adrenalin, and she knew it was only a matter of minutes before he succumbed to his injuries. She helped him further into the building, then turned and fired the Ruger with just one hand, putting a dozen rounds out through the doorway and around the doorframe. She switched to another twenty-two round magazine and used the weapon as a crutch to aid both her own leg injury and the dead weight of her mentor.

The building was derelict, and parts of the ceiling had fallen, with the wooden floorboards that had once been above, now jutting at angles. Pigeons and jackdaws fluttered in the rafters above the fourth floor, their wings clapping loudly. Natasha pressed on over the fallen bricks and timber, the discarded rubbish from various fly-tippers and rough sleepers over the years. She turned and saw a figure in the doorway. She fired the silenced .22 rifle and the man responded with a barrage of gunshots that sounded more like cannon fire within the confines of the building. Outside, she could hear emergency sirens as paramedics and armed police flooded onto the scene. The man fired again, and this time Reno sagged to the ground and Natasha returned most of the magazine in retaliation. She pulled at him, and he scrambled on the timber and bricks, and they reached a doorway with part of a wooden door remaining. Natasha kicked it inwards, and it splintered and fell. She tugged at Reno and together they fell inside the brick-walled room and onto an earthen floor amongst decades old beer cans and cider bottles.

"We're trapped..." Reno said fatalistically.

"Never..." Natasha replied, casting her eyes over the room. There was light emitting from the far wall, the brick-work crumbling revealing a hole in the wall just twelve inches in diameter with weeds growing through. She looked at Reno, then went back to the door and fired at the advancing figure, who took cover and returned a volley of fire that pinged and ricocheted off the brickwork around her. She knew that the man was King and was disappointed that Caroline Darby had not joined in the fight. She returned to Reno and dropped the empty rifle on the ground before taking the pistol out of his hand. "I've always known," she said.

"What?" he asked weakly. He was lying on the ground, his back propped against the wall and the earth around him was already sodden with blood.

"You killed my parents," she said. "They were marks in a contract and you delivered on that contract."

"I'm sorry," he said, looking at the hurt in her eyes.

"Why didn't you kill me?" She paused, just long enough to fire two shots down the length of the building. King was ahead of three armed police officers in tactical gear and carrying carbines. Two officers returned fire and she was lucky to dip back into the room with her life. She pulled the remains of the door off the ground and let it drop in the doorway, giving the men less to see of the room and their targets within. "You always drowned the children of your marks," she said breathlessly. "Why did you spare me?"

"I was going to," Reno replied. "But there was something about your face as you were sleeping that made me change my mind."

"You watched me sleeping?"

Reno nodded. "When the Bratva found out that I'd spared you, they saw that you were turned out onto the streets and made me perform my next five contracts without payment. I found you on the streets of Paris and had an intermediary act through a lawyer, sending you to Switzerland and after a few years, I contacted you."

"And whored me as a killer."

"Trained you. And gave you skills that would one day earn you a great deal of money."

Natasha looked at him tearfully. "I want to say, thank

you and fuck you at the same time." She wiped the tears from her eyes with the back of her hand and aimed the pistol at his head. "I was always going to do this eventually."

"I know. I've been waiting..."

The gunshot rang out in the confines of the room and Reno's head snapped backwards spraying the brickwork behind him with blood, bone fragments and brain matter. When his head slumped forwards, he looked peaceful and rested still. Vapour rose from the large hole to the back of his skull, clearly visible in the cold air, and blood dripped into his lap with a patter, patter, patter, which slowed to a sporadic drip by the time Natasha had squeezed and wriggled out through the tiny hole in the wall, leaving blood and skin and threads of clothing on the rough, broken brickwork.

FIFTY-NINE

Harley Street, London

"YOU'RE QUITTING?" Caroline asked unable to contain the surprise in her voice. "But we're not done here yet."

"He's done, you can see it in his eyes," said King, munching on grapes.

"Thanks, I'm still here," said Big Dave. "Anyway, I don't mean I'm done..." He glanced at the message that had just arrived on his phone. "... I just have other fish to fry."

"Like what?" Caroline persisted.

"Family shit." He looked at King and asked, "Are those for me?"

King ate another grape, then dropped the bag onto the bed. "They are now."

Big Dave had been taken to the A & E at Kingston Hospital where two .22 bullets had been removed. One in his left shoulder and the other from his ribs, just in line with his heart. A combination of muscle and the bullet's subsonic velocity had given him a chance, and as King had later said, luck had been kind to him as well. The Security Service had transferred Lomu to a private clinic to convalesce. There had been an account running with the private hospital since the Second World War when wounded allied agents could recuperate and be debriefed in secrecy, and it provided a medical service that was second to none with a brigade of chefs and a menu to rival The Savoy.

"Anything we can help with?" asked King.

"I just need time," Big Dave said. "I need to return to Fiji, and I haven't been home since I was recruited by the army. I wasn't welcome, but I guess they need me now." He shrugged. "My sister keeps calling and texting. I stayed in contact with her after my mother remarried."

"We haven't finished here," said Caroline.

"You are," Big Dave replied. "It hasn't all got to be tied up with a bow. You need to grieve for your aunt. You need to make sure that your parents are safe. And you need to accept that whatever you do in this game, there will always be unfinished business. The French DGSE have reported her showing up in Lyon attempting to use a safehouse they have under surveillance tracking Russian GRU agents."

"But they lost her."

"And the fight will be there for another day. There'll always be another fight." Big Dave paused. "And after I deal with my family problems, I'll be back to do whatever needs to be done."

King swiped the bag of grapes off the bed and delved in. "I need a break, too," he announced. "Time to evaluate."

"We can't leave this," Caroline retorted. "I'm going to find the bitch that did this. And you know what she did to your sister, her children and her husband."

"I don't need reminding," he replied curtly. "But there's more to it than this assassin. For what I've done to Russian intelligence and the Bratva, they aren't going to leave it alone. And the CIA director, Robert Lefkowitz, whatever his plans, ran one of our government ministers as an agent and manipulated us into an operation on Russian soil." He paused, recognising the fact that he had taken the bull by the horns and gone after Zukovsky and the location of the Paradigm Shift, when he should have taken a breath and looked for the play. Although they had already taken care of that. They knew that he was being hunted by the Russians and shared just enough intelligence for MI5 to think that the CIA were helping an ally. "Lefkowitz and his stooge, Newman appeared to offer an olive branch when it was really a branch of poisonous thorns."

"And then there's Simon Mereweather," said Caroline.

"He's at reception with Ramsay," said Rashid as he walked in and nodded at Caroline and Big Dave. "I think they're checking how many meals the big man is having a day, and whether he's behaving himself with the nurses."

"Many, and no," grinned Big Dave. "And what *about* Mereweather?"

King scowled. "He ordered the SAS leader, a man called MacPherson to slot Zukovsky when the mission was completed or turned out to be a bust."

"Wow," Big Dave said quietly, shaking his head. "And you had no such orders?"

"No."

"Nothing like being out of the loop, is there?" Rashid commented flatly. "And if it was down to the SAS team, then we'd be looking at a deniable stash of lethal chemicals being used in Ukraine."

"He's okay though, that McPherson bloke. He was getting in just as I was getting out. Came in as a captain and was invited back after his four-year Rupert tour. He seemed to be a straight shooter." Big Dave paused. "He wouldn't have confided in you if he had received an order like that, that's just the way the SAS operate. That's how we all operate, isn't it?"

King shrugged. He couldn't have given a damn about MacPherson, but Simon Mereweather should have had more faith in him, and King suspected that MacPherson had taken on the order as an unofficial interview for MI5. The man had to be nudging forty and soldiering was a young man's profession. A new career in intelligence would be right up the man's street.

Rashid started on the grapes and Big Dave frowned. "What did you bring me?" he asked.

"Er, I went in on the grapes with King," Rashid said quickly.

"Is that why you wouldn't come in on me with this?" Flymo asked, stepping into the room and handing Big Dave a bottle of Mount Gay rum. "The Caribbean's finest," he said.

"But I'm not from the Caribbean."

"I know, but what the hell do they make in Fuji?" Flymo grinned.

"Fiji," Big Dave corrected him irritably.

"Whatever. Couldn't even find it on a map, mate." Flymo paused. "Good to see you are doing well. I only popped up quickly to say hi. Mereweather and Ramsay are off to Hereford and I'm flying them there by Flymo Airways in the service's Sikorsky after they've checked in on you."

"Well, see that they both get to use the sick bags, won't you?" King said gruffly. He stood up and said, "I've got to be somewhere. He broke a sprig of grapes off the vine and grinned at Big Dave. "Good luck with your family problems. I'm here to help if you need me..."

King walked out of the room and into the corridor. The walls were covered in expensive-looking wallpaper and the tiled floor was colourful mosaics forming a pattern he was too tired to see. There were paintings on the walls that looked expensive to King, and as a one-time artist with little time these days to hone his craft, he recognised talent and would wager that some of the art belonged in museums or galleries and wondered whether wealthy benefactors had donated the pieces. He had heard that two of the wives of one of the wealthiest Saudi princes had given birth at the hospital in recent months, and that the President of a former Warsaw Pact nation had been treated for his enlarged prostrate in the past few weeks. So, he imagined that funds were never an issue for the hospital, and if they ever ran into lean times, then Sotheby's would auction some of the art off quite happily.

King saw Merewether and Ramsay ahead of him getting out of one of the lifts. The lift was gilded and had stained glass panels and looked straight out of a nineteen-thirties hotel, and indeed there was a lift operator who could have passed as a bellhop in a period film.

"I thought you would be staying for a while longer," said Mereweather. "We thought we'd do a debrief and round-up in Dave Lomu's room, it's quite secure."

"I have to be somewhere," King replied curtly, with no intention of stopping. Mereweather strayed into King's path and was met with a cold look of indifference for his trouble. "Careful," he said. "I don't like being hemmed in."

"MacPherson acted on my orders. You were operating way beyond your remit and although I went along with your judgement to shut down the Paradigm Shift program, I couldn't go along with chancing Zukovsky getting away, and nor was I prepared to close on the promises you made to him. We are not in the business of paying off a man who tried to destroy our nation." He paused. "You had gone through personal tragedy, a trauma. You wanted to end this Russian threat and find the assassins at any cost. I was worried that your judgement was becoming clouded. And yes, as far as the deal with Zukovsky was concerned, I was worried that you were going soft."

King stared at him. "Anything else?" he asked, then barged past and headed down the corridor, not looking at either man as he said, "As I stated, I have to be somewhere..."

SIXTY

Heathrow Airport, London

KING FOUND him in a bar in Heathrow's Terminal 5. He was sipping a bourbon in *The George*. A taste of a British pub for foreign businessmen who never made it to the real thing and didn't know any better. When he looked up, King felt some satisfaction that the man's façade had slipped, if only for a moment.

The two MI5 security guards accompanying him peeled away, as they had been briefed to, as King walked over. Both men were dressed similarly to King. Not a tie or suit jacket in sight. They were tough men who enjoyed a ruck. They both played rugby and boxed. One of the men was a Brazilian ju-jitsu champion. Just the sort of men to send a message, although King was sure that the athletic-looking American could probably handle all they could throw at him.

"This isn't a proper English pub you know..." King said, pulling out a chair and sitting down almost a full metre from the table. Enough distance to be out of the chair and on the man in an instant, although King was sure that the man wouldn't try anything. He glanced to his right and saw the two armed-police officers, a common sight in the airport lounge, cradling their Heckler and Koch carbines. The two officers had been read in and were watching the suspect. The American wasn't going anywhere.

"The beer's warm and over-priced, and the service is lousy, doesn't that count?" asked Newman.

King ignored the man's comment. He was finding it difficult to find patience and humour within him today. Today was a straight-talking kind of day. "We've got some of the best minds in the business, but they're struggling with this one."

"And what about you?"

King shrugged. "I'm just a blunt instrument, apparently. But I've got *your* number, mate." He paused. "All that bullshit about mending bridges between the CIA and Security Service. You fucked us over."

"That's the game we're in."

"You like playing games, don't you?" King stated flatly. "Well, how about we have a little game of our own?"

Newman glanced at the armed police officers, then looked back at King. "Call off your dogs," he said. "I'm not going to give you the satisfaction of making a sudden move, and besides, I have diplomatic immunity. You can't arrest me without a shitstorm coming your way, and you especially can't arrest me now that I have passed through passport control. This is a technical no man's land, especially for a diplomat who has passed through and is awaiting his flight home."

King nodded across at the two armed-police officers and gestured for them to leave. The two plain-clothed security guards had done what MI5 officers generally did while waiting and had got themselves a couple of coffees and were watching intently. They looked like they wanted Newman to give them an excuse.

"You've been working Campbell since his days at Yale. That must have given Lefkowitz a real kick; having secured a career politician at the beginning of their career."

"Before my time, but yes, I gather he was pleased with the recruitment."

"And now that man is in government, in one of the top four political jobs, no less." King paused. "And you sent him after the Russians early on."

"Not me, but yes. Campbell was feeding the Russians what we wanted him to, and he was getting a lot in return. As an asset, he earned his money from the Russians, but got his warm, fuzzy, glow of self-worth and Western patriotism from the work he did for us."

King nodded, mulling over the situation. Campbell mustn't have known which way was up. A simple slip-up, a mistruth or a moment of carelessness and he would be discovered. Politics was a difficult enough career to navigate at the best of times – and not many came through unscathed or untarnished - but working for a foreign intelligence service while knowingly both deceiving and playing another must have been like balancing on the edge of a precipice with his eyes closed. King wondered whether the man found it a blessed relief now that the charade had been uncovered. But King couldn't have cared less how the man felt, Campbell had blood on his hands hiring Reno and his accomplice through the Russian mafia intermediary. King had already been warned off by Simon Mereweather, but frankly, after his insurance policy with MacPherson in Russia, he no longer cared what the party line was. Right now, he wanted justice for his sister and her family, and for the attack on Caroline's parents and the murder of her aunt.

"I am surprised by your visit," Newman commented, sipping some of his disagreeably warm beer. "The smart play would not have been to show your hand but raise the stakes. If we didn't know you were aware of us running Campbell, you could have used that to your advantage. Now, we have no option but to cut him loose. Unless, of course, you want to go in with us and share the asset?"

"I've had enough of games."

"Then, you would appear to be in the wrong profession."

"Too right." King paused. "But that's on me."

Newman shrugged. "So, what more do you want from me? I mean, I have diplomatic immunity and you need to grant common courtesy. That's how it works between our two great nations."

"Then extend me that same courtesy," said King.

Newman shrugged. "Very well. Director Lefkowitz knows all about you. He knows that you're the kind of man who likes a challenge. More than that, even. You're the kind of man who walks into a trap, just to see how it gets sprung. He knew that you would plough head on if he made it interesting enough. The hacking threat, the mention of Zukovsky. What would be more inviting than that? Campbell took care of the Russian end. They found a way to get a man to Zukovsky and we provided the narrative. By the way, you have a guard at castle Tay that has a penchant for kinky sex with whores and who now has the funds to indulge in his perversion. And the Russians thought that Zukovsky would come good on another matter, and of course they are now going to be disappointed."

"So, the chemical weapons stash was your target all along?"

"Yes."

"But it relied upon us destroying it. It could have so easily have gone another way."

"Not with you on board." Newman paused. "You've got to admit, Robert Lefkowitz certainly has the measure of you."

"But to what end?"

"Disarray." Newman smiled. "The Kremlin, the GRU the FSB... they're all conducting mole hunts and turning their organisations upside down looking for a traitor. Yes, it's a good thing the gas wasn't used on the Ukrainians, but the deception has undermined the Russian President's confidence in his own machine. His own paranoia will be his undoing."

King stared at the young man opposite him. Part of him held respect for him and the man he served. MI5 hadn't seen the deception coming, and in part, King knew he had to take much of the blame. He had gone off full tilt and hadn't even considered the possibility of another angle being played. It had been an impressive gambit. But another part of King wanted to break the man's neck right there and then. Their ally had tricked them, and King now suspected there would never again be the old status quo they craved, merely a new age of wariness and occasional common interest.

King clasped his hands together then started a slow clap. Several drinkers and diners nearby watched the display, but King was unperturbed. "Bravo," he said, noticing how uncomfortable Newman looked at the unexpected display. "The CIA win this round."

Newman started to squirm and reddened in his cheeks.

"King," he said, looking around him. "I don't think this is appropriate."

King gradually slowed his clapping, then stopped the display entirely. The drinkers and diners gradually returned to their mobile phones, tablets and conversations. That was the thing about airports – nobody remembered people for long. "Appropriate? No, I think it's you lot who don't know what appropriate is." He stood up, looking down on the smart young man. "I'll be seeing you," he said.

"No hard feelings?" Newman offered.

King ignored him and walked away, not looking back. Newman watched, then smiled as he checked his watch and finished his beer, then got up from the table and picked up his cabin bag and made his way through the crowds of people heading for the boarding gates. Newman did not see the two MI5 security officers hurry to his table and collect the empty glass in gloved hands and store it in a sterile plastic zip lock bag to preserve the man's DNA. And he did not see them deliver it to King, who was watching from the atrium above and planning his next move. He had vowed to fight smarter and dirtier from now on, and the first people on his list was a young CIA officer called Newman and his dying mentor, Robert Lefkowitz.

AUTHOR'S NOTE

Author's Note

Hi – thanks for reading and I hope you enjoyed the story as much as I enjoyed writing it! If you don't want to miss news of new releases, the chance to win giveaways or hear about promotions I'm running, then you can sign up to my mailing list here:

www.apbateman.com/sign-up-now

I would like to thank Sebastian Junger and his wonderfully chilling description of the experience of drowning in his book *The Perfect Storm*, and would like to extend my gratitude to his publishers Fourth Estate/Harper Perennial for allowing me to use the passage.

As the reader you've already done your part and read this story, and I thank you for that. However, if you have the time to leave a short and honest review on Amazon, you'll make this author happy! I'm hard at work on another thriller as you read this, so I look forward to entertaining you again soon.

A P Bateman

Printed in Great Britain
by Amazon

25234334R00212